Mark Seaman spent more than thirty years as a successful Radio and TV producer/presenter before turning his attention to writing full time.

In recent years he has written and directed a number of pantomimes and plays for the stage and has been fortunate to receive several awards for his scripts and productions, many of which are staged both at home and abroad.

Mark's first novel, *A Corner of My Heart*, received excellent reviews and he is excited to have joined the talented stable of authors at Austin Macauley for this, his second novel, *The Family Tree*.

Mark is married with three children.

For Ayshea, Melissa, and Ben. The fruit of our own family tree.

Mark Seaman

The Family Tree

AUSTIN MACAULEY PUBLISHERS™

LONDON * CAMBRIDGE * NEW YORK * SHARJAH

A CIP catalogue record for this title is available from the British Library.

ISBN 9781528998581 (Paperback)
ISBN 9781528998598 (ePub e-book)

www.austinmacauley.com

First Published 2021
Austin Macauley Publishers Ltd
Level 37, Office 37.15, 1 Canada Square
Canary Wharf
London
E14 5AA

My thanks go to K D M Snell for his support, along with my wife Sandra for her endless patience.
Also, to C S Lewis and John Lennon for their words and inspiration.

Preface

Have you ever had a dream where the imagined and reality intertwine? One of those trance-like illusions that engulfs your mind completely and so disturbs your senses that, even as you wake and adjust to your surroundings, you're still not entirely sure as to whether you are physically in the moment or continuing to play out a role in some other worldly experience induced through sleep and your unconscious psyche? Or perhaps you've experienced a daydream where, although cognisant of your surroundings, your subconscious thoughts are transported to a different place in time even though your physical body remains rooted in the present? And, as these imaginings establish themselves as both equally bizarre yet vivid in their content, they begin to take on a terrifying authenticity of their own?

I have experienced those dreams for myself, many times. But for me it didn't end there. My night-time slumbering and daytime flights of fancy have now become so intertwined that both appear as real to me, presenting their own nightmare illusion of fantasy and distorted truth.

C.S. Lewis so adeptly addressed man's inability, on occasion, to recognise the difference between reality and the imagined in his book "***God in the Dock***," where he states –

"If a man doubts whether he is dreaming or waking, no experiment can solve his doubt, since every experiment may itself be a part of that dream. Experience proves this, or that, or nothing, according to the preconceptions we bring to it."

I have found this statement to be increasingly true for myself and, as I write this, am no longer sure whether my life is grounded in reality or being lived out in the increasing dominance of my subconscious where both fact and fiction have now become inexplicably interlinked and disturbingly surreal.

Chapter One

My name is Charles Benton; Charlie to my friends and family and I live in Gunthorpe near Peterborough with my dad and mum, Peter and Irene. Dad is 52 and, although quite tall and traditionally slim, is beginning to show early signs of a contented middle-aged spread. Mum says this is because he doesn't get enough exercise apart, that is, from walking to and from his car before heading off to work or when arriving home again. He is employed as a senior sales rep for a local plastics and moulding company, having begun his working life there after leaving school and never looked to move on. As a youngster, he started in the warehouse but has successfully negotiated his way up the ladder of promotion until reaching his present position. He has an easy-going nature about him and is not overly ambitious as demonstrated by having spent his entire working life to date with the same company. If pushed on why he hasn't moved on or sought to do something more challenging with his life, he always volunteers the same reply.

"My greatest ambition as a young man was to marry your mum and provide a roof over her head. I've accomplished both so why should I set myself further targets that I'm not really interested in achieving. I like my job, my clients and I know my limitations. So long as I've got enough money in my pocket to pay the bills and buy my season ticket to watch Peterborough play, I'm a happy man." Then he'll laugh, adding. "Why would I want anything more, when I already have your mum and support the best team in the land? They're not nicknamed The Posh for nothing and she's always been top of the league for me as well."

As for Mum, she's different altogether. She's fifty but looks younger and has kept her hair longer than many women of her age, often tying it up or back to expose her soft clear complexion which still demonstrates none of the customary signs of early ageing such as lines around the eyes or natural creases in the skin. She may be shorter than Dad but has a greater appetite for life than him and, like me, enjoys filling each moment with some form of meaningful activity, getting the most out of the day and all it has to offer. Mum's not unhappy with Dad though, nor does she complain about his apparent lack of ambition. To be honest, I don't think I've ever heard them have a real argument or witnessed them fall out in any meaningful way.

She worked as a receptionist for a building company in Nottingham before the two of them got married. They met when he was employed as a junior sales rep and sent on a training course to Nottingham to learn something about one of the companies Dad's firm did business with. While he was there, he went out with one of the senior salesmen to see the manager of the company Mum worked for about a big order they were hoping to get. The story goes that while they were waiting in the reception area, Dad got chatting to Mum. They got on well and kept in touch, with Dad driving up to Nottingham on the occasional Sunday to see her. He even went a couple of times for the whole weekend, which was when Mum said she knew he must be getting serious.

She told me this arrangement went on for some time until Dad said he couldn't afford to keep travelling up to Nottingham anymore and wouldn't it be easier if they got married and she moved down to live with him in Peterborough.

"A real romantic your dad," she laughed. "He always had a way with words; maybe that's why he's such a good salesman?"

Once they were married, she got a job in Peterborough working in a solicitor's office answering the phone, typing letters and so on. They wanted children but nothing happened for a while until she fell pregnant with me, almost after they'd given up on the idea of having a family.

"We were so excited the day we found out I was expecting. It was like a real answer to prayer," she said, before adding, "Albeit quite a long time after we'd first asked God for a baby."

Mum was more than happy to give up work when I eventually did come along but always thought she would like to go back to doing something for herself once I was older and started senior school. More recently she's found herself a part time job at another solicitor nearby which she enjoys, and which gives her the opportunity to employ some of her former admin skills again.

I've just turned twenty and am studying Genealogy and English Local History at Leicester University. It's one of only a couple of universities to offer this particular course and, being based in Leicester, means I can get home at weekends if I want to or when my washing needs doing. Mum teases me when I arrive back with a bag full of dirty clothes but I think she's pleased in a way that I'm not too far away and that she and Dad can keep half an eye on me.

"Oh, I see the washing machine at the university is broken again Pete, poor Charlie has had to lug this lot all the way home for his mum to do."

Although they rib me, I know they're happy to have me at home occasionally as well.

My course covers Topography, Landscape, Family History, and other associated areas of Genealogy, and we have some great tutors at uni who really know their stuff.

I had an idea recently for part of the course work to include my own family's history and to research our family line. I felt it would provide genuine purpose towards this particular area of my studies as well as offering the opportunity to discover more about our own family at the same time. One of my senior tutors, Professor Everson, encouraged me, saying he thought it was a good idea and that he would help support me in my research as far as he was able. Of course, I needed to check with Mum and Dad that they were happy for me to investigate our family history as well. And, although I felt sure they wouldn't object, when the time came to talk it through with them, I suddenly felt nervous about how best to broach the subject. I thought about what I might say on the train as I headed home one Friday afternoon after my final lecture, eventually deciding the best approach would probably be just to go for it, after all the worst they could say would be no.

I unpacked my bag and stuffed my dirty washing into the laundry basket before making my way downstairs. I could hear Mum singing to herself as I opened the kitchen door. She was standing over the cooker preparing our evening meal.

"Hello, love, everything alright?"

"Fine, thanks; I've put my washing in the basket."

"Mmm, now there's a surprise."

I walked across the room and squeezed her arm.

"Mum, what do you know about our family?"

She turned and smiled. "That's a strange question to ask the minute you walk in." She leant forward and kissed me. "Well, let me think. I can tell you that your dad's an idiot, has been for most of his life if that helps."

"No, I'm serious. I mean our family history?"

She looked down to check the contents of her saucepan. "Why, what do you want to know for?"

"It's for my uni work. I'm thinking of researching our family tree as part of my degree course. That's if it's alright with you two?"

She turned and, looking at me over the top of her glasses, frowned.

"Well, if I'm honest, I'm not sure your dad and I would be too happy to have our dark family secrets brought out into the public domain for everyone to pour over."

"Mum, it's only a bit of research for a family tree, I'm not planning on writing a book about it."

She glanced briefly at the bubbling contents of her saucepan before turning her head back to face me, a large smile wreathed across her face. "I know that, you daft brush, I was only joking."

I heaved an internal sigh of relief.

"Actually, if you do decide to look into our history," she continued, "do my side of the family first. There's a bit of a mystery about my great-great-grandfather that's never been proved one way or the other, that's if the rumours are to be believed."

"How do you mean?"

"Well, Granddad William, or Grampy Bill as we called him when I was younger, said that *his* grandfather had been murdered, but he was quite old when he told us that and he didn't seem to know much about it either, apart from the fact that he'd apparently been a vicar somewhere in Kent. He certainly couldn't remember the circumstances or any of the gory details, that's if it really happened in the first place of course. I've told you before he was known for telling tales about all sorts of nonsense as he got older and most of them turned out to be a load of old bunkum." She laughed. "He had a colourful imagination, did Grampy, and liked nothing better, when I was a little girl than filling my head with some scary story or other as I was about to go to bed. Granny Anna would tell him off, but he'd just laugh and give me a cuddle, telling me he was only joking."

"Even so, a murder, there's a story in itself; you've never told me that one before."

Mum moved to the table and began chopping carrots. I took a piece and sat down opposite her.

"What else do you know about him?"

"Don't eat all that carrot or there'll be none left for your tea."

I laughed and took another slice.

"Charlie I'm serious, I'm not cutting this lot up just so you can stuff your face with it before it's even cooked."

I hastily swallowed the half-chewed piece of carrot. "Okay sorry, last bit I promise. Now what were you saying about Grampy?"

"Where was I? Oh yes, about his grandfather supposedly having been murdered. Mind, you've got to remember he was around eighty when he told us that." She smiled. "Like I say, he was always coming out with some tale or other about things that had or hadn't happened in our family. We never knew whether to believe him or not. I remember Mum telling me once that one of his favourite stories was that he'd taken on practically a whole troop of German soldiers in the trenches during the First World War and shot them all himself. Mum said Gran would roll her eyes and laugh at most of the things he came out with telling us not to believe a word, especially that particular tale as he'd never even been a soldier." Mum paused and grinned. "There was a letter apparently from the Army saying Grampy had been unfit to serve because of breathing problems brought on by the coal dust he'd inhaled during his time down the mines. And, of course, even if he had been fit enough to sign up, they probably wouldn't have taken him anyway, what with mining being a reserved occupation. You couldn't just send anyone down a mine in those days; they had to know what they were doing." Mum shook her head and smiled again. "I think the fact the army wouldn't accept him on health grounds was the thing that bothered him most though, it made him feel less of a man in some way. Maybe that's why he made up some of the stories he did, to convince himself, as well as others, of what he might have done had he been allowed to join up." Pausing again, she turned and looked at me. "To be honest, Charlie, considering his health problems, we were all surprised that he made it to the age he did." She smiled again. "He was a lovely old man though, and for all his bluff and bluster, he really cared about his family. Mum told me once he said he'd had to survive so he could look after Granny Anna in her old age. He said that she'd looked after everyone else for most of her life and now it was her turn to be cared for and it was his job to do it." I noticed a tear form in Mum's eye as she embraced the memory. "It broke his heart when she died." Mum shook her head again and looked at me. "There's a picture of him somewhere holding you as a baby. You were just two when he died. He'd bounce you around on his knees for ages making you laugh. More, more you'd say, and off he'd go again rocking you from side to side."

"I don't remember that, but he sounds like a character."

Moving back to the cooker she turned down the heat under the saucepan. "He was."

"So, is it alright if I have a go at researching our family tree then?"

"Only if you promise to do my side first?" She put her hand to her face and pushed back a lock of hair from her eyes, laughing as she did so. "Your dad's lot are as boring as him."

I stood up and pinched another slice of carrot, clenching my fist around it in the vain hope Mum hadn't seen me.

"I'll tell him you said that."

"Be my guest, you'll only be confirming what I've told him myself." She waved her knife at me. "And if you think I didn't see you take that piece of carrot, Charlie Benton, then you're as daft as he is. Now get along with you, out of my kitchen."

I moved towards her and kissed her on the cheek.

"Love you, Mum."

She smiled, adjusting her pale blue patterned apron as she did so.

"You too, although for the life of me I can't think why?"

"Alright if I call Simon?"

"Yes, but don't be long, I'm expecting your dad to call soon. He says he might be home early this evening."

"Okay."

I walked into the lounge and, picking up the phone from the coffee table, flopped down full length onto the sofa. It was good to be home, surrounded by familiar things and with the smell of something delicious wafting through the air from the kitchen as Mum prepared our evening meal. Simon and I chatted merrily about everything and anything as friends do for a few minutes until I heard the lounge door open, it was Mum. She entered, wiping her hands on a tea towel, and with a look of obvious displeasure on her face.

"Come on, love, I said not to be long, your dad's going to call soon remember? And get your shoes off that settee."

I sat upright, swinging my feet round onto the floor as I did so. "Sorry, Mum, just coming." Smiling sheepishly, I turned back to the phone. "I've got to go mate, Mum's expecting a call, see ya."

Placing the phone back on the receiver I apologised again.

"Sorry about that, Mum, I wasn't thinking."

"We're not made of money, Charlie, and that's a new settee so we don't need your muddy shoes all over it, okay?"

I stood up, playfully throwing my right arm out in front of me.

"Ja mein Fuhrer."

"I'm serious, Charlie, your dad and I have worked hard for what we have and all we ask in return is that you respect our wishes, and our home."

I walked over to her and took her in my arms.

"Sorry, Mum, I was only joking. You and Dad are the best, really."

"Well, just think next time that's all."

I smiled and gave her a kiss.

"I'm seeing Simon at the pub later; alright if I bring him back for a cuppa after?"

"Only if you promise not to make a mess on my settee." She grinned and shook her head.

"Just as well I made a fruit cake, isn't it? Don't they feed you at that university?"

I patted my stomach. "I'm a growing lad, remember? At least that's what Nanny Mary used to say whenever we went to her place, she always had a cake on the go. Anyway, there's more important things than food to spend our money on at uni."

"Like beer I suppose."

I put my hand to my head and grimaced. "Mum, how could you? I was going to say books and pens and the like but, I suppose alcoholic sustenance could be included as one of the essentials of student life as well."

Feigning disgust, she shook her head in mock derision.

"Go on clear off with you, you're as bad as your dad, an answer for everything."

I blew her a kiss as I left the room. "Thanks, Mum, I'll take that as a compliment. Love you."

Chapter Two

Simon and I had a good session in the pub that night, both responding with gusto to the effects of the contents of our pint glasses. The trouble with alcohol is the more you drink the more you believe your conversation has value and makes sense, determining your ideas and discussion to be both enlightened and profound, when in reality you are more than likely to be talking absolute rubbish. The two of us had grown up together as friends, attending the same primary and secondary schools. We were the same age, bar a couple of weeks with Simon being born on the 20th June and me on the 3rd July. He never let me forget he was two weeks older either, especially if we disagreed about something.

"You need to remember, Charlie, I've got a bit more life experience than you and so, in all probability, am right and you're wrong."

We teased each other about all manner of things as we grew together, as only really good friends are able to do. One of our favourite topics as we got older was the opposite sex, especially once we reached our mid-teens and realised that girls had a lot more to offer than just a ponytail to pull on. Mind, for all he would attempt to pull rank on me when choosing which girl to ask out he never seemed to fare any better than me in his efforts at wooing them into submission.

Even as a youngster, I had an interest in social history and so when I discovered Leicester University offered a degree course in English Local History, I knew that was what I wanted to study. Simon preferred politics and successfully applied to The London School of Economics for a degree course in Political and Social Science, and with the two of us commuting on a fairly regular basis to Peterborough we were still able to meet up on occasional weekends and during holidays. We both shared a passion for the countryside and in how it had shaped society over the centuries; also, in how modern civilisation was reversing earlier trends and seeking to reshape the rural landscape along with its surviving community. I felt strongly about the role of family history and associated local industry in the changing geography of our environment, while Simon felt that politics and science held sway for the way ahead.

The one thing we did agree on was that neither end of the spectrum should be ignored. The future needed to respect lessons learnt from both the past and the present, which in itself will become the past in years to come. The world, we felt, could only move forward in preparing for whatever lay ahead by carrying with it the best from its history and allowing those experiences to help shape the future, a future Simon and I were determined to influence and play a vital role in.

"It sounds like the two of you have old heads on young shoulders," our parents said when we told them what we wanted to study and our reasons for doing so. Laughing, they added. "That shouldn't be interpreted as wise heads though."

Whilst we laughed along with them, the two of us knew where our hearts lay and ultimately, I like to think, our families were proud of us and of the choices we'd made. That said, after a few pints in The Blue Bell, you would be forgiven for thinking the two of us had little, if any, physical clarity about what it was we actually wanted to achieve after gaining our respective degrees.

"We'll change the entire thinking about political, industrial and family history when we've finished."

"And how its ancestry continues to shape the dynamic of the country, along with its place in the modern world. Same again is it?"

This particular night ended with me turning down the now traditional one for the road. "Come back to ours and have a coffee instead. I've had enough beer for tonight." Simon looked at me through the bottom of his glass as he drained its contents. "You sure? I'm paying."

"No, you're alright. Anyway, Mum's made a fruit cake and I could just go a large slice of that."

After another meaning of life conversation over our coffee and cake Simon left and I stumbled upstairs falling clumsily into my bed still the worse for wear. I knew I would regret it in the morning along with the comments from Mum and Dad and the thick head which would accompany both my remorse and determination never to do it again. At least that's what I would promise Mum at the breakfast table when she would chide me about the noise I'd made coming in, even though I'd presumed myself to be as quiet as a mouse. Another illusion instituted by the false assurance alcohol promotes after consuming one pint too many!

Dad would smile behind his newspaper, recalling his own youth and the odd occasion he'd also seen the bottom of one too many glasses on a night out with his friends celebrating a win by his beloved Posh. Mum would catch the two of us winking at each other and give us both an icy stare which we would acknowledge as time to end any further attempts at defending our laddish behaviour.

To be fair, they both knew I was just letting off steam away from my studies and, much as I liked a pint with Simon and my university friends, I accepted it for what it was and not something which would have any real detrimental effect on my revision or determination to do well in my exams.

This particular evening felt different though, despite the fun Simon and I had had. The thought of a family member having possibly been murdered, no matter how long ago, stayed with me and was something I was determined to find out more about. As I clambered into bed, pulling the pillows under my head in an effort to make myself more comfortable my thoughts were still occupied by the supposed fate of my long since departed ancestor.

I was dozing towards oblivion when I felt a tug on my arm. Opening my eyes I looked around, the light from the streetlamp outside my window casting a bright golden glow across the room. It appeared I'd forgotten to close the curtains properly when getting into bed. As I lifted myself up, placing my feet on the floor and still wondering if I had dreamt the tug on my arm, I looked down and noticed something large and dark lying on the carpet. My instinct was to shout out but as I opened my mouth the cry inside of me became stifled, giving way to little more than a surprised gasp. As my eyes adjusted to the light, I could see the shape of what appeared to be a body lying face down in front of me. I could tell it was a man with the back of his head balding slightly and thick sideburns running down either side of his face. My mind raced as I tried to make sense of the scene before me. What or who could it be, and how had they got into my bedroom?

Rising from my bed and moving towards the light switch I heard a moan and, turning towards the body again, noticed the man's head lift slightly off the floor and look up at me. His eyes appeared dark and sunken and there was blood flowing freely from a wound across his forehead. Again, I wanted to shout out but with my head spinning and the air inside my lungs stifled momentarily I could hardly breathe let alone call for help. I stood rooted to the spot as my body shook and a state of dread and panic ran through me. The man coughed and gurgled as the flow of blood increased and ran down the side of his face. He reached out a hand towards me and spoke, his voice cracking, displaying the obvious pain he was in.

"Help me, Charles."

I looked around, not knowing what to say or do as his hand brushed against my leg, his fingers reaching out to grasp me as he repeated his plaintive cry.

"Help me, Charles."

My head started to swim and my chest tightened as everything began to go dark around me. I sensed myself losing consciousness as I fell towards the floor.

Chapter Three

The alarm by the side of my bed rang out the next morning, its loud clanging bell rousing me from troubled sleep, and as I instinctively threw out an arm to turn it off my hand connected with the carpet. I opened my eyes to find myself lying by the side of my bed. Suddenly the events of the previous night overtook me once more. I jumped up and looked around for the man I'd seen lying at my feet a few hours earlier along with the stain of blood from the wound to his head. The bright morning sun was now pouring through my still open curtains and, in that moment, with its rays warming my back, dispelled any lingering doubts I may have had regarding what I'd witnessed as being anything other than a bad dream. I shook my head in effort to clear it and looked at myself in the mirror. "Dying men lying on the floor talking to you and bleeding all over the carpet, you're losing it Charlie boy. Better lay off the booze for a while, it's clearly messing with your brain."

I washed and dressed and made my way downstairs to the kitchen where Mum and Dad were finishing their breakfast.

"Oh look, Irene, Lazarus has risen from the dead. Good morning, sleepy head. A bit too much to drink last night then was it?"

I grinned, accepting their jibe as deserved.

"Morning, Dad, Mum. Not really, just didn't sleep well. I had the weirdest dream."

Rising to put the kettle on Mum smiled at me. "I'm not surprised after you and Simon polished off half that fruit cake between you last night. Going to bed on a stomach full of beer and cake is a perfect recipe for strange dreams I should think. Tea or coffee?"

"Coffee I think, ta. Sorry if we woke you up, we tried to be quiet."

Dad got up and winked at me, placing his breakfast things on the draining board.

"Oh you didn't disturb us, Son, we're used to having people crash into tables and chairs while we're trying to sleep."

I knew he wasn't really upset but also that Simon and I had obviously made a noise and so owed them an apology at least. Picking up the packet of Rice Crispies on the table I poured some into a bowel.

"Yeah, sorry about that. I told Si to keep the noise down but he walked into the table and knocked over a chair. We thought we'd keep the kitchen light off until we closed the door so as not to wake you."

Dad laughed. "Well, that worked, didn't it?"

I poured some milk onto my cereal as Mum passed me a fresh cup of coffee; its aroma filling my senses as I reached out and took the steaming mug of liquid in my hand.

"I should be careful with those Rice Crispies, son, all that Snap, Crackle and Pop, might be a bit noisy for you? Never the best thing for a hangover."

"Yeah, yeah, very funny, thanks, Mum. And I haven't got a hangover, just a bit of a thick head that's all."

Dad smiled at Mum, nodding in my direction. "Nothing new there then."

He moved to Mum, kissing her on the cheek and patting me lightly on the shoulder as he passed by.

"Well, some of us have got work today even if it is the weekend. We can't all be struggling students lazing around and drinking our life away."

"That's not fair," I said, fighting to swallow a mouthful of cereal. "It was just one night for goodness sake. I'm working really hard for this degree, you know that. I was only talking to Mum yesterday about an idea I've got to look at our family history as part of my course work."

"I know she told me." He laughed. "I also understand she gave orders to look at her side of the family because she says my lot are not very interesting?"

I raised my cup to my lips and smiled at Mum.

"I couldn't possibly say, but she did tell me something interesting about one of her lot that I want to follow up."

Dad waved his hands in the air in a pale imitation of a supposed ghostly apparition. "Oh yes, the family murder, I've heard that one as well."

I picked up another spoonful of cereal. "Well, I haven't."

Mum sat down next to me.

"I told you yesterday Charlie, Grampy's anecdotes couldn't always be believed; he probably made the whole thing up. It'll be just another of his tall stories I'll bet."

Dad looked at his watch and moved to the door.

"Well, there'll certainly be one murder in this family if I don't get off to work. See you both later."

I waved my spoon at him and mumbled goodbye through another mouthful of Rice Crispies.

The next few minutes were spent in silence as I finished my cereal and Mum sipped her tea. I enjoyed these times alone with her when Dad was at work; it reminded me of when I was younger and just happy to be in her company. Perhaps being an only child had created some special bond between us, a deeper, more profound relationship than if I'd had to share her with a brother or sister.

Mum put down her cup and looked at me.

"So, what was this dream about?"

Pushing my bowl to one side I recounted the events from the night before.

"It was really weird. I suppose it was because of what you said yesterday." I ran my fingers through my hair, scratching my head as I struggled to find the right words. A feeling of anxiety overtook me once more as I recalled the detail of what had happened, along with the very real sense of panic I'd experienced at the time.

"I dreamt somebody touched me and when I looked down to see who it was, I saw a man lying on the floor."

"What did he look like?"

"I don't know I couldn't see him properly he was lying face down. But as he lifted his head, I saw blood running down the side of his face and he sort of gurgled when he tried to speak."

Mum smiled and shook her head; clearly struggling to take my story seriously. "So, did he actually mange to say anything in the end, this mysterious stranger?"

"Yeah, and that was the weird thing, it was like he knew me."

"Knew you?"

I felt my body shudder. "He asked me to help him."

"Help him? How?"

"I don't really know, but he said my name. Not Charlie but my proper name, Charles."

Mum stifled a laugh. "What did you say?"

I ignored her obvious amusement and continued.

"Nothing. I remember feeling nervous though, and everything spinning away from me like I was going to faint or pass out."

"Then what?" her tone softening a little as she sensed my disquiet?

"Then nothing. I don't remember anything after that." I shrugged my shoulders. "The next thing I knew the alarm went off and it was morning. Only, I wasn't in bed, I was on the floor." I looked at her. "And before you say anything, no it wasn't because I'd fallen over from the effects of the couple of beers I'd had earlier."

She took my hand and leaned across the table towards me. "As if."

I shook my head and smiled at her.

Smiling, she squeezed my hand as if to reassure me. It was the same smile she used to give when I was a little boy and found myself in trouble or worried about something. It was a smile designed to encourage me that all would be well.

"Like you said, it was a dream and not a very nice one by the sound of it. And, although I'm not saying you and Simon had overdone it earlier, it does sound as though the combination of beer, cake and talking about our dear departed relation all merged together to addle your brain a little, that's if it wasn't addled enough already." She laughed. "Maybe a few early nights and staying away from the pub for a couple of days might help as well? But I don't suppose for a moment you'll listen to your mum's advice on that score, will you?"

I smiled gingerly back at her. "There was one thing though…" My voice trailed away as I struggled to complete the sentence.

She squeezed my arm again. "What is it, Charlie, what's the matter?"

"Nothing, I'm fine it's just, well…" I took a deep breath and blew out my cheeks. "It's just, well, the whole thing felt like déjà vu, you know, like I'd been there before, met him before. I mean obviously not in my bedroom of course but…" my voice trailed away again.

"As I said before, going to bed on a stomach full of fruit cake and alcohol along with a story about some long departed relative who may, or may not, have been murdered is likely to cause anybody a few strange dreams, even nightmares, as appears to have been the case on this occasion. Maybe next time you'll listen to your parents when they advise that too many late nights and too much to drink isn't the best recipe for a good night's rest." She paused, stroking my hand as she did so. "Try to let it go eh, Son, and put it down for what it was, a case of overindulgence and a vivid imagination."

I took her hand and kissed it.

"Fair enough, but remember, I'm only young once so the odd late night isn't going to kill me, even if it does result in a few bad dreams along the way." I laughed. "There's plenty of time for me to get old and grumpy like you and Dad later."

She slapped me playfully on the arm.

"You won't need this grumpy old woman to do your washing and ironing anymore then will you?"

"Ah, well, that's different of course. I wouldn't want to deprive you of the pleasure of supporting your poor overworked son when he has so much revision and studying to do."

"That'll be at The Blue Bell then, rather than at home or in the halls of Leicester University?"

We laughed and took each other's hand again.

"Seriously, Mum, thanks for listening, and for the advice."

"And thank you for confiding in me. I hope you'll never feel too old or too wise to seek your mum's counsel?"

I let go of her hand and stood up, walking across the room and placing my cereal bowl in the sink.

"So you and Dad are happy for me to research our family tree then, yeah?"

"Of course we are. It'll be nice to know a little more about our history. And you know I was only joking yesterday when I said about looking at my side first don't you, unless of course you were thinking of doing your dad's lot at the same time?"

"No, that would take ages and I only need to offer it as a part of my work. It'll help demonstrate I can do formal research and bring a paper together through having contacted all of the appropriate agencies and then collated the required information into the correct order. The genealogy side of things is just the family history part of my course. We're also studying landscape, the countryside and so on, so I'll just do your side for now." I smiled at her. "Anyway, I really do want to know if there's been a murder in the family now, that's if I go that far back of course, although I can't imagine I won't with a carrot like that dangling in front of me."

She watched as I moved back to the table and sat opposite her again.

"We don't always say it Charlie, but your dad and I are really proud of you, I hope you know that? Yes, I know we joke about you being out late with Simon and your other friends, but deep down we think you're great, a real credit to us."

I felt my face colour up.

"Just goes to show what good taste you've got."

"No, I'm serious, we really are proud of everything you've achieved so far in getting to university and in doing this course. It's not something we would ever have done, or even thought about for ourselves." She laughed. "Well, certainly not your dad anyway; not unless they did a course on Peterborough United football club, then he might have had half a chance." She grinned. "No, I think it's safe to say your brains come from my side of the family, only don't tell him I said that or we'll both be in trouble."

"Normally I'd agree with you," I said, teasing her. "But maybe I should check again first, just to be sure, after all there are obviously some dark characters from your family's past that are going to come to light." I grinned. "Who knows what I might discover about the Pearce family and beyond as I delve back in time, you might be related to Doctor Crippin or Jack the Ripper?"

"Well, if I am, you better hope I don't decide to keep the secret to myself and do away with you and your dad in the process." She laughed. "Well, your dad anyway."

We spent the next half an hour enjoying each other's company, talking about nothing and everything while we cleared the breakfast table and washed up. As we put the last of the dishes away Mum gave me a hug.

"Thanks for that, Charlie. It's nice to spend time just the two of us, we seem to do it less and less these days. Oh I know all the reasons; what twenty-year-old boy, or man I should say, wants to be seen with his mum all the time but, even so…" She hugged me again.

"I know, same goes for me, Mum. You're alright for an old codger."

She stepped back and flicked me with the tea towel.

"Cheeky thing. Not so much of the old if you don't mind."

"Alright if I go upstairs and make some notes about starting this research, or do you need me for something else?"

"No, you're alright, you carry on."

"I'd like to talk to you in more detail about your parents as well at some point if that's okay? And anything I might not have heard about Grampy or Granny Anna before would be great as well. It's a pity I didn't start this a couple of years ago while your mum was still around; I bet she could have told me a few tales about the two of them, and about your dad. She was always happy to say how proud she was of him, but never really wanted to talk about his time in the army or about how he died." Pausing momentarily, I smiled. "She was great Nanny Mary; I really miss her at times."

Mum nodded, her speech faltering slightly. "I miss her too Son, and you're right, she was a special lady."

"Sorry, I didn't mean to –"

She raised her hand to interrupt me. "It's fine Charlie, it's good to talk about her. And yes, you're right she could have told you a few tales about Dad, although I'm not sure she would have given that much away. She always remained protective of him, especially about his time at Dunkirk. It was only during the last few years of her life she even opened up to me about some of what they'd been through together. I suppose she became aware of her own mortality towards the end and recognised it might be the time to talk about certain things that, up until that point, she'd chosen to keep just between her and Dad. I was glad she did though." Mum looked directly at me and nodded. "And so yes, maybe there are a few new stories I can tell you about their lives, especially now you're older and putting together this family tree."

"I think I'd have liked your dad, even from the little I do know, sounds like he was pretty special, same as Nanny."

"He was. Mind I can't remember that much about him myself, being so young when he died."

We leant forward and gave each other a hug.

"Thanks, Mum, I'll look forward to it."

I made my way upstairs feeling excited about the prospect of researching Mum's family and planning in my head how I would start. I had, by now, completely forgotten about my ethereal encounter from the night before and so was surprised to feel a sudden chill run through me as I entered my bedroom. It felt as though I'd walked into the coolness of the open air rather than the warmth of my own room. My body shuddered as I recalled the events from the night before. Instinctively I looked to the floor but there was nothing, only the carpet and a pair of socks I'd dropped when getting ready for bed.

As I lifted my head and glanced towards the mirror on my wardrobe door, I felt the room become warmer again. I stared at my reflection. "Get a grip, Charlie boy. Maybe Mum is right; a couple of early nights and abstinence from the booze for a while might be just what you need?" I looked at myself again and laughed. "Then again, perhaps not."

Chapter Four

I returned to Leicester with renewed enthusiasm for both my studies and the associated work that lay ahead. I was also grateful for Mum and Dad's blessing in allowing me to research our family tree; their support and encouragement meant a lot and provided me with the added impetus I needed to forge ahead with the project. Keen to make start I made an appointment to talk with Professor Everson who headed up the course on English Local History. He could appear a bit odd, even self-obsessed at times in his attitude towards the whole subject of Genealogy and of the overriding influence he felt it had on the shaping of modern society; also, as to how it should be viewed in the twentieth century.

"The past cannot be understated in its shaping of the modern world and man's place within in it," he used to say. He had a real passion for family lineage and ancestry and in how one influenced the other.

"What our forebears chose to put in place many years ago still effect the decisions we make today, even those conclusions that were made long before our own grandparents where born. Just look at Parliament for instance; how many of our laws and precepts have remained on the statute books for a hundred years or more without any thought of change, for better or for worse?"

He was a difficult man to get to know, certainly outside of the classroom, but I liked him all the same. A bit of a loner by nature and happy in his own company, he was never one to stay and chat with students after a class, at least not about anything that involved any social activity away from our studies. Some maintained it was because he was about to retire and so didn't want to get overly involved with the new intake. I don't know if that's true or not, but I certainly don't remember ever having had a conversation with him about anything other than my course work and his part within it. There wasn't much he didn't know about his subject though and I was sure he would be pleased to think I was going to explore my own family's roots in greater detail as part of my studies. He was from Kent originally himself and so I hoped this might further encourage his support for my project, especially once he became aware that one of my ancestors had been a parish priest in the county and had, perhaps, been murdered there as well. And so it proved on the day we sat down together to discuss my proposal.

"Really, that's fascinating Benton. I only wish I was ten years younger and could fully embrace the opportunity of advising you on the various aspects of your research but, as you know, I retire at the end of this term so Professor Smalling will have to be your mentor and guide on this particular area of your work. He will be the one to assist in your investigations and in bringing your conclusions together."

I was already aware of most of the practices for gathering the necessary information regarding a family's history from earlier work we'd done, but still thought Professor Everson might be keen to support me with any additional advice or insights he deemed relevant, even if it was only until the end of term.

"Naturally, I'd be happy to run through the rudiments of gathering the necessary detail regarding one's family forbears with you again if that will help? And of course, with any relevant information I might be able to supply regarding Kent as a county. As you are aware, I grew up there as a boy."

I smiled as I watched him put a match to the pipe clenched firmly between his teeth and suck on it furiously in an effort to ignite the small parcel of tobacco he'd stuffed into it during our earlier exchange. A cloud of smoke suddenly appeared and a spark from the pipe lifted lightly into the air before dropping onto his brown nylon shirt and singeing a small hole in it to accompany the already established network of similar trademark burns in the material. His creased trousers and crumpled tweed jacket, along with its well-worn leather patches on the elbows, also betrayed a man who had lived for too long on his own with no one to care for either him or his general appearance. For all of that he still displayed a genuine, almost youthful, zeal for his work; his eyes taking on a steely gaze of fervour and dedication to his duties whenever he was engaged in discussion with a student about his great passion for ancestry and its associated local history.

"You'll never truly know what you were put on this earth to do until you've tested it against what others have achieved before you," was another of his favourite quotes, along with, "How can you make a difference to what is and is to be until you truly know and understand what has been before?"

I'm not sure we always understood the meaning of those quotes, but we never doubted the passion with which they were delivered. There was a genuine excitement in his tone when he spoke, and woe betide you if you didn't share that same enthusiasm. It was this obvious commitment for his chosen subject that I wanted to tap into and draw on, even if it was only to be available to us students for just a few more weeks.

"That would be wonderful Professor, thank you very much."

Not wanting to appear overly pushy or as though he might be seeking to sideline Professor Smalling, the new kid on the block, he backtracked a little, realising his personal eagerness to be involved had perhaps exceeded his professional obligations.

"Of course, any assistance I might offer lad will need to be in line with whatever Professor Smalling has planned. He will be leading the course once I have retired, and so it makes sense for me to assist you only in conjunction with his thinking and timetable rather than the other way around. Perhaps you should speak with him first?"

"Of course, but it would still be nice to have your wisdom and input available to me Professor, especially your intimate knowledge of Kent."

I knew I'd achieved the right tone as a satisfied smile spread across his face and another cloud of smoke rose from his pipe as if sending out the signal that a meeting of the minds had been achieved; one that would bring harmony, learning and the desired result for all parties.

I made plans to talk to Mum and Dad at length about their family memories the next time I was home. In the meantime, I began setting out my priorities for the rest of the research I would need to undertake. I also spoke with Professor Smalling who was equally keen to encourage my efforts in exploring Mum's family history but reminded me this would be viewed only as part of my overall course work, and that I shouldn't become so focused on it that I let other areas of my studies slip.

"The danger with getting overly involved with any one particular aspect of your research Charlie is that it becomes all consuming. This in turn can result in the greater reason for the project, the gaining of your degree, getting lost along the way. You may well learn more about the history of your family, but not as much about yourself and the other areas of your studies as you might have hoped, or, indeed, about what it was you originally set out to achieve."

He was right, of course, and equally as passionate about seeing his students succeed as Professor Everson, although in every other area of their character and personalities they remained poles apart. Whilst Professor Everson displayed every student's perception of what an older university tutor would look like, staid in both character and appearance, Professor Smalling portrayed the complete opposite.

I liked him from the start; he was young and ambitious and dressed in similar fashion to his students, wearing open neck shirts, sweatshirts and casual trousers, even jeans on occasion. He talked in the language of today, a language we understood and could immediately identify with. He was happy to share a story or joke with us as well, although he was a stickler for application and attentiveness when it came to our studies. He had an air of authority about him we all respected, and soon learned never to overstep the mark in our relationship with him, either in or out of the halls of study. He also had a talent for reading us individually, quickly making it clear to each one of us where he thought the focus of our attention, with regards to our work, should be directed. This wouldn't necessarily be the areas of a module we were particularly drawn to or that readily appealed to us but more on the syllabus as a whole. He knew we needed to gain the right grades throughout the entire course and not just in the areas that we enjoyed or thought we could do well in.

"Don't ignore, or take for granted, any part or component of your studies Charlie and thereby lose out in the bigger race itself. Remember, it's the complete package that will get you across the finishing line not just the bits you like or enjoy." He smiled, recognising he'd lapsed into a metaphor about his other great passion outside of genealogy and local history, that being sport. He had run distance for his school as a student as well as playing cricket and football at a decent level, and so never missed the opportunity to use a sporting analogy when seeking to encourage us in our work and studies.

"You know what I'm saying Charlie, you have a talent. Just don't get side-tracked and have reason to regret it later."

I returned his smile. "Thank you, sir, I'll remember that. I'll wear my running shoes in future to stop me going off track so to speak."

"And sarcastic remarks like that will definitely see you struggle to get out of the starting blocks with me lad."

He winked at me and laughed.

"Seriously, Charlie, I think it's a great idea that you look into your family history and that Professor Everson is willing to help guide you in that, but you still need to remember what I said about viewing it only as part of your course work. I would hate to see other areas of your studies suffer because of it, okay?"

"I hear you, sir, and thank you again."

Even though I agreed Mum's family tree would only make up a relatively small part of my course work I was still hugely excited by the prospect and sensed, for the immediate future at least, that is where the greater part of my attention would be focused.

Chapter Five

The next few weeks seemed to fly by as I settled back into university life along with putting together the list of organisations I needed to contact about our family's history. Each day I grew more determined to get to the bottom of what really happened to dear old George. I knew I couldn't overlook any part of the detail if I was to discover the truth about his alleged murder or, as Mum had intimated and was more likely to be the case, that the whole story had been one of Grampy's tall tales.

I decided to visit all the usual venues such as The General Register Office and The Public Records Office in London as they would hold much of the detail I required regarding any family births, deaths and marriages that Mum couldn't remember as well as confirming the ones she could. I knew it would be long and arduous work but that was also part of the fun and appeal for me. Pouring over dusty reference books or studying reels of microfiche to uncover some particular detail about an individual or an event from the past always gave me a real sense of achievement and of a job well done. Equally, discovering some previously unknown truth about a person or moment in history also never failed to enthral me. I think this was part of the reason I'd been attracted to studying English Local History in the first place. Mum and Dad said even as a youngster I'd been interested in history and geography; wanting to know what places would have been like in years gone by and how people would have lived their lives in earlier times. The countryside, in particular, held a fascination for me. Mum told me as a boy I would often look out of our front room window at the rows of houses opposite and ask what life would have been like there a hundred years or so before.

"What was here before our houses were built, Mum?"

"Fields I suppose, Charlie, I don't really know."

"Well, if there weren't any houses and it was just fields, who would have lived there?"

"I don't know sweetheart, maybe no one."

"Well, they must have lived somewhere. What would houses have been like a thousand years ago?"

"I'm not sure Charlie, maybe they would have been made out of mud or wood. Why don't we go to the library and have a look in the history books there?"

Discovering the library for me was like opening up Aladdin's cave with its treasure trove of reference books that chronicled the history of our culture, the landscape, its geography and how community and associated living conditions had changed over the years. As I got older my interest in topography and family history grew and was further nurtured at school; also, in the books I read and programmes I chose to watch on television. And as my enthusiasm for this area of learning developed, I felt increasingly this was more than just a passing phase; rather it was fast becoming a passion that would stay with me for life. Once I found out there were colleges and universities which offered the opportunity to study these subjects and to gain a degree in them I knew I had discovered my path in life. Even though I wasn't entirely sure what a degree in English Local History was at that time, or what it might offer me in the way of employment opportunities when deciding my eventual career path, I still reasoned that in gaining it I was, at least, making a statement to the outside world where my heart lay. And, hopefully, once I'd attained this sought-after degree a corresponding door of opportunity might open for me along the way.

After a fortnight of hard work and preparation at uni for what lay ahead I went home to talk with Mum and Dad about what they knew or could remember about our family history; information I hoped would further assist in my research. It felt strange that, even with such an obvious passion for ancestry, I'd never really sought to ask about the origins of my own family. This was to be a new adventure. Little did I know at this stage how the discoveries I was to make in the weeks ahead regarding our forebears would not only disturb the settled roots of our family tree but shake the very core of my own existence forever?

Mum greeted me with her traditional welcome as I walked through the back door that Friday afternoon. She was kneeling down looking for something in the cupboard under the sink as I entered the kitchen and didn't even look up to make sure it was me before she spoke.

"I hope you've brought me a nice bag of dirty washing to do. My line doesn't look the same without your socks and pants hanging from it."

"Mum, you might have checked it was me. I could have been the window cleaner."

She looked over the cupboard door and smiled. "I thought you were the window cleaner. Didn't you know I wash his socks and underwear as well, along with his window rags whenever he calls? He gives me a discount."

"As if."

"Exactly, as if! Of course, I knew it was you. For a start nobody else, apart from your dad, walks straight into the house without knocking first, and certainly not round the back."

"I suppose." I closed the door and put a plastic carrier bag on the kitchen table. "There you go, your wish is granted, my washing."

"That's not a lot. Don't say you haven't been wearing clean clothes every day?"

"Of course I have. One of the other lads at uni has started using the local laundromat in town so I went down there and did some of my stuff with him."

"Wonders will never cease. Not that I'm complaining you understand, but isn't my washing machine good enough for you anymore?"

"Of course it is, but you're not as pretty as the girl who works there on the evening we go."

Mum stood up and washed her hands at the sink. "I'm sorry?"

"I didn't mean you're not pretty, I just meant that you're my mum and she's a bit of alright if you get my meaning?"

"So you don't mind *her* seeing your underwear then, if you get my meaning?"

"That's what in the carrier bag. We only do our T shirts and stuff like that there."

"And does she provide an ironing service as well?"

"Of course not, we just hang them up to dry in our rooms and then put them under the mattress to press them flat."

"What a great idea, I must start doing the same with your dad's shirts, he'll be thrilled. I might even get rid of my iron altogether."

"I wouldn't, they look just as creased the next morning."

I walked over and gave her a hug, planting a kiss firmly on her cheek.

"No one looks after me like you Mum, you're the best. Anyway, you'd only worry if someone else started washing my stuff, especially my pants. You'd be telling me to buy new ones every week in case they thought you sent me out all the time in the old faded ones I've got at the moment."

"And whose fault is that? I told you to buy some new ones the last time you were home."

I gave her another kiss and moved towards the kettle.

"Cup of tea?"

"Go on then. How are you getting on with our family tree? It sounded like your tutors are behind you from what you said on the phone?"

I filled the kettle and plugged it in. "Yeah great. Professor Smalling likes me to run everything past him though. I think he finds it difficult with Professor Everson being so keen to support me as well."

"Is that going to be a problem?"

"Not really. Professor Everson retires at the end of term so won't have any input after that. And research methods have changed as well since he started at the uni back in the 50s. There are easier ways to find stuff out now. Technology, computers, and the recording of data have come a long way in the past thirty years. Not that he's against the modern methods of research, it's just that he prefers the old-fashioned way of endless visits to libraries, poring over old documents and the like when there's things like microfiche that you can scroll through in half the time and get the same information. Belt and braces he calls it." I laughed. "Once he's gone, it'll smooth the way for Professor Smalling to set out his own agenda. I still like him though."

I put two mugs on the table and looked around me. "Where do you keep the tea bags now, they were on the side last time I was at home?"

"I've put them in the cupboard with the salt and pepper. Your dad managed to knock them on the floor last week and then blamed me for leaving them out. Mind, he's already had to ask twice where they are himself, and when I remind him why I've moved them he just grunts."

"Nice to know you're still crazy about each other?"

"Oh he's crazy alright."

We sat for the next twenty minutes chatting and enjoying our tea together. Much as I liked living independently at uni it was always good to get home again, for a while at least, and spend time with Mum and Dad. That was part of the reason I was so excited about exploring our family tree. It would be something I could do for them whilst continuing with my studies at the same time. Draining my mug, I stood up and picked up my shoulder bag.

"What time will Dad be back? I want to pick both your brains about the family before I start trawling through the records and looking up birth certificates, marriage licences and so on."

"About six I should think. We're not planning on doing anything this evening or tomorrow for that matter so we can talk then if you like?"

"Great. Alright if I have a bath? It was a bit hot and sticky on the train."

"Of course, there's a tank of hot water."

"Thanks, Mum."

"You're welcome." She squeezed my arm. "It's exciting isn't it?"

"What is?"

"This family tree thing. I wonder what you'll find out, nothing too horrid I hope."

"Well, if it's true about a murder in the family that's not exactly going to be a barrel of laughs is it?"

"Oh I should forget about that. I shouldn't have said anything in the first place. That'll just be Grampy winding us all up. Like I said before he liked nothing better than to tease us or pretend he was privy to some great secret about the family, which he never was, or at least not that I can remember."

I swung my bag over my shoulder and moved to the door.

"Well, I hope there is some truth to it; a good murder will make all the research worthwhile. And who knows what else we might discover from our family's murky past?"

"Charming. Go on get off with you and try not to make too much mess in that bedroom of yours, I only just vacuumed in there this morning."

I waved my hands above my head. "Was that to get rid of the dark and terrible evidence of the bodies hidden under the floorboards?"

"I'll bury *you* under the floorboards Charlie Benton if you don't clear off."

Smiling I closed the door and walked along the hallway to the stairs. The late afternoon sun shining through the stained-glass panelling in the front door reflecting a myriad of colours against the wall opposite me. I watched as my shadow, initially in front of me, moved level and then behind me as I made my way up the stairs. Reaching the top, I turned briefly and looked back down to the hall below. As I did so I thought I caught sight of another shadow moving against the wall but dismissed it immediately as a trick of the light, a reflection from the colours glimmering through the glass panels in the front door as they shimmered and danced their way up the stairs. I smiled again remembering how, as a young boy, I had, on many occasions, sat on those same stairs counting the colours displayed through the glass; it was like having my own private prism. I would sit there for ages in a world of my own allowing the coloured beams and reflections to carry me off to imaginary places and magical kingdoms. Distant lands where I could be king of all I surveyed until Mum or Dad's voice would shatter my childish fantasy and jolt me back to reality.

"You'll hurt your eyes if you keep staring at the sun through that door, Charlie my lad."

"But I'm the king of Sunland and these lights are my orders sent out to my people as thoughts in space."

"Well, if I may interrupt those thoughts your majesty, the only land I want you to be king of this evening is the land of nod. Now upstairs with you, it's time for bed."

How many times had we engaged in such make-believe conversations as I was growing up? I couldn't remember, but the light reflected in those different panes of glass still fascinated me and took me back to those halcyon days as a young boy growing up surrounded by love, encouragement and the playful teasing of my parents.

Still embracing these memories of youthful contentment, I entered my bedroom only to be struck once again by a passing chill in the air; one that made my body shiver. I glanced across the room and noticed my window was open and so immediately assumed my involuntary shudder had been caused by the obvious change in temperature. Looking around the room, my mind reverted to the days of my youth once more. I visualised my cabin bed with its small writing desk where I used to sit and pour over my school books devouring all I could about social history and the way in which people had lived and worked in years gone by. It was no coincidence that I'd carried this early desire to discover more about life's communal landscape into my adult years, and now sought to make my way in life through that same, long held, passion for history and the events of the past. I looked at the walls, now tastefully decorated in soft greens and creams, Mum's choice; a decision made by her once I'd left for uni, but formally painted white with a dark blue border to match the kit of my footballing heroes, Tottenham Hotspurs. I'd chosen this mainly to wind Dad up who would berate me for not sharing his passion for his beloved Peterborough.

"I thought I'd brought you up better than that Charlie. You could at least pretend to support your old Dad. What will my friends think when they find out his son is a traitor to the cause?"

"Probably that he's got more sense than his dad I should think," Mum would say, winking at me at the same time.

I would chime in with, "Chivers for England," which would only add to Dad's discomfort. We both used to support the National team whenever they played and Martin Chivers was a regular for England in the early 1970s, as well as being my favourite Spurs player at the time. I also had a poster of him on my wall along with the rest of the team who did so well in the early '70s, winning both the EUFA and Football League Cups. Eventually as my interest moved more towards the countryside and social history so my desire to support Spurs, or indeed any football team, waned. After a while I didn't even bother to look for their results on a Saturday afternoon anymore, something else Dad struggled with for a while as we had, up until that point, always sat down together, while Mum prepared the tea, to see which of our respective teams had enjoyed the best result on the day.

As I stood there recalling those happy times I felt another chill run across my shoulders which caused me to shudder again slightly. Looking across the room I noticed the curtains ripple on the breeze as it entered through the open window. I moved to close it and as I did so I heard the same voice, from deep within, call out to me again as it had before.

"Help me, Charles."

I shook my head. "You're getting paranoid now Charlie boy, hearing voices and the like. Nobody's called you Charles for years, not since you ran into Dad's car on your bike as a youngster and broke the headlight."

"Happy days," I reflected, smiling to myself as I closed the window and began to unpack my bag.

Chapter Six

That night, during our evening meal, I began to ask Mum and Dad about our family's history and what they could remember regarding their own parents and family line. As we talked, I began to feel for Dad with the majority of the conversation being focused on Mum's side of the family.

"I'll leave you two to chat while I do the washing up," he said at one point after listening to Mum and I talk in some depth about a particular memory from her past.

"No, Dad, I want you here as well. What you have to say is equally as important as Mum; you might remember something about her relatives that she's forgotten or doesn't think is relevant."

"Charlie's right, Pete." She reached out and took his hand. "And I want you here as well. It may be my side of the family we're talking about but it's still *our* family, okay?"

"Well, in that case, I'll have a couple more of those potatoes if we're not clearing the table just yet."

Mum laughed, "Typical man, always thinking of his stomach."

I looked at them and smiled. Whatever I might find out about our family history in the days ahead I was just glad to be a part of it and, more especially, to have the two of them as my parents.

I pushed my plate to one side and picked up my notebook.

"So, Mum, tell me some more about your parents, especially when they were younger?"

"Let's clear the table first; I don't want to be doing it at midnight which is probably what'll happen if we leave it until after we've finished talking. We can chat while we're washing up."

"Do you mind if I finish my dinner first?" Dad spluttered through a mouthful of potato.

She laughed again. "If we wait for you to finish eating, we probably will be here until midnight. You carry on, Charlie and I will work around you."

"Charming."

Mum and I looked at each other and laughed as we left the dining room and headed for the kitchen, leaving Dad to wave his fork in protest at the two of us.

Squeezing some washing up liquid into the sink I watched as it mixed with the hot water from the trap creating a small mountain of bubbles.

"I'll wash, you talk and dry up."

Mum smiled. "There's a contradiction in terms if ever I heard one."

"You know what I mean."

We stood and watched as the sink filled with the hot soapy liquid.

"There's some new rubber gloves under the sink."

"That's fine, I like the feel of hot water against my skin," I said, rolling up my sleeves.

"So where were we?" Mum asked, taking a clean red and white striped tea towel from a kitchen drawer.

I put the first pile of dishes into the water displacing the stack of bubbles to one side as I did so.

"I was asking about your mum and dad. And don't worry if I've heard some of the stories before, it will be good to put them into context with anything else you can tell me that I don't already know."

Dad entered the kitchen carrying his now empty plate.

"That was great, really lovely, thanks."

"Good, I'm glad you enjoyed it. There's some ice cream if you want it." Dad placed his plate on the work surface by the sink.

"Nothing else for me thanks." He patted his tummy. "Those extra spuds have filled the gap perfectly."

Mum smiled. "If you could put the mats and the tablecloth away while Charlie and I finish here, that would be helpful? We won't be long."

"No problem, I'll be in the lounge when you're ready."

I turned and smiled, lifting a hand to my face to scratch my nose and leaving a trail of bubbles across my cheek which Mum wiped away with the tea towel.

"Thanks." I looked at Dad again. "That's fine, you take it easy, I'll do this lot." I nodded towards the other plates and remaining pieces of cutlery still left to wash.

"Oh no, you don't; you go and sit down Pete," Mum countered. "I don't want the two of you out here together throwing bubbles over each other and onto my nice clean kitchen floor."

I looked down at my wet hands now dripping their soapy covering onto her gleaming lino.

"Sorry, Mum."

"Well, don't just stand there apologising, put your hands back in the sink."

Dad winked at me as I turned, suitably chastened, back to my duties.

"Yes, Mum."

"I'll leave you to it then." I heard the kitchen door creak as it closed behind him.

Mum drew alongside me picking up a handful of clean knives and forks from the draining board.

"Sorry, Charlie, we don't seem to be getting very far do we?"

"That's fine, don't worry about it. Do you want to finish this lot first and we can start again when we sit down?"

She leant across and gave me a kiss. "Might be best, and less messy," she added, glancing down at the floor again.

I nodded guiltily. "Yeah, like I say, sorry about that."

"It'll be fun learning more about our family tree, I'm looking forward to it. Are you sure it's alright to do this as part of your course Charlie? I feel as if we're taking advantage of your studies for our own ends?"

Having finished the washing up I stood and watched as the last of the bubbles disappeared down the plughole creating a whirlpool of frothy liquid as they did so.

"It's fine, Mum, really, I'm looking forward to it as well. Remember it was my idea in the first place." I turned to her and smiled. "And to be honest having you and Dad on board is going to make it a lot easier for me. I've got a fixed point to start from, somewhere solid to begin my research, which is great." I wiped round the sink and squeezed the last of the water from the dishcloth. "Honest, Mum, don't worry about it, you're helping me out big time."

"So long as you're sure, I wouldn't want your dad and I to cause you any problems or get you into trouble?"

Moving to pick up the kettle I stroked her arm. "You're not, okay? Tea all round is it?"

"Thanks, I'll get the mugs."

Dad was sitting in his favourite armchair reading the newspaper as we entered the lounge, mugs of hot tea in our hands with steam rising invitingly from them.

"All done?" he asked, folding the paper and dropping it by the side of his chair.

"All done." Mum placed a mug onto a cork coaster set on the arm of his chair. "We really should get you a new chair Pete, it looks so old and tired next to the new one and the sofa."

"When we can afford it. Anyway, I like this chair." He rubbed his hand gently along the slightly worn light brown fabric. "We go back a long way."

"My point exactly. We got it when Charlie was eight, so that's twelve years ago. I said it should have gone when we got rid of the other chair and settee."

Dad raised his mug to his lips and smiled. "You just sit there on your shiny new sofa and I'll stay here on my favourite dusty old chair and then we'll both be happy, alright?"

Mum shook her head. "We'll have this conversation again soon Peter Benton, you mark my words. One day you'll come home from work and find that chair gone."

"And if I do then I'll be right behind it."

Mum sat on the sofa patting the seat next to her for me to join her. "Well, if I'd have known that I'd have got rid of it long ago."

I sat down, carefully placing the other two mugs of tea on matching coasters on the coffee table, my notebook and pen clasped firmly under my arm.

"If you two have finished, I would like to find out at least a little bit about our family before bedtime?"

Dad laughed. "Well, that's easy; your mum was born in 1936 so she's fifty." He looked at her grinned. "Mind on a good day she'd get away with late forties."

"You can talk," Mum retorted. "You're two years older than me and look every day of it."

It was good to hear the two of them tease each other as I knew deep down how much they cared for one another. Equally I wanted to get on and so jumped in before they could continue. "Listen, either play nicely and help me or it'll be early to bed for the both of you, okay?"

Mum squeezed my arm and smiled apologetically. "Of course Charlie, sorry, where do you want to start?"

I took a sip of tea and opened my notebook "Like I said earlier, with your parents. And, remember, I want you to pretend I've never heard these stories before, so don't worry about repeating stuff I might already know."

Mum sat back and stroked her hand across the dark blue crushed velour of her prized new settee.

"Okay, well, Dad was a miner as you know; he started at the colliery when he was sixteen. He worked at the same pit in Nottingham as Grampy, Newstead, that's where he met Mum. And Grampy was born near Nottingham in 1878 and started in the mines in 1892 I seem to remember he said. He was just fourteen then, at least that's what he told us, but as you know Grampy made up so many stories I can't promise you that's true either, although it may well be as children did start work much earlier in those days."

Dad leant forward nearly knocking his mug from the arm of his chair.

Mum looked at him and sighed. "Be careful, Pete, for goodness' sake. You spill tea on your old armchair if you like but not on the carpet and certainly nowhere near my new furniture."

"I was only going to say that your granddad may have told a few porkies over the years, but he was definitely a miner, that much at least we know is true."

"Yes, he was; I'm just saying I'm not sure if he was actually sent down the mine itself at fourteen. Although as I say employment laws were very different back then. I suppose it wasn't that many years earlier that children had been sent up the chimneys, so who knows, perhaps he was working underground then?"

Carefully placing my mug on its coaster to avoid any chance of an accident I chipped in. "Actually Mum, you'd be surprised, in the very early day's boys as young as ten were sent underground, although things did change over the next few years when the required ages for some areas of work were raised. I think it was in 1900 the law was changed, but I'm not sure off the top of my head. It was certainly around that time though. I can check that side of things for certain when I do some more research and look at the different dates and anniversaries that may have a bearing on our own particular family's history."

Mum grimaced. "Really, how awful, poor little mites, I thought it was bad enough with Dad becoming a miner at sixteen." She raised her shoulders and shuddered. "Anyway, Dad and Mum lived near the colliery in what was called the new village. Originally when the pit opened in 1874 miners and their families who were moving to the area to live and work were housed in what was then known as the old village. Grampy told us the colliery itself had started life when two shafts were sunk near to Newstead Abbey which, apparently, had once been the home of Lord Byron, but again you'll need to check the detail for yourself."

Mum paused and touched my arm. "Am I going too fast for you, Son?"

I looked up from my notebook. "No, you're fine, I'm just taking down those dates to check out; much of the other stuff I've heard before, either from you or Nanny Mary before she died."

"So you don't want all this then?"

I smiled and scratched the side of my head with my pen. "Really, Mum, it's fine, just keep going. Like I said, pretend I've never heard any of this before. It won't do any harm to double up on what I know already, and I can always leave out what I don't need and check on the rest later. Honest, it's great, really."

She looked uncertain but smiled back at me and took another drink from her mug. "If you're sure? So, where was I? Oh yes, Dad. Well, like I said he became a miner at sixteen, so that would have been…1924, that's right, and he stayed there until he signed up for the army in 1939 when he turned thirty-one. Of course, mining itself was a reserved occupation during the war as I've said before, so miners weren't traditionally allowed to join up, but as Dad was working in the offices for the union by then he got special dispensation." Mum paused again briefly, a wistful look on her face as she embraced a particular memory and one I didn't feel appropriate to ask about.

"He married Mum in 1934 when he was twenty-six." Smiling at me she placed her empty mug on its coaster.

"Mum was four years older than Dad as you know." She paused again. "It was something that always concerned her, as traditionally women were usually a bit younger than their husbands back then, especially if they were planning on having a family. She told me Dad laughed when she'd mentioned it, saying it didn't bother him and that he quite liked being married to an older woman. He teased her and said being older would mean she would have more life experience like his own Mum, and that she'd probably be a better cook and housekeeper for it as well."

Dad leant back in his chair and stretched his out arms. "Wish I'd thought of marrying an older woman then before I proposed to you."

Mum flashed him an acerbic glance, smiling playfully as she did so. "I wish you had as well."

46

Keen to keep the conversation flowing I jumped in. "Well, you didn't, and anyway if you had, you wouldn't have had me and then we wouldn't be having this stop start conversation, would we?"

Mum smiled and rubbed my arm. "You're right, Charlie, sorry." She paused to gather her thoughts again. "So, Mum and Dad got married in 1934 as I said, and they had me in 1936." Pausing again, she stared into the distance for a moment.

"Are you alright?"

"Sorry, what? Yes, I'm fine. I was just remembering something Mum told me Dad had said when I was born. She was thirty-two when I came along. They hadn't been sure at first if they could have children, and then when she did fall pregnant the doctors had been a bit concerned for her, what with her being slightly older and having high blood pressure. She had it all her life. That was the cause of her heart problems later, and again when she died of course."

"Yes, but she made it to eighty-one love; that's not bad for someone with a dicky heart and high blood pressure."

"I wasn't saying it was, I was just telling Charlie what happened that's all."

I took a deep breath. "Mum, Dad, listen. I really don't want to sound uncaring or ungrateful but if the two of you are going to pick each other up every time you disagree over a particular event or something the other one has said about a family member then my course will be over before I've had a chance to complete it."

I looked at Dad. "By all means chip in if you think Mum has missed something, and Mum, please don't take offence if Dad says something you don't agree with. I just need to get the basics down for now, so I have something to refer to when I begin my research proper, alright? We can have the wider conversations about who said what to whom and why once we have everything set down formally in front of us, okay?"

They looked at each other sheepishly.

"Sorry, Son. It's just difficult for your mum and I to simply blurt out a load of detail and not be involved; it's our family we're talking about remember? Well, your mum's anyway, but I was there for much of it as well."

It was my turn to say sorry. "You're right, both of you. I apologise. And of course I love to hear these stories as well; it's just that for now I need to look at this as a piece of course work without any of the emotional involvement if you know what I mean."

Mum stroked my arm again. "We do, and we'll try." She smiled at the two of us. "We'll all try, yes?"

Dad and I nodded our agreement and sat back in our seats as Mum took up her story once more.

"Now where was I before I was so rudely interrupted?" She threw us an affectionate grin. "Oh yes, I was telling you what Dad had said when I was born." Turning to me, she smiled awkwardly. "I know this might not be a particular bit of information you need to know Charlie, but just let me say this one thing and then I promise I'll try and keep my little detours to a minimum, okay?" I grinned and shook my head.

"Mum told me he said I was a gift from God and that he was doubly blessed now as he had two women in his life to love and care for." She paused and looked towards the floor, clearly embracing the moment. "Mum told me that story a few times over the years. I think it helped when she was feeling low or thinking about him not being here anymore." She took a handkerchief out of her cardigan pocket and gently blew her nose, the sentiment of the memory overtaking her. "Still, they're together again now."

I suddenly realised this wasn't going to be an easy task for either of them, especially Mum. How could I ask for only the bare facts and figures about their family history, their flesh and blood, my flesh and blood, in such a clinical and apparently cold-hearted way? I shifted uncomfortably in my seat.

"Mum, I'm sorry, I should have realised this might be tough for you, I'll choose another family, a family I don't know."

Putting her hanky back in her pocket and clearing her throat she turned to face me.

"You most certainly will not Charles Benton; I've been looking forward to this."

That was the first time in as long as I could remember that she, or anyone for that matter, had called me Charles, apart from my tutors on occasion and of course the mysterious voice I'd imagined crying out to me in my bedroom.

"We both have, haven't we, Pete?"

Dad straightened himself in his chair and nodded in agreement.

"We certainly have. We really want to help you, Son, you just need to be a bit patient with us that's all."

I laughed. "I know, just so long as we all remember this is part of a three-year course and not a thirty-three-year one, okay?"

I felt a sharp but playful slap to the back of my head.

"If you continue with that attitude my son then it won't be finishing your degree you'll need to be worrying about, it will be finding somewhere else to live."

"Okay, Mum, point taken."

We all laughed as Dad picked up his mug and waved it in the air.

"Another cuppa?"

"Yeah thanks, Dad, that would be great."

"Irene?"

"Thank you."

Rising from his chair Dad picked up the empty mugs.

"You two carry on without me, it's your mum you really need to speak with anyway, Charlie."

I looked up at him.

"And before you start, I know you said you wanted both of us to contribute, and we will, but it's your mum's side of the family you're discussing, and I can tell you from personal experience there isn't much she doesn't know about them, or anything else for that matter." He looked at Mum and smiled. "Am I right, your ladyship?"

She acknowledged his slightly backhanded compliment with a sarcastic smile of her own.

"Glad to see you've learnt something in the time we've been married."

We watched as Dad left the room.

"He's a good man, Charlie, and he loves us both very much, never doubt that, I don't." She laughed openly. "Well, maybe sometimes."

I rolled my pen around in my fingers. "So, you started to tell me about your mum and dad and when you were born?"

"Sorry, yes. You have to remember I was only four when Dad died and I hadn't really seen much of him in the previous year either, not after he signed up, what with his training and then being sent to France."

"Before we talk about that, Mum, tell me some more about his work at the mine, about him and Nanny Mary when they were younger, or at least what you can remember?"

Mum put her hands to her face and closed her eyes briefly to focus.

49

"Like I said, I was only four when he died so my personal memories of him are pretty vague." She paused. "Actually, I do have one specific memory of him from when I was really young, his smell."

She smiled, noticing the look of surprise on my face.

"That might sound strange, but he always had a musty smell about him when he came home from work. I suppose it was a mixture of sweat and coal dust from the mine. Mum said he would pick me up when he came in from his shift and give me a hug, much to her consternation." She smiled to herself for a moment before continuing. "She would tell him off for picking me up in my clean outfit or nightdress and making it grubby with his soot-covered hands. 'Wait until you've had a wash at least before you pick the baby up,' she would say, adding that he would smile and tell her she was next for a sooty hug and a kiss. Then he'd wave his dirty hands in the air causing her to shout again in playful protest before running away." Mum looked at me again and smiled. "I'd forgotten that, Charlie, so thank you."

"For what?"

"For bringing back those memories of happy times. And they were happy times, not only because Mum said they were but because, young as I was, I can remember laughter in our house, a lot of laughter." She paused again before laughing herself.

"And, of course, after he'd had his wash he would pick me up again and start cuddling and tickling me, and kissing me as well. Thinking back, I remember his kisses always felt scratchy, but now of course I realise it was his whiskers rubbing against my skin not his lips."

"Did your mum tell you much about his time working in the mine; for instance, did he enjoy it do you know?"

"I'm not sure if enjoy is the right word. In fact, I'm not sure any of the men really enjoyed the long hours they spent underground in those cramped and claustrophobic conditions, but they were close, always looking out for each other, watching each other's back so to speak; at least that's what Mum told me whenever we spoke about those days. It was a difficult and dangerous job being a miner Charlie, especially back then. And because of the obvious risks it was one none of them ever took for granted. As I said before, towards the end of his time at the colliery, Dad was working topside, as they referred to it, so I think that made him even more aware of the dangers his friends were facing below ground. He wanted to do his best when representing their concerns to the pit owners and help make the conditions and the environment they worked in safer, and better for them."

"It can't have been easy?"

"It wasn't, although I was too young at the time to be aware of any of that of course."

"Tell me about living in the village, or at least what you can remember, and anything your mum might have told you as well? I never really talked to her about their time at the colliery. I really only saw her when we went to visit, apart from the last couple of years, but she was quite poorly by then and not really up to long conversations about the past."

"That's right." Mum paused. "Well, we stayed in the village for a while after Dad was killed but then moved to be near her friend Peggy in Papplewick a few miles along the road."

"I've heard you mention Papplewick before as the place you and Nanny Mary moved to."

"Nice little town it was, still is I should think, although it'll have grown a bit over the years of course." She laughed. "Famous for its pumping station, which helped provide fresh water to Nottingham until around 1969, and also for being the place where one of Robin Hood's merry men, Alan-a-Dale, is buried, or so the story goes." She looked at me. "Funny how some things stick in your memory."

"You said you moved there to be near your mum's friend?"

"That's right. Peggy lost her husband in the war as well, a few months after Dad, but they'd known each other for a long time before that when Dad and her husband Walter had worked together at the mine. Walter left the colliery before the war started but kept in touch with Dad as they were good friends. And of course, once the two of them joined up Peggy and Mum had another reason to stay in touch. After she moved to Papplewick the only time either of them went back to Newstead was for the centenary celebrations in 1974. They would have both been around seventy then." Mum paused again. "Gosh I hadn't realised how much I'd forgotten over the years, or at least not thought about." She looked at me. "I hope this is helpful?"

"It's great Mum, honest. I won't need all of it for the family tree of course but it's really interesting to know, and it'll help fill in some of the background when I'm looking at specific dates and places later on. Tell me some more about the time she and Granddad John lived in Newstead, when he worked at the mine?"

"It was a close-knit community in the village and not just amongst the miners but their families as well. I suppose in part because it'd only been in existence since 1874 when the first shafts were sunk. Before that Newstead village as an entity hadn't existed at all, so anyone living and working there at that time did so because they were a part of that tight knit mining fraternity."

She was interrupted by Dad, who, pushing open the door with his foot, entered carrying a tray.

"Tea is served." He paused and flicked his foot behind him to close the door.

"Be careful, Pete, or you'll have that tea all over the floor."

Dad looked at me and shook his head. "Oh ye of little faith. I learnt my footy skills from watching the Posh."

Mum laughed. "That's why I said be careful."

Dad scowled playfully as I came to her defence.

"She's got a point, Dad."

"I shall ignore your petty insults and rise above them."

Mum and I smiled at each other as Dad placed the tray on the coffee table.

"I've bought some chocolate biccies as well. I thought it might help with our memories."

"Why would it do that," Mum countered, suspecting his real motive?

"Haven't got a clue, but it sounded like a good idea at the time."

Laughing, I took a biscuit from the plate. "And me. I'll have one, thanks."

Dad picked up his tea in one hand and, taking a biscuit in the other, sat back in his chair.

"Don't let me interrupt you, feel free to carry on."

I nodded and, turning back to Mum, took a bite from my chocolate digestive. "You were saying about living in the village?"

She looked at me disapprovingly. "Don't speak with your mouth full, Charlie."

"Sorry," I replied, spitting crumbs down my sweater. I looked across to Dad who was laughing. Mum stared at the two of us.

"You're just as bad, don't encourage the boy."

He glanced at me and winked. "Yes, Mum; sorry, Mum."

Taking a sip of tea from her cup she shook her head at the two of us.

"Now, where was I? Oh yes, Newstead. Well, Dad had grown up only knowing life in the village, what with him being from mining stock as well. And Grampy had worked at the colliery since 1892, so mining had pretty much run in the family one way or another for as long as anybody could remember, certainly in those early days anyway." She paused. "Hang on, if the shafts were sunk in 1874 and Grampy was born in 1878 four years after they opened and he was fourteen when he first started at the mine that would have been…1892; yes, so that is right. Granny and Grampy got married in 1902 when they were both twenty-four. They didn't talk much about their early times at the colliery; people didn't back in those days. I think it was a bit of a generation thing, you know like in the war when men went off to fight but didn't really discuss their experiences when they got back. It was just the way things were back then."

Dad moved forward in his chair. "Mum's right. I remember my dad not wanting to talk about what he did in the war either. I was nearly twelve when he came home for good; he'd been away for pretty much all of the campaign, only getting back for occasional leave before that. I would ask him from time to time what it was like, but he would just smile and say he'd done what he had to and that, hopefully, the world would be a safer and kinder place to live in now. He never discussed the actual fighting though, although he did tell me once he'd been caught in a hand grenade blast. I remember he was having a bath by the fire one night when I was a lad and I noticed what looked like candle wax on his back. He said a hand grenade had gone off near to where he'd been standing which had killed one of his friends and that some of the shrapnel had ripped through his uniform and scarred his back, but he wouldn't say any more than that, not to me at least, and so we never talked about it again."

I smiled. "I love the idea of him having a bath by the fire. Was that the same tin bath your mum used to put you in?"

"Yes. During the week it was hung on a big nail on a wall by the outside loo and was only brought into the house at bath time on a Saturday night. Mind, I can remember Mum also soaking the washing in it at times, especially if Dad's clothes were particularly dirty when he came home from work at the garage. That said, she would have done them outside, weather permitting, so they could go straight on the line to dry once she'd put them through the mangle and squeezed out as much of the water as possible." He laughed. "Funny how some things like that stay with you over the years."

"An outside loo, I bet that was fun?"

53

Dad took a drink from his cup and grinned.

"I'm not sure fun is the word I'd use to describe running out in the freezing cold of winter when you're desperate for a pee or whatever and having to sit on a cold wooden seat to do your business. And toilet rolls were also a luxury we couldn't always afford when I was very young either. I dread to think how many sporting headlines or news announcements of the day got imprinted on my bum back in those days. Mum would tear an old newspaper into squares and carefully thread a piece of string through them with a big knitting needle before hanging them on a nail banged into the wall next to the toilet." He laughed again. "Many a time I sat there lifting the paper carefully from the wall before tearing a piece off to make sure I wasn't sharing it with a spider who'd taken shelter behind it. Such was life in a two up two down in Peterborough in those days. Happy times, I think. Not that we knew any different."

I grimaced. "Sounds great. Thank goodness for modern life in the 1980s and the luxury of an inside loo with proper toilet paper is all I can say."

Mum set her cup down on the tray. "Well, it wasn't me who drifted away from the subject this time Charlie. So much for you wanting to remain focused."

She was right. I'd allowed my concentration to wander but had also enjoyed Dad's trip down memory lane.

"You're right, Mum, sorry. What were you saying?"

"I was telling you about Grampy and Granny Anna not being very forthcoming about their early life at the colliery."

"That's right. What about *your* dad, did he tell you or Nanny Mary anything about those early days? You know, about what conditions were like in the pits or how the young boys got on who worked there?"

"Not really, or not that I can remember, I would have been too young. So even if he had spoken about it, it would only have been to Mum anyway. That said, he did talk with Grampy about life at the colliery. Granny Anna said the two of them would sit around the fire for hours discussing all the fors and against about being a miner once Mum and Dad got married." She smiled. "But those conversations were nearly always just between the two of them, women weren't encouraged to join in or have an opinion." Mum paused and looked into the distance. "It all seems an age ago now and yet think how things have changed, even over the past few years. Oh I know we've just had this awful strike, but even so look at how much better off we are these days, at least we're not still sending children up chimneys *or* down the mines. Like you said before Charlie it was only around the turn of the century that things really began to improve for youngsters."

"You're right, before that they could be working at the pits from ten or even younger. The law only changed to prevent that around the mid-1800s." I blew out my cheeks. "I wasn't even making my own bed at ten."

Mum smiled. "I'm not sure making your bed is a priority even today looking at the way you leave it sometimes when you get up in the morning."

"Very funny ha ha, point taken."

"Anyway, as I was saying, I think Grampy thought himself lucky not to have started working there until he was nearer fourteen." Mum shook her head. "I still find it hard to believe little ones of that age and younger were being sent down those black holes to do a man's work, and under such awful conditions. Mum said Grampy told her he was one of the lucky ones as he began working on the surface when he first went there, grading the coal that had already been brought up. He said some of the other young lads were sent straight underground, with their shifts often starting in the middle of the night, poor little souls. And of course, in those days there was no proper machinery to help with the actual mining of the coal itself either, they had to dig it out by hand using pickaxes and shovels with the only light to work by being provided by lamps and candles. Grampy said these would have been held in the air for hours on end by the young boys so the miners could see what they were doing in digging out the coal. There was no electric lighting back then and certainly not deep underground in the mines themselves."

"It must have been awful. Were there many accidents?"

"As I said, Grampy didn't really like to talk about it, at least not that side of things, but what Mum could remember from the limited conversations they did have on the subject was that yes, there were accidents, and not just in Newstead, but at all the collieries, some of them were really serious."

Dad leant across the arm of his chair towards Mum. "Do you remember that time we went up to stay with your mum a few years ago? We spent a day driving around so I could get a proper feel for the area." Mum smiled and nodded as Dad turned to me. "I'd only been there a few times before, mainly on business and in the early days when your mum and I were first courting. I didn't really know much about the area then, or what it was like to have lived in a mining community." He turned back to Mum and smiled. "I seem to remember I was more interested in you in those days than in what your dad and granddad did for a living."

"I'll take that as a compliment," Mum replied, laughing. "But yes, you're right, we went up for a long weekend. Gosh, I'd nearly forgotten that." Mum looked across to me. "You stayed with your school friend I seem to remember?"

"Yeah, Barry, but it sounds like I might have enjoyed coming with you."

Dad laughed. "Well, you didn't say so at the time. You said you couldn't think of anything more boring than being dragged around by your parents for a weekend while they relived their courting days. I also think there was a school disco on that you and Barry wanted to go to? And, if I remember rightly girls had just started to appear on your radar as well."

"Could be. Jenny Porter I think her name was. I wonder what happened to her."

Mum gave me a gentle push. "Sounds like it could have been serious if you're still able to remember her name."

"I can remember her name but not a lot else, so it can't have been that serious. I was only about fifteen after all."

Dad sat back in his chair and rubbed his chin. "As if we could forget. That was the first time you asked to borrow my razor, and then cut yourself trying to shave off that bit of bum fluff you were just starting to develop on your chin."

I laughed and stroked my own chin. "Scarred for life and all because my father didn't teach me to shave properly. Still, it shows how times have changed; I'd love to pay a visit there now. I might even head up that way as part of my research."

"Well, if you do, you'll be able to discover the history of the place for yourself. The colliery's over a hundred years old now and, like so many pits these days, its future is under very real threat. I don't think Mrs Thatcher is going to back down now, especially after the battles of the past few years." He looked at Mum and smiled recalling the very real tensions that had touched our family in recent times, and which had so dramatically affected the wider mining community.

"Mining families are a proud race Charlie and every generation remembers the one before, along with the part each played in chronicling their history, whether that be in Nottingham or wherever a colliery was established."

"Flippin' heck, Dad, you sound just like Arthur Scargill."

Sitting upright, Mum looked straight at me. "Your dad's right though, Charlie, and although we may not be miners ourselves we are from mining stock, well, at least I am, and proud to say so. Everything that's gone on over the past few years between the government and the miners has been awful. Families falling out with each other, father set against son, it's terrible. Many of those wounds have yet to heal, and I'm not sure some of them ever will. The government should be ashamed of itself treating hard working families like that."

I could tell she was becoming emotional recounting the events of that desperate time and of the effect it had had on her, and more especially her own mum whose health and heart were already beginning to fail back then.

"I'm sorry if this is difficult, Mum; do you want to leave it for tonight? I should have remembered how upset it had made you and Nanny during the strike."

Mum took her handkerchief from her pocket as Dad leant forward to squeeze her hand.

"Your mum's okay, Charlie, it's just sometimes conversations like this can bring back a few of the darker memories as well as the good ones." He could tell Mum was struggling and so moved the conversation on. "You were asking about accidents in the mines?"

I realised what he was doing and willingly took his lead. "That's right. You said all of the mines experienced accidents?"

"They did. In the very early days, accidents might have been caused by walls or roofs collapsing in the shafts or in the mines themselves. The supporting structures back then were mainly wooden and wouldn't have been as safe as they are today. So yes, there were and always have been accidents in the pits. The most common in those early days seems to have been with men being crushed by the tubs of coal as they rattled along the makeshift rail tracks underground, or if they failed to stop properly. Sadly, some of those accidents would prove fatal."

I looked at Mum who appeared to have recovered her composure.

"Sorry, Charlie, it all just came back to me that's all; you know, what with my growing up there, at least during my early years." She smiled at me. "I'm fine now, promise. Just ignore your silly old Mum."

I leant across and gave her a kiss.

"Listen, I can find out most of the actual history about the colliery from the library, or if I decide to go there, so let's not worry too much about that sort of detail for now. Tell me a little more about your dad's time working there, or what you can remember at least, if that's okay?"

"Of course." She took a breath and smiled. "Well, as I said earlier, he was born straight into the mining community of Newstead and first went down a shaft himself in 1924, aged sixteen. It seems so young now but of course, as we know, he was already two years older than Grampy when he went underground for the first time that's if, as we said earlier, that particular story was true?" She looked at me thoughtfully for a moment before casting a glance towards Dad. "Would I be right in saying although you had to be twenty-one in those days to be legally considered an adult, boys of sixteen were still thought of as men when it came to working down the mines, or pretty much anywhere else for that matter?"

Dad nodded. "Absolutely; I remember your mum telling me she would watch them walking up the road at the end of a shift, with the only difference between the boys and the grown men being their size and the jackets that hung a little more loosely from the shoulders of the youngsters. Apart from that they all looked the same; covered in the same black dust and grime from the pit; their teeth gleaming white against the backdrop of their dirty faces as they spoke, gesticulating and joking with each other as they made their way home. She said Bill told her once when she asked him how it felt to watch the youngsters disappear down a shaft for the first time, knowing what they were about to experience that he'd said, 'They may have gone down as boys, but they came up a few hours later as men, or they didn't survive.'"

Mum smiled knowingly. "Your dad's right, Charlie, I heard that story from Mum as well." Pausing, she shook her head reflectively. "And although I know lots of youngsters leave school at sixteen these days as well and go out to work it still seems strange to think those young lads back then couldn't vote, drink or get married, but were still thought of as being old enough to put their lives at risk at the coal face. It's hardly the same as working behind the till in Woolworth's is it?" She paused again, a smile returning to her face. "Having said that it wasn't all bad, dirty and demanding though the job was. Like I said there was a strong feeling of community in the village and we children certainly never felt deprived or anything less than loved. I can still just about remember May Fairs and summer fetes when I'd run around in the fields, playing with the other children and making daisy chains, oblivious to any of life's greater challenges beyond my own little world. Mum always tried to protect me from the harsh realities of a life spent as a miner's daughter, certainly in the late 1930s and early '40s when times were often quite tough. I think that's part of the reason we moved to Papplewick after Dad died. She wanted to make a fresh start for both of us. It wasn't that she didn't have friends in Newstead, or that we weren't happy there, it was more that whenever there was an accident at the pit or maybe a miner would lose his life Mum would be reminded of her own loss, of Dad's death, albeit under very different circumstances. It just took her to a place she didn't want to be, and so the potential for a new beginning became all the more attractive, especially once Peggy suggested we move nearer to her."

As I sat listening to Mum speak I realised I was becoming as embroiled in her story and corresponding life journey as much she was and, interesting though it was, I knew I needed to bring her narrative back to the specific memories she had about her father before we lost the thread of our conversation altogether.

"You were telling me about your dad, and what your mum might have said about *his* time at the colliery?"

Mum raised her eyebrows and smiled at me. "I'm sorry, Charlie, I keep going off track, don't I?"

"It's fine really, but if there is anything specific you can remember about his time at Newstead, that would be great as well?"

"Of course."

Dad smiled encouragingly as she paused to collect her thoughts.

"Well, he spent fifteen years there in all, most of it down the mines, although, as we said before, he also worked topside for a while, which is why he was able to get that special dispensation, allowing him to leave and join the army. Dad was a good organiser and leader, much loved and respected by the other men by all accounts. His shifts were amongst the most productive Mum told me once. He seemed to be able to get the best out of everybody who worked alongside him. By 1939 though, things began to change with The Sheepbridge Company becoming the new owners of the colliery. It was a successful mine by then with a steady output of coal. Apparently, it had what were described as favourable geological conditions. I think that meant the seams were healthy and there was still plenty of coal to be brought up. Anyway, the new owners took a shine to Dad and promoted him to working in the office. Mum said he felt a bit of a traitor putting on a shirt and tie and watching his mates heading off to the pit for their underground shifts." She laughed as the memory overtook her. "Although I remember her saying as well that he wasn't opposed to the extra bit of money the promotion provided, and nor was she. Quite a lot of things were in short supply in those days and an extra bit of cash in your purse or pocket could make all the difference when it came to putting food on the table for a hungry miner and his young family. And of course, if he hadn't started working in the office, he probably wouldn't have got his dispensation allowing him to leave and sign up; he would have been held to his contract as being in a reserved occupation. The Country would have struggled without the coal the miners brought out of the ground during the war, and it wasn't a job just anybody off the street could have done, you needed to know what you were doing." Mum stared wistfully across the room as if trying to pluck some particular episode from her memory.

"It's funny; I don't really remember him coming home in his shirt and tie but, young as I was, I can still just about remember him picking me up with his sooty black hands and rubbing his whiskers against my face." She dropped her head and stared at the floor for a moment before looking up at me again.

"I remember his smile as well. He always seemed to be smiling, at least when he was with me." She laughed. "Perhaps it was just that his teeth looked whiter through the coal dust on his face? Whatever it was, I do remember his smile."

I could tell Mum was tired now and that I was unlikely to get much more from her this evening. I closed my notebook and rubbed her arm.

"Thanks, Mum, you've been really helpful; you too Dad." He looked at Mum and grinned, appreciating my sensitivity towards her.

"Anything to assist the studies of the brightest young mind at Leicester University."

It was my turn to smile. "I'm not sure about that, but I'll take the compliment all the same."

Mum moved to pick up the cups and place them on the tray.

"Leave that Mum I'll do it." I arched my shoulders, stretching out my arms as I did so. "And then I think, if it's okay with you two, I'll turn in, I could do with an early night. You must both be tired as well, especially you Mum after all that talking?"

Dad sat back in his chair and laughed. "An early night, you the great late-night reveller, are you not feeling well?"

"Yeah, yeah, very funny. But I want to make a couple of extra notes about some of the things you've said before I forget that might be useful for my other research." Tucking my notebook under my arm I bent down to pick up the tray.

Mum shifted forward on the sofa. "Are you sure you're alright carrying that lot?"

"I'm fine, no sweat. I'll leave them on the draining board."

Dad jumped up and opened the door.

"There you go, Son, sleep well."

"Cheers, Dad." I looked back over my shoulder. "Night Mum, and thanks again."

"You're welcome, Charlie." She blew me a kiss. "My pleasure, really."

I winked at her. "All the same…"

"Goodnight, Son, love you."

"You too."

I heard the door close behind me as I made my way towards the kitchen, wishing one of us had left the hall light on earlier, as the only illumination now available was that from the streetlamp reflecting its glow through the glass in the front door. I pushed open the kitchen door with my foot allowing the small amount of light from the hallway to reveal the outline of the table and chairs in front of me. Placing the tray on the table, and turning to switch the light on, I dropped my notebook on the floor. As I bent down in the dark to pick it up, I felt a little giddy; the sort of sensation you get when you move your head too quickly and become unbalanced. I stood up slowly, taking a deep breath to steady myself. As I did so the room began to spin and move away from me, becoming even darker and changing in appearance. It took on a shape and design I didn't recognise; the walls turning to thick dark stone casting murky shadows across a grey slate floor. I felt my heart racing and a bead of sweat run down my back. I tried to shout out to Mum and Dad but my mouth was dry and the words stuck in my throat.

Shaking my head, I blinked rapidly in attempt to clear my vision but to no avail as everything began to close in around me, the shadows becoming longer, reaching out like icy black fingers, twisting and turning towards me as though drawing me in to take hold of me. I couldn't breath and felt as if I were suffocating, the very air from my lungs being sucked from me. As I stood, unable to move, my legs buckling and my body trembling in both dread and fear, I heard a voice calling out to me, it was a voice I had heard before; its tone desperate and pleading.

"Help me, Charles."

I closed my eyes, praying for some assistance of my own to come and rescue me from the terror I was experiencing. Suddenly I became aware of light shining all around me and I instinctively opened my eyes to see what it was. I was back in our house, with Dad standing beside me. He had followed me into the kitchen, turning on the light as he entered the room.

"Are you alright, Son? What are you doing standing here in the dark; you look like you've seen a ghost?"

I attempted to speak but the words stuck in my throat again. "I'm…"

Thankfully, Dad jumped in before I embarrassed myself further.

"I just said to your mum we'd forgotten to leave the hall light on and that you'd be struggling to turn it on with your hands full carrying the tray."

I swallowed hard in an attempt to clear my throat which thankfully responded. "Sorry, yes, thanks Dad, I was…" My voice trailed away again as I wrestled with my thoughts. Should I tell him what had just happened; or rather what I thought had happened? I felt embarrassed, not entirely sure if he would believe me if I did say anything.

He looked at me quizzically. "You were what?"

I smiled and shook my head as if dismissing my own words. "Nothing, I was just thinking that's all."

"In the dark?"

I tried to make light of my obvious embarrassment. "Well, you and Mum are always going on about me wasting electricity and leaving all the lights on, so I thought –"

He interrupted me. "Now you're just being silly, Charlie. I mean yes, you could occasionally turn off some of the lights you leave burning for no good reason, but neither of us expect you to walk around in the dark you idiot."

I put my hand to my forehead as a trickle of perspiration ran down the side of my face.

He moved towards me. "Are you sure you're alright, Son?"

I felt trapped, both by the question and his closeness in proximity, and so moved to pick up the cups, taking them to the sink and placing them on the draining board. I spoke without turning, not wanting to visually engage with him in case he asked again about my frame of mind or wellbeing. "Yeah, I'm fine, just tired like I said."

"Well, if you're sure," his voice fading as he turned and walked back towards the lounge. "See you in the morning, Son."

"Night, Dad." I stood motionless for a moment staring ahead of me at the newly decorated kitchen wall with its rose patterned paper butting up against the pale blue wall units housing the breakfast bowls and dinner plates. I noticed a small space between the paper and side of the unit. "Not like Dad to leave a gap when he's decorating, he must have missed it." I smiled to myself, grateful for the distraction. "Better not tell Mum or she'll tease him rotten." I knew if I did and remembering what a perfectionist Dad was about his DIY, he'd probably strip the whole wall bare and start all over again. As I stood there the events of the last few minutes overtook me once more. I looked down at the sink not really noticing it as I become lost in a stare. Suddenly, there it was again, that desperate cry resonating in my head.

"Help me, Charles."

I felt my body shudder as I battled to take control of my thoughts and bring my mind back to the safe reality of my physical surroundings.

"You're losing it Charlie boy, better get a grip or it'll be the funny farm for you." I turned and walked to the door pausing only briefly to look back at the familiar surroundings of the room. I tapped myself on the side of the head in admonishment. "You see it's just a kitchen you pillock, a bloody kitchen that's all." Turning off the light I allowed myself a wry grin. "Even if Dad has only done half a job in decorating it." I made my way slowly up the stairs not entirely convinced I had fully exorcised the earlier demons from my mind.

I struggled to sleep that night, tossing and turning; my thoughts running wild with all that Mum had told me and by the recurring memory of what had taken place earlier in the kitchen. Eventually, my eyes becoming heavy, I drifted off, sheer mental exhaustion and the physical need for rest getting the better of me.

Chapter Seven

I woke with a start the next morning as the bell on my alarm clock rang out loudly, rousing me from my stupor. I'd been dreaming of walking through a field by a river and of looking up at the sun which had caused me to blink as it shone erratically through the branches of a large tree blowing in the breeze. A bell had been pealing, and as I looked in the direction of where the sound was coming from I noticed a church spire in the distance. As I turned away the ringing got louder, no longer a regular and ordered toll but more a desperate clanging noise now fully demanding of my attention. I sat bolt upright in my bed as my subconscious mind was shaken violently into the reality of another day. A sense of panic swept over me as I struggled momentarily to clear my thoughts and recognise it had been my alarm clock that had woken me and not the ringing of a church bell as my dream had suggested. I reached out and grabbed at the alarm, turning it off and cursing it as I did so. "Bloody thing."

There was a knock at my door, it was Dad.

"Alright if I come in, I heard your alarm go off?"

I rubbed the sleep from my eyes and coughed to clear my throat which felt dry.

"Yeah of course."

Dad entered dressed in his suit. "Morning, Charlie, are you okay?"

"I coughed again and apologised."

"Yeah, sorry, I've got a dry throat, must have slept with my mouth open."

"I didn't mean that, your alarm has been ringing for ages. Your mum and I were beginning to think something was wrong?"

"No, I'm fine, just in a deep sleep that's all. I had a really weird dream as well."

Dad looked at his watch. "Tell me about it later, I'm off to Kettering and I'm running late already; I don't want to get stuck in traffic."

"Okay, have a good day then."

"See you later, Son, look after your mum."

As the fog began to clear from my brain I realised what day it was. "Hang on, Dad, it's Sunday. You worked yesterday as well; surely you're not working the whole weekend?"

He grinned and shook his head. "I am this weekend. I got a call yesterday just before I left work asking me to go and meet the boss of this new company setting up locally. It could mean a lot of business for us and, apparently, he'll be at the factory himself this morning. Strike while the iron's hot and all that."

"Well, I hope they're paying you overtime then?"

He laughed. "Something like that, see ya. I'll get back as soon as I can."

I watched as he closed the door and fell back into the warmth of my bed, pulling the blanket up under my chin. I lay there for a moment recalling the dream I'd been having before the alarm had woken me from my slumbers. It had felt so real as if I'd actually been there. Wracking my brain I tried to make a connection with anything I might have been thinking about recently that could have created such a vivid image. After a few minutes of reflection and with no flash of inspiration forthcoming I reasoned the dream had probably been initiated through my recent studies at uni and ongoing interest in the countryside and its topography.

I felt myself drifting towards sleep once more when a loud bang echoed in my head; it was the front door slamming shut. "Better get up," I thought, recognising Mum would be downstairs waiting to have breakfast with me despite the fact she would have been up for more than an hour already having, no doubt, prepared a full English for Dad before he left for work. She was always the same if one of us had to make an early start. "You can't go out on just a bowl of cereals or a piece of toast when you've got such a long day in front of you. What would anyone think of me sending you out on an empty stomach?"

I recalled how Dad and I would tease her in response. "You're right; they'd probably send the food police round demanding to know what sort of a woman lets the men in her house go out starving and then be happy to see them begging for a crumb or a crust from people on the street."

I stretched, throwing back the bed covers and smiling to myself. It felt good to have such an easy relationship with my parents and to know how much they cared for me. I was aware of a few of my fellow students at uni who didn't enjoy the same bond with their own parents and looked forward to term time as a means of escape from the family. I on the other hand relished both spaces, viewing them in equal measure as friendly and welcoming. My thoughts were disturbed by a voice calling to me from the bottom of the stairs. It was Mum.

"Are you up, Charlie? Would you like a cooked breakfast? There are a couple of eggs and sausages left that your dad couldn't manage." I smiled to myself again, knowing she would have purposely cooked extra as an excuse to feed me up.

"You're a growing lad," she would say, "And always look so thin when you come home. Goodness knows what they feed you at university?"

Rolling on my side I pulled myself out of bed.

"Coming, Mum, I'll just have a quick wash and get dressed. And yes, a cooked breakfast would be great, thanks."

"Bacon and beans as well?"

"If it's going?" I knew it would be, along with some cooked tomatoes and a couple of slices of toast.

"Tea or coffee?"

"Coffee please, it'll help wake me up. I'm feeling a bit dopey today."

"Don't be long then."

I pushed my feet into my slippers and headed for the bathroom. As I washed and dressed, I thought of some of the things I wanted to ask Mum about her own Dad. I knew she would be happy to tell me everything she could remember about him but also recognised the need to be sensitive in my line of questioning. She'd always struggled with losing her father at such an early age and had carried an additional burden of grief for her mum as well as she got older. She told me Nanny Mary had felt the unwarranted but, no less, genuine sense of guilt in having lived on for so many years following Granddad John's death in the war. She said it had been the sadness of his passing coupled with the guilt of her own longevity that her mum had found the hardest to countenance at times. Although Mum tried to comfort and encourage her, she also recognised that something had died within her the day he was killed; something that would never be reconciled or healed no matter how much love and attention she received from other quarters.

"We were born to be together Irene," she'd told her. "If he's not here, then neither should I be. My heart may be beating but it was broken forever the day he died."

I thought about this and of the love Mum still felt for her parents as I finished dressing, encouraging myself to be as gentle as I could – when it came to seeking additional information from her about our family's history.

The delicious and unmistakable smell of bacon and eggs being prepared greeted me as I reached the bottom of the stairs, the appetising aroma filling my senses as it wafted invitingly along the hallway from the kitchen.

Pushing open the door I was greeted by Mum, head down over the cooker stirring pots and keeping a watchful eye on my toast as it browned gently under the grill.

"Oh, you're up then?"

I smiled at her obvious attempt at humour.

"Smells lovely, Mum, just like you, if you get my drift?"

She threw me a wry glance in between juggling a saucepan of beans and the frying pan with its sizzling contents of bacon and sausage.

"I'll take that as a compliment, I think. The kettles boiled and the coffee's in the mugs, I'll have one as well."

I placed my notebook and pen on the table and moved to fill the mugs. "Have you eaten?"

"Sort of. I had a bit of toast with your dad earlier, but I'll have a bit of something with you as well."

"Don't fancy a fry up then?"

She looked up briefly from the cooker. "Well, I did have a sausage with my toast earlier if I'm honest, hence this extra one I'm cooking with the bacon for you now. Sit yourself down, won't be a minute."

A full English breakfast in our house is one of life's great gastronomic delights and no one prepares it like Mum. I have never fathomed how she can fry sausages, bacon, two eggs, tomatoes and a piece of bread separately in the one frying pan and yet bring them all together at the same time, along with a saucepan of beans and two slices of toast, still warm, ready for a thick knob of butter to spread on them.

I put the two steaming mugs of coffee on the table and sat down, my mouth already watering in anticipation of the feast to come.

A plate full of colourful and equally delicious looking food was placed in front of me.

"There you go, Son, get that lot down you. Hopefully it will keep you going until lunchtime."

I looked at the feast set before me and puffed out my cheeks. "Until tomorrow lunchtime I should think. Thanks Mum, this looks fantastic."

She squeezed my shoulder. "It's nice to be able to spoil you Charlie, enjoy."

I shook some salt and pepper on my food and began the demolition process of reducing the contents of my plate. Mum sat opposite me with a satisfied smile on her face at my obvious appreciation of her culinary efforts. I watched as she carefully buttered her toast and took a sip of coffee from her mug.

"I've been thinking about Dad this morning, Charlie, as you asked me to, and as to what I could remember about him, especially after he joined up. It is his time in the army you wanted to talk about isn't it?"

I nodded, swallowing a mouthful of sausage and egg as I did so.

"If that's okay, and maybe some more about your early life with him in Newstead as well, if there's anything more you can remember? I know you were really young when he left." I smiled. "Are you sure this is okay, Mum? If it's going to upset you I can…"

She shook her head.

"We've already spoken about that." She took a deep breath. "It will do me good to talk about him. That's if you don't mind me reaching for my hanky at times? Anyway, now Mum's gone it's up to me to keep his memory alive, for all of us."

"Thanks, but only if you're sure?"

"I'll be fine." She leant across the table and rubbed my arm, nodding towards my groaning plate of food. "Now you tuck into that lot and I'll do the talking, at least until you've finished your breakfast."

"Okay." I loaded my fork with more sausage and egg. "Tell me what you remember about your home?"

She took another sip from her mug and thought for a moment. "Well, Newstead itself consisted of around a hundred and fifty houses, maybe less, but they were all pretty much the same. They had a kitchen, what they called a parlour and a pantry, along with two or maybe three bedrooms. They weren't big houses but certainly big enough for us, and for most of the young families who lived and worked there in those early days." She smiled at my efforts to take notes and cram forkfuls of her delicious fry up into my mouth at the same time.

"Why don't we do this after you've finished, you'll get indigestion if you keep going like that?"

"I'm fine honest, you carry on."

She shook her head in mock disapproval. "Well, don't blame me if you get pains in your stomach later on that's all I can say. Now, where was I? Oh yes, our house. It had an outside lavvy and, the same as your dad said last night, a tin bath that everyone in the family shared on a Saturday night. I have a vague memory of that when I was young." She laughed. "That was the best bit about being the smallest in the family as I got to go in the water first; you know while it was still warm and clean. There would only be a few saucepans of hot water in it anyway, barely a few inches deep, so we never had a proper soak. It was in, stand up to get washed, sit down, wash off the soap and out. Oh yes, and an extra jug of water over my head if Mum had washed my hair. Then I'd stand in front of the fire while she rubbed me down with a towel that had been placed over the fire guard earlier to warm through. I loved the feeling of that soft warm towel going around me and Mum pulling me in towards her, holding me close as she rubbed my hair and dried me off." She laughed. "And of course, there was always plenty of coal to keep the fire going."

I stopped eating long enough to make a couple of notes and to spread some butter on a piece of toast. "It sounds a bit basic to me, although I do vaguely remember enjoying bath times as well when I was a youngster?"

"And you had a lot more hot water in the bath as well, along with all of your toys to play with." She paused and shook her head. "They were different times Charlie but, I suppose we didn't know any different and were just grateful for what we had. I think children, certainly when they're very young, are more accepting of their lot; they don't question things so much, at least not like youngsters seem to do today." She shook her head again and laughed. "Sorry, there I go again, heading off in a different direction. What was I talking about?"

"Life in Newstead."

"That's right. Well, as I said the village was first made up of just houses for the miners and their families but, after a while, some of them were turned into little shops or pubs as there was no early infrastructure in place like there is today when a new estate is built. One house that was converted into a pub was called The Brown Cow. Grampy said he used to go in there sometimes with his mates, but they weren't really pubs as such, at least not like the ones you go in. They were known as Shebeeners and didn't have a formal license to sell alcohol either. One of the first properly established pubs was The Station Hotel which was built around three years before Grampy was born, so that would have been around 1881."

I put my knife and fork down for a minute to give my stomach a brief respite. "What about transport? I don't mean for getting around locally but more for people coming to the area to work or family visits and the like?"

Mum chewed her lip in thought for a moment. "There were two railway stations in the village I seem to remember, The Midland and The Great Northern."

I picked up my knife again to butter another piece of toast. "Flipping heck, Mum, this is great, how do you know all this?"

"I'd forgotten I did if I'm honest, but your dad and I were talking last night after you'd gone to bed and things just came back. Mum had spoken to me about a lot of it over the years of course after we moved away and, young as I was, I suppose I picked up stories about the village just through having lived there. And Papplewick wasn't that far away remember, so news of what was happening in Newstead still did the rounds locally." She paused as the memories came back to her. "Also, with mining being the biggest employer in the area we were taught about its history in school, along with how the village and the pits had come into being, not only in our area but right across the Midlands and up into Yorkshire as well. Like I said before, miners are a proud people and so passing down stories and shared experiences of colliery life was an important and natural part of a youngster's education, both inside and outside of the classroom."

"Do you have any other stories about life there you can remember?"

She laughed. "Gosh, I'm not sure, it was all such a long time ago and I haven't got Mum here to remind me outside of what your dad and I were discussing last night." She paused again to gather her thoughts. "I suppose it was the same as anywhere else really, we didn't know any different, it was just home. When you're little you just imagine everybody is the same as you, so for us living in that small mining village and seeing our dad's coming home each day grubby and covered in coal dust was the norm. It's just what we knew. I think I became more interested when Mum and I moved away after Dad had been killed. I was a bit older then and maybe better able to appreciate what a special time it had been for us as a family living there."

She looked at me and smiled. "I do remember when Mum and I first moved to Papplewick to be near Peggy; we started to go to church with her for a while. Peggy was part of a singing group and so we used to go and support her when there was a special service or local event she was involved with. I asked Mum about the church once; St James' it was called. It was really old, built around the

12th century – and very imposing, or at least it felt that way to me as a little girl. It had high ceilings, stained glass windows that sort of thing, loads of history about it. Anyway, I asked Mum why our church in Newstead wasn't the same and she said it was because it was relatively new compared to St James and had only been built in around 1928; before that there had been just a couple of small chapels where people gathered for Sunday services and the like. I suppose, as with the Shebeeners, they'd probably started life in someone's house and grown from there. It was at times like that I realised how new the actual village itself really was." Mum took another drink from her mug and smiled at me. "Remember what I said yesterday about the mine only being established there in the early 1870s?"

I nodded, also taking a large gulp of coffee from my mug.

"Well, that meant it was only around sixty years old when Mum and I moved away. Everything was still really new and only just beginning to establish itself but, as kids we didn't know that, we just assumed the village had been there forever, like all youngsters do wherever they live, until they're told different."

I finished scribbling down what she was saying and looked up.

"Thanks, Mum, all of this is really helpful, especially the specific years and so on, although as I said before don't worry too much about that as I can check most of them against the information held in the public records office and so on. In fact, I should be able to find all of the various dates I need regarding who lived where and when along with any associated births, marriages and deaths from the recorded census details for that period. And of course, when I go further back to try and discover the truth about the alleged murder in the family, if indeed there was one." We smiled at each other. "I'm really excited by all of this, Mum, especially as it's *our* family I'm investigating. It's going to be really interesting to see what else I can uncover over the next few weeks."

Mum laughed. "Just so long as you don't discover anything too outrageous. I don't want to be the subject of sly conversations and gossip amongst our neighbours."

"So having a murder in the family isn't racy enough for you then?"

She nodded her head and grinned. "I suppose you have a point there, – it can't get much racier than that can it?" She leant forward in her chair and took a breath. "You said you wanted to know about Dad, and how he died?"

"If that's okay but, like I said, if you think it'll be too painful for you then I could probably find out most of that detail from the war records as well, although they won't include your personal memories and stories about him of course." I paused briefly. "That won't make a big difference to the family tree itself, it's just interesting for me to hear about it?" Her smile encouraged me to continue. "I know he was killed at Dunkirk, but that's about it. I certainly don't know any of the physical detail of what happened. I didn't like to ask before, you know with you being so young at the time and him being your dad and all. Silly really I suppose that we don't think to talk about these things while we can but, well…"

I sensed myself digging a hole and felt my cheeks turning red with embarrassment.

"It's fine, Charlie, really. It'll probably do me good to talk about it. I wish now I'd asked Mum more about what actually happened myself but, like you say, we don't. We try to be sensitive, and then of course once the person's gone it's too late to have that conversation. So please, don't worry, let's just see how we get on, okay?"

I nodded and smiled, recognising this wasn't going to be easy for her but was more than grateful she was willing to try.

I pushed my now empty plate to one side and, leaning back in my chair, rubbed my full stomach. "That was delicious, Mum, really good, thanks."

"You're more than welcome. Like I said before, it's nice to be able to spoil you every once in a while."

She stood up. "Now, let's clear this lot away and then I'll tell you what I can remember about Dad."

We spent the next ten minutes washing and drying the breakfast things and talking generally about how much I was enjoying life at university and of what she had planned for the back garden once she convinced Dad of the benefits to be gained in having a fishpond.

"Let's go through to the lounge and talk Charlie, it's more comfortable in there." Putting the last of the plates away, I nodded my agreement.

"Great."

I followed her along the hallway and into the lounge where the sun was shining through the front window, casting differing shadows across the carpet as it caught items of furniture in its path and spread its welcoming light across the room. I ran my foot across the red and grey patterned design as if trying to capture the sun's rays under my shoe.

"I love the sun."

Mum smiled as she sat down on one end of the sofa. "You always have. I remember when you were a little boy you would run around with your fishing net trying to trap it like the colours at the end of a rainbow." She laughed and threw her head back embracing the memory. "You would ask me for an empty jar or container to put it in, so you could bring it out to cheer yourself up on cloudy days or when it rained. You always did have a vivid imagination."

"And here I am still trying to catch it all these years on." I pretended to grasp a handful of the golden rays of light as they stretched across the carpet and furnishings, illuminating the room. Laughing back at her, I waved my clenched fist in the air. "Have you got a jar handy for me to put this in, Mum?"

She shook her head again, grinning at me as she did so. "You daft thing. Honestly, I wonder about you sometimes I really do."

I moved to sit opposite her in Dad's chair. "I won't be in trouble for sitting here, will I?"

"I won't tell if you don't. But you're right, he can be quite protective of that old chair. I don't know why though? As I said last night it's certainly seen better days and is definitely ready to be replaced, but he won't hear of it." She gestured towards the other armchair and sofa. "And it certainly doesn't do anything for the rest of my lovely new suite."

We both settled into our respective seats as I turned the pages of my notebook.

"So, come on then tell me about your dad, or at least what you can remember, and about him joining up?"

She paused briefly allowing her mind to step back in time.

"Well, as I said yesterday, I wasn't even four when he left, but I do have a vague recollection of him in his uniform." She leant forward and picked up a small plastic bag from the side of the coffee table. "And these brought back a few memories as well. I sorted them out earlier before you were up. They're old photos of him and Mum just before he left. I think you may have seen some of them a long time ago, but I haven't had them out for years, certainly not since Mum died."

She took out a handful of small black and white photographs of her parents, presumably taken shortly after her dad had signed up. There was also a couple of him holding Mum, as a little girl, in his arms and another with her standing by his side wearing a floral-patterned dress. Her hair was in ringlets tumbling down the sides of her head with a clip holding the fringe off her face.

"That was my Shirley Temple look," Mum laughed.

"Shirley who?"

"Oh come on, Charlie, you must have heard of Shirley Temple? I'm sure I've spoken about her before. She was a child film star in the 1930s and was famous for her curly hair and ringlets. Mum thought she was great, so that's why I had my hair like that for a while as well. As you can see it wasn't to last." She put her hand up to her light brown, slightly greying hair which hung straight and long just beyond her shoulders. "I'd give anything for those curls now, but they just seemed to grow out by the time I reached my teens. Mind they were never naturally as tight as in those pictures. Mum used to spend hours putting rags in my hair at night so it would be curly in the morning." She laughed. "The things we girls do to make ourselves pretty, or at least what we do to our children, poor things." She nodded towards me. "Just as well you weren't a girl Charlie, goodness knows what I might have done with you, especially now in the '80s with big hair being the in look?"

I laughed and looked down at the pictures spread across the coffee table. "You look like you were happy though Mum?"

"I was, and so were Mum and Dad. As I told you yesterday, I do remember a lot of laughter in our house." Mum pointed to the floral dress she was wearing in the picture.

"That dress was yellow, and those flowers were red and blue. It was my favourite; I loved all the different colours. Mum said I still wanted to wear it even when I'd obviously grown out of it. Apparently, I got very upset when she gave it to a neighbour for her little girl who was a bit younger and smaller than me. She said I'd wanted to go to the lady's house and demand it back because it was *my* dress and not hers." She picked up two more photographs and smiled at them lovingly before handing them to me.

"I think these are from around the time Dad left. Mum told me later that after he'd finished his training he was given a few days' leave so he could come home and say goodbye to us; that's when these were taken. He took some copies out to remind him of us while he was away, including one of me in that flowery dress; he liked me in it as well."

"When did he actually leave?"

Mum closed her eyes in thought. "I think it was near the end of November, a couple of months after the war started."

74

I watched as she folded her arms and pulled them into her chest as if to provide some form of physical comfort before continuing.

"Mum told me in later years that after Dad had left she would say a prayer with me for him every night when she put me to bed. I think it was partly to keep his memory fresh in my mind, what with me being so young, but also because she had quite a strong faith and wanted to remind God to keep a hand on the man she loved, that we both loved."

Mum looked at me and smiled, lowering her arms and placing her hands on her knees. "It's funny isn't it, but even the most devout of atheists will sometimes say a prayer of sorts when all seems lost and every other cry for help seems to fail or fall on deaf ears."

Pausing again, she shook her head gently. "Anyway, we didn't hear from Dad again for some while after that, I think it was almost a month before we received his first letter Mum said."

I sensed her becoming emotional. "You okay, Mum?"

"I'm fine, Charlie, just a bit…you know."

I nodded my understanding and shook my biro to make sure the ink was running okay.

"Did he get home again before he was killed?"

Mum paused, her expression becoming more solemn. "No, we never saw him again."

The next few moments were spent in quiet reflection until I broke the silence. "We can stop for a while if you like Mum, if you're finding it too much?"

She looked at me and smiled, a tear forming in her eye. "I didn't mention this before Charlie; I wasn't going to either, didn't think I'd be strong enough but, well, this seems to be the perfect time."

I looked at her and shook my head quizzically. "Didn't mention what?"

She got up and walked to the sideboard; her hand pausing as she moved to open a drawer. She spoke without turning to face me.

"I've kept these locked away since Mum went; she passed them on to me a few days before she died. I didn't know if or when I'd be able to look at them again, but, like I say, this seems to be the right time."

I felt a thread of excitement run through me, although I equally sensed whatever it was she was about to share was not going to be easy for her.

"I'd never known about them before, but she wanted me to have them." She took a deep breath and opened the drawer, taking out an old biscuit tin and stroking it lovingly as she moved back to the settee. "This was Mum's. It's where she kept her treasures as she called them, her keepsakes, including the photos we were just looking at. She'd shared some of them earlier, before she passed away, but not these." She opened the tin and showed me the contents. In it was an empty packet of Woodbine cigarettes, a very sad looking red rose, a bright green hair ribbon and three brown envelopes. I shook my head again.

"I'm not sure I understand. Are they Nanny Mary's?"

Mum, clearly emotional, took a deep breath. "I said this might not be easy Charlie so bear with me." She sat down and took the items from the tin one at a time, describing each one as she did so. "Mum told me this was the last packet of cigarettes Dad had smoked before he left. He'd thrown it away, but she rescued it and kept it as a reminder of him." She put the cigarette box back and picked up the hair ribbon.

"This was the last thing Dad bought me before he left. I don't remember, but apparently he'd taken me out a few days before and I'd seen this ribbon in a shop and liked it." Mum laughed. "Mum said he bought it and tied my hair back with it to show her when we got home but, being Dad, who never was very good at dressing me or doing my hair properly hadn't tied it tight enough, and so by the time we got back it was hanging off the very ends of my hair and about to drop off." She took another deep breath and fought back a tear as she stared – at the ribbon in her hand. "Mum said I wore this every day for the next few weeks, telling her I wouldn't take it off until my daddy came home again. She said she couldn't remember exactly how long I kept it in my hair but that it was a long time."

It was hard to imagine my mum as a little girl, wearing ribbons in her hair, but I could see from the look on her face that the memory was very real to her. I watched as she folded the ribbon, placing it back gently in the tin, before, equally as carefully, picking up the rose.

"Mum and Dad went for a drink the night before he left; a neighbour came in and kept an eye on me while they went to their local, The Kings Head I think she said it was called. Anyway, there were a few of their friends in the pub that night, with some of the other men about to go off to war as well. Apparently, a young girl came in selling roses and Dad bought this one for Mum. Maybe a local flower seller had got wind of couples saying goodbye and saw a chance to make some money, but it obviously worked as Mum said she sold quite a few."

She smiled, holding the flower in the palm of her hand to make sure none of the few remaining petals fell away. "Mum kept it pressed in the pages of a book for a long time after Dad left before putting it in this tin for safe keeping along with her other treasures, and that's where it's been ever since."

I stared at the fading rose laying limp in her hand and tried to envisage how different it would have looked on the night Granddad had bought it for Nanny Mary, and of the circumstances surrounding their parting. It was hard to think of my Grandparents as a vital young couple deeply in love, or of the emotions they would have experienced that night knowing they were about to be parted for goodness how long with him heading off to war. I wondered if he might have acted differently had he known this was to be the last time he would see his wife and young daughter, and as to what Nanny Mary might have said to try and stop him leaving had she been aware this was to be their final goodbye. I looked up at Mum who was still caressing the flower in the palm of her hand as if it were some precious jewel.

"And you didn't know anything about this tin or its contents until just before she died?"

She shook her head. "Like I said only the photos; but no, none of this." She nodded towards the tin. "I suppose we all hold on to the odd memento of a special time or relationship and these where Mum's, her private memories of the man she loved and of their last few days together."

"And the envelopes; presumably they're letters of some sort?"

Mum placed the rose carefully back in the tin and lifted out the three slightly faded envelopes. I watched as she embraced them lovingly to her chest.

"Yes, and the most precious memories of all. Mum told me she'd thought of destroying them when she became ill as some of the content is quite personal, things about the two of them and their relationship. But she realised if she did any remaining physical evidence of Dad's life and their time together would be gone forever."

Mum placed her hand flat against her nose and mouth in an attempt to control her emotions. "She said by passing them on to me it would keep his memory alive and, that as an adult now with a family of my own, I would understand, from reading them, just how much they'd loved each other, and me. She also said it would give me an insight into what Dad was thinking about and experiencing during those last few weeks of his life."

She paused again. "As I said, I had thought of not showing them to you, to protect Mum and Dad's privacy if you like, but then realised that would have been as unfair on you as it would have been on me had she chosen to destroy them before I'd had a chance to read them. I needed to overcome that feeling for myself, as Mum had, so as to be able share them with you, not only so you could use them to help with your research but, more especially, so you can share them with your own children when the time comes and let them know about their great grandparents; what sort of people they were and of the lives they lived." She held the envelopes out towards me. "What better evidence could you offer them than these personal keepsakes along with their shared truths and wonderful memories, and all of it linked directly to their own family's history?"

I was taken aback by what Mum was saying and touched by the honesty and bravery of her actions in deciding to make this disclosure.

"Are you sure about this, Mum? I mean, yes of course I'd love to read them and hear what they have to say but I'm also aware this is your mum and dad we're talking about. This is not only about them, but rather it's the two of them physically speaking to each other, or at least your dad speaking to your mum, privately, perhaps even intimately."

"And that's the point I'm trying to make, Charlie." She nodded towards the tin. "Mum passed all of these items onto me to cherish and to learn from, and now I'm passing them onto you to do the same; to help you discover who your Grandparents really were and so, in years to come, you won't just think of them as simply an old lady you visited from time to time and a man you never even met." She looked down at the faded brown envelopes again. "I know you'll honour and value their content just as much as I do."

"Of course I will."

She smiled. "You won't get nearer to discovering the truth about this particular period of our family's history than by reading these letters."

I recognised this wasn't easy for her and was determined to honour her bravery and conviction in deciding to share these precious insights from her parents all too brief love story.

"Thanks, Mum. I've always thought of Granddad John as being special from the way you and Nanny Mary talked about him, even though it wasn't much or very often. And now, thanks to these letters, I've got the opportunity to find out more about him for myself. That's if you're absolutely sure you're happy for me to read them?"

Mum placed the envelopes back in the tin and, standing up, passed it to me.

"I'm sure, although I don't think I can actually sit here in silence while you read them, so it might be better if you look at them on your own." She looked down at me and nodded towards the tin again. "And while you're doing that I'll go and busy myself with the washing and ironing."

"That doesn't seem fair?"

"Really, Charlie, it's fine." She forced a grin. "Anyway, the ironing won't do itself, and it'll still be there next week if I wait for you or your dad to do it."

I looked up and smiled. "Well, if you're sure? Thanks Mum."

"They're each numbered one to three so they can be read in order. The first is the one he wrote to her on the day he left. Mum said she found it on the dining table propped against a vase after the two of us had waved him goodbye at the front door. The second is the one I mentioned earlier, sent about a month after he'd left, and number three is the one he wrote in France just before he was killed."

We looked at each other for a moment, both sensing the enormity of the journey we were about to embark on as a family. In taking these first few tentative steps towards discovering more about our ancestry we were also putting in place the first part of our family tree.

Mum ran her fingers through my hair. "Love you, Charlie."

"You too."

She moved towards the door. "I'll leave you to it. Like I said I want to get this washing and ironing sorted and there's another couple of jobs I want to get on top of as well, so take as long as you like."

Recognising her need to reflect on all we'd discussed and that she wanted to stay out of the away until I'd finished reading the letters, I nodded my understanding.

"Thanks again, Mum."

I watched as she left the room, closing the door gently behind her. Sitting in silence for a moment I stared at the open tin and its treasured contents. Here before me was not only a piece of personal family history but, more heartbreakingly, all that remained of a tragic love story between two young people whose lives had been ripped apart in one horrifying moment of violence and war. I picked up the first envelope and carefully removed its contents. The pages inside, as with the envelope itself, had faded slightly and turned a light coffee coloured shade of brown. I slowly unfolded the two sheets of paper inside and was taken aback momentarily as a small additional piece of paper fell to the floor. I picked it up, noticing a large cross marked in the middle of the page. Underneath the cross was a short note.

Please give this big kiss to Irene and tell her everyday how much her daddy loves her and how proud he is of his little girl.

I was immediately overcome with emotion realising he was talking about my mum, the woman who had brought me into the world and cared for me for so many years but, to him, was his daughter, his own precious little girl; someone he had loved unconditionally and sought to protect in the short time they'd spent together. I suddenly became aware of how tough this voyage of discovery was actually going to be, not only for me but, for all of us, and especially Mum. In the past I had been the journeying inquisitor researching the lives of those I didn't know and wasn't particularly concerned about. It had been easy for me to remain detached when compiling the detail of their existence but, this was different, these were people I did know and truly cared about. This was *my* family. I was about to embark on a very different journey and one that would change my life in ways I couldn't even begin to imagine.

I placed the small piece of paper on the arm of my chair and sat back to read the letter itself. As I stared at the words in front of me, I was struck by how neat the writing was, a phrase that could never be attributed to my own attempts when putting pen or pencil to paper. I smiled, recalling the times Mum, Dad and my tutors had commented at my own sloppy efforts at writing in long hand.

"It looks as though a spider has found its way into a bottle of ink and then, in making its escape, has staggered across the sheet of paper in some sort of drunken fume induced haze." I knew their accusations were well founded as I had always felt the need, when making notes, to get down all the relevant facts and information in double quick time so as not to forget, or leave out, any salient detail, thus resulting in a perfect example of their appraisal of my handwriting.

As I looked down at this precious document, a shiver ran through my body causing the paper to tremor slightly in my hand. This was triggered, in part, by the knowledge I was about to discover something about my Grandparents and their relationship both private and personal, something, that until this moment, I had never even considered or been aware of. At the time of writing, more than forty years previously, the contents of these letters had been intended for their eyes only, reflecting their personal feelings for one another without thought or consideration that one day they might be viewed by others, and certainly not their own children and grandchildren. I drew a deep breath, exhaling slowly and deliberately in anticipation of what I was to about to read.

My darling Mary,

Saying goodbye to you and Irene today will be the hardest thing I will ever have to do. Thank you for letting me dress her this morning and for giving us those precious few minutes alone together. It made me wish I had done it more often, rather than simply assuming it was part of your role as her mother. Although, in the few times I have helped before, I recall how often I would choose the wrong dress or place an incorrectly coloured ribbon in her hair causing you to make comment which would result in my becoming defensive, arguing my corner about making such an innocent mistake. And I'm sorry for that as well, as I am for so many other areas of our life together that I have, in the past, been mistaken in or taken for granted. Perhaps it is because of this awful war, along with the realisation of how quickly one's life can end, that I have become more acutely aware of just how precious every second spent in each other's company truly is, no matter how brief or fleeting that moment may be.

Irene is such a pretty young girl and already demonstrates your own loving and affectionate nature. I am so proud of you both. As for you my beloved Mary what can I say other than I love you, and although I may be travelling far away in the weeks to come my heart will most certainly remain here at home with you and our beautiful daughter. We don't know what the future holds my love, either for ourselves or for the world at this dark and terrible time but be assured I will do my part to help secure the victory Mr Chamberlain and his government have determined we should achieve. I know you were keen for me to stay at the colliery but, as a man, I felt compelled to seek the dispensation made available to me and sign up for active service. Had I not done this I know, in the years to come, I would have felt I had failed not only my fellow man and Country, but more especially myself. How could I ever have looked at you and Irene again knowing I hadn't heeded the call to protect you both, and others, from this awful threat to our peace and security posed by Hitler and his army. I ask you again to forgive me for feeling this way, and for answering the call to serve the greater good?

My darling, there is one other thing I need to say, and this will be as hard for me to write as it will be for you to read.

If I do not come home again, as I hope and pray I will, I want you to know that my final thoughts will be of you and Irene and in praying that God will protect you both and provide for you. I won't say anymore now as I don't want to upset you further. Our parting today will be hard enough for both of us. Kiss my pillow each night and hold it to you as I will surely do the same with the pictures of you and Irene that I will carry with me always.

Your loving husband,
John.

P.S. I have been putting aside a little extra money for a while now knowing this day would come. You will find four pounds and two shillings in your sewing basket. I hope it helps if times become especially hard in the weeks ahead.

I sat staring blankly at the pages of faded writing in front of me, my heart and mind numb with emotion. These were the actual words my grandfather had written to my Nan on the day he'd left for war. I'd always been passionate about family history and in how our societal and industrial landscape had been shaped across the years by men and women like my grandparents and their forebears but, with this tangible evidence of that shaping and move towards change here in my hand, my zeal for the subject and its detail became even more profound and resolute. I was suddenly aware that other events in history I had read about and studied in recent years were every bit as authentic and valid to the families involved with them as the story unfolding in front of me was to mine. I now knew for certain I had been right in choosing English Local History as my core subject at uni and, whilst the final destination for my life's work was still undecided, I was at least heading in the right direction, both personally and professionally. Accepting that truth and feeling more positive in myself because of it I picked up the second letter. This one had been written, as Mum had said, around a month after my grandfather had joined his troop and left for the front. I opened it carefully in case of another unsuspected enclosure, but there was none; instead, just three short pages of clearly hastily composed words that, for all the obvious pressure under which they had been written, were still none the less as eloquent and heartfelt as any well planned sonnet or poem to a loved one might have been.

My dearest Mary,

I am sorry not to have written before but life and events have simply overtaken us since leaving Blighty. Also, because we have been on the move for much of the past few weeks it hasn't been possible to have our letters collected for posting. I don't think any of us were prepared for the intensity and ferocity of the fighting we have encountered in the time we have been here. Hardly an hour has gone by that we haven't been under fire or returning it. I cannot tell you exactly where we are in case this letter is intercepted by Gerry on its way to you. I do pray though that it reaches you safely and that you and dear Irene are both well? I am sure she will have grown even in the short time I have been away. I look at the pictures we had taken together before I left each evening and thank God that he has allowed me to survive another day; another day that prayerfully brings us closer to being together again. I miss you both so much.

The fighting has become particularly intense of late with a number of our troop being wounded, including one lad I had become friendly with who was shot yesterday. I went to visit him last night in the field hospital, but sadly he died before I had a chance to speak with him. He was only a young bloke, twenty-one, and recently married. He hadn't been here long either and had just received news from home telling him his wife was pregnant with their first child. He was so excited and had written back to her saying how happy and proud he was. It's sad to think that when she receives his letter it will be alongside the news that he is gone and that he will never see his baby or hold it in his arms. It made me realise once again how fragile our lives and time together are on this earth and of just how precious you and Irene are to me, never doubt that my darling. Even though fighting and death are all around us we try to keep our spirits up as best we can. The sergeant, who is a top bloke, does his best to encourage us by telling jokes or teasing us about how easy we had it at home before joining up and how the army will make real men of us. I'm not sure how the lads working underground at Newstead would feel about their lives being described as easy knowing how hard they work and of the very real dangers they face each day. I miss them too, but am grateful to be here and to play my part in protecting their freedom and the lives of those they hold dear.

I will try and write again soon Mary, hopefully with better news. In the meantime, give Irene the kiss I long to give her myself but, for now, can only place on her picture. As for you my beloved, I hope you know how much I long to hold you in my arms again and embrace you. I miss the smell of your body and the look in your eyes as we join together in a loving embrace under the blankets on our bed. Keep my side warm and ready for the time when I am home again and able to fill you, once more, with my love. Continue to hold my heart close my darling as I do yours.

God bless you both,
Your loving husband John.

I read the last few words through a mist of tears forming in my eyes. How many times had I sat with my Nan over the years and viewed her as little more than a loved but ageing family member? To my shame I freely admit I had never imagined or considered her as being the youthful and vital recipient of this stated physical love and desire by my granddad. Does any youngster choose to think of their parents sharing such intimate relations, let alone their Grandparents? After all, love and sex are the domain of the young aren't they? Surely our parents and the generations before were never of an age to enjoy each other's bodies, or indeed any form of physical contact; even watching them kiss, for many a child, is a step too far! I knew this be true for myself and of the effect it had on me as a youngster whenever I witnessed Mum and Dad share more than a fleeting peck on the cheek. And yet here I was caught up in a love story far deeper and more vibrant than any I had read about in the past or could imagine, and with the lead characters in this particular tale of romance being none other than my own Grandparents. I have been given a lot of advice over the years from my parents and teachers alike to assist in my growing towards adulthood but I knew that, from this moment on, nothing would have a more direct influence on my learning about life and relationships than the few minutes I had just spent in reading these letters. I felt a major shift had taken place in my thinking about how, in future, I would view others, especially the older generation. No longer would I regard them as merely aged relatives or unknown figures from the past when carrying out my research for a history project; from now on I would view them for what they truly were, vibrant and passionate human beings with a very real-life story of their own to tell. Yes, perhaps they had aged physically in years, but their opinions and the contribution they'd made towards today's society was no less vital or valid than that of my own peer group, or indeed any other generation. If anything, I would now consider their outlook on life as being of even greater value, bringing as it did, a perspective based on already proven life skills, experience, personal bravery and inventiveness.

As I sat in silence embracing this newfound determination to better respect my ancestral forebears I heard the lounge door open behind me.

"How's it going?"

"Wow," I replied, turning to face Mum as she entered the room. "I've only read the first two, but my goodness what a story. I'd never thought of Nanny Mary like that, as a young Mum with you as her little girl."

"How do you think it made me feel when I read them?"

I leant forward as she moved closer and squeezed her hand. "I can see why you didn't want to share them, but I'm grateful you did, they are very powerful. I only wish I'd known your dad; he sounds an amazing man. He obviously loved you both very much?"

She looked down and gestured towards the open tin. "You wait till you read the last one, it upsets me just thinking about it."

"I can read it later if you like?"

"No you're alright, I just came in to see how you were getting on. I'm in the middle of some ironing at the moment so I'll finish that and then come back and join you."

"Are you sure, I'm really happy to leave it for another time?"

"No, really, Charlie, it's fine. Like I say I want to get this bit of ironing done, and it'll be easier for both of us to talk once you've read them all."

I picked up the letters. "Promise you'll come back and talk about them though when you've finished?"

She nodded cautiously. "I will but, as I said before, what I can't promise is I won't get upset." I noticed her eyes beginning to fill once more. "See, I'm going already." She sniffed back her tears. "Sorry, I'll do my best."

"Please don't apologise, Mum. Seriously, I've been getting a bit misty eyed as well."

She leant over and stroked my head. "That's alright then, we can have a cry together."

We smiled at each other, both of us sensing the poignancy of the moment.

"Love you, Mum."

She smiled and moved towards the door. "Love you too, Charlie."

"This is turning out to be quite a day," I mused as the door closed behind me. I placed the first two envelopes and their contents back in the tin and held the third in my hand for a moment. I stared down at it, Nanny Mary's name and address still clearly visible on the front. I ran my finger over the pencilled writing and, closing my eyes, tried to imagine what would have been going through my grandfather's mind as he wrote these words and how he might have been feeling. My body shuddered as the sound of gunfire and men shouting filled my head. I opened my eyes, a slight sense of apprehension overtaking me as I looked down at the brown envelope in my hand. Another voice spoke out to me, this time it was a voice I knew well, my own. "Pull yourself together, Charlie boy, don't go getting all weird again. It's only a letter for goodness sake, no matter how emotional its content might be."

I carefully removed the letter from the envelope, slowly unfolding the three pages inside so as not to damage them. As with the previous letters the pencil writing on the envelope and paper was neat, albeit a little faded by time but still clear enough to read.

My precious darling Mary,

I miss you and Irene terribly and wish I could be at home holding the two of you in my arms. Today we are preparing to make our way towards the beaches at Dunkirk in the hope of being evacuated with the rest of our boys as Gerry have pretty much overtaken Calais and Lille where we had been holding up. The fighting has been intense with German planes bombing our lads and the allied troops almost non-stop for the past few days. Many of our boys have been killed in the attacks along with scores of local civilians as well. We have been heartened to hear of so many small fishing boats making the journey across the channel alongside the Navy's bigger ships to help with the evacuation. Our lads from the RAF have been doing their bit as well and we cheer every time one of them flies overhead or shoots down one of Gerry's planes. The buggers have been bombing our boys on the beaches for days now and sending in their smaller planes to shoot them on the sand or in the sea as they wait to get on one of the boats or ships and away from this hell hole. I couldn't tell you where we were stationed in my earlier letters Mary because we didn't want Gerry to know, but with them pummelling us from every side now I don't think it will make any difference and I was desperate to let you know how much I am thinking of you both. We have to be brave and remember we have God on our side, even if it does feel as though he might have forgotten us at times, as we battle against this awful evil. Deep down though, I hold on to the hope he hasn't. It is tough though my darling when we come under yet another barrage from Gerry and are forced to witness the horrifying carnage that results from it along with the terrible loss of so many lives. I have witnessed many chums being killed in recent days Mary and it is hard to imagine the sorrow their families will feel when they learn that their son or husband has died in this terrible battle. They can be assured though that every one of them was a hero and fought bravely to the end.

Hopefully I will be one of the lucky ones and make it on board a boat to safety, but in case I don't I need to say a few things to you my darling. If I am not spared I want you to know that you and Irene will always be in my heart wherever I am, in this life or in the next. From the first minute I saw you in the social club that night I knew there would never be anyone else but you for me. It was as if you were the only girl in the room. I couldn't take my eyes off you, and on the day we were married I was so proud and, I admit, more than a little nervous. I knew then I was the luckiest man in the world, and nothing has changed in the time we have been together to make me feel any different. Then when Irene came along she just seemed to complete us as a family. I had my two girls to love and care for and I knew I'd never need, or want, anyone else.

Now I need to tell you something that is really hard for me to say Mary, but you must hear it. If I don't get home again I want you to know if you ever meet someone else in the future who you think will look after you and Irene properly and care for you both then I am telling you it is okay for you to be with him. I know you will be angry with me for saying this but in time you might feel differently, and I just want you to know I am saying it is alright and that you mustn't feel guilty because the most important thing is that you and Irene are cared for. Nobody will ever love the two of you like I do but I don't want you to be lonely or struggle to manage on your own. I have to go now my darling as we are on the move again. Please kiss Irene for me and be happy. You have such a beautiful smile please don't hide it away if the worst happens.

May God bless you both and I pray we will be together again soon.

With all my love,
John.

I sat motionless staring at the slightly crumpled pages in my hand trying to imagine how my Nan had felt in reading them that first time; knowing, as she probably did by then, that her man wasn't going to be one of the lucky ones, that he was dead, and wouldn't be coming back. I wondered how many more desperate letters of hope for a safe return had been written by other brave soldiers on those beaches, only for their final goodbyes to be lifted from their blood soaked uniforms by their colleagues, the authors blasted to death like my grandfather, as the fires of hell rained down on them from every angle. I thought about the German soldiers and considered how they might have felt firing endless rounds of ammunition from their machine gun posts into the midst of those terrified young men running desperately across the once peaceful sands of Dunkirk in search of shelter, only to be met by a wall of white hot metal and shrapnel ripping apart both their bodies and their lives. As a student of history I was all too aware that similar atrocities had been performed by other warring nations across the years and that total innocence is a difficult claim to make for either side involved in such carnage but, in that moment, I was struck by the ultimate futility and senselessness of such brutal aggression. I thought back to The Great War and how on the first day of The Battle of the Somme, 1st of July 1916, almost sixty thousand British soldiers had fallen under the might of the German artillery. Maybe I'm naïve or perhaps it's the arrogance of youth that allows me to believe there must be a better way to reconcile our differences. As I sat there reflecting on all I had read I heard the door open behind me again. It was Mum.

"Tough stuff eh?"

"You're not kidding." I turned to face her, placing the letter back in the tin.

"I can't begin to imagine how he must have felt writing that letter knowing he probably wouldn't be coming back. How do you even begin to say the things that really matter to the people you love above all else in such a finite and desperate time?"

I watched as Mum walked towards me and sat on her new settee, stroking it, almost without thought, as she did so.

"I don't know, Son, really I don't." She looked at me for a moment before turning slightly as if to gather her thoughts. "I've told you already I don't have many memories of Dad, being so young when he left, but the ones I do have are mainly of him playing with me and laughing as I said earlier. He laughed a lot, I do remember that." She smiled. "In later years, as I grew up and asked Mum about him she would say the same thing, that he always had a smile on his face and that he would try and see the best in people even if he didn't necessarily always agree with them. She did tell me once though how he'd come home early one day without that usual grin on his soot covered face. He said one of the men had been crushed by some equipment in the mine and that he'd stayed with him until help arrived, but that by the time it appeared it was too late to save him. Sadly, there were a number of accidents like that in those early days; things weren't as safe or well designed as they are today. Mum knew it must have been serious for Dad to be so quiet but, even then, he tried to remain positive, at least for her. He knew she worried something similar could happen to him and so tried to reassure her that he hadn't been in any danger himself. He told her they should count their blessings and be grateful for each day spent together. Mum told me she'd argued with him, asking what blessing there was to be had in worrying about your husband going down a filthy hole in the ground every day to make money for somebody else while they got by on low wages and lived in a house where the few possessions they owned were forever covered in soot and dust. She said even then Dad had forced a smile and told her they were the lucky ones. He said there were plenty of other folk in the country who would have been glad of a roof over their head and a regular wage coming in no matter how mucky their surroundings."

Mum paused and gave a reflective smile.

"She wasn't really angry with him of course and, to the greater extent, enjoyed the sense of community in Newstead the same as every other family living there. She was just scared the next time there was an accident it might be her man that was hurt or killed, although she also recognised the truth in what he'd had said about others who would be grateful just to have a job, no matter how hazardous, and for the money and security it provided."

I watched as Mum stared into the distance and grinned, her eyes lighting up as she recalled the story. "Do you know what he said to her then?"

I shook my head.

"He said, how can I do anything but smile when I have you to come home to everyday. You put this smile on my face Mary Pearce and as long as we're together that's where it stays."

Mum's eyes filled with tears.

"She told me that story a few times over the years and especially as she got older. I think it helped remind her of happier days when they were young and had their whole lives ahead of them, even if it did include the possible threat of danger at times." Mum looked at me, her face glowing with pride.

"And that was your granddad Charlie; a man who loved your Nan, his friends and his family, and carried a smile on his face for as long as he lived."

She shook her head. "Do you know I'd almost forgotten all of that until just now? It was only as I was talking to you it all came back."

"Well done for remembering. He was obviously a special man."

"He was." She paused briefly. "I don't think I've ever told anyone else that story, apart from your dad."

"And she never met anybody else?"

Mum looked at me quizzically.

"You know, what your dad said about giving Nanny Mary permission to marry again if she ever met the right person?"

Mum nodded her understanding. "It's not that she never found someone else Charlie, it's more that she never put herself in the position to meet anybody in the first place. For the first few years after Dad died she said she had enough to do with bringing me up but, the truth was, as she told me later, she never wanted anybody else." She paused for a moment as if considering whether to continue with her story. "I'm not sure whether you'll understand this Charlie, not because you're not wise enough but rather because you're maybe too young to fully grasp the sort of feelings they had for each other; you haven't met *your* soul mate yet, you've never truly been in love, not in the way the two of them were." Pausing again, she smiled. "I asked Mum the same question once when I was a teenager. I told her I was old enough to look after myself and that she should get on and think about herself for a while; that she was still young enough to find someone else to share her life with if that's what she wanted to do. She told me if she looked for the rest of her life she would still be searching on the day she took her last breath as there would never be anybody to take Dad's place. She said when he died a part of her had died with him, and the only reason she was able to continue living was because of me. I'd been created by the two of them and she vowed to honour that part of their relationship, in loving and caring for me, as she knew he would have done if she'd have gone first." Tears forming in her eye again she looked directly at me.

"I think if I hadn't been born, Mum would have followed Dad very quickly, not through taking her own life but because they were just two peas from the same pod. Quite simply, she would have died from a broken heart. To be honest Charlie, like I said, I think a part of her did die the day she heard he'd gone, but she'd promised him she would care for me and she wasn't going to break that promise no matter how heavy her own heart was feeling."

I shifted in my chair. "I never knew any of that Mum. I'm sorry she was sad for such a long time."

Mum smiled. "Oh she wasn't sad all the time, far from it. Yes, there was a part of her that remained broken and missed him every day, but your Nanny had a bigger heart than most of us and she learned to survive. And, once your dad arrived on the scene, she had another reason to keep going as well. She had to play both parenting roles then, making sure he cared for me and looked after me properly. And of course, once you were born, she found new reserves of energy all over again, certainly in the early years of your life. She would pick you up and carry you around telling you all about your granddad and how proud he would have been of you. It's just a pity that as you started to grow and become old enough to appreciate some of those stories her own health began to fail and she became more inward looking and less talkative about the past, except maybe with me on occasion. That said, she still found reasons to laugh and enjoy life Charlie, she just wished Dad could have been there to enjoy those moments with her that's all."

"What about Grampy? He and your dad were close, weren't they? I know you told me whenever you spoke to him about what had happened to Granddad John, he would say he'd died too young and that it was all very sad. Even you and Dad never really talked about the two of them together in any great detail apart from the odd story here and there."

Mum looked down, pausing for a moment. "No you're right, and certainly not while Grampy was still alive that's for sure." She took a deep breath. "Outwardly yes, he would say he was sad that Dad had died so young but, we all knew it went deeper than that. The truth was it hit him much harder than he liked to admit, and he couldn't bear to relive that terrible time or talk about his true feelings about what had happened with anybody." She turned towards me, her voice breaking a little with emotion.

"Grampy adored Dad. He liked him from the minute your Nanny took him home for tea that first time. They struck up an immediate rapport, becoming friends rather than simply father and son in law once he and Mum got married." She took a deep breath. "Mum told me that after Dad was killed at Dunkirk Grampy changed. He would still put on a face for outsiders but found it hard to smile naturally anymore with those who knew him well. He was proud of Dad in so many ways; proud he was a miner, proud they shared the same values, and proud of the fact Dad had signed on to work at the colliery at sixteen when he could have looked elsewhere for less demanding work as a lot of young lads were doing by then. Grampy felt a ready affinity with Dad, especially with the two of them having gone down the mines at such a young age." Mum laughed. "Even though Dad had taken his daughter away, for Grampy, mining still came first. He was working in the offices by then due to his failing health and hadn't been down a mine for years, but the pits still meant everything to him along with the welfare of his friends and fellow workers. He said he knew Dad would be a credit to the colliery and that even in his early twenties he was a born leader in the making. Your Nan told me once he'd first heard about Dad during the general strike in 1926 when he was only eighteen. Apparently, he'd already taken up a role in the union, The Nottingham Miners Association I think it was called back then. The General Secretary at the time, a man named George Spencer, was negotiating on behalf of the local miners with the colliery owners to get the best deal for the men, and Dad, young as he was, was a part of that team." Pausing for a moment she shook her head slightly. "I can't begin to imagine what the two of them would make of the industry today, especially with all the troubles over the past few years. It would have broken their hearts to have witnessed the division going on between families during the strike. And as for Mrs Thatcher, well, I hate to think what they would have said to her, especially Grampy. He would have been livid I can tell you. He'd have stood alongside Arthur Scargill and the other miners full square defying the Government and anybody else trying to force the men back to work. Dad would have been the same, although he would have wanted to look out for Mum and me as well. He would have hated to see the hardship so many families put up with, living hand to mouth and struggling to survive."

I nodded in recognition of the point she was making.

"I remember you talking about it at the time and saying you were glad that neither was still alive as it might have caused some division between the two of them."

Mum took a breath and smiled knowingly.

"Well, Grampy was old school; he knew how tough things had been back in the early days. He used to tell Mum stories about the men who'd been down the pits for years already when he started at fourteen. They'd told him how lucky he was to be joining then as they could remember times when lads of ten and younger had been sent underground, pushing truckloads of coal along the tunnels or standing for hours holding lamps to light the way for those cutting out the coal itself. We've talked a bit about that before, remember?"

I shook my head in disbelief.

"It's hard to believe they were treated so badly and forced to work under those conditions."

"I don't know if anybody really thought of them as being treated badly as such, it was just the way it was in those days, and families were grateful for the money it brought in. Don't forget, back then children were still going up chimneys, so being sent down a mine was seen as just another mucky job that had to be done and, rightly or wrongly, children were the ones chosen to do it. It was even more of a 'them and us society' back then Charlie, nothing like today. Even Mrs Thatcher and all the conditions she'd imposed on the miners would've probably been viewed as being almost reasonable back then compared to what they had to put up with in those early days."

"So why might Grampy and Granddad have had different views about the strike then?"

Mum thought for a moment. "It isn't so much they would have had different views, it's more as I was saying, that they lived through different times; had different experiences and expectations. Yes, they were both miners to the core, but my dad recognised things were changing and, although he was a union man, I think he might have fought as hard for the rights and needs of his own family as he would have done for the men in taking the action they did."

"You mean he might have gone back to work; been a scab wasn't it they called them?"

Mum turned to me; a look of sadness etched across her face. "I don't know if I'm honest Charlie. Mum used to say it was the one time she was grateful neither of them was around, as she knew Grampy would have died first before considering returning to work, whereas she thought Dad might have argued for some form of compromise. For him, being able to clothe and feed his family was equally as important as putting up two fingers to the Coal Board and Mrs Thatcher. She said whilst Grampy would have been the first one on the picket line she thought Dad might have struggled with the tactics adopted by some of those on strike. Do you remember when the Yorkshire miners moved across the County border and picketed the Nottinghamshire workers to join them and make it a countrywide strike?" I nodded. "Well, some said that was a form of intimidation and put unfair pressure on the Nottinghamshire men to get involved. Mum said Dad might have struggled with that sort of action and been torn between showing loyalty to his colleagues and his desire to look after his family." She put her handkerchief to her face for a moment. "It wasn't a good time Charlie as you know, but it did make Mum and I think about the two of them again. We had conversations only the two of us could share, apart from the ones you and your dad might have overheard when she was staying with us." She smiled. "We would shout at the radio and television about what was happening, each protesting Dad and Grampy's beliefs even though they weren't there to hear us. We wanted to remain loyal to their cause."

I laughed, recalling the occasional outburst I'd witnessed during that period.

"Dad and I did smile a couple of times when you two went off on one, but I hadn't realised how personal it was to you both, at least not in the way you've just described."

Mum looked up, gently shaking her head.

"That whole episode brought back so many memories for Mum, many of them difficult ones, especially when she thought about losing Dad at Dunkirk and the effect it had had on the mining community of Newstead, as well as on us as a family of course. Dad was so respected and loved by everyone, it really hit her hard. I think that was another part of the reason we moved to Papplewick; she wanted to get away and start again as I said before."

I looked at Mum appreciating, perhaps for the first time, how difficult those dark days of just a few years ago must have been for her and Nanny Mary.

"To be honest Charlie I sometimes think it was the miners' strike that finally finished her off. Yes, her heart was getting weaker by then, but I believe that whole sorry episode just brought back too many memories for her, both good and bad. And so, after a while when it all became too much for her she simply gave up the fight."

We sat in silence for a moment. "I'm sorry."

Mum smiled at me, her eyes glistening with tears. "Nothing for you to be sorry about, Son, it was just her time, although perhaps not entirely as she would have chosen."

I attempted to lighten the mood. "I bet she used to tell you how pleased Grampy had been when she first brought Granddad home, especially with him working at the colliery as well?"

"Oh yes, he definitely approved of her choice there. He was as pleased as punch it was a miner taking his daughter out and especially one who was in the union." She laughed. "And he was equally as pleased when they announced they wanted to get married. Mum told me although he was a man of few words when it came to declaring his feelings, he took her to one side a day or two before the wedding and told her she'd done well for herself, and that he couldn't be happier for her, or more proud of her. He said he thought Dad would go on to have a big future in the union, and not only in Nottingham but on behalf of miners up and down the Country. And I think in a way he did, at least until the war came along and he joined up."

"So why didn't Grampy like to talk about him so much after he'd died if he was so proud to have him in the family, it can't only have been because of what happened at Dunkirk?"

Mum paused, considering how best to reply.

"Part of the trouble for Grampy was that after he'd stopped going down the mines himself, because of his bad chest, he began to feel less of a man in some way. Yes, he still worked in the colliery offices, but it wasn't the same, at least not in his mind. He was a pit man at heart and working topside never held the same attraction or sense of value for him. And I think, with the start of his health problems coinciding with the beginning of the First World War and precluding him from being considered for service then also led to him feeling a failure in some way, even though they probably wouldn't have taken him anyway with mining being a protected occupation as we talked about before. There was no modern thinking about the changing roles of men and women in the workplace in those days Charlie. Men went off to work and, traditionally, that was hard physical work of some sort while the women stayed at home and brought up the children, along with everything else they did. Mind, that often equalled much of the physical work carried out by their men, especially during the war, even if it wasn't recognised as such. But, maybe that's a story for another day." She smiled. "Anyway, I think after his disappointment in not being able to serve in the First World War because of his health and then Dad being killed at Dunkirk the two things combined, leaving him unable to express his feelings in any coherent way, and so it just became easier not to talk about it."

"But that's silly, he couldn't help not being well."

"You and I know that Charlie, but you couldn't tell that to Grampy. The years of working behind a desk after his time spent in the pits left him feeling inadequate in some way as well, as though he wasn't a real man, not unless he could come home with his hands and face covered in coal dust like the other men. That coupled with the fact that when another war came along his son-in-law got special dispensation from the authorities to sign up for military service reminded him yet again of his own perceived failings both at work and, as had been the case in 1914, of not being able to put on a uniform and fight for his Country. Granny told him he was being silly and that no one else thought of him in that way but it didn't make any difference to Grampy, or to his thinking." Mum looked away and bit her lip before returning her gaze to me. "He told her once, after Dad was killed, that he felt guilty to be alive; that he should have been there as well, standing alongside Dad and the others on the front line. She reminded him he was sixty-two at the time and wouldn't have been allowed to fight at his age but, like I said, it made no difference to Grampy, he still felt he should have been there helping to protect Dad and to bring him home safely to Mum and I." She paused again. "It was as if, with both his own father gone and now his son-in-law as well, he felt he was the only man left in the family, and for all he wanted to protect and provide for us his health wouldn't allow him to do so." Mum shook her head gently. "I think looking back with hindsight that knowledge and sense of loss, on so many levels, crippled him every bit as much as his failing health."

I leant forward and took her hand. "That's really sad. I hadn't realised he'd been so unhappy."

She took her handkerchief and squeezed it tight in her hand. "Frustrated rather than sad I think Charlie, but still not easy for him, or for Granny. But, as I say, it was only a few of us who saw that side of his character, as far as everyone else was concerned he was just Bill, the cheery old ex miner who liked his pint and a game of dominoes at the social club." She took a breath and looked directly at me. "And as for you, well, he adored you. He used to say how much you looked like Mum. I could never see it myself, I always though you looked more like your dad's side of the family."

We smiled at each other as I squeezed her hand again.

"Talking of Dad, he is okay with me just looking at your side of the family for now isn't he, I would hate to upset him?"

She laughed. "I shouldn't give it a second thought. Your Father's never been the best at keeping in touch with his relatives. To be honest Charlie, if I didn't keep the Christmas card list up to date I don't think half of them would ever hear from him again. The only reason they get one at all is because I put the cards and the address book in front of him each December."

"Like Father like Son eh, Mum?"

"You said it. I think you men are all the same when it comes to remembering special days and events. Family and football may begin with the same letter, but they certainly get twisted around when it comes to their order of importance, or they do in your dad's case that's for sure."

"Just as well I was a Spurs fan then. At least Spurs and Santa Claus start with the same letter, so maybe there's hope for me yet?"

"If you were as quick at helping around the house as you are with your witty remarks my lad then there might be some hope for you."

I held up my notebook. "Seriously Mum, thanks for all of this. I know some of it won't have been easy for you, but I do appreciate it. And even though it's only the dates and timeline of events we actually need for the family tree itself it all helps me to get to know my family better, to understand more about them and where I'm from, if that makes sense?"

"It's been good for me as well, Charlie; made me think a little about some of the things I might have taken for granted perhaps in the past. It's a pity in a way that we haven't spoken about a lot of this before, but I don't think families do really. We all seem to get on with our lives from day to day, often with the really important things never actually getting discussed or talked about until the moment's past or it's too late."

I nodded my agreement as she picked up one of the letters.

"Was it helpful to read these as well?"

I blew out my cheeks.

"They certainly gave me a feel for what your dad and mum went through at the time that's for sure. It must have been really difficult for them, especially for your mum after your dad was killed." I forced a smile, not wanting to upset her further. "But yes, it was helpful to read them, so thank you again."

"What's next?"

"How do you mean?"

"Well, is there anything else your dad and I can help you with; any more information about the family you might need that we would know about?"

I lifted my pen and scratched the side of my head with it considering my reply.

"I'm not sure really, you've told me so much already. Any other dates or family connections we haven't talked about up till now I can find out from the various registers for those particular years when I get back to uni; although like I say, you've certainly given me loads to be getting on with. The real challenge begins once I go back further to your great grandfather, Thomas Anderson and beyond; then I'll need to go to the General Records Office for Family History in London. I'll also need to look at the different Census results for those years as well. The Land Registry will provide me with much of that information."

I scratched my head again and thought for a moment.

"Oh, there is one thing I forgot to ask that will save me a bit of time. When was it again that Grampy and Great Granny Anna got married, I forgot to write it down before?"

Mum chewed her lip in thought for a moment.

"1902." She nodded and grinned. "They were both twenty-four with their whole lives ahead of them, and with Grampy, like most men Granny said, determined to change the world, or at least his bit of it." She smiled ruefully. "Then, after he retired in 1938, she hoped he might slow down a bit, but he wouldn't hear of it. He kept himself just as busy as when he'd been at the colliery, certainly until his health began to fail more seriously anyway. Mind, then he went on to outlive Granny by four years, so what do we know?" Shaking her head, she added, "Sadly she never got to meet you, but I know she would have adored you the same as Grampy did. She was such a lovely lady, always had a sweet in her pocket for me when I was little. She'd hand it to me and tap the side of her nose as if to say, 'Don't tell your mum, it's our little secret.' I think in part that's why Grampy made such a fuss of you because he knew how much she would have cared for you as well. It was as if you reconnected them in some way. I would often overhear him talking to himself about you, as if she were actually there in the room with him."

"He's a smashing little lad alright love," he'd say, "I'll be sure to give him a big hug from you at bedtime, you see if I don't."

Mum smiled at me again. "Yes, he certainly thought the world of you Charlie."

"I wish I could remember more about him, sounds like he was a real character?"

Mum laughed. "He was certainly that alright."

We sat back in our seats taking a moment to absorb all we'd discussed.

"Are you ready for something to eat? Shall we have lunch?"

"A sandwich would be great if that's okay, all this talking has made me a bit peckish?"

"I'm not sure talking has anything to do with it, you're always hungry."

I stood up and laughed. "Cheek. Come on I'll give you a hand."

I took Mum's arm and helped her from her seat. "Up you come old girl."

"Not so much of the old if you don't mind."

We embraced and moved towards the door.

"Your dad and I are really proud of you Charlie, of what you're doing. I just hope we're helping?"

"Absolutely." I opened the door and followed her into the kitchen.

"Bread or rolls? I bought those nice crusty ones you like, or there's a sliced loaf?"

"Rolls thanks Mum, two if that's okay."

She took a bag out of the bread bin and held it up. "Of course it is, that's why I bought this lot."

"Great, I'll make the drinks. Hot or cold?"

"A glass of water for me thanks."

We spent the next few minutes preparing our food and chatting about Dad having to work at the weekend before returning to the subject of our family's history.

"Do you know anything about Great-Great-Granddad Thomas," I asked, placing Mum's water on the table in front of her?

"Thank you. Not really except that he was something to do with farming in Kent. I know he was married to a woman called Sarah and that Granny Anna was their daughter of course. She told me once that they moved to Nottingham to be near her sister Ruth after Thomas was killed in some terrible accident, I think she said. But to be honest Charlie I was only young when she told me those things and by the time I was old enough to be interested she was getting on herself and her memory wasn't as sharp as it had been so we didn't talk much about those early days again." Mum took a bite from her roll and thought for a moment. "I also seem to remember she said her mum had married again, to another farmer from Nottingham, but I can't remember his name or what happened to him."

"What about Sarah? Do you know what happened to her?"

"Again, not really, although I think Mum said she died of tuberculosis when she was quite young, maybe in her early fifties? Apparently, it killed quite a lot of people around that time. It was pretty widespread both here and abroad." Mum took a drink from her glass. "Sorry, that's probably not much help, but it was a long time ago."

"No that's great, it gives me something to look for, somewhere to start at least." I reached for my notebook, and as I looked at the words written down in front of me my heart missed a beat. They were words I knew well yet wasn't responsible for writing. *Help me Charles.* The book fell from my hand to the floor.

Mum sat upright in her chair. "Are you alright Charlie, you made me jump?"

I didn't know how to answer. "Yeah fine, I… I just dropped my book that's all."

"Well, I can see that but –"

I interrupted. "Sorry, it just caught me by surprise." I bent down and picked up the book, opening it slowly, fearing what I might find. As I turned to the same page, I held my breath, it was blank. Was I seeing things now as well as hearing strange voices in my head?

"Are you sure you're alright?"

I felt my hands shake and a bead of sweat run down my back. "Yeah, I'm okay, really. I must have moved my head too quickly bending down. You know that dizzy feeling you get sometimes when you do that? Really, just give me a minute."

Mum looked at me, obvious concern showing in her expression. "Well, if you're sure, but you do look a bit pasty faced."

By now I was beginning to feel embarrassed along with a growing need to end this line of enquiry, no matter how well intended.

"Honestly Mum, I'll be fine. I think I'll take this upstairs though if that's alright?" I nodded towards my plate and glass. "Maybe have a bit of a lie down for a while until my head stops spinning." I looked at her. "Sorry, we were doing so well."

She shook her head. "Don't apologise to me Charlie, it's you I'm worried about."

I squeezed her hand and stood up. "Really, it's nothing, just feeling a bit woozy that's all."

"Well, if you're sure? I'll tidy up here, you just take yourself upstairs."

I placed the notebook under my arm and picked up my glass and plate. "See you later."

"Just be careful you don't drop something. Would you like me to help?"

With my head racing and desperate to escape, I snapped back at her. "I said I'll be fine, okay?"

She stared at me, taken aback by my outburst. "Where did that come from, I was only offering to help."

I took a deep breath and smiled, recognising I had responded unreasonably to her genuine sense of concern for me.

"I know. Sorry Mum, forgive me? I really will be alright if I just put my head down for a few minutes." I smiled and nodded towards my plate. "And as for this lot, I promise not to break your precious tea set."

She grinned. "I'm not worried about that. I never use the best china when you're around anyway, past experience has taught me otherwise."

We smiled at each other, the earlier flash of tension between us passing as quickly as it had arrived. I put down my glass and opened the door. "Thanks Mum, love you."

She watched as I balanced my load again and walked into the hall. "I'll get the door. Feel better, Son."

I made my way slowly up the stairs and, with a slight feeling of trepidation, opened the door to my bedroom. I felt confused, struggling to compare what had just happened in the kitchen to the other desperate pleas for help I'd encountered in recent days. On those occasions the cries for assistance had been audible, resonating in my head, not visual and staring up at me from the pages of my notebook.

I finished my lunch and lay on the bed, the soft pillow providing me with both the comfort and reassurance I craved as my head sank back into its inviting embrace.

I lay there for some time considering all that had happened in recent weeks. Yes, I loved the work I was doing and the challenges it afforded me on so many levels, but these bizarre imaginings and strange voices in my head were beginning to trouble me. Was I overdoing it perhaps, attempting to burn the candle at both ends; too many nights out with Simon coupled with all that was going on at uni? And of course, there was the added stress of focusing my research on Mum's family, and in making sure all the appropriate detail was in order, not only for my degree but, more especially, for her. I certainly didn't want to let her down, not after making such a big thing about the family tree being the high point of my studies. I nodded in agreement with myself at this hastily conceived piece of logic. Yes, that was it, I'd been pushing myself too hard and, consequently, my imagination had been working overtime in an effort to keep up. I looked around the room, taking comfort in its familiar surroundings; my dressing gown hanging on the back of the door, my books on the shelf along with the record player and my much-loved collection of albums. I smiled and berated myself for hanging onto so much vinyl when CD's were clearly becoming the in thing. Pushing my head back into the pillow I watched as the sun flickered through the branches of a tree outside my window creating animated silhouettes across the white painted ceiling above me. I felt my eyes closing. As I drifted towards sleep, I revisited the earlier conversation I had had with Mum, recalling how foolishly I'd reacted to the blank pages of my notebook. Perhaps Paul Daniels had visited our kitchen and conjured up the words I had imagined written there? I smiled, concluding it was me that would need help if I carried on giving credence to these illusory fantasies.

Chapter Eight

I returned to Leicester with a renewed sense of excitement about all that lay ahead of me; making early appointments to discuss the next phase of my research with both Professor Smalling and Professor Everson. I knew my work would ultimately be judged by the former but also wanted to tap into Professor Everson's extensive knowledge and experience of my chosen subject, especially with him being the one who'd encouraged me so readily when I'd first suggested including Mum's family tree as a part of my course work.

Knocking on his study door late one afternoon shortly after my return to uni I was pleasantly surprised to hear his cheery voice answer almost immediately from the other side. "Come."

I walked in and, as on numerous previous occasions, was immediately reminded of Michael Caine's study in the film **Educating Rita**, along with his role as Dr Frank Bryant. Not that Professor Everson was a drinker or struggling in his enthusiasm for teaching as Michael Caine's character had been, but rather in the general dishevelled appearance of the room and of the man himself. There were books set in differing piles lying around, along with papers covering his desk that appeared to have been shuffled and then dealt in no particular order across it. Professor Everson himself was a slim man and the belt on his trousers always appeared as though it was two sizes too long, being tucked back into itself to stop the end from hanging down in front of his waist. His jacket also appeared to be too large for his narrow frame and his tie was never quite straight either, the knot appearing slack and pulled to one side of his collar. He also had a habit of running his fingers through his grey and thinning hair whenever he became actively engaged in a discussion. This led to many a student wondering if he actually possessed a hairbrush or comb. That said, you couldn't help but like and respect him, both as a man and as a teacher. His general appearance may have left a little to be desired but his knowledge and passion for his chosen subject could never be doubted or called into question. He was a man with a lifetime of experience which he was more than happy to pass on and encourage in his students. He had been at the university for many years and was one of the founding Fathers behind the setting up of the degree course in English Local History and, although nearing retirement, his enthusiasm for the course and desire to see it continue was obvious for all to see. As Professor Smalling had remarked to us students on more than one occasion, without Professor Everson's input, help, and encouragement he might never have been in a position to inherit the mantle of Head of Studies for this particular course himself.

"What Andrew Everson doesn't know about the subject isn't worth hearing and what he can't teach isn't worth learning. I say that from the privileged position of having worked alongside him these past couple of years not only as a colleague but, more especially, as a willing and grateful student of both his craft and wisdom on so many levels."

As I walked towards his desk Professor Everson beamed at me, raising his gaze above his half-moon glasses. "Ah Benton, how are you getting on with your family tree? Have you made much headway?"

I stood opposite him and smiled.

"Sit down lad, sit down."

I looked down at the chair in front me which was currently home to a small pile of books. He glanced at them and laughed.

"Not sure how they got there. Here give them to me." He reached out his hands as I passed the books over to him and watched as he placed them on the side of his desk.

"So, where have you got to?"

I sat down, taking my rucksack from my shoulder and placing it at my feet by the side of the chair.

"Well, sir, I've had a long chat with Mum about what she can remember, and I've got some good stories from her, including some I hadn't heard before. I've also got a few dates and events to check out as well." I moved forward a little. "But, before I follow them up, I wanted to pick your brains, if that's alright with you Professor? I just want to make sure I'm following the right procedures and don't miss a trick so to speak, as the outcomes will obviously have an effect on my overall grades, as you know."

I watched as a look of appreciation spread across his face. "That's very kind of you Charles but, as I have said already, ultimately, your work will be judged by Professor Smalling and the examining panel which, as you are aware, from the end of this term, I will no longer play any part in."

"I know that, Sir, and I have every intention of seeking Professor Smalling's advice as well. Like you, he's been equally encouraging towards this part of my work. It's just that I know how passionate you are about content and detail, and I really don't want to miss any opportunity for getting that side of things right, especially with this particular area of my research, if that makes sense?" I smiled. "After all, with this being Mum's family tree, I've got my parents to impress as well."

He nodded his head and returned my smile. "If flattery were an additional part of your degree, Charles, I would have to give you an A plus." He leant forward and folded his arms together, placing his elbows on the desk. "Of course, I am happy to help lad, but I must emphasise once again the need for you to refer all we discuss to Professor Smalling and, if any part of that referral does not gain his sanction or tacit approval then you must discount it. This is a challenging period for the two of us as well, and I don't want to be perceived in any way as interfering or seeking to usurp his teaching methods with regards to your studies. I intend to do all I can to ensure the smooth handover of responsibility for this course to his safe keeping, both for its long-term future and for the good of the university as a whole. I trust you understand that?"

I nodded my agreement. "I do Sir, and I promise I won't act on anything you might say to me without running it past him first and gaining his approval."

He unfolded his arms and leant back in his chair. "Good, I'm glad we're both clear on that." He sat still for a moment before leaning forward again and bringing his chair tight up to the desk. "I am touched though that you want to speak to me about this Charles and, if I'm honest, more than a little excited by your plans. I'm not sure we've had a student before, so intent on making his own family's history such a major part of their course work." Cupping his hands under his chin he smiled. "So, what have you discovered so far?"

I bent down and took my notebook from the rucksack.

"Well, sir, Mum has told me quite a bit about her own parents, along with a few dates regarding other family members' births, marriages, and deaths that sort of thing, or at least as far back as she can remember. It's more when I go further back in time that I'd really be grateful for your advice Professor, if that sounds okay? You know, like how much detail I might need to include regarding each family member and so on?"

He looked at me and drew a deep breath. "Much of what you are asking lad can be answered by Professor Smalling, indeed it would be remiss of me to inform you otherwise. That said, there is one thing I have learnt over the years that I am happy to pass on and, although others may offer similar advice, can never be overemphasised; and that is, as to the amount of background detail and information you may be required to demonstrate as having been researched in support of your findings and corresponding conclusions." He looked at me, determination set firmly in his gaze. "You can never have too much Charles, even though some it may not physically be required for your end of year exams. That may appear as obvious to you but believe me I have lost count over the years of students who have presented what they presumed would be enough to get them through, only to fall at the final hurdle because they lacked some, ostensibly, minor fact or piece of information necessary to complete their paper. How many times have I said, the one thing you can expect when it comes to your finals is the unexpected? As my scout master used to say, *in omnia paratus*, be prepared for all things."

Whilst I'd anticipated much of what I was hearing I still nodded my appreciation at this well-intentioned piece of advice, accepting both its wisdom and the sentiment in which it was proffered.

"Those who put in the hours and work during the early stages of their studies reap the rewards of their endeavours at the end." He placed his hands flat on the desk and smiled. "It may be an old saying Charles but it still rings true; *carp diem*. Seize the day lad and all it offers, and you won't go far wrong."

I smiled inwardly at his use of Latin to encourage me. He was well known for quoting phrases and themes from a variety of historical greats and differing foreign languages when seeking to emphasise a particular point to his students, with Latin being a firm favourite.

"Thank you, Professor, I'll bear that in mind."

We looked at each other, neither quite sure what to say next. Eventually he broke the silence.

"I think the best thing to do for now is to take what you've gathered so far to Professor Smalling and see what he makes of it. By all means tell him you have spoken with me, and of course feel free to use me again as a sounding board in the weeks to come if you feel that might be useful; providing, as I say, he has no objections."

I rose to leave placing my notebook back in my bag. "Thank you, sir."

He offered me his hand. "Good luck, Charles, I'm sure you will do well, you're a good student. I hope one day to read a paper by you on some new theory for taking forward the study of local history along with all it encompasses."

I shook his hand and smiled, grateful for his belief in me. I wondered if he might have wanted to say more in his support of my work but felt, perhaps, a little constrained by the growing awareness his time as lead tutor was coming to an end, and that Professor Smalling should now be viewed as the main focus of attention for all matters regarding my degree. That said I still made a mental note of his remark about never having too much detail when compiling a piece of research, especially if it contributed towards an exam or a wider assessment of a students work. My focus on gaining this degree was absolute, not only for myself but also for those, including my family, who had so readily invested their time and faith in encouraging me.

I confirmed my appointment with Professor Smalling a couple of days later. His study was very different than that of Professor Everson's, set out more as an office, with its contemporary angular furniture, filing cabinets, and uncluttered surfaces, including a modern and highly polished grey metal desk.

His study may have been starker in appearance than his senior colleague's but the greeting I received was no less effusive and welcoming.

"Come in, Charlie, good to see you, how's it going?"

Even the fact he called me Charlie as opposed to Professor Everson's preference for Charles, or my surname Benton, encouraged me to feel immediately relaxed in his company.

"Fine, thank you, sir."

"How did you get on with your parents? Is this family tree idea of yours still a goer?"

"Absolutely, they were really helpful. Professor Everson has been really encouraging as well." I knew as soon as I'd spoken, I'd got my timing wrong.

"Professor Everson? I thought we agreed I would be your first point of contact from now on, after all it'll be me who'll be running an eye over the detail of your research and conclusions before you sit for the finals themselves."

"Of course, sir." I felt my face colouring with embarrassment. "I didn't mean anything by that, other than he'd been encouraging about my plans to continue with the theme of putting together Mum's family history. He made it very clear I should speak to you first in future about any thoughts or ideas I might have, and certainly about anything you considered personally to be relevant in helping take my work forward."

I sensed he was still smarting, not from a bruised ego but rather that I had seemingly gone behind his back and broken a bond of trust between us.

"Please, Professor; don't think badly of me, it just came out the wrong way. I am absolutely clear that *you* are my tutor *and* point of reference for all matters regarding my work and in the putting together of my family tree."

Sensing my discomfiture, he smiled.

"That's alright Charlie no harm done. Professor Everson is an inspirational guy, I recognise that." He nodded and smiled again. "He's helped me to get to grips with life here at the university as well during the time I've been here, along with its traditions and routines. Just remember to run things by me first in future though, okay? We can't have two threads of work and research going on or there'll be a conflict of interest and that'll affect the amount of time you spend on it and, potentially, the marks you receive for your efforts."

I returned his smile. "And I get that too, sir, I really do. Again, I am sorry if I offended you in anyway."

He waved away this renewed attempt at rectifying my earlier verbal misdemeanour.

"You didn't and we're fine. Now let's stop all this apologising and get down to business."

He pointed towards two vibrant green hessian style easy chairs set to the side of his desk. I smiled to myself, thinking how well they fitted in with the modern look and feel to the rest of the room.

"Here, sit yourself down and tell me where you are as far as family members and any information you've uncovered about them is concerned? Have you decided how far back you actually want to go with this family tree of yours?"

"Well, I was thinking of –" he interrupted.

"Sorry, Charlie, before we start, I was just about to get a drink. Do you fancy a tea or coffee?"

I put my bag by my chair and took out my notebook. "A cup of tea would be lovely, thank you, sir."

"Great." He got up and moved to the door. I sat looking at my notes as he spoke to one of the office administrator's outside.

"Could we have a couple of cups of tea please, Sandra?" There was a pause. "Thanks."

I was aware of him walking behind me and back to his chair. "Sorry about that but I'm parched. Now, where were we? Oh yes, about how far you wanted to go back in time."

"Well, as you might remember the initial idea for me doing this was sparked by my mum telling me that her great-great-grandfather was a vicar from Kent who we think might have been murdered? Mind, nobody really knows that for sure as my great grandfather was apparently a bit of a lad and would often come up with what might best be described as colourful tales about the family. So we don't really know if that story is true or not, but it'd still be interesting to discover the link between Mum's later family, who were miners from the Midlands, and what connection, if any, they had to do with a vicar in Kent almost a hundred and fifty years earlier? I thought the association with mining would be worth following up as well, what with the strike of a couple of years ago and so many pits looking to close down. There's a lot of history there on its own."

He leant forward placing his elbows on his knees and supporting his chin with his hands. "You're not wrong there Charlie that's for sure, although whether current history will get you any better grades is up for debate, but the combination of family history and the changing landscape between the South of England and the Midlands is an interesting theme I'll give you that. Nottingham wasn't it you said your mum's family came from originally?"

"That's right. Then it gets a bit muddled between there and Kent and as to why they moved. But I guess all of that'll become clearer once I get down to doing some more detailed research, at least I hope so."

There was a knock on the door. A middle-aged woman entered carrying a tray containing two cups of tea and a plate of biscuits. I smiled inwardly, thinking how out of place she looked in Professor Smalling's modern study with her plain brown dress, faded red cardigan and hair swept back up into a bun on the top of her head.

"There we are Professor. I've bought you a few digestives as well, I know you like them." She placed the tray on a small white plastic coffee table set between our two chairs.

"You spoil me Sandra, you really do." He touched her arm by way of recognition at her efforts to please him as she moved away from the table. "Thank you."

Her eyelids fluttered as she pursed her lips and offered an embarrassed smile. She was clearly appreciative of his attention, albeit polite on his part and certainly not intended to flatter or encourage her in any other way.

"I've put a pot of sugar there as well so you can help yourself." She turned and smiled towards me. "I didn't know whether your guest took it or not."

I looked up. "Thank you."

Turning to leave she nodded. "You're welcome." Her eyes moved to Professor Smalling again. "Let me know if I can do anything else for you Professor?"

I smiled to myself again presuming her offer to provide him with any more than a simple tray of refreshments was an invitation he was highly unlikely to accede to, whether her intentions were honourable or not. She smiled at him again, hopeful perhaps for some further compliment or word of encouragement. He meanwhile was busy picking up a biscuit, clearly oblivious to her attentive gaze. He replied without looking at her. "Thank you, Sandra, I'll call if we need anything."

She smiled again, a little less assuredly this time, as she left the room closing the door quietly behind her.

"Help yourself to sugar and a biscuit Charlie, otherwise I'll stuff them all myself and that won't do me any good." He patted his stomach. "I need to lose a bit of weight not put it on."

"I don't take sugar in tea thank you, sir, just coffee."

I helped myself to a biscuit though but avoided dunking it, my preferred option, and took a bite; the crisp consistency of it feeling dry in my mouth as I chewed on it. I attempted to swallow but felt some of the biscuit stick to the roof of my mouth and so took a sip of my tea to clear it.

"So, back to what you were saying about how far you're intending to go with this research of yours. To your mother's great-great-grandfather I think you said?"

"That's right, sir, the vicar from Kent. Well, according to Grampy he was a vicar anyway."

He gulped a mouth full of tea from his cup and laughed as he helped himself to another biscuit. "That's the one you said told a good story yeah?" He nodded at the biscuit in his hand. "Told you I liked these. Have another one or I'll never manage my lunch."

"I'm fine thank you Professor." I took another mouthful of tea to wash down the last of my digestive.

"So, what about the research itself, are you on top of that?"

"I was thinking of all the usual places, libraries, census results and the General Register for Family History in London?"

He finished his biscuit and drained his cup. "All good venues, yes. You'll need to look at individual birth and death certificates as well of course. They'll provide you with the timelines you're looking for and will also give you a guide as to which particular census results you want to be looking at in any ten-year period. Once you've got those you can go further and look for marriage certificates and any children from those marriages as well, that's if you're intending to include all of them, or perhaps just the ones that are relevant to the particular side of the family you're looking to follow? They're the ones you'll need for your course work, although you might decide to expand a little on your research of course, just out of interest, especially as it's your own family you're looking at. And if you do, then marriage certificates will also give you links to former generations, listing parents of the bride and groom and so forth, but you'll already be aware of that." He laughed. "Just try and stay focused Charlie. I know from experience how easy it is to go off at a tangent and discover a load of information that, interesting though it may be, has bugger all to do with the job in hand, if you get my drift?"

I smiled, acknowledging both the humour and sense contained in his remark.

"I just want to get it right really Professor; obviously for my work here, but it'll also be nice for Mum to get to know a bit more about her family as well, or at least as far back as I decide to go. I know that means a lot to research but, that's part of the fun for me." I smiled. "But yes, I will stay focussed." Pausing momentarily, I looked at him. "Someone told me once you can never have too much detail or information, so I want to do a good job for all concerned."

He leant back and laughed, putting his hands behind his head as he did so.

"Nice one, Charlie, but I think we both know who you're talking about there. Professor Everson told me that one as well when I first arrived, and he hasn't been embarrassed about reminding me of it over the past couple of years either. One of his favourite mantra's I think."

I could feel myself colouring up again.

"It's fine; don't fret yourself lad, its good advice, just a little worn around the edges with repetition that's all." He leant forward again. "Listen, Charlie, you're a good student okay, we all have high hopes for you. Your passion for Genealogy and family history is obvious for all to see. You just get out there and do your thing and when you get stuck or need some advice you know where I am. Hopefully, most of what you'll need to be aware of should be covered here in the weeks ahead anyway, and what isn't readily available through us you can go off and discover for yourself." He smiled. "Don't be too hard on yourself either, not about the course itself or what you want to achieve for your family. In fact, and I don't mean this to sound uncaring in any way, your mum has to come second in all of this, at least over the next few weeks while you're doing all the initial groundwork. Your first responsibility is to yourself and to your work here lad. Once you've gained your degree you'll have the rest of your life to talk about your family and its history, but for now just get your head down and deal with what's in front of you, okay?"

I recognised the sense in what he was saying and nodded my understanding and agreement.

He leant forward and, placing his elbows on his knees for support, clasped his hands together under his chin. "And don't forget, once you've collated your research, you've still got to write everything up in chronological order ready for your finals, so you've got more than enough to be worrying about for now without adding your mum into the mix as well."

There was a momentary pause in our conversation as I smiled and nodded again.

"You'll be fine, Charlie."

I rose from my chair offering my hand as I did so. "Thank you, Professor, I'll do my best."

Standing to face me he took my hand and shook it firmly. "I know you will." Then, winking at me, he added, "Go get 'em Charlie, and make us all proud of you."

"I'll try."

I felt his hand squeeze mine as if to emphasise his support and encouragement for my plans.

As I closed the study door behind me, I experienced a fresh wave of enthusiasm for the task ahead. I also resolved, as advised, not worry too much about keeping Mum and Dad up to speed over the next few weeks regarding any early results of my investigations. Smiling to myself, I made my way back along the corridor. As I walked, I could hear Mum's voice in the back of my mind gently berating me. "Come on, Charlie, don't keep it a secret from us, tell us what you've found out?"

I decided I would need to have a conversation with them both before I started my work in earnest if I wasn't to fall into the trap Professor Smalling had intimated; that of being more concerned about pleasing my parents than the board of examiners. I knew they would understand, but also recognised that keeping them, and Mum especially, at bay in the days ahead would still prove a challenge. Heading back to my room my mind whirred with excitement as I began to formulate my plans for the days ahead.

Chapter Nine

The next few weeks raced by in a blur as I journeyed between uni and the various libraries, record offices, and other locations garnering the necessary information about Mum's family and its recorded history. I would start each day by looking through my notes and thumbing through the various photos and other information Mum had passed on to me so as to bring myself up to speed before getting my head down and beginning the next phase of my research. These mornings would often turn into full days however as I delved further into the life of a certain family member's history uncovering, perhaps, an unexpected certificate of birth or marriage which, in turn, would lead me to some new discovery or particular area of interest I hadn't been anticipating. I would then have to rein myself back and focus once more on the specific individual or historical piece of evidence I was meant to be recording. This in turn would, hopefully, provide me with the appropriate facts or detail required to complete my dedicated line of enquiry. However, even in maintaining this strict regime I still found my days becoming longer and more arduous, and by the time my head finally hit the pillow at night both my mind and body were equally exhausted. Even then I would leave a notepad by my bed to jot down any thoughts or ideas that might come to me as I lay there seeking precious sleep. That said, and for all I was tired, I still maintained a growing sense of excitement and achievement as the days rolled into weeks. And yes, as suspected, Mum and Dad were keen to know all I'd discovered each time I went home, although Dad quickly recognised and accepted the need for me to focus the results of my efforts towards my exams rather than attempting to satisfy their own curiosity.

"Leave the boy alone, Irene, he'll tell us what he can when he's ready. All this work is for his degree remember, not for our entertainment. He's come home for a break not to answer a load of questions from the two of us, isn't that right Charlie?"

"Well, I –" would be about as far as I would get before Mum interrupted.

"Oh shut up, Pete. Charlie doesn't mind me asking, do you son?"

And so it would go on. Eventually though she got the message and, to the greater extent, we maintained a friendly alliance with me promising that, once I had completed my research, I would reveal all I had discovered to them in one sitting rather than passing on little bits of information piece meal.

When I began the physical routine of tracing our family tree I presumed, mistakenly, that some of it might prove a little monotonous, with my having to wade through endless documents and paperwork each day in an effort to trace an individual or follow a particular time line, but nothing could have been further from the truth. Every page I turned or piece of microfiche I studied opened a new world to me, even when it didn't directly involve a member of my own family. Each name I came across, along with their corresponding detail, created a new path of interest for me. These were real people who had lived full lives and helped shape the world that I inhabited today. This simple truth alone encouraged my passion for genealogy and family history to a new level; making me realise once again how fortunate I was to be able to follow my chosen avenue of learning so freely and with so much encouragement from both my family and tutors at university. Every birth or death certificate I reviewed took me to a certain place in thought and time as I tried to imagine the sense of joy these individuals would have felt in welcoming a new life into their home or the sadness, perhaps, at the passing of that same loved one as their life reached its end. Some of those who had died had lost their lives at an early age, either through untimely illness, disease, or by way of an accident. Others had died at birth, and all affected me in ways I hadn't anticipated or expected. After all, these were people and events, as a young man living in the mid-20th century, I had never seen reason to consider at any serious depth before. There was plenty of time for the greater meaning of life and death stuff as I grew older, got married and had a family of my own. And, although I'd shared in Mum and Dad's sense of grief in the past when hearing of the loss of a close family member, for me at least, death itself was still a long way off and not something I felt I needed to consider for some years hence. Suddenly though, in reviewing the lives of so many others who had come and gone before me over the years, I was struck by how brief our time on earth truly is. I wondered if all these individuals, whose stories I was now learning about had enjoyed their lives, realised their dreams and fulfilled their potential, or had they been constrained by lack of opportunity and family circumstances, thus falling short of all they might have become. Had they been disappointed by the life afforded them in the time and space in which they'd existed? I smiled to myself, recalling the words my favourite Beatle, John Lennon, had once remarked about life; in that worrying about the future instead of living in the moment would serve to hold us back rather than carry us forward.

"Life is what happens to you while you're busy making other plans."

As I scrolled through the apparently endless list of names on the various census forms, I pondered how many had relatives living today who only existed because of them and yet were now, as with my own ancestors, no more than a fading entry on a family register. Is that all we're born for or to become, simply a name on a list as having once existed but now gone and seemingly forgotten, our lives recorded as no more than a footnote in a book gathering dust on a shelf in a records office?

Surely there has to be more to life than our simple coming and going? If not, then why had my grandfather John given his life at Dunkirk? Indeed, why had any man or woman ever laid down their life in conflict to protect or save another? Or perhaps the bigger question to consider is why does any woman give birth at all, if all that results from her labour pains is the knowledge that in the shortest span of time her child will be gone again, and the best that can be hoped for in the whole sorry process is that history will continue to repeat itself ad infinitum for generations yet to come. These and many other uncertainties about the true meaning of life began to trouble me deeply as I spent long days continuing my research in the halls of the General Family Records Office, the National Archives and the Land Registry Building.

Eventually I resolved I had enough to worry about without adding yet another layer of new and potentially unanswerable questions to my ever-lengthening catalogue of things to consider. For now, at least, I decided the greater meaning of life would have to wait a little longer, and certainly until I'd finished my exams.

Those weeks spent researching my ancestry also confirmed I had, without doubt, chosen the right subject to focus my energies on. Genealogy and all it encompassed captivated me as no other topic ever had before, even if it was presenting me with as many new questions about the purpose and reason for our being as it was in providing any appropriate answers.

I may not have been entirely sure as to the greater reason for man's existence on the planet but our connection with it and its corresponding landscape truly fascinated me, as did the parallels for our joint subsistence. Also, in how, as members of the same human race we each need to respect and support one another if life, as we know it, is to continue in any meaningful way.

Once I had compiled the obligatory information regarding my family's history dating back to great-great-great-grandfather George's birth in 1814, along with a little about his forebears, all that remained was to check with my tutors that I had enough detail for the examiners to grade and consider before arranging it in sequence ready for my finals. Of course, on a personal level, it was George I was really interested in. However, I recognised this held little relevance for the examining board, other than their duty to consider his more general role and positioning in Mum's family tree.

Even respecting this maxim, I was still excited to discover that, far from being simply associated in some way with an unexplained death a hundred and forty years earlier, it had been George himself, as Grampy had intimated, who had been the victim of a gruesome murder. Although physical information about the exact circumstances were pretty sketchy, records did demonstrate beyond any reasonable doubt that he'd been killed by would be thieves in his church.

Of course, I would like to have discovered more about what had actually taken place on that fateful day, but I also needed to remember by going back five generations in my family's history I now had more than enough detail for this particular area of my chosen course work. I also needed to include my dissertation on Landscape and Topography, both of which held equal status as far as my finals were concerned. I decided to speak to Professor Smalling first this time, reminding myself that, as my head of year and senior tutor, he would have much of the say in signing off my work ready for its final consideration by the examining board. That said, I would also ask if I might be allowed to talk through my findings with Professor Everson as I knew he would be interested in all I had discovered during my lengthy investigations.

I sat opposite Professor Smalling nervously picking at my fingernails and listening to the rain drive against his study window as he carefully read through my notes that Thursday afternoon. This meeting felt more formal than our previous encounter with both of us sitting at his desk rather than the more relaxed setting of the easy chairs sipping tea supplied by the lovely Sandra.

"Well, you certainly haven't skimped on the detail, I'll give you that." He looked across the desk at me and smiled as a clap of thunder reverberated outside, causing me to jump a little in my seat.

"Don't look so worried, Charlie, this is good stuff," he said, thumbing through the paperwork in front of him. "Of course, it'll need knocking into shape properly; making sure the dates and events correspond exactly and so on but, all in all, yeah, a good start." He winked at me before flicking through the pages again. "Some of it's a bit slap dash in its presentation at the moment but, like I say, it's early days. I'm sure you're aware of what needs to be done to hone it and tidy it up; and don't forget, I'm here to help if you get stuck."

"Of course, and thank you, Sir." I moved forward in my chair. "There is one thing I struggled a little with. It was when I was doing the physical research; I found some of it provided me with slightly differing results to those I'd been expecting. Not about specifics such as births and deaths of course, they're all constants, but more odd pieces of information about looser timelines, such as when a particular event occurred that sort of thing." I scratched my head to think of an example. "Some of the stuff concerning what happened during my family's time at Newstead Colliery for instance. Areas of that appeared to differ occasionally from what my grandparents had told Mum and which she'd passed on to me. Things like when a certain part of the village, say a pub or school was established. The date itself might correspond with the records but not necessarily with what Mum had said and so I needed to check it again. No big deal, just time consuming, but still important of course when connecting dates and corresponding events. The same thing happened when I was looking at some of the information about my great-great-great-grandfather George and his family when they were working on the farm before he went into the church. For example, the date his mother Alice began working on the farm. Also, child labour and the ages at which they started work in those days. They weren't always recorded as meticulously as – they would be today. Not that we have child labour as such any more of course, but you know what I mean?"

"I do, but that sort of associated detail matters less than physically knowing who a person is, or was, along with their date of birth, death and overall place in your family line." He sat back in his chair and smiled again.

"As I said, all things considered Charlie you've made a good start, well done. So, what's next? Are you going to write all of this up or talk to your parents first about what you've discovered? It doesn't really matter as you've still got plenty of time for both, but I can imagine how eager they must be to hear where you've got to with all of this." He shifted forward, his expression becoming more considered. "That said, I'm also keen for you not to lose focus. Remember what I said before; your ultimate responsibility is to yourself and in the gaining of this degree."

"I know. I think I'll write it up first or at least get all the dates and information into chronological order before I talk it through with Mum and Dad. After all, their interest in the physical detail of what happened to who and when is very different from that which you and the examiners will be looking for, certainly in how it's structured and presented anyway."

I smiled and shifted a little awkwardly in my chair. "Would it be alright if I showed the results of my research to Professor Everson? I absolutely accept that you're my first point of contact in all of this but, as you know, he's always shown a keen interest in my work, and it would be nice to let him see where I'm up to, if that's okay with you?"

I watched as he rose and walked to the front of his desk, his head bowed slightly. I grimaced, expecting the worst as he looked down at me considering his reply. – Pausing, he stroked his chin thoughtfully.

"It isn't necessary for you to refer every conversation you have with Andrew Everson to me, Charlie. Really, I don't mind, so long as you remember all that we've discussed before."

I interrupted. "I know Professor Everson is retiring at the end of term but, as I said, he's always been supportive of my ideas and it would be nice just to let him know how much his enthusiasm for my work has helped and encouraged me, the same as yours has Sir."

"I understand that, Charlie, and thank you for asking." He stood up and walked back to his chair. "Andrew is a great man and an inspiration to us all, students and tutors alike. As I've said before, I have much to be grateful to him for myself, so yes of course share your findings with him. All I would say is keep in mind the methodology the two of us have agreed in how best to present your final work. Consultation and shared passion are always laudable but don't see it as a licence to change what we already have in place." He smiled. "I want the best for you as well Charlie, so just continue to play by the rules, if you get my drift. Okay?"

I stood up and stretched my back.

"Not the most comfortable of chairs I know, sorry about that."

"It's fine, Sir, just a bit stiff that's all."

He looked up and smiled. "I'm away for the next few days, so why don't you take that time to speak to Professor Everson and begin honing these notes of yours into some form of documented order ready for writing up? You might even choose to run through the timeline with your parents once you're happy with its detail and the order in which it plays out?" He stood up and laughed. "Just don't go making wholesale changes, okay? We can work on your final conclusions together when I'm around again, if that sounds like an idea?"

I smiled, offering him my hand which he grasped and shook firmly. "You're going to be alright Charlie; you're a good lad and a credit to the university. I have high hopes for you, we all do."

"Thank you, Sir, I appreciate that." I looked straight at him. "Doesn't stop the nerves though. As the finals get nearer so the pressure to succeed increases and my confidence in being able to get it right decreases."

He laughed again. "That's the way it should be. A few nerves are always a good thing; helps keep you on your toes and your brain active at the same time. If these courses were easy there'd be no point in having them. The idea is to test you on a number of levels and equip you for the next thirty or forty years of your working life." A broad smile spread across his face. "And its great fun for us tutors as well, watching you lot crap yourselves in the same way we did all those years ago when it was our turn to stand where you are today. What goes around comes around, Charlie." He leant across the desk and punched me playfully on my arm. "Now bugger off and let me get on with my work."

I shut the study door behind me and smiled inwardly as I made my way down the corridor. I liked Professor Smalling and, for all his teasing, felt he really did understand my feeling of nervousness coupled with a genuine desire to do the best I could in the weeks ahead.

As I reached the front door and stepped into the rain, I decided a hot shower and a couple of pints with my friends were in order. I'd worked hard over the past few weeks and an evening off felt like a guilty pleasure well-earned before having to put my brain into gear once more and turn this latest research into some semblance of order ready for my finals.

After a quick shower and something to eat I set off for the pub, dodging into every other shop entrance along the way in an effort to avoid the rain which was still falling quite heavily. As I made my way along the high street, head down and focussing on missing the puddles in front of me I quite literally bumped into

Professor Everson who was also taking shelter from the rain in a local Bookmakers doorway.

"I didn't know you were a betting man Professor," I said, with a smile on my face?

"I'm not." I sensed he hadn't fully appreciated my attempt at humour. "I'm just avoiding the worst of this foul weather for a moment or two." He looked around him. "I hadn't even noticed it was a betting shop."

"I was joking, Professor, I didn't really think you were one for the horses."

He smiled and flicked the rain from the collar of his jacket. "Ah I see, a joke, yes, very good Benton."

I decided to move the conversation on; my attempt at levity clearly having fallen on stony ground.

"I'm glad I've run into you, Sir; I wanted to show you the results of my research into Mum's family tree. I've pretty much got all the detail I need now and thought you might like to see it?"

It was his turn to make a joke.

"Well, you certainly did run into me Charles, quite literally it seems." He looked directly at me and laughed.

"Very good, Sir, touché and all that." There followed a short awkward silence between us, neither quite sure how best to move the conversation – forward. After a few seconds he smiled and nodded.

"Yes of course, I'd be happy to look at it with you. That is, presuming you have already spoken with Professor Smalling about it?"

"Absolutely Sir. And I checked he was happy for me to speak with you as you suggested I should when we spoke before."

"Then yes, I would like that."

The rain was falling heavier now and we both moved a little further into the doorway as a man came out of the shop. I moved to one side to let him pass.

"Sorry, mate, we're just getting out of the rain for a minute."

The man smiled as he squeezed past. "Don't blame you; nice day for ducks yeah?"

Smiling, I nodded in agreement as he brought his collar up around his chin and moved quickly away. Professor Everson and I looked at each other, hunching our shoulders in mutual accord in response to the man's comment; it was indeed a day fit only for ducks to enjoy.

"You were saying Benton, about my viewing your research. I'm free tomorrow afternoon if that fits in with your plans?"

"That would be fantastic, thank you, Professor." I shuddered as a trickle of rain ran down my back. "Your passion for family history seems to have rubbed off on me as well Sir; I've really enjoyed my work over the past few months, and I have you to thank for much of that."

He looked at me, a smile of appreciation on his face. "Thank you, Charles. And yes, it is a bit of a passion if I'm honest; maybe even an obsession if you talk to my wife."

We laughed as a clap of thunder broke overhead.

"Well, it doesn't look as if this rain is about to stop anytime soon so I think we'll just have to make a dash for our chosen destinations and put up with getting wet in the process." He pulled his jacket collar further up around his neck. "My car is just around the corner if you'd like a lift to wherever it is you're off to?"

"That's very kind of you Professor but I'm only going to the pub a couple of doors down. Meeting up with a few friends."

"Ah yes one of the benefits of student life, being able to put the world to rights in the local hostelry over a couple of jars of scrumpy, I remember it well."

"Jars of Scrumpy?"

"That was my favoured tipple back in the day, but I'm not sure they'll have it in The High Cross. Mind, I'm more of a beer man these days." He laughed. "And a couple of halves are more than enough for me now. The days of pint glasses and drinking games are definitely a thing of the past, certainly for me."

"It'll probably be just a couple of halves for me as well, Sir. We poor students have to watch the pennies you know."

He laughed again. "We used to say the same when I was your age but, somehow, always found enough for a drink or two. Anyway, have a good evening and I'll see you tomorrow."

"You too, Sir, and thank you."

I watched as he made his way down the High Street, a newspaper held above his head in some form of vain attempt to keep the rain from soaking him further. I smiled as I thought about him being a student and how different university life must have been some forty or so years earlier. Although I was a lot younger than Professor Everson, I was equally aware how quickly time passes and, having spent the past few weeks looking at Mum's family history, I also recognised that whilst my great-great-great-grandfather George had been born in 1814 this was in fact only five generations before my own arrival on earth which, in the overall span of time, is hardly even a blink of an historian's eye.

I stood in the doorway, internally debating these issues of life and death, as the rain beat down from a seemingly endless grey sky. Suddenly a car went by and sent a wave of water towards me as it drove through a large puddle. I jumped back in surprise and, roused from my daydream, pulled my jacket up over my head and made a dash for the warmth and welcome of the pub just a few yards further down the High Street.

Our meeting the next afternoon went well and Professor Everson was every bit as encouraging about the results of my latest research as I'd hoped he would be. I knew his opinion wouldn't hold any particular sway when it came to the final marking of my papers, but it was good, all the same, to gain his approval and to have him recognise the effort I'd put in; also, to know he felt I was still headed in the right direction.

"This really is excellent work, Charles, along with plenty of corresponding detail, I commend you on it. You've also included just the right amount of background information regarding the investigative road you've travelled and how that led you towards making some of your conclusions." He waved his hand across the pages of notes spread across his already cluttered desk. "This will all help assist in demonstrating to the board how you've taken each element of your studies seriously and not simply majored on the personal interest you have in establishing your family tree. That said, you will have to expand a little on the reasoning behind your decision to use your Mother's family line as a part of your research. It may not be entirely original in its concept, but it is inventive all the same, so well done. Genealogy in its broadest sense is a wide-ranging topic and you need to bring a number of shared areas of mutual interest together; the landscape, the general topography and of course the more intimate family history side of things as well." Smiling broadly, he looked up and clasped his hands together. "I like it, Charles, I like it a lot, as I'm sure Professor Smalling did as well; although, like me, I am sure he also reminded you there is still work to do in bringing all of your conclusions together into the required chronological order ready for your finals."

"He did and thank you, Sir, I appreciate your comments."

"Just one other thing I would remind you of lad, and I know – other tutors would say the same: your Mother and Father. When you come to talk to them about what you've discovered please don't feel a need or duty to explain more than you have already outlined here, at least for now. If they, or you, want to seek additional information or detail about the background and history of some of the individuals named in your research, then fine, you can do that at a later date. For now, and for the remainder of your course your loyalties lay in impressing only your tutors and the examining board. Once you have gained your degree, as I'm sure you will do, then is the time to afford yourself the luxury of delving further into your past, should you decide that is something you wish to do. We are both clear on that aren't we?"

"Of course, Sir; Professor Smalling made a similar comment when we spoke the other day." I looked directly at him. "The only thing is, I was thinking of…" my voice trailed away.

"You were thinking of what, lad?"

"Well, it's George Anderson himself, Sir, my great-great-great-grandfather. You see, now I know the area in Kent where he lived and was apparently murdered, I was hoping to take a trip down there during the summer break to see it for myself."

He stared at me momentarily considering his reply. "I don't see a problem with that, so long as it is only out of personal curiosity or to confirm the detail of what you have already discovered." Pausing again he nodded. "I do understand your desire to investigate that particular side of the story further Charles but, as before, my advice would be not to allow it, nor indeed any other form of potential distraction, to shift your focus from the real job in hand, that being, in gaining your degree. There will be little in Kent, certainly on an academic level, that you'll discover which might add anything to the specific detail required for your finals that is not already outlined here. It's the individual names, dates of birth, marriages, and so on that makes up the person's family line and interconnection that we are interested in, at least on the formal side. Also, in your ability to collate and provide said information in chronological order via a concise and detailed report, documenting your reasons for the research along with your final conclusions. These are the factors by which you will be judged. The board will have little interest in who your ancestors' friends and neighbours were, what they did for a living, or of their personal relationship with your family, unless a direct link or blood line can be demonstrated." He laughed. "Even if there is the potential whiff of intrigue surrounding a part of it. There is plenty of time to play Hercule Poirot and investigate the apparently unrecorded revelations regarding the demise of this particular family member once you leave university. Agreed?"

I smiled, appreciating both his wisdom and council, although I knew, whether relevant or not, a trip to Kent was already, for me, a firm intention.

"Thank you, Professor, I really do appreciate your advice and the encouragement you've shown me."

I sensed a genuine feeling of mutual respect pass between us as we held each other's gaze and shook hands.

"Good luck, Charles. I hope you have a good weekend sharing all your news with your parents. I'm sure they must be very proud of the work you are doing?"

"I hope so, Professor, and thank you again."

I closed the study door behind me gratified with the support I'd received from both my tutors. I also felt a rush of excitement at the prospect of revealing all I had discovered to Mum and Dad over the next few days. My only hope was they wouldn't ask questions I couldn't answer or, as had just been pointed out to me, weren't relevant, at this stage, to my degree.

Chapter Ten

Mum and Dad were standing on the platform as my train pulled into Peterborough that Friday evening.

"See you've brought another bag of washing for me then," Mum said as I threw a bin liner of dirty clothes into the boot of the car, along with my shoulder bag and books.

"That's a bit presumptuous, how do you know its stuff to be washed?"

Leaning against the car door she laughed. "I can smell your socks from here. Honestly, you men are all the same; you put on a clean shirt to go out in but never think to change your socks until they walk away on their own."

I looked at Dad who was smiling as well. "Help me out here Pop?"

"No point, Son, I've given up. I just do as I'm told, including putting on a clean pair of socks every day." He looked at Mum. "Which I might add I do without any reminder from you thank you very much."

As I bent down to ease myself into the back of the car Mum leant forward and gave me a kiss.

"It's good to have you home, Son."

I smiled as she climbed into the front with Dad. "It's good to be home."

Closing her door, she turned to look at me. "I'm really looking forward to hearing all about the results of this latest research of yours Charlie." She laughed. "And yes, I know you haven't wanted to speak to us that much about it over the past few weeks until you were ready, but I've been excited about this whole family tree thing ever since we first talked about it, so it'll be good to finally hear what you've discovered."

I pursed my lips and shook my head.

"Sorry, Mum, I haven't brought it with me. I didn't think I'd have room with all those dirty socks as well."

"Charlie Benton, you better have brought it with you, or you'll be taking all that washing back to Leicester the same as it arrived, dirty socks and all."

We laughed as Dad pulled away, turning onto the main road for home.

"So, have you uncovered much new about your mum's side of the family then that we didn't already know," he enquired, glancing in the rear-view mirror to gauge my response?

"Not really, well not the first couple of generations that we've already spoken about, but obviously there's more to tell the further back we go. What really interested me on a personal level though was how many other people they'd all have got to know or been involved with during their lifetime. I mean, generally we all tend to think only about the individuals we know in *our* particular circle of friends and family, yeah? But the reality is we meet all sorts of people along the way, and sometimes we might help them or do something that changes something about their life that we never fully become aware of."

Dad glanced at me in the mirror again. "Sounds a bit deep."

"Not really if you think about it. Let's take politicians for instance, they don't know us individually, yet they create laws that affect us all, perhaps for generations to come, and yet they'll all be dead and buried long after introducing those laws but, in a way, they'll still be dictating how we live in fifty or a hundred years' time."

"I'd never really thought about it like that before Charlie, but I suppose you're right."

"I really became aware of how the things we choose to do can affect others when I was reading about your dad and his Father-in-law Mum, when they were working in the mines. It was really fascinating to learn about the different owners of the collieries and how they viewed their workers, the unions, and so on."

"And we're really looking forward to hearing all about it as I said, but first let's get you home and fed; you must be tired and hungry after that journey?" She laughed. "And, after carrying all of that dirty washing of course?"

It was good to get home again, with the opportunity to relax for a while, having focused my attention, pretty much, entirely on work and research for the past few weeks. And although I knew I'd spend much of the next few days talking to Mum and Dad about the discoveries I'd made, I was also grateful that, here at home at least, I would find none of the additional pressures to get that detail as accurately defined as would be the case at uni. There I would be expected to place all my ducks neatly in a row without error ready for my finals. Putting all of that to the back of my mind, for now at least, I determined to make the most of the next few days and just enjoy my time at home. I laughed to myself, remembering the advice Professor Smalling had given me about not letting Mum dictate the conversation or its detail with regard to what I'd uncovered.

"It may be her family, Charlie, but it's your degree. There'll be plenty of time after you leave university to go back and record it in a style more suited to her wishes or thinking. For now, only focus on what you need to do to get your grades."

Of course he was right, but this was Mum we were talking about and she could prove a far more intimidating opponent than any university tutor once she made her mind up about something. Even so I did raise the point as we sat down to supper that evening reasoning. If I didn't speak up now, I would have no chance once we started talking in any depth later on.

"Listen, Mum, I know you want to find out as much about your family as possible, and I'm really happy to tell you everything I've learnt so far, but please remember this research is for my finals. I have to present it in a way that pleases the board first and ticks all of their boxes if I'm to get my pass, okay?"

"Of course, I know that Charlie. I'm not sure why you feel the need to tell me it again, or am I missing something?"

Dad leant across the table to pick up the bowl of potatoes.

"He means don't be pestering him for information that he might not have to hand just now or that isn't relevant to his degree. It may be *your* family tree but there might be bits his examiners don't need to see or know about, no matter how interesting or important they might appear to – us." He laughed as he put the bowl back on the table. "Especially you. Pass the cabbage love?"

Mum lifted the bowl in mock derision as though to throw it at him.

"I'm not stupid, Pete; I do know all of this is for Charlie's exams." She looked at me and smiled. "It will just be nice to learn a bit more about the family, or at least as much as he can tell us." She turned to Dad. "If that's alright with you, Mr know it all?"

I jumped in before Dad could respond.

"Thanks Mum, it'll be nice for me to talk about it as well, I'm looking forward to it. Up until now it has stayed mainly on the paper apart from talking it through briefly with my tutors to make sure I was headed in the right direction. It'll be good to bring it to life a bit." I paused and patted my stomach. "Great meal, thanks Mum, can't remember the last time I had a proper roast with all the trimmings."

"Don't they serve real food in Leicester then?"

Dad grunted. "I shouldn't imagine a roast dinner is a priority at university is it Charlie? Burgers and beer sound a bit more like it to me, am I right, Son?"

I grinned back at him as I piled another spoon full of carrot onto my plate. "I couldn't possibly say."

We spent the next few minutes catching up on family issues and talking about Dad's job which had seen him travelling a little further from home than he would have liked in recent weeks.

"They say it comes with the responsibility of having a senior position within the Company, but the truth is it's just a way of getting more for less out of everybody."

"I told him to complain but he won't."

"There's no point in rocking the boat Irene, it's just one of those things. Anyway, if I refuse, someone else will take on the extra work, and next time they're looking at redundancies whose name will be at the top of the list? The one that didn't go the extra mile, that's who."

"I'm sorry, Dad; sounds like you're having a bit of a rough time."

"Anything for a quiet life, that's your dad's problem. He's never been ambitious and the people at the top know that so they just pile more work onto his shoulders. He's not getting any younger either."

"What's my age got to do with it? I just don't like an atmosphere that's all. Why cause an argument over a couple of extra trips away?"

"Until the next time."

"Come on you two play nicely."

They looked at each other and grinned.

"Charlie's right, love. Look, if they ask again next month, I'll say something, okay?"

Placing her knife and fork together on her empty plate she peered over her glasses at him.

"Alright, but if you don't I will."

We ate our sweet of homemade apple pie and custard in much lighter spirits, after which I offered to help Mum with the washing up while Dad finished a report he'd been working on.

"I'm sorry about earlier, Charlie, but I do worry about your dad. Even now he's working when we should all be spending time together."

I tried to inject some humour into our conversation. "What like washing up the supper things? Anyway, he's finishing that report so we can spend the next couple of days together remember?"

She shrugged her shoulders as she placed the dinner plates into the washing up bowl causing warm soapy water to run over the edge into the sink.

"I know but …"

"He's fine, Mum. Don't beat him up for being the man he is. He just likes to get things right, same as me with this research. We both like to see a job through to the end that's all. He's still the man you married."

Mum looked up and flicked some bubbles at me.

"Another know-it-all in the family. I'm not sure this university education is actually doing you any good if all you can do is join forces with your dad and criticise your poor old Mum."

I leant forward and squeezed her arm. "I'm not criticising you I'm just sticking up for him, if that makes sense?"

She laughed. "I'll remember that the next time you want a roast dinner."

We spent the next few minutes laughing together and generally catching up with events from the past couple of weeks. I'd forgotten how much pleasure I got from spending time with my parents and smiled inwardly at the prospect of our being together over the next few days, simply relaxing in each other's company.

"You look tired, Charlie."

"I'm okay, just haven't been sleeping so well lately. It's probably all this research, I don't seem to be able to put it down at the end of the day. It's still running around my head when I get into bed."

"Well, worrying about it in the middle of the night won't help; it'll still be there in the morning."

"I know, but it's not just the work it's…" I looked down at the tea towel in my hand and stuttered to a halt not wanting to finish my sentence.

"It's what, Charlie? What were you going to say?"

I looked up and forced a weak smile.

"This is going to sound stupid."

"Now you've got me worried. What's stupid?"

I took a deep breath.

"Well, ever since I've started looking in detail at your, *our* family, I've been having these strange dreams, a bit like the ones I told you about before but, in

130

the past few weeks they've become more vivid and real to me, almost as though I'm a part of them. It's like I'll research some information about one of our family members and then dream about them, seeing them clearly in my mind, perhaps sharing a conversation with them even though I've never actually met them and don't know anything about them apart from what I've read or researched." I looked at her and shrugged my shoulders. "Told you it was stupid."

Wiping her hands she took me in her arms. Even as a grown man it still felt good to be held by my mum.

"It's not stupid, Charlie; you've just been overdoing it that's all, same as your dad. You both care too much about what you do and neither of you know when to say enough. I'm not surprised these people are coming to life in your dreams; after all, you read about them all day and then, by your own admission, you can't let them go at bedtime, so of course everything gets churned around in your head and is still there when you go to sleep."

I stepped back and smiled at her.

"Thanks, Mum. When you say it like that it does make sense, well, sort of anyway."

Rubbing my arm she moved towards the kettle.

"Listen, Charlie, I was going to ask about what you've found out so far but, after what you've just said, I'm not going to, at least not tonight."

"Mum, I'll be fine, I just –"

She interrupted. "You'll just nothing my lad and that's an end to it. You go and sit down with your dad and I'll make us all a drink, then when you've finished it you can get yourself off to bed for an early night." She squeezed my shoulder and smiled. "Our family tree can wait another few hours, after all it's waited this long."

True to her word, Mum didn't raise the subject of my research during the next half an hour as we sat and enjoyed our hot drinks together. She also made it clear to Dad that anything to do with my uni work was definitely taboo as far as being the topic of conversation for this particular evening.

"So, when *are* you going to dish the dirt on your mum's family then?"

"Not tonight, Pete, that's for sure."

Dad shifted in his chair. "But I thought…?"

"Well, don't, Charlie's tired and I've already agreed with him that any information he has about the family can wait until tomorrow, isn't that right, Son?"

I swallowed my mouthful of hot chocolate and laughed.

"Don't bring me into your lovers' spat."

Dad smiled and shook his head. "We're not fighting Charlie; it's just that, as ever, I'm in the wrong. I clearly haven't quite got the hang of reading your mum's mind yet."

"Sarcasm won't win you any fans either Peter Benton."

"Yes dear, no dear, sorry dear."

I decided to change the subject before they really did fall out.

"So what's gone wrong with the Posh, eh Pop? I heard they got stuffed a couple of weeks ago?"

"Just unlucky that's all, they were better at home during the week though. They always seem to play better at home recently, especially if it's an evening kick off. Something about playing under the lights I think."

Mum laughed. "Or maybe it's because the lights are so bad the other team can't see the ball?"

"Flipping cheek; you've already told me off once this evening and now you want to attack my football club." He grimaced as though in pain. "A man can only take so much you know Irene."

I smiled and shifted forward in my seat. "Well, I'm off to bed if that's okay with you two love birds? Like we said earlier Mum, I am feeling knackered and it's been a long day, what with the journey down from Leicester and all. I think I could do with just getting my head down." I stood up and yawned as if to emphasise my tiredness. "Night Mum, and thanks," I said, bending down to kiss her on the cheek.

"What are you thanking me for, I haven't done anything?"

"Yes you have. And you've provided the inspiration for part of my degree as well, or at least your family has."

Dad leant forward in his chair.

"And I for one look forward to hearing all about it." He smiled and rubbed his hands together. "I do hope there's some dark and sinister secret in there somewhere, something your mum will be ashamed of that I can tease her about. It'll give me a chance to get even with all the things she says about the Posh."

"I don't know about any dark and sinister secrets, but I do hope it'll be more interesting than your stupid football team. And of course there's great-great-Granddad George and the mystery about his alleged murder, I presume that'll be dark enough for you if it turns out to be true?" She turned to me and smiled. "I must admit even I'm looking forward to hearing more about that particular episode in our family's history; that's presuming you've managed to find out anything more about it?"

I stretched my arms and yawned again.

"All will be revealed tomorrow Mum, all will be revealed tomorrow."

She looked up and smiled.

"I'll look forward to it, goodnight, Son," she said, adding with a wink, "Sleep well."

I recognised this as a reference to our earlier conversation in the kitchen and nodded, grateful for her concern.

"Thanks, Mum, I'm sure I will. Night, Dad."

"Night, Son, good to have you home."

"It's good to be home, see you later."

I closed the door behind me and stood for a moment listening to the two of them talking to one another.

"The boy's exhausted, Pete; I just hope all of this work hasn't been too much for him, especially as so much of it has been surrounding our family."

"He'll be fine after a good night's rest. And as far as reading up about your family is concerned, I bet he's enjoyed every minute of it."

I smiled and moved towards the stairs. I'd enjoyed my work over the past few weeks although I knew some of what I'd discovered wasn't going to be easy to talk about, especially with Mum. All families have secrets or things that have happened to them over the years they might not choose to make public, and our family was to prove no different.

As I reached the top of the stairs I sensed a shadow move across my bedroom door causing me to shudder as if I'd been caught by a sudden chill. I stood for a moment to gather myself, reasoning it to be no more than a reflection caused by the tree outside the upstairs window catching the light of the streetlamp beyond and throwing its silhouette across the landing. I admonished myself, remembering what Mum had said about becoming too preoccupied with the results of my research. Also, how she hadn't been surprised that the characters and stories I'd uncovered regarding our family were dominating my waking thoughts and night-time slumbers as I struggled to place them in some semblance of reasoned order. I shook my head. Yes, I wanted to do my best for all involved but right now I was tired and wasn't going to allow any more random thoughts to access my mind and wreck my chances of a good night's sleep.

As I stood in the bathroom cleaning my teeth, I felt the same chill breeze pass over me I'd experienced just a few minutes earlier on the landing. I looked in the mirror, but instead of seeing my face and the airing cupboard behind me there was nothing, just a black space. I dropped my toothbrush and gripped the sink with both hands as a wave of nausea overtook me and my head began to spin. I instinctively closed my eyes in an effort to stop the room from turning, and as I did so I heard a distant voice calling out to me.

"Help me Charles."

I recognised it immediately; it was the same desperate cry I had heard before. I stood motionless almost afraid to breathe as a feeling of complete panic ran through me. Opening my eyes tentatively I glanced in the mirror again; the room was bathed in light once more and there behind my reflection was the airing cupboard just as it had been moments before.

I looked at my face staring blankly back at me in the mirror.

"The sooner I get this family tree sorted and out of the way the better," I told myself, attempting to shrug off the events of the last few minutes as nothing more than the effects of tiredness and exhaustion. I stared hard at my reflection, desperately fighting against the growing sense of unease and foreboding that currently held me in its grip.

As I got undressed, I thought about the day to come and of the stories I would share with Mum and Dad about what I'd discovered over the past few weeks; also, how much pleasure it would bring them, in learning more about our family's history. I eased myself into bed and immediately felt more relaxed as the soft welcome of my pillows and warmth of the blankets embraced me, relaxing both my body and mind as I drifted towards unconsciousness.

I turned on to my side, mumbling words of encouragement to myself. "A good night's rest and everything will look better in the morning." Closing my eyes, I encouraged kindly sleep to overtake me. I prayed I wouldn't be disturbed again by the same unsettling dreams which had so troubled me in recent weeks; it was a prayer that, sadly, wasn't too be answered.

My alarm woke me with a start and I leant across the bed to turn it off feeling anything less than rested. Although I'd managed to get to sleep fairly quickly much of the rest of the night had been spent tossing and turning with the names and accounts of my ancestors vying for precedence in my tired and addled brain.

I dreamt of being at Dunkirk and fighting alongside my grandfather John; the Germans raining death down upon us whilst we and the other allied troops scurried about the beaches like ants attempting to avoid this evil boot of aggression from trampling us out of existence. I also dreamt of pushing cart loads of coal along the deep underground tracks at Newstead colliery and of attending a service at my great-great-great-grandfather George's church in Kent.

The trouble with fitful sleep and half-awake dreams is, whilst they appear to make sense in the still dark hours of the night, come the next morning and the bright light of day they appear as elusive and distant as the night itself. But, if that's true, and accepting these imaginings to be no more than figments of my overactive and exhausted mind, why is it they are appearing as more real to me as each night passes, creating an increasing aura of authenticity in both their content and momentum.

I turned over and looked at my clock. Another half an hour in bed sounded inviting. – I pulled the blanket over my head, closing my eyes and mind to the world once more.

Chapter Eleven

It was almost eleven o'clock before I sat down with Mum and Dad, ready to reveal all I had discovered about our family over the previous few weeks.

"All those late nights at university must be catching up with you Charlie. I've never known you to stay in bed so late, even after a night out with Simon and your other friends; you've always been a bit of an early bird."

"It's not that Dad, it's more like I said to Mum yesterday, I'm just not sleeping very well at the moment, and even when I do get off, I'm having these really weird dreams."

"I told him it's all connected with this work he's been doing for our family tree. I feel guilty now suggesting it. You should have chosen a family we didn't know. It would have been a lot easier and not put so much pressure on you Charlie."

"It's fine Mum really. Anyway, it's been easier in a way looking at your family because I had a starting point rather than beginning from scratch with a timeline and group of people I didn't know at all." I smiled at them both. "And it's been nice finding out a bit more about my relations as well, even if they are a bunch of nutters."

"Charlie! That's not very nice."

Dad laughed. "I thought you'd discover there was madness in the family, Son, well on your mum's side of it anyway, I've suspected it for years. You should have researched my lot, a different breed of person altogether."

Mum's eyes widened as she stared at him in mock disbelief.

"Oh yes, a different breed alright, certified most of them, or at least they should have been if you're any example to go by."

"And I love you too."

We laughed which lifted my spirit and put any remaining thoughts about the previous night's unrest and disquieting dreams to the back of my mind. I positioned myself centrally on the sofa surrounded by sheets of paper and other research material as Mum and Dad sat patiently in their chairs on either side of me.

Mum smiled and nodded towards the paperwork spread around me. "I feel quite excited now. Just tell me there's nothing too awful in what you've found out, Charlie? Did Grampy invent all those stories about there being a murder in the family?"

I opened my notepad and smiled at her knowingly.

"Maybe not. It seems that –"

Dad interrupted. "Was it George, was he the victim?"

"It certainly looks that way, at least as far as I can tell from what I've discovered so far."

Mum leant back in her chair. "And I always thought Grampy had made it all up, or at the very least was exaggerating, knowing what a great storyteller he was."

Dad laughed. "A great fibber, don't you mean?"

I shuffled forwards in my seat.

"Like I said, we'll come to George later if that's okay? Now, do you want to hear what I've found out or not?"

They glanced at each other briefly then, suitably chastened, turned back to face me.

"Sorry, Son, it's just that I've never really thought of your mum as coming from a family of murderers before."

"Pete, that's enough, let the lad tell the story in his own way." She looked at me again. "Sorry, Charlie, no more interruptions I promise." She glowered at Dad. "*We* promise."

Dad put his hands in the air as if to acknowledge defeat.

"Thanks. Listen, I don't mind you asking questions, as long as you accept I might not be able to answer all of them, or may not have the particular piece of information to hand that you want to know about, okay?" They looked at me quizzically.

"What I mean is, some of what you might want to know about isn't necessarily required information for my degree and so won't be included at this stage. If the examiners think I'm waffling or trying to bluff my way through a question by giving them some unnecessary detail or over egging a particular aspect of my work in an effort to cover up a greater hole in my research then they'll mark me down. So for now most of what I'm going to tell you will be just the hard numbers and facts, although I'll try to give you as much background information as I can, or at least as much as I can remember anyway."

Mum leant forward and smiled.

"For the next couple of hours Charlie you have our complete attention, we're all ears." She threw a swift and dismissive glance towards Dad. "Don't say a word Pete, not a word."

He shook his head. "As if?"

I felt a bead of nervous perspiration run down my back. I didn't want to let them down in what I was about to disclose, but equally recognised my greater loyalty lay in the attention to detail required for my exams.

"Okay, let's start with your dad, John Pearce. As we know he was born in 1908 in Nottingham. His Dad was Henry Pearce, also a miner, and his mum was Winifred. She was a farmer's daughter and was working in a local textile factory when she met Henry."

Mum jumped in. "That's right. I think she made lace and…"

It was my turn to interrupt. "Mum please. The side of your family we're tracing is the one that takes us back to great-great-great-Granddad George if you remember, so we need to leave Henry, Winifred and that particular branch of your family to one side for now, okay? As we agreed before, if we want to look at the wider family history at some point we can do that at another time, but for now we just need to focus on the line that takes us back to George."

"Sorry Charlie you're right, I was just…" She looked at me apologetically and drew her hand across her mouth. "I know, shut up Mum."

I smiled. "Well, perhaps not shut up exactly; just maybe hold back a bit."

She nodded her understanding,

"Your mum was Mary Coulson born in 1904 to William Coulson a miner, and to Anna Anderson daughter of Thomas and Sarah Anderson who we'll come to later. Now Grampy and Nanny Anna…" I paused for a moment and looked up at my duly attentive parents.

"What is it, Charlie?"

"Well, this may sound silly but can I just call them all by their proper names for now and not keep referring to them as my grandparents or great-grandparents as it sounds a bit odd, at least as far as the way I'll need to present it at uni. I won't be referring to them as Grampy or Nanny Anna when I construct the family tree itself for my finals, even though the tutors are aware it's my own family I'm using. I'll just give you their names, dates, and any appropriate detail about their circumstances for now, yeah? That'll be what the examiners will be looking for. It doesn't really matter to them whether or not they're actually related to me, certainly as far as my grades are concerned. But equally, I don't want you to think I'm being uncaring about our family, it's just…"

Mum put her hand up.

"You tell us in whatever way is best for you Charlie. As you say we can look at it through ancestral eyes once your work is finished and you've gained your degree, which I might add your dad and I are convinced you will, right love?"

Dad grinned. "You betcha."

I moved a little more comfortably in my seat. "Thanks. To be honest this whole family tree thing feels a bit odd anyway, at least doing it as a piece of work about my own family. There were quite a few things I thought would be interesting to follow up on but knew they'd be dismissed as not relevant for my course work and finals, so I've left them out for now and made a note for us to look at them again separately once I've finished at uni."

I turned the page of my pad and picked up a piece of paper from the sofa to cross reference the information with my earlier notes. "Okay, where was I?" I scratched my head. "I think I'll start again if that's okay. Right, your dad." I laughed. "I mean John Pearce. I couldn't find out much about his time at school apart from the fact he went to a local one near to Newstead. Traditionally around that time children left school at about fourteen and started work, but John didn't start at the colliery until 1924 when he was sixteen, so maybe he did something else before becoming a miner. We can always look at that another time, for now it's his years at the pit that we'll concentrate on if that's –"

Mum interrupted again. "I think he worked for a local grocer for a while after leaving school, but I don't know what he did exactly or how long he was there." She looked at me and grimaced. "Sorry, Charlie, I'm doing it again, aren't I?"

I nodded at her. "Look, I know you know most of this, Mum, and what I'll talk about when I get to his time in the army and Dunkirk and the like but, if you can just let me go through what I have in front of me for now, that would be great. Like I said before, it's more for me and my tutors at this stage than it is for you and Dad. I just want to make sure I've got everything in the right order. The fiddly bits around the edges that are only really of interest to us can wait for now, okay?"

Mum smiled. "Absolutely, and it'll be good to hear it again anyway, or at least what you feel able to share. Like I say I do know a little bit about Dad's early life, but again that's only from what Mum told me. She said he wasn't very forthcoming about his younger years, and as for his time in the army well, we've already talked about some of that."

"That's right, and I was really moved by those letters you showed me, especially the one he wrote just before he died. It made it all the more real when I came to look it up as part of my research. Anyway, the point is if I'm going on about stuff you already know just ignore me, unless you think I've got something totally wrong, in which case please shout out."

Mum smiled. "Charlie, stop worrying about offending us, I'm sure it'll be fine. You were the one who was concerned about giving too much detail and now you're telling us to ignore the bits you've got." She leant forward and squeezed my hand. "You just tell us what you've learnt and leave us to worry about whether or not we've heard it before."

"Thanks." I sat back for a moment reflecting. "It's funny, but when I'm talking to my tutors it feels okay just to set everything out in a matter of fact sort of way, but when I'm talking to you two well, it's different, you're my parents and this is our family we're discussing. It seems strange to refer to them as just a series of names and dates on a piece of paper."

As I looked at my notes and the names written down in front of me, I recalled how I'd felt when I first began searching through the births and deaths registers looking for information about Mum's family. I remembered how I'd been troubled in seeing the names of so many other individuals who, alongside my own relations, had come and gone over the years; once living full and vital lives but who were now little more than a distant memory or, perhaps, had been forgotten completely. I drew a deep breath as a feeling of melancholy overtook me.

"Are you alright Charlie, you look like you've lost a pound and found a penny?"

I looked up and smiled, nodding my head as I did so.

"Yeah, I'm fine." I paused and took another deep breath. This wasn't going to be as easy as I'd hoped.

"Actually, if I'm honest I've found some of this a bit sad." I nodded towards my notebook. "I know I said earlier about them only being a list of names and dates on a piece of paper but, the truth is, as I was looking through all the various family registers and so on I was really struck as to how these were not just a list of nondescript names; but in fact were real people who had lived real lives, and

I'm not just talking about our relatives but all of them. I must have looked at hundreds if not thousands of names and every one of them belonged to someone who had spent time on this earth. Babies who'd died almost as soon as they were born, and others who'd lived to a great age; they'd all existed, mattered to someone, but were now gone? And so I wound up asking myself, what was the point of them being here in the first place?" I glanced at my parents; a look of concern on their faces.

"I mean we all hope our lives are going to count for something and that we'll make a difference in the world, but the reality is most of what we achieve is pretty insignificant in the greater scheme of things."

Dad glanced at Mum and then back towards me. "That all sounds a bit negative, Son. All a bit doom and gloom for a young man with his whole life in front of him; supposedly excited about discovering his family's history along with their place in society. I thought you were planning to be a part of the great movement forward; you know, gaining this degree of yours and going on to right all the wrongs in the world?"

"Oh don't get me wrong, I am excited about lots of things it's just…" My voice faded along with the smile on my face.

Mum squeezed my hand again. "It's just what, Charlie?"

I shook my head. "I'm sorry, I don't mean to appear negative, it's just that in all the names and lives I've researched over the past few weeks I can really only remember the ones that were, or are, connected to our family. And yet didn't all of those other lives count for something as well? Will anybody else, other than their own immediate family, have reason to remember them or to celebrate their existence and the time they spent on this planet?"

Dad pursed his lips.

"I don't think I've ever heard you talk like this before Charlie, and I don't really know what to say to you in reply other than, perhaps, the point *is* to celebrate the life we're given and make the most of the opportunities that come our way while we can rather than condemn the whole process out of hand." Moving back in his chair he stroked his chin thoughtfully. "Listen, Son, you've a heart for people and their place and value in the world, also for history and the great outdoors. You can question it if you like, but your mum and I have watched this passion grow in you, especially over the last few years. And, if you've been given that desire then surely you owe it to yourself and others to embrace it; to go on and make the difference in the world only you can, and not just for those

141

who are here today but for those who follow you as well, whether they remember your name or not."

Mum gestured her agreement.

"Do you remember we went to Tetbury once for a long weekend when you were younger? And while we were there, we visited the Westonbirt Arboretum?"

I smiled at her and nodded.

"Well, I've always maintained that was the day you developed your love for history and the countryside. You kept going on about how the man who founded the place had not only created it for himself and his family to enjoy but also that he'd planned ahead, planting certain trees and bushes in areas that in a hundred years and more, certainly long after he was gone, would be the height and shape they are today ready for us to get pleasure from. You've said on more than one occasion how that visit inspired you to want to do something similar with your life, something different that would also be remembered by others in the years to come just as he had. Do you remember that, Charlie?"

I smiled again. "Robert Holford, that was his name. And yes, I do remember." I felt embarrassed by my earlier outburst.

"I'm sorry, you're right, life is exciting, or at least it should be." I paused and, taking a breath, considered the wisdom of what Mum had said. "I guess I'm just tired after the past few weeks of focusing solely on my research and work." I laughed. "Maybe I should have built in some additional time to simply enjoy the journey along the way as well."

Dad sat back in his chair.

"You're Mum and I were talking about that very thing only the other day. We were saying how hard you've been working and that you needed to take a break at some point or you'd burn yourself out." He smiled. "Sounds like we were right."

"I agree." Leaning forward Mum took my hand again. "I thought you looked tired when you arrived home."

I felt like a little boy being reprimanded for some minor misdemeanour, and yet equally recognised this wasn't critique being proffered in a judgmental or disapproving way. I knew I was loved and that they only desired the best for me. Also, that if I was wise, I would listen and respond in a positive way to what they were saying. Mum glanced at Dad and then back towards me.

"Listen, Charlie, the summer break is not far away, why don't you take a few days out just for yourself and relax, let us spoil you?"

142

I felt humbled by her suggestion.

"Thanks Mum, I appreciate that. And you're right, I have been overdoing it a bit of late; I just want to do a good job. I feel like if I let up now I might miss out on something or fail in some way."

Dad stood up and took a step towards me.

"Stop being so hard on yourself, Son." Looking down at me he smiled. "If you don't ease up a little, then you really will miss out, you'll make yourself ill and then where will you be?"

"I know, Dad, but it's hard to let go. It's like I've come this far and if I stop now then all the hard work I've done already will count for nothing."

"That's daft, and I think if you take a moment to think about it you'll agree."

Mum let go of my arm and moved back in her seat.

"We're not saying you should stop or give up, Charlie, we want you to get this degree every bit as much as you do; even more perhaps as we're the ones who've watched you put in so much effort over the past year or so." She paused. "All we're suggesting is, that you take a few days off to relax, recharge your batteries so to speak ready for that final push. All work and no play remember?"

Dad tilted his head towards Mum as he moved back to his chair.

"She's right, Son, a few days without your head being stuck in a book studying will do you the world of good. You'll come back all the fresher for it as well I promise you."

I recognised, not only the wisdom in what they were saying but, that I was tired and taking a few days off certainly sounded a welcome alternative to checking the detail of my research yet again for the umpteenth time.

"Actually, I have been thinking of going to down Kent, to Sowfield, to find out a bit more about old George. I thought if I went to his church there might be a bit more information in the parish records about what happened to him. All I've really been able to discover so far is that he was killed, apparently trying to stop a robbery. It's all a bit vague though as far as any tangible evidence is concerned, or at least from what I've uncovered so far. The church would probably have kept its own record of events, or there might even be some locals from the area who've heard a version of the story as it was passed down over the years from family members and the like."

Mum leant forward. "So he was murdered then?"

"That's what it looks like but, as I say, the exact circumstances as to what actually happened are not entirely clear."

Dad laughed. "That doesn't sound like much of a break to me; taking yourself off to Kent to do even more research."

"It's not work as such, Dad; I'm just interested to know what happened. Anyway a few days of taking in the fresh air of the Kent countryside won't do me any harm will it?"

"I suppose not, but even so I'm not entirely sure that's the sort of rest your mum and I had in mind. What do you say love?"

"I agree but, like Charlie, I am interested to know what happened, and as he says a few days away from all the pressure he's been working under certainly won't do him any harm." She turned to face me, an inquisitive glint in her eye. "So what *can* you tell us about him being killed?"

"I'd rather not say for now, Mum, if you don't mind, at least not in any detail that isn't based on proper research and the facts to back it up, you know what I'm like. I'm not trying to be secretive or precious about it; it's just, like I said, everything's a bit vague as far as any physical evidence is concerned, and so I'd rather wait until I've been down there and done a bit more digging around, if that's okay with you?"

She looked disappointed. I smiled and decided to move the conversation on.

"Anyway, all that's a long way down the family line; I haven't told you what I've found out about the other members of our tribe yet have I? We'd only got as far as your dad if I remember rightly, and even then I'd only just started before _"

Dad interrupted, laughing as he did so. "Before you went off at the deep end about the meaning of life you mean, or the lack of it?"

"Yeah, yeah, very funny, I've apologised for that." Pausing briefly, I looked directly at them. "And yes, I promise to take a break from my uni work for a while as well, okay?"

"So long as you do."

I laughed. "Fair enough. But remember, if you really do want to know the truth about the dark dealings surrounding George's grisly end then I will need to make a few enquiries about him while I'm down there."

"Of course we want to know what happened, all we're saying is try and find a bit of time for yourself as well. After all he's been dead for a hundred and forty years already so waiting a bit longer won't make any real difference will it, either to him or to us?"

"I know, you're right, but I'd still like to go." I looked at Dad. "They serve a good beer in Kent as well, what with all those hop fields and local breweries."

Dad threw back his head and laughed. "Ah, so now we know the truth, it's a pub crawl you're planning, nothing to do with the supposed murder of our dear departed family member." He winked at me. "Mind, I've heard those rumours about the local beers as well so maybe I should come with you, just for moral support of course?"

"Charlie certainly doesn't need any more training from you in the art of drinking beer thank you very much. I've seen him the worse for wear on more than one occasion already following a night out with you."

"How dare you woman. It was only a couple of pints and a chat about football that's all, what could be more natural between a father and son. What do you say, Charlie?"

I laughed. "Don't bring me into this, although I think Mum may have a point." I tapped my notebook. "Anyway, enough about that, do you want to hear what else I've found out about our family or are we going to talk about beer for the next couple of hours?"

Standing up Mum looked down at the two of us. "Of course we do, and I'm sorry we seem to have gone off track again, but you know what your dad's like?" She winked at him. "Shall I make a drink before we start?"

Dad got to his feet as well. "Good idea love, but you sit down I'll do it. Charlie can make a start and I'll catch up when I come back. After all it's your side of the family we're talking about."

"Tea or coffee, Son?"

"Coffee, thanks."

"Irene?"

"Tea please."

We watched as he left the room.

"Your dad and I aren't telling you what to do, Charlie, I hope you know that? We're just worried about you and about how hard you've been working of late that's all."

I got up and, moving towards her, crouched down to kiss her lightly on the forehead. "I know you are, Mum. You and Dad are great, and I promise I will ease off a bit, but I really do want to go to Kent though."

Leaning forward she ran her fingers gently through my hair in the same way she had so many times when seeking to comfort me as a young boy.

"And we're not saying you can't; just don't overdo it while you're down there, okay?" She took my face in her hands and kissed me on the cheek. "We both love you very much Charlie."

We looked at each other in silence for a moment, all earlier doubts about the greater meaning of life instantly dismissed as I recognised a far deeper truth about the reason for human existence in the world, that of giving and receiving unconditional love.

"Love you too Mum."

She kissed me again and smiled. "Now, are you going to tell me about our family or not?"

I moved back to my chair. "Okay, here we go." Picking up my notebook I flicked through its pages. "Now clearly we know quite a bit about your dad already from your short time with him and from what your mum told you. And, we have those very moving letters she kept that he'd written to the two of you before he was killed, so I won't say any more about him personally for now. I also won't bother about you and Dad at this stage either, except to confirm he was born in 1934 and you in 1936. You were married in Nottingham in 1961, to please your mum no doubt, although you'd already committed to living here in Peterborough by then to be near Dad's work. You were twenty-five when you got married and Dad was twenty-seven." I looked up. "You told me you didn't think you were going to be able to have children at first after a few false alarms but then your little miracle, me, came along in 1966 and you've known nothing but happiness and joy ever since. I know we don't need that particular fact for the family tree but how could I not mention the brightest event in yours and Dad's life together so far?"

Mum laughed. "It seems wrong to correct you about an error in your facts so early on, so we'll discuss the bit about you being the fount of endless joy in our lives later."

Smiling I turned back to my notes. "Fair enough. Now remember, it's just your side of the family that we're interested in, the line that takes us back to George Anderson." I took a deep breath, a mix of trepidation and excitement running through me. I wanted to get this right for both of us. "So, things we already know, and forgive me for repeating myself but I just want to run this from top to bottom for now. Your dad, John Henry Pearce was born in Nottingham in 1908. His parents were Henry and Winifred Pearce, also from Nottingham and a mining family. I think you told me once your dad had been

146

given the middle name of Henry after his father, but that he preferred to be called Harry?" Mum nodded, clearly enjoying the moment and not wanting to interrupt my flow.

"Right then, and your mum was born Mary Alice Coulson in Nottingham in 1904, four years before your dad. Her parents were Anna and William Coulson, Grampy Bill and Granny Anna to you and me, but for research purposes, and as we agreed earlier, we'll call them by their given names." I stopped and put my notebook down. "I know what I said about not changing the subject and sticking to the facts but there is a question I've been meaning to ask you about your dad and Grampy for a while now, about their time working together in the mines."

Mum shifted in her chair. "I've told you before, Charlie, I don't know much about those early days, only what Mum said really."

"I know, but I was wondering how they got on with each other as men rather than any specific detail about the two of them individually, what with them both being miners and so on?"

She looked a little confused. "I'll try, what is it exactly you want to know?"

"Well, you always said Grampy was a big union man and one for taking on the bosses whenever he felt the miners were getting a rough deal or being taken advantage of."

"That's right. I remember Mum saying Granny would tell her to keep out of his way if there was trouble brewing at the colliery. Apparently, he was well known for his fiery temper." She smiled. "She said nobody was safe once he had the bit between his teeth."

"So what did he make of your dad then, 'cause I seem to remember you saying he wasn't as belligerent as Grampy and that he'd try and find some common ground with the colliery owners during a dispute rather than go for all out protests and strikes?"

"Funny enough he really liked Dad, they got on well, or at least they did once he'd got used to another man coming first in his daughter's life." She laughed. "Of course they had their differences, especially in the early days, but I think, in the end, Grampy came to realise that Dad and others like him were the future for the coal industry. Mind, that was an admission he struggled with, certainly early on, having held dear to his more militant views towards management over the years but, which now, were being seen by many as both outdated and better left in the past. Changes were already beginning to take shape as far as mining was concerned in the run up to the war, both in the pits and in the way they were managed. I'm not saying Grampy backed down from his principals of putting men at the coal face first, but I do think he recognised the world was changing, and of course he'd lived through the general strike of 1926 and had witnessed first-hand how that had affected miners and their families. Being invalided out of the pits and having to work topside made a difference to his thinking as well. I think he also struggled more than he let on with his failing health. Mum said it wasn't so much the asthma and his other chest problems that frustrated him, it was more the mental side of things that dragged him down; his perceived loss of standing in the community and amongst his peers. You and I might see it differently Charlie, but you need to remember he was a proud man and so things like not being able to provide for his family in the manner he would have chosen would've really upset him. And of course not being able to take his place on the front line alongside his fellow men to defend his Country, in either of the wars, bothered him as well. He might just have scraped in during the First World War if his health had allowed but by the time the Second World War came along he was too old to sign up anyway. Even so it still troubled him. Granny said he would become very down about it, even depressed at times, and no matter how much she tried to reassure him he would still argue he was less of a man than his friends and work colleagues."

Mum paused, taking a deep breath as tears filled her eyes. "I'd almost forgotten this Charlie, but I can remember her saying to me once that when telegrams arrived telling friends and neighbours their loved ones had been lost in battle he would sink into even deeper despair, protesting that it should have been him as well, laying down his life for his family and Country." I watched as she took her handkerchief and wiped her eyes. "Granny would say at times like that she was grateful for his bad chest, and that she'd rather have him at home with his limitations than to receive a telegram saying he'd been killed in some foreign land and never see him again." Mum smiled ruefully and shook her head. "She said he would get angry with her and tell her she was being selfish and that she didn't understand what it was like to be a man, especially one who was being denied the opportunity of having his life truly count for something, even if it did mean losing it." She paused again. "He told her once that the torturously slow death of ignominy he was suffering was more painful to him than any German bullet or bomb could be, no matter how hard that was for her to understand. She was hurt by that; at the thought he would prefer to be shot to pieces in battle somewhere rather than be safe at home with her and the family." Mum stared into the distance. "Perhaps he was right, as she certainly didn't understand." I looked on in silence, a feeling of regret sweeping over me once more that I'd chosen my own family for this project.

"You alright, Mum; are you sure this isn't going to be too much for you?"

She leant forward and took my hand. "I'm fine Charlie, really I am. It's just…well, sometimes you remember things you thought you'd forgotten, and then they come back to touch you again, that's all." She shook her head and laughed. "That's a very long-winded answer to your question isn't it, and it doesn't really tell you very much about how Grampy and Dad had got on together either does it?"

"Not exactly but –"

She interrupted. "Sorry, let me start again, and I'll try not to go off track this time." Pausing briefly to collect her thoughts she smiled at me before continuing. "So, as I began to say, I think Grampy recognised Dad as the new broom who would sweep away the past and hopefully help create a bright new future for the coal industry and for those who worked in it. Although, God only knows what would have happened had they both been here to witness the events of the past couple of years, what with the strike and Arthur Scargill's call to arms. I think there may well have been a falling out between them then." Pausing again she blew out her cheeks. "And goodness knows what the two of them would be like now with the Government's hardened attitude towards the coal industry and all these proposed pit closures. I know Grampy would have been distraught to think of his beloved Newstead colliery being under threat. Mind, I think even Dad, reasonable as he was, would have sided with Grampy over some of what Ian MacGregor and Mrs Thatcher have done of late." Shaking her head, she sighed. "Even towards the end of her life Mum would talk about the differences she and Grampy had had over the pits. She used to say he would get angry with her for supposedly siding with Dad when he talked about the need for change; that they were both too quick in agreeing with management in how that change should happen. He'd say those of Dad's generation hadn't lived through the same hardships and losses the early miners and their families had experienced in the late 1800s, and that it was their protests and strikes that paved the way for the better pay and working conditions that Dad and others like him enjoyed now. Mind, even with those improvements he'd still argue there was a lot to be done to bring real parity between miners and other trades employing manual workers." She paused and gazed into the distance. "I remember a few months before she died Mum said there could well have been a split in the family had our two respective fathers still been alive to witness what went on during that awful strike. I know she wasn't well by then, what with her heart problems and so on, but, as I've said before, I still believe the events of that dispute caused her health to deteriorate a lot sooner than it might have done otherwise. I think she felt the injustices and unreasonable employment demands, as Grampy would have described them, that had been inflicted on the miners by management and the pit owners over the previous hundred years or so were brought to a head in that conflict. For her, it was a moment in time when the proud tradition and history of coal mining in this country reached a nadir, with both sides becoming so entrenched in their views and demands that a place for Dad's more reasoned approach would have found itself beyond getting any sort of a hearing, fair or otherwise. Certainly Grampy would have argued that." She paused again as if shaping in her mind what she wanted to say next. "I believe that strike tore the heart out of the mining community as a whole and has acted as a trigger for, maybe an end to the coal industry itself. And I think Mum recognised that as well, and it all just became too much for her." She smiled and looked at me, her eyes moist with tears.

"Maybe you shouldn't ask me anymore questions about my family memories Charlie or I might lose it altogether and we really will be here all day." She looked at her watch. "Talking of taking a long time, where has your father got to? How long does it take to make a cup of tea for goodness sake? I could have prepared a full meal in the time he's been out there." As she finished speaking so the door swung open.

"And about time, what have you been doing out there growing the tea leaves and coffee beans?"

"Sorry, I forgot to turn the kettle on at the wall. I thought it was taking a long time to heat up."

"I said I should have made it."

I smiled at the two of them exchanging playful glances as Dad placed the tray of drinks on the coffee table.

"No, you're fine, sweetheart, I can manage." He grinned, picking up his mug and moving towards his chair. "How's it going then, have I missed much?"

Mum and I looked at each other and laughed.

"Actually no. Charlie made the mistake of asking me about the relationship between Dad and Grampy, well, at least as far as their differing views over the way the mining industry should be run. And I'm afraid I developed a bad case of verbal diarrhoea after that going off at a tangent and telling him far more than he needed or, probably, wanted to know."

"Don't do yourself down Mum it was really interesting, and remember, I'm the one who asked the question, so I've only got myself to blame." Leaning forward to pick up my drink I winked at her.

"Thanks for the coffee Dad. Now, shall I continue from where we left off?"

Taking a sip from her cup, Mum nodded her agreement. "Yes please."

I spread my papers out on the sofa again.

"This may look a bit messy but remember, it's still only a rough edit, it'll all be in order ready for my exams."

Dad looked at Mum and smiled. "You know what you're doing, Son, we're just happy and proud to be a part of it, aren't we love?"

Mum smiled, a genuine look of affection on her face.

"Very proud."

I cleared my throat as a slight nervous tremor ran through me. Suddenly I felt more concerned about getting my facts right for the two of them than I did about presenting my findings at uni.

"I think as I said earlier, the best thing for now is just to give you the basics regarding family births, marriages, deaths, and so on in chronological order. Also, maybe one or two highlights about their lives. After that we can expand on any additional detail and talk about it separately, along with anything else I might have discovered that you'd be interested in. That'll also give you a chance to chip in with anything you feel I might have missed out or got wrong. Does that sound okay?"

They nodded in unison. "Great, otherwise we'll be stop starting again like we did before Dad came in with the drinks." I laughed. "Sorry Mum, like *I* did before Dad came in with the drinks."

She acknowledged my apology with a smile. "Whatever's best for you, Charlie?"

I cleared my throat again. "Okay, so I got as far as your granddad, William Coulson. He was born in 1878 in Nottingham. His Dad was Edward Coulson who was born in 1850. On Grampy's birth certificate it said Edward was a miner at Newstead colliery as well, but as the colliery only opened four years before Grampy was born in 1874 we're not sure what Edward did before that. I did dig a little deeper and found some information suggesting he might have worked as a general labourer for a time, but that's maybe something we can look at again in the future if we want to? We do know though by the time Grampy was born Edward and his wife Nancy were already living in Newstead. That would have been the *old* village which was built in 1875 to house the early miners and their families. It changed and became the *new* village a few years later during the late 1880s and early 1890s when better facilities were established for the rapidly growing community. I think I alluded to that the last time we spoke. Anyway, looking at the records it shows there was something like twelve hundred men working at the colliery by that time." I looked up from my notes. "I'm not sure where Edward and Nancy lived before that, although it doesn't really matter because it's only your direct family line we're following Mum. That said, and just to complete this particular story about Grampy's parents, Nancy was born in Nottingham as well in 1854. On Grampy's birth certificate it said she was a textile worker. Nottingham and pretty much all of that area around the Midlands including here in Leicestershire became hot spots for families to migrate to who were looking for work. The whole region witnessed a growing number of factories and companies at that time which were expanding their businesses and taking on extra workers for the flourishing textile, lace, and hosiery industry, as you intimated earlier Mum. Of course, all that's gone into decline in more recent years with modern technology and machines able to do the same work for a lot less money, and without the need for anything like the old workforce, so the bosses are able to save all round."

I looked up and smiled at the two of them, pleased that I'd got through so much detail without further interruption, yet also aware that in not just sticking to the basics, as intended, I had already overstepped my own line about not going into too much detail at this early stage.

"It's funny hearing you say some of this Charlie, because it brings back memories of stories Grampy and Granny used to tell me when I was younger about how hard things had been for them when they first got married. Conditions were tough in those days for young couples starting out and they weren't paid much either for all the hours they had to work. Granny had moved up from Kent to Nottingham with her mum after Great Granddad Thomas died and…"

I jumped in. "Mum you're doing it again, you're getting ahead of the story, I haven't got that far back yet."

Mum looked at me apologetically. "Sorry Charlie, I got carried away in the moment, I won't do it again." She smiled. "Or at least I'll try not to."

Dad shifted forward in his chair placing his empty mug on the tray. "Otherwise, you really will get carried away, and it won't just be in the moment, will it Son?"

I laughed. "I'm only glad I'm not related to Professor Smalling or any of the examining board. I'd never get my preparatory work finished at all if they interrupted as much as you have."

Mum put her hand to her mouth. "Alright Charlie, you've made your point, my lips are sealed."

Dad laughed. "Until the next time."

Feigning a look of playful frustration, I turned back to my notes.

"Okay, so we know about Grampy and his parents. Now, Nanny Anna as we know was born in Kent in 1878 the same year as Grampy." I looked directly at Mum. "Her Mum and Dad were Sarah and Thomas who we'll come to in a minute, alright Mum?"

She nodded meekly and, raising her hand, drew an imaginary zip across her mouth.

"Nanny Anna married Grampy and…" I stopped and shook my head.

"What's the matter, Son, is something wrong?"

"No, Dad, it's fine. It's just…well, now I'm doing it as well."

"Doing what?"

"Referring to them by their family names, Grampy, Nanny Anna and so on. I said to Mum right at the beginning I wanted to do this on a more formal basis, just using their given names as I'll do at uni."

Mum looked at me and unzipped her mouth. "May I say something?"

I returned her smile. "Go on then, as if I could stop you anyway."

"Well, and it's only a thought so tell me to be quiet if you like, but at this stage does it really matter? I mean we both know when you come to put it down in black and white for your exams or have to explain it to your tutors then of course you'll present it in a more formal context, but for now why don't you just refer to them in whatever way feels easiest? In other words, if you talk about Grampy Bill then so be it, and if you refer to him as William Coulson then we'll go with that as well, what do you think?"

I moved my head slightly from side to side pondering the wisdom of Mum's words.

"She's right, Son, it doesn't matter to us either way. Surely, it's more important at this stage just to get their place in your mum's family line correct, all the more formal stuff can wait until you get back to Leicester."

I nodded.

"Yeah, okay, I see that. Thanks, it does make sense and its lot easier as well if I'm honest, at least as far as this part of the story goes." I took a deep breath, puffing out my cheeks as I exhaled.

"So, to continue. Grampy married Granny Anna..." I smiled inwardly, having fallen back immediately into the trap of over familiarity when referring to family members. "They married in 1902 when they were both twenty-four. William had already been at Newstead for the best part of ten years by then having begun his working life in 1892 at the age of fourteen. He could have started a couple of years earlier at twelve because the law stating children had to be at least thirteen before going down the mines wasn't changed until 1900. In fact, in the years before 1842 there was no real law at all in place to prevent children of almost any age being sent underground to work, not until Parliament stepped in and raised the minimum age to ten and above in 1860. I think we talked a bit about that earlier?"

Mum shook her head. "Different days Charlie, different days. Grampy used to tell us stories he'd heard when he was younger about children who'd been put to work doing the most terrible jobs at no age at all and nobody said a word, it was just accepted. He said little ones as young as eight or nine would work in the factories crawling under work benches and the like to clear away the dust and dirt that would get into the machinery and cause it to break down." She smiled ruefully. "We've all heard tales of children being sent up chimneys to clean them. And the smaller the better it seems, because they were the ones who could get into the narrow channels and up around the bends. Grampy said even though the age was eventually raised for child labour, along with the conditions they were forced to work in, the Government was still slow to enforce the changes because they didn't want to upset the owners of the very factories and mines where the youngsters were working. And of course the employers were more than happy to keep the wages of their workers low. They knew regular work was hard to come by, especially for the majority of families who would have had little or no formal education, so any form of income was gratefully received, even if it did mean sending your children out to work for long hours every day, and often under the most appalling conditions. The phrase 'beggars can't be choosers', was never better expressed than when referring to those dark days."

There was a natural pause in our conversation as we embraced the appalling truth of what Mum had just said; a truth which became all the more shocking as we acknowledged this was not just a community of individuals with whom we had no point of reference, but rather, these were people who, in all likelihood, were directly linked to our own family. Mum sat forward in her chair and placed her hands on her knees.

"You know I don't think I've ever truly thought about it like that before, at least not as far as our own family is concerned." She looked at me. "But, hearing you talk about those times again Charlie and realising these are the same stories Grampy and Granny used to tell all those years ago has brought it all back to me. As a young girl I chose to let most of it go over my head, but revisiting it now and understanding most of it would have been based on circumstances and conditions they had both probably experienced has really touched me."

I attempted a smile. "And we've only gone back around a hundred years; we've still got another forty or fifty to go yet until we get back to great-great-great-Granddad George. Things in Kent weren't much better than they were in the Midlands back in those days either, just more of the same if you weren't born into money or hadn't had a proper education. Many of the men employed in the mines down there worked under the same conditions as their Northern counterparts. One of the main differences there though was, if you weren't employed in the mines or the cotton mills, as you might have been in the Midlands, you'd probably be looking for work on the land or in the orchards collecting apples and other fruits ready for market." Smiling I leant across the settee to pick up a particular sheet of paper. "I know we agreed not to move away from basic dates and so on regarding the family until we had them all listed but, as we've already drifted a bit, I did find out something quite interesting regarding the fruit fields of Kent in the early part of the 1800s that could have been written today." I looked at the two of them and laughed. "If I don't tell you now, I'll probably forget it."

I knew I was breaking my own set of conditions again but did feel the point I wanted to make was apposite.

Dad smiled and stretched his arms above his head, arching his back as he did so. "Sorry, Son, just a bit stiff. I think it's all the sitting in the car I've done this week." He looked at Mum. "I don't know about you love, but I'm finding all of this really interesting?"

"Absolutely." She smiled at me. "I just wish you'd stop apologising and putting pressure on yourself to get everything exactly in order. Your dad and I are just thrilled you feel able to share all of this with us. As we agreed earlier, if we think you've got anything wrong or want to ask about something in particular then we can. In the meantime, we're just happy to listen."

Dad smiled and nodded his accord.

"You just keep going, Son, we'll tell you when we've heard enough or get bored."

"Pete!"

"Joking." He leant his head to one side and winked at me.

Mum moved to sit upright in her chair and tapped the face of her watch. "Sorry to interrupt but if I could just say one more thing? As we started a little later than we thought can I suggest after Charlie has told us about this particular event we break for lunch. I don't know about you two but I'm getting a bit peckish."

"Good thinking, love. Sound good to you, Son?"

I nodded. "That's fine with me."

Smiling, Mum moved towards the edge of her chair. "That's settled then. Now, what was it you were going to say about Kent Charlie?"

I looked down at my notes.

"Well, the 1800s were a time of varying challenges for most fruit producers in Kent. Although there was plenty of enthusiasm for fresh fruit in the early part of the century there was also problems with getting it from one end of the country to the other as transport links still weren't very good, and the Government displayed little appetite to restrict imports from abroad. And they certainly weren't of a mind to raise tariffs on those imports and make home produced fruit more attractive and affordable. That's what I meant before when I said some might liken it to the arguments we have over imports of food today, certainly as far as the Common Market is concerned, and for those who argue we should only be buying British. It seems a lot of the country were feeling the same way in the early part of the 19th century as well. It was also difficult for poorer people to make things like chutney or jam at that time because sugar was very expensive, and bread and jam would have made up a fair portion of the diet for those on a limited income back then. And, if people weren't making their own jams and preserves it meant fruit growers and farmers could be left with whatever they hadn't managed to sell at market going to waste, especially the softer fruits. Equally, with the advent of a more efficient rail system by the mid-1800s the demand for locally grown fruit and veg at both ends of the country became easier to meet, and so the market expanded rapidly. And of course this was welcomed by the poorer families I mentioned earlier, who also saw a corresponding drop in sugar prices which allowed them to make more of their own jams and pies and not have to worry about any uneaten fruit just rotting and having to be thrown away. It also meant there was additional *jam* to be made by the Kentish fruit growers in the shape of healthier profits for producing larger crops, including the growing demand for softer fruits like plums, cherries, and so on which had a much shorter shelf life." Looking up I put my notebook and papers to one side. "It's interesting isn't it when you look back and presume that everything has changed for the better over the years but, then realise, that actually, things have remained pretty much the same, bar their name and place in history." I smiled. "Anyway, at that point, and, talking about food, it seems a good idea, as Mum suggested, to stop for something to eat, although I would like something a bit more substantial than bread and jam for my lunch, if that's okay?"

Mum stood up and laughed. "Well, I'd better go and see what there is in the cupboard then hadn't I? I presume you don't want a proper meal though? I was planning on doing that this evening."

"No, that's great Mum, thanks. Something like beans on toast'll be fine for now."

She shook her head. "Honestly, you'll look like a tin of baked beans at this rate, that's all I ever seem to be cooking for you these days."

"I like beans."

Dad picked up the tray and moved towards the door. "Beans on toast sounds fine for me as well love. Any chance someone could open the door?"

"Here you go Dad, I'll get it."

"Thanks." He turned to Mum. "I'll wash these things up while you get the lunch ready."

I held the door open as they walked past me. "And I'll lay the table after I've been to the loo."

Mum and Dad headed for the kitchen while I made my way upstairs. As I entered the bathroom, I felt a cool breeze run across me, causing my body to shudder involuntarily. I glanced towards the window to see if it was open presuming this to be the cause of the apparent draft; it was closed. As I stood washing my hands I felt another chill move over me. I looked up slowly from the sink towards the bathroom mirror fearing what might greet me as I recalled the earlier vision I'd experienced only a day or two before. As my gaze met with the mirror I sighed with relief; there was nothing other than my own nervous reflection. "You're losing it mate," I thought, admonishing myself for allowing my mind to consider anything other than the facts before me; that being of a puff of air catching me unawares, no doubt caused by the draught from the door as it opened and then closed behind me. I looked at myself in the mirror again and laughed, berating myself as I did so. "You're spending too much time living in the past with all this family tree stuff; too many ghosts and stories about murdered relations that's your trouble. The sooner you get this lot sorted and put to bed the better for everyone." Running my fingers through my hair I smiled at my reflection. "Okay handsome, time for lunch."

As I turned and reached for the door my feet became inexplicably rooted to the spot. Unable to move, I felt the same chill wind I'd experienced moments before passing over me again. My body shuddered as a now all too familiar voice greeted my ears. "Help me Charles." I shook my head not wanting to accept what I was hearing. As I did so I was back in the moment, my feet able to move and the door handle turning freely in my grip. I moved quickly out of the bathroom onto the landing where I paused momentarily, gathering my thoughts and attempting to rationalise what had just happened. Leaning against the wall to steady myself and with my mind racing I heard Mum's voice calling from the kitchen below.

"Come on Charlie if you're going to lay this table, I'm about to put the beans on."

"Coming Mum." I took a deep breath and made my way slowly down the stairs stroking the familiar pattern of the wallpaper as I did so; grateful for the sense of security it afforded me. Mum had wanted Dad to decorate the stair walls and landing for some time, but he'd never quite got around to doing it, and in that moment, I was pleased he hadn't. I ran my hands across the floral pattern, taking emotional refuge in the safe haven of this simple piece of décor. As I reached the bottom of the stairs the smell of beans on toast being prepared wafted along the hallway, greeting my nostrils and offering me yet further assurance that all was well. I tapped the side of my head and smiled as I entered the kitchen. "Just get these next few weeks out of the way, Charlie boy, and you'll be fine."

Chapter Twelve

The three of us sat down after lunch ready to continue our trip down memory lane, or perhaps not as we were about to enter previously uncharted territory as far as our family history was concerned. From here on in the majority of the information I would be sharing would be from what I'd discovered exclusively through my research rather than from what any of us could remember from the various stories we'd shared or been told of by Mum's parents and other family members over the years. Mum and Dad settled in their chairs waiting for me to begin. I carefully laid out my papers on the sofa once more and turned the pages of my notebook.

"So, we've gone back as far as Grampy and Granny Anna…" I looked at Mum. "Please don't think I'm being dismissive of them, it's just that we need to move on now from their place in the family tree, okay?" She smiled and remained silent for which I was grateful.

"Granny Anna died in 1964 aged 86…"

"Two years before you were born." I looked up. "Sorry Charlie, but she so wanted your dad and I to have a baby before she died. She was heartbroken to think we might not be able to have children of our own after struggling to conceive in those first couple of years after we got married. And then just a year after she died, I fell pregnant with you." I smiled as she took a hanky from her pocket and blew her nose. "She would have loved you so much."

Although I was keen to move on I sensed Mum's sadness and allowed her the moment. "And I'm sure I would have loved her just as much from what you've told me about her." Mum sniffed and rubbed her nose again. "Go on Charlie don't worry about me. At least your tutors won't be crying every time you talk about a member of your family passing away."

I smiled again, unsure what to say in response.

"Keep moving Son or she'll be blubbing all day." Dad winked at me and then smiled lovingly at Mum to reassure her.

"Okay, so Granny Anna passed away in 1964 and Grampy followed her four years later in 1968 aged ninety." I looked up at Mum and laughed playfully. "And yes, before you say anything, I do remember him even if my memories are a bit vague as I was only two when he died. But from the photos I've seen of him holding me and from and all that you and Dad have said about him he was clearly a special man."

Mum looked down and tugged at the edge of her handkerchief. "I know I've said this before Charlie, but his heart broke the day Granny died. I'm surprised he lasted another four year after she went if I'm honest, especially when you consider he'd been invalided out of the mines at thirty-six because of all that soot he'd breathed in when he was younger. Granny said his heart broke that day as well. Much as he tried to put on a brave face about it, she said once they moved him out of the pits and up to the colliery offices he changed; lost his confidence, his spark. Maybe not in public, but at home certainly, he was never quite the same."

The three of us fell silent. I, especially, was moved as I'd never heard this particular story before, but it served to encourage me yet again that I'd made the right decision to research Mum's family tree. As well as documenting all of these facts for my degree I was also gaining new insights about my family and its history that may otherwise never have been spoken about or revealed to me.

"Go on, Charlie, sorry. Although I can't promise I won't do the same again if something else comes back to me." She smiled. "I'll try not to though."

"That's fine, and I'll try not to get angry with you if you do." I threw her a playful grin. "Actually, if I'm honest, it's really good to have you and Dad here to fill in some of the blanks, you know, to tell me the stuff a Census or family register can't. The detail you get from them is pretty lifeless and dry, all very matter of fact, so it's good to get a bit of background information to go with it as well; to get know what sort of people they really were, even if I won't be using much of it for my finals. And, like we agreed earlier we can always go back and look at it all again in more depth later on if we want to. I'm already making a mental note of some the things I want to know from you both once my exams are out of the way."

Mum smiled. "We'll look forward to that."

"Okay then, moving on to Thomas and Sarah." I turned the page in my notebook. "Thomas Anderson was born in Kent in 1846 and was son to the man we're all really interested in knowing about George and his wife Elizabeth." I looked up and smiled. "Thomas grew up in the village of Sowfield where his dad, George, was the vicar of the local church, St Mark's. I managed to find out that Thomas attended the parish school there. Well, not exactly a school as such, it was more of a makeshift one which had been set up in a local woman's house. Her name was Nancy Fielding, which has absolutely no bearing on the story of our family whatsoever; I just thought it was quite apt considering the wide-open spaces of the surrounding countryside."

Dad threw me a weary grin.

"Sowfield itself was quite small and very rural, bordered by large expanses of open land and working fields. Whilst the church appeared well founded and established from what I was able to discover, there wasn't a lot else going on in the village itself. However, with St Mark's being centrally located and proving very popular with both the landowners and local farm workers alike there soon became a growing demand for the village to have a school of its own. The community was obviously still expanding in the early to mid-1800s and so it was the perfect time for Nancy to arrive and offer her services as a teacher." I looked up from my notes. "It's a bit sad about her really. I found out from the records office that she moved to Sowfield from another village nearby, where she'd also been a teacher, after her fiancé died. He was killed in a farming accident when one of his horses apparently kicked him in the head, so to make a fresh start she moved to Sowfield but remained a spinster for the rest of her life." I paused briefly. "I don't know why I looked that up really; I think I was just interested in the school that Thomas attended, and it went on from there."

Mum frowned. "That is sad."

"That's what I thought. I guess she just never found anyone else she wanted to marry. Anyway, it appears she began teaching in her front room until a proper school was built in 1856 when Thomas was ten. He started full time work at fourteen on one of the local farms four years later in 1860. Sarah, Thomas's wife to be, was born in 1852. Her father was a blacksmith and she worked on the same farm as Thomas, which is presumably where they met. They got married in 1875 when he was twenty-nine and she was twenty-three, and then Granny Anna came along in 1878. Records show they had another child before Anna, a boy, but he died shortly after being born. There was no name or specific detail of the cause of death recorded, other than his date of birth and that he died a few days later. Perhaps he'd been premature and not strong enough to survive, I don't know, but Granny Anna was their second and only other child."

I looked up as Mum shuffled uncomfortably in her chair.

"Go on, Mum, you obviously want to say something."

"Sorry, Charlie, but yes, listening to you say that reminds me of Granny telling me once that her mum had lost another baby before she was born, although she didn't say it had been a boy. Perhaps Great Nanna Sarah hadn't wanted to talk about it, other than just to say the baby hadn't survived?" She shook her head. "I'd quite forgotten that until now." She stared ahead as if collecting her thoughts. "I wonder what would have happened to him if he'd have lived." She looked at me again. "I also seem to remember her saying her dad had died in an accident a couple of years after she was born and that was the reason the two of them had moved up to Nottingham. But I wonder now if she'd also struggled with the memory of losing her first child as well." She turned to me and smiled apologetically. "Or is that what you're about to tell us? Sorry, have I jumped the gun again and stolen your thunder?"

I nodded my head. "Only a bit, but you're right about Thomas, he was killed in a farming accident in 1880 in really tragic circumstances. And yes, you're right again about Granny Anna as well, she was just two when he died. The records say he fell under a horse drawn plough and died from his injuries. I should think he was probably sliced in two if he fell under one of those heavy sharp blades, not a nice way to go."

"And not a very nice picture to paint either, thank you very much."

"Sorry, Mum, just allowing my imagination to run on a bit."

She shuddered and hunched her shoulders. "Yes, well try reigning it in a little if you don't mind and stick to what you actually know."

I laughed again. "Okay, sorry."

"But presumably I'm right though in saying that's why Sarah and little Anna, as she was then, moved away? I think her sister was already up that way, wasn't she?"

"Spot on, well done."

Mum shook her head and smiled. "Honestly, the things you forget but that are still there in the back of your mind somewhere."

Dad laughed. "Thereby hangs a tale or two."

"What does that mean exactly?"

Dad looked at me and winked. "I couldn't possibly say."

I shook my head. "Now come on you two play nicely, that's if you want me to finish this story today?"

They laughed. "Sorry, Son, go on, you were saying about Sarah moving to Nottingham?"

I looked down at my notes again searching for my place.

"That's right yes." I paused for a moment scanning the page. "Got it, here we are. So, Thomas was killed in 1880 and Sarah moved to Nottingham the next year to make a fresh start with Anna who was almost three by then. Sarah's sister Ruth lived there with her husband Arthur." I looked at Mum. "Actually, I'm hoping you can help with this next bit as I couldn't find out how Ruth and Arthur first got together, other than they were married in Nottingham in 1874. She was a couple of years older than Sarah having been born in 1850. Can you throw any light on how she met Arthur, and was he the reason she moved away from Kent?"

She smiled. "Strangely enough I can. Granny told me Ruth first met Arthur when he was on holiday in Kent. He was a miner himself and had gone there to get away from the pits for a while and to get some fresh air before returning to the soot and grime of the mines. Apparently quite a few miners would try and get away for a break, to the countryside or maybe the seaside, even just for a few days, finances allowing of course. They felt the clean air helped clear the dust from their lungs and put a bit of colour back in their cheeks after spending most of their days underground. Anyway, it seems Arthur had some relations in Kent who lived nearby to where Ruth and Sarah lived and the two of them met during his stay, a sort of holiday romance I suppose you'd call it nowadays, or at least it was for them. And it seems after he went back to Nottingham they kept in touch, and eventually he wrote to her and proposed and she accepted; and that's how she came to move to Nottingham. I remember thinking how romantic that was. I wonder what happened to all the love letters between the two of them. I'd love to read the one where he proposed to her."

I nodded and smiled. "Thanks Mum, that's great. I won't actually need that for my course but it's good to know all the same. It's funny to think Arthur went all the way down to Kent to get away from the pits when it was around that time the first coal mines were being established in the county itself. I presume you know Sarah married again after she moved to Nottingham?"

"Yes, well, sort of. Granny told me she'd married again, but as she was only young herself when that happened and with her mum dying a few years later she said she lost touch with him." Mum paused and looked to the floor.

Dad shifted forward in his chair. "Are you alright love?"

She looked up and smiled at the two of us, tears filling her eyes.

"I'm fine, it's just…" She took her hanky out of her pocket and held it to her nose.

"It's just that I'm finding this all a bit emotional that's all and, well, I hadn't thought I would." She shook her head and sniffed. "Silly really isn't it? I mean their all gone now and…"

Dad dropped to his knees in front of her and took her hand.

"No, it's not silly, you're not silly, they're your family." He took her face in his hands. "I just hope you make as much fuss about me when I go."

Mum wiped her eyes and laughed. "Ah well, that'll be different altogether, although I suppose I might miss you a bit." She gave him a playful shove.

Dad moved back to his chair feigning hurt. "Charming!" They held each other's gaze for a moment, a look of genuine affection between the two of them.

"Shall I stop Mum? You don't actually need to hear all this if you don't want to, or at least not today, we can talk about it another time?"

She leant across and squeezed my hand.

"Don't be daft, Charlie, of course I want to hear about it, about them. It's just remembering things I thought I'd all but forgotten, and then having them back in the forefront of my mind again." She squeezed my hand again and smiled.

"For you this is history, much of it you won't have heard before anyway and, even if you have, it will only have been in passing or when you were a lot younger and so won't really mean anything to you, but for me…well, for me it's real. These are people I knew or heard about when I was growing up. And whilst much of what you're telling us is about events that happened a long time ago, those things really did happen, and they happened to people I actually knew and loved, well, most of them anyway." She let go of my hand and moved back in her chair. "Or, at least up to this point. After we get beyond Thomas and Sarah and the little I know about them, then it'll all be new ground for me as well." She wiped her eyes again. "So hopefully I won't need to cry anymore." She smiled and nodded towards my notebook. "Go on then, continue with the family saga."

"Okay, if you're sure." I looked down and ran my finger across the page in search of my place. "So, we were talking about Sarah having married again." I took a breath and coughed to clear my throat. "As we said she moved to Nottingham to be near Ruth in 1881, almost a year after Thomas was killed. I suppose coming from a farming background she began to move in those circles again and met a farm worker called Walter Cooper who she married in 1883 when she was thirty. Anna would have been still only five then hence her not remembering any great detail about Walter, at least early on. As you said earlier, after Sarah died in 1904 Anna lost touch with Walter pretty much altogether. The record of Sarah's death stated she died at fifty-one of heart failure. I suppose today we would say that was young and they might have been able to help her had she been born a few years later but, back then, it wasn't unusual to go at that sort of age or even younger, certainly if your heart wasn't strong?"

Mum nodded. "Actually, now you say that Charlie, I do remember Granny saying her mum had been a poorly lady, subject to colds and coughs that sort of thing. Maybe she just had a weak heart all along and it was never discovered? As you said they didn't have access to the same medical facilities that are around today, no NHS or X ray machines or any of the other paraphernalia we have to help diagnose those sorts of things." She looked at me. "Sorry, Charlie, I interrupted again."

She was right, but I also recognised the need to be sensitive and allow her the opportunity to express her thoughts and feelings as we travelled this family journey together. Some of the detail we were discussing was very personal and I didn't want to upset her for the sake of a few minutes' patience and understanding on my behalf. "That's fine, don't worry, it's all useful stuff to know even if it is only for our own consumption." We smiled at each other as I continued. "Anyway, poor Sarah died in 1904 just two years after Granny Anna had married Grampy, so presumably that's another reason she didn't remember too much about Walter, what with her being newlywed herself and having left home a couple of years before?"

Mum jumped in again. "Do we know what happened to Walter?" She looked at me and put her hands in the air. "Sorry, sorry, I've done it again."

I laughed. "Stop apologising Mum, like I said it's fine." I glanced at Dad who was also smiling. "It just means we'll move at a slightly slower pace that's all."

"Thank you, and I am sorry, but I'm also quite excited to know about them all now and what happened to each of them."

Dad shook his head. "Well, if you shut up long enough for the lad to speak then you will."

I decided to move on quickly to ease the potential for further upset between the two of them, no matter how well intentioned.

"In answer to your question Mum yes, we do know what happened to Walter, although that's a bit upsetting as well. Again, according to records he was sent to a sanatorium in 1909, five years after Sarah died. Apparently, he was admitted there for being violent and mentally unstable and, from what I could find out, he never recovered, or at least not enough to be released back into the outside world. It seems he died there three years later in 1912 aged fifty-nine." I looked up. "I didn't bother to research his family records though as it wasn't relevant to your family tree, what with him being Sarah's second husband and not a direct relative to your blood line. Still sad though, and for his own family of course; probably another reason why Granny Anna would have lost touch with him."

Mum nodded. "I wonder if he never recovered after losing Sarah and that's what tipped him over the edge so to speak."

Dad's eyes lit up. "Or perhaps he was a bit of a nutter already when she married him, and that's what caused her heart to fail?"

"And who asked for your opinion? A bit of a nutter, is that the best you can do?"

"Well, you never know. As you said yourself, they didn't have all the modern technology we have today to help diagnose those sorts of things. There was no NHS to stand by you then was there? Poor bloke probably lost the plot and was put away for being a bit strange."

"Pity you weren't born then as well. They might have locked you away for being strange. I'd have certainly signed the paperwork I can tell you."

"Love you too."

"Honestly, you both want locking away. I'm here trying to tell you about the history of our family and all you can do is argue with each other."

Mum sat upright in her chair. "We're not arguing Charlie, I'm just putting your father right on a few things, as I seem to have to do more and more these days, isn't that right *dear*?"

"Whatever you say *darling*. What could I, a mere mortal man, say in my defence against your great and all-consuming female intuition and wisdom?"

"Exactly."

I watched the two of them grin playfully at each other.

"Shall I continue, or is there to be a second round in this lovers' spat?"

Mum laughed. "Don't sink to your father's level at an attempt at humour Charlie, it doesn't become you."

I laughed and looked down at my notes again. "I'll take that as a yes then to me carrying on. Okay, so we won't worry about what might have caused poor Walter to lose his marbles and become incarcerated in the asylum, sad though that may be. Are we agreed we can leave him there, not literally of course but as far as our interest in him and his place in Mum's family line is concerned?"

They winked at each other and nodded at me.

"Good." I turned the page of my notebook and was surprised to discover how near to the end I was. "We're getting there." Fixing my eyes on the name before me I continued. "And so, we reach the potential climax of your family story Mum, or at least as far as we're taking it for now. The life and death of your great-great-granddad, The Reverend George Anderson, vicar of St Mark's Church from the village of Sowfield in Kent."

Mum shifted in her seat, waving her hand in the direction of my now dishevelled pile of notes and papers strewn across the sofa. "Before you start, I just want to say thank you for all of this. I know it's your work, and of course it goes without saying your dad and I hope you will pass your exams with flying colours, but I'm still really grateful that you chose to research *our* family. Listening to what you've had to say has brought back all sorts of memories, some happy and some perhaps a little sad." She smiled and took a deep breath. "And who knows what you're about to tell us regarding dear old George, but whatever it is I just want to say thank you anyway." She looked at me, tears filling her eyes once more. "I'm really proud of you Charlie, and of everything you've discovered and told us so far. It's shown me how precious family really is in our life's journey. And right now they don't come any more precious to me than you."

Dad nodded his agreement and smiled. "That goes for me too, Son, although maybe not expressed in the same flowery language as your mum, but yeah, you're alright."

I was moved by their show of affection and, unsure of how best to respond, made a sad attempt at humour. "I love you too, that is presuming I do pass my exams with flying colours, otherwise I'll be seeking adoption on the grounds of instability and insanity in the family. And remember with dear old Walter hovering in the background I would probably win my appeal."

"Even though, as you've already pointed out, he's not a blood relative," Dad quipped.

I scratched my head. "Fair point. Okay, I may have to think again about that one."

Mum thumped the arm of her chair with the flat of her hand. "Oh come on you two stop your bickering, I want to hear about George and what happened to him."

I smiled and, looking down at my notes again, gently smoothed out the page in front of me that had become slightly crumpled under my hand.

"Here we go then. George Anderson was born in 1814. His father was Samuel Anderson an agricultural worker, born in 1788. His mother was Martha Anderson, formerly Martha Green, a seamstress born in 1791. Samuel died in 1828 from Dropsy. This was assumed to be an excessive swelling of the body's soft tissue caused by an accumulation of water in his system. Today of course it would be treatable but in the 19th century there wasn't a lot that could be done, and certainly not for dear old Samuel as the record of his death attested. George's mother, Martha had an even shorter life. She died in childbirth in 1820, six years after George was born. According to the records the baby died at the same time. All a bit tragic really and not the best of starts for poor George either."

Dad leant forward. "If his mother died when he was only six who brought George up for the next few years, was it his dad? Presumably Samuel still had to work? And surely even in those days George would have been too young to be sent up the chimneys or left to fend for himself while his dad was away from the house? I can't believe they had any form of childcare back then?"

I nodded. "You're right, certainly about George being too young to work, at least officially but, equally, I couldn't find anything out about who might have cared for him, certainly not in those very early days after his mum died."

Mum pursed her lips in thought. "Sad though all the same."

"It is, but, as we only need to know who they were for this particular part of the family tree it isn't something we need to focus on. It's George's story we're interested in remember? If we want to go any further back down the family line then that's work for another day, certainly as regards my research for uni is concerned anyway."

Mum shrugged her shoulders. "I know but…"

"Don't I know but Irene, just let the lad continue."

I winked at Dad.

"Alright then, so George was born in 1814 but we don't know a lot about him after that until we meet him again at St Mark's, although it's fair to assume he probably did some sort of training for the clergy in the years before, maybe working as a curate in another parish nearby or at St Mark's itself. And, if that's true, then perhaps he'd been looked after by someone associated with the wider church when he was a lad after his mum had died and while Samuel was out at work? I've no idea if that's what happened of course but it's a possibility and would make sense."

"You would have thought that sort of thing would have been documented somewhere?"

"They are these days Dad but back then things were different. Records were not kept so well, and until books like the Clerical Directory came along in 1858 a lot of the personal detail about individual members of the clergy was still pretty hit and miss. Certain parishes might list their own vicars or ministers in the local Clerical Guide, but as to their personal details or the history of a particular priest's upbringing or early training well, that wasn't always formerly logged or recorded, certainly not as it would be today. That said these were still significant times as far as world history was concerned. Even in the thirty-two years George was alive there were some amazing discoveries and events that took place. For instance, in the year he was born, 1814, Napoleon was deposed and exiled to the island of Elba. Mind, he escaped the next year and took control of France again until he was defeated for a second time at the Battle of Waterloo when he was parcelled off to St Helena where he stayed until his death in 1821. George was only a young lad of seven when that happened." I felt my long-held passion for history rising as I recounted some of the other major events from the period. "Honestly, we think we're living in historic times now what with putting a man on the moon and so on but back then some of the things that happened are still influencing us today, even if there have been some amazing advancements along the way. Things like photography for instance; the first photos were produced around 1826 and look how that's grown over the years. Braille was first published in 1829." I laughed. "The battle of the Alamo took place in 1836, although I don't think John Wayne was there at the time, and, Queen Victoria came to the throne in 1837. All that happened in the first few years of George's life. And of course in the year before he died, 1845, the great potato famine began. So although he only lived until he was thirty-two a lot of things happened during that period that have gone on to take their place in the history books of today. News travels much faster these days as well, so we can't know how much of what happened back then would have reached the sleepy idyll of the Kent countryside in the time George was alive anyway. That said, newspapers were around then of course so he would have caught up with most of what went on, albeit it might have taken a few weeks to reach him, as opposed to our watching the news on TV from around the world today, when things are reported almost as they happen."

I looked up. "Sorry, I just love history, along with the thought that when all of these things were going on they were every bit as important to people like George and others as the news and events of today are to us."

Dad laughed. "You always did like history, Son; even as a lad you would ask how old something was or where it came from."

Mum smiled and nodded. "We used to say, you had an old head on young shoulders."

"Well, I have the two of you to thank for encouraging me in that; I don't think I could have done all of this without you."

Mum shifted forward in her chair. "We're just happy you followed your dream Charlie, and long may it continue."

I scratched my head. "Sorry, I've lost my thread again, gone off on a bit of a tangent; where was I?"

"Talking about George. Did you find anything else out about him, or about him being killed and who might have done it?"

"All in good time Mother, all in good time." Turning the page in my book I paused to catch my breath. I was enjoying myself and felt in full control; also, in watching my parents' deepening interest in what they were hearing. I felt a fleeting sense of pride sweep over me, which passed as quickly as it had arrived, remembering that Mum and Dad were a willing and captive audience to my endeavours; the examining board, however, would listen with a very different set of ears to the results of my findings and, conversely, be much harder to impress.

"What I can tell you is he married Elizabeth Moor, daughter of Henry and Rebecca Moor. Henry was a local landowner with an interest in the church, so this would make sense for all concerned, with his daughter choosing to marry a priest. This was beginning to be a time when those with money were moving into the Ministry themselves, either by entering it formally and putting on a dog collar or, in supporting a local church and its parish financially through their wealth and social position. The so-called Landed Gentry of the day liked to be seen by others as holding sway within the local, and wider, ecclesiastical community. They might even have financed the building of a chapel on their land if they thought it would improve their influence and standing with the local authorities and powers that be. I shouldn't have thought it would have done Henry's reputation any harm at all to have his daughter marry the local vicar, and the same would be true for dear old George himself. For him to have had both the physical and financial support of a well-heeled landowner would certainly have given him a bit of a leg up the proverbial clerical ladder."

Dad laughed. "A marriage made in heaven so speak."

Mum and I looked at each other and shook our heads.

"You should go on The Comedians Dad; Frank Carson would love you."

"Frank Carson is welcome to him with jokes like that."

I smiled and turned back to my notes.

"Anyway, as I was saying, George married Elizabeth in 1844. She was twenty-two at the time having been born in 1822. George was eight years older than Elizabeth which wasn't unusual in those days; the man could often be a good deal older than his wife, especially in the case of what we might call, an arranged marriage, or should I say a marriage of convenience, which normally meant there was money or position to be gained by one party or the other.

"Elizabeth gave birth to young Thomas in 1846, two years after she and George were married and, sadly, the same year of his untimely end." I paused and looked up. "And this is part of the reason I want to go down to Kent, so I can find out more about what actually happened to him."

"Is there a question about whether he *was* murdered then, I thought you said he had been?"

"It's not so much w*hether* he was murdered or not, it's more about the circumstances surrounding the how and why he was killed that I'm interested in."

Mum hunched her shoulders and shuddered. "Ooh it's like the plot from an Agatha Christie murder mystery isn't it?"

Smiling, I continued. "The reason it caught my attention is because the records to hand simply state he was killed by a person, or persons unknown, who were presumed to be robbing the church, but it doesn't give any particular detail as to the circumstances surrounding that assumption."

Mum shuffled forward in her chair again. "How interesting, and you say there wasn't any more information about it other than what you've just said?"

"Not that I could find from what was available, no. Remember the records I'm looking through are pretty basic at this stage, you know, just the fundamentals about any births, marriages, deaths, that sort of thing. If you want to go off-piste so to speak you have to search through the local police and community records themselves, which is why I'm keen to make the trip down there. I pretty much have enough information for my course work already, along with all the other family names and dates we've been talking about but, well, I want to know what actually happened to the old boy, don't you?"

Dad stood up. "I'll get the car keys and drive you down there now if you like?"

I laughed. "Thanks Dad, but even I'm not that keen."

"I was joking, but I do need to stretch my back, and a visit to the loo wouldn't go amiss either."

Mum glanced at her watch. "Look at the time; the afternoons all but gone, I'd better start thinking about tea." Getting to her feet she looked down at me. "Sorry, Charlie, is that alright with you? I didn't mean to sound dismissive of all you've been telling us, it's really interesting, and yes, we would like to know what happened to George, wouldn't we Pete?"

"Absolutely."

"And we can talk more about you wanting to go to Kent later, but for now you must be exhausted with all that talking? How about we call it a day and make a fresh start again tomorrow?"

Leaning forward I closed my book. "Sounds fine to me Mum, and yes, I am a bit knackered." I looked up at her and smiled. "I'm also hungry so don't let me keep you from the kitchen."

Laughing, she cuffed me gently across the ear. "You're always hungry you cheeky thing. Just for that you can wash up as well as laying the table."

"My pleasure."

The two of us talked animatedly about all we had discussed during the day whilst we lay the table together and prepared tea.

"I'm sorry about earlier Charlie, when I got upset about some of what you were saying, it's just…well, some of it overwhelmed me a bit that's all."

"And like I said at the time there's no need to apologise, it's your family after all. It must feel strange trying to process so much detail in one go, especially when you remember most of it happened so long ago."

Mum nodded. "You're right. And I think although I've dealt with the sadness of my dad dying and got used to him not being around, suddenly having to re live it again and place it in context to the rest of what's happened to our family over the years, it just came as a bit of a shock. Same with Grampy and Granny.

Of course, I accept their gone, but to talk about them so openly and to think about their lives again, along with the struggles they faced over the years, well, it just got to me a bit that's all, but I'm sure I'll be fine now."

"Actually, it was good for me to see you and Dad react the way you did to some of what I was saying. I mean, up until today much of the information I've uncovered has been just that, a lot of facts about a group of people who, although I might have heard of most of them, held no particular relevance to my own life, other than they were my relations. But to actually read those letters you showed me earlier and to hear you talk about them and the rest of the family as you did has brought them alive for me in a way I hadn't really thought about or appreciated before, and I thank you for that."

I noticed Mum becoming quiet again and moved to give her a hug.

"Love you Mum, and no need to apologise again, okay? I think we've all learnt something today, and not just about our ancestors but maybe about ourselves as well." I stepped back. "Listening to you talk about Grampy I can see a bit of him in me."

Mum looked at me quizzically. "How so?"

"Well, in his desire to see something through for a start. He clearly loved being a miner and was really frustrated when he had to give it up because of ill health. I'm not saying he didn't give of his best when he moved up to work in the offices but, from what I've found out and from what you've told me about him, his heart clearly remained underground along with the other men. I also get the feeling his enthusiasm for the union was really more a reflection of his passion for those he worked with and wanted to support. He wasn't bothered about the politics, as so many in power appear to be today, he was more interested in just getting the best deal for his fellow workers, his friends as he saw them. And holding sway in the union was a way of him being able to fulfil that desire, to fight for the rights of those friends and colleagues that he cared so much about."

Mum smiled. "That's very perceptive, Charlie, but you're certainly not a union man."

"True, but I do like to think I have the same dedication, perhaps even stubbornness as him. Look at this family tree stuff. You and Dad have both told me not to push myself too hard with all the work I've been doing, even that you were concerned it was all becoming a bit of an obsession, when really all I wanted to do, and still want to do, is my best, to get everything right, even if I don't always know when to step back and look at the bigger picture. You might call it an obsession, but I like to think of it as focus and commitment, and I think Grampy might have argued the same regarding the way he felt about the mines and the men who worked in them."

Mum looked at me for a moment, pausing to wipe her hands on a tea towel.

"I've never really thought about you and Grampy as being alike before. In fact, I've never truly aligned any of my family directly to you, or to me for that matter, apart from having the same hair colour or facial features, things like that. But now you come to mention it I suppose there are similar character traits between the two of you." She leant forward and kissed me on the cheek.

"I'll have to revisit my family tree properly once you've finished it to see what other comparisons I can make between the two of us and our ancestors." She turned, laughing as she did so, to check on a pan that was beginning to boil on the cooker.

"I don't think you should research your dad's ancestral heritage anytime soon though. I'd hate to think of any similarities between you and his side of the family. I wouldn't be surprised to find he was related to some very strange people."

We were still laughing as Dad entered the room.

"What's so funny?"

Mum and I looked at each other, with her the first to respond.

"Nothing."

"The two of us laughed again as Dad stood in the doorway shaking his head."

"Mad, quite mad."

"That's just what we were saying wasn't it Charlie?"

Shaking his head again, Dad turned to leave. "I only came to see if there was anything I could do to help, but as you've both clearly lost the plot I'll leave you to it." He glanced over his shoulder as he closed the door behind him. "Just shout when tea's ready."

We dutifully called him twenty minutes later to join us again. It felt good to be together, enjoying one another's company along with Mum's delicious home cooking.

True to my word and Mum's instructions I sent them both off to the lounge after our meal while I cleared away the tea things. I felt it was the least I could do, especially after they'd listened so intently to my earlier ramblings and responded so positively to all I'd had to say.

"You really don't have to do it all yourself Charlie, I was only joking before when I said you should clear away."

"No, you're fine Mum really. You and Dad take yourselves off into the front room while I do this. It'll give me a chance to think through some of the detail we spoke about earlier, especially about my heading down to Kent for a few days, I'd really like to do that."

"It does sound interesting I'll give you that, and it would be nice to know exactly what happened to poor old George. Although I must admit that's mainly because I'm interested for my own selfish reasons."

I spent the next half an hour washing up and putting away the tea things alongside making myself a cup of coffee. My mind wandered to and fro as I waited for the kettle to boil considering all that I'd discovered about my family in recent weeks and thinking again about my proposed trip to Sowfield. I was brought abruptly to my senses as the switch on the kettle clicked and turned itself off, releasing a spray of steam into the air from its spout. Pouring the water onto the coffee granules I watched as they melded together with the boiling liquid to form a dark brown sludge in the bottom of my mug. I added some milk, sugar, and more hot water which, when combined, created a pleasant aroma and turned the mug's contents to a light caramel colour. As I stirred my coffee, pondering all that lay ahead in the weeks to come, a feeling of excitement swept over me. A trip to Kent, hopefully, to discover the truth about the alleged murder of our dear departed family member and the pulling together of all the research I'd undertaken in readiness for my finals; I couldn't wait to get started. Smiling contentedly to myself I switched off the light and made my way towards the lounge door which Mum and Dad had left slightly ajar. Pushing it open with my foot I entered the room.

"All done folks, anyone want a drink, the kettles still hot," I said, holding up my mug to prove the point?

They both turned to face me. "Not for me, Son, thanks, I don't know about your mum though?"

Mum smiled and shook her head. "I'm fine as well thank you love."

"I'm off to bed then if that's okay? See you in the morning."

Mum patted the seat next to hers on the sofa. "Aren't you going to join us for a while, it's still early?"

I forced an expansive yawn. "No, you're fine; I'm a bit tired after all that washing up."

Mum picked up a cushion, feigning to throw it at me. "Cheek, we offered to help; you were the one who insisted on doing it all himself."

I laughed, raising my arm in pretence of deflecting the imaginary cushion heading my way. "No seriously, I could do with an early night; I'm a bit knackered if I'm honest. I think the past few weeks have caught up with me, and there's a couple of bits of my other work I want to read up on, so I'll head on up if that's okay with you two?" I took a sip from my mug. "And, it'll give me a chance to make a few more plans about this trip to Kent as well."

Dad shifted further round in his chair. "You're definitely going then?"

"Yeah, got to really haven't I? I mean, in a way, old George is the main reason we started this whole family tree thing in the first place. Seems silly to have come this far and then, for the sake of a couple of days down there, leave the most vital question of all unanswered and not fully resolved. And, as we discussed earlier, a few days away won't do me any harm either; it'll give me a chance to clear my head before I get down to preparing the rest of the stuff I've been working on ready for my finals."

Mum smiled. "I agree, well, at least with the part about you taking a few days off."

"Thanks."

"And we'll help out with the train fare and accommodation expenses while you're down there."

I moved towards the middle of the room. "Really, Dad, that's kind of you, but I've got some money saved up and I should be…"

Dad raised his hand, interrupting my flow. "Please, Son, your mum and I have already talked about this, and we're both agreed it's something we'd like to do, to help, if you'll let us?"

Mum moved forward in her seat. "Your dad's right, Charlie. You've worked so hard over the past year or so and already incurred a lot of expense on this course –"

Dad interrupted again, laughing as he did so. "Even if most of those expenses have come about in meeting the cost of take away meals and beer!"

I laughed as well. "Oh come on, Dad, not all of them. Well, not quite anyway."

"Seriously, Son, we want to. We're both really proud of all you've done to date, you know that, and so it would be our pleasure to help out in this way."

"But you've both done so much for me already, really I –"

It was Mum's turn to interrupt. "Please, Charlie; let us do this for you. We're both aware of how hard you've been working of late, and hopefully it will take a bit of the pressure from you, at least financially." She looked at me, a sense of pleading in her expression. "Please?"

Puffing out my cheeks, I raised my eyes in grateful thanks. "Well, if you're sure, then yes, that'd be great."

Dad laughed again. "No, thank you, Charlie; at least if we help with your train fare you won't be asking to borrow your mum's car to take down to Kent." He looked directly at me. "And before you do, the answer is no. Your mum has a few meetings over the next couple of weeks and, whilst she might tell you it's alright and that she'll organise lifts and so on, I know she likes to use her car rather than rely on others."

I took another sip of my now rapidly cooling coffee. "The thought hadn't even crossed my mind. Anyway, your car is much more comfortable for a long journey like that."

"Now you are having a laugh. You've got about as much chance of taking my Granada as flying down to Kent on a rocket."

I waved away his protestations. "I'm joking. Anyway, I like the train, I travel on it pretty much every other week remember? It'll give me a chance to do some work as well, certainly on my way back at least if my searches down there prove fruitful." I smiled again. "Seriously though, thanks again for the offer of the dosh, it'll really help; one less thing to think about."

"Have a tot up and let us know what you need and I'll get the cash out for you, probably easier than giving you a cheque, better just to have the money in your pocket."

"Thanks, Dad, Mum."

Mum gave me one of her maternal smiles. "You're welcome Charlie, just pleased to help."

I turned to leave. "And on that happy note I'll say goodnight again." I took a last swig from my mug and moved towards the door. "Night both."

"Goodnight, Son."

I closed the door behind me and headed for the kitchen with my empty mug. As I flicked the light switch there was a flash, the room remained in darkness. "Great," I thought, "bloody bulbs gone now."

As I edged forward in the dark towards the sink, I felt the room begin to spin as it had before. I reached out, placing my hand on the table to steady myself. As my eyes adjusted to the light, I looked down at the floor which began to alter both in shape and appearance; no longer was I looking at Mum's patterned lino but rather the same grey slabs I had seen during my earlier experience of a couple of weeks ago. The kitchen walls also took on a similar appearance, changing from their familiar patterned wallpaper to a darker stone effect. Gripping the edge of the table I shook my head in an attempt to clear it. I heard a voice call out to me; it was a voice I was becoming all too familiar with and yet was still unknown to me.

"Help me Charles."

I forced myself upright and, without thinking, threw out a hand towards the light switch, hoping that in some miraculous way the bulb would illuminate where previously it had failed to do so. As I struggled to find my feet, so my unspoken prayer was answered and the room became bathed in light once more. I blinked in the sudden brightness and saw I was back in the familiar surroundings of our family kitchen, lino, patterned wallpaper, and all. Reaching out I stroked the draining board in simple appreciation of its physical presence and the sense of wellbeing I gained from finding it there. I stood for a moment regaining my balance and clarity of thought. Perhaps Mum was right, maybe I had been overdoing it of late, hence these recent visual imaginings and strange voices in my head. I flicked the light switch on and off a couple of times, partly to make sure it was working properly, and to reassure myself that all I had experienced over the last few minutes had been no more than a momentary illusion and should not be connected in any way with the reality of my present surroundings. I glanced around the room again, confirming all was as it should be. Turning to leave I patted the light switch gently as if to admonish it for having failed me earlier, and to further reassure myself that all was well. I tapped on the lounge door as I made my way to the stairs.

"Night Mum, night Dad."

The warm reply that emanated from the room further comforting and encouraging me. "Night Charlie, sleep well."

I began my ascent, satisfied once more that all was calm in the world again or, at least, in this small part of it. Holding onto the banister I made my way up the stairs, delighting in the vibrant shafts of colour displayed across the carpet from those reflected through the stained glass of our front door. Momentarily I was transported back to my childhood, with memories of the nights I would sit on these same stairs staring down at the differing silhouettes and shadows that would dance around in front of me as the moon or streetlight reflected their glory through the door's brightly coloured panels. Smiling to myself I remembered how, on more than one occasion as a youngster, I'd allowed my thoughts to run riot and found my boyhood imaginings taking on a more sinister turn; one where fictional knights in shining armour would stride through this rainbow coloured land set before me to rescue my imagined hero, only for them to morph into eerie monsters or strange alien beings and find me shouting for someone to come and rescue me. Mum, on hearing my cries, would immediately rush to my side to offer the support and comfort I so desperately craved, reassuring me that all was well and that I was safe. Maybe the strange illusions and fitful dreams I'd experienced in recent weeks were no more than a return of those same boyhood fantasies come back to haunt me, initiated by overwork and tiredness?

Reaching the top of the stairs and turning on the landing light I grinned, reprimanding myself as I did so. "It's what Mum's always said, you've got a vivid imagination, perhaps a little too vivid it appears if recent events are anything to go by. Next thing you know, you'll be calling out to her like you did as a kiddie, asking her to come and give you a cuddle and tell you everything's alright." Looking in the mirror on the landing wall I admonished myself once more. "You'd better get a grip of yourself or it'll be the funny farm for you, and then where will you be? Up the proverbial creek without a paddle that's where."

Entering my bedroom I reached for the light switch, smiling to myself as I flicked it on and off a couple of times to make sure it wasn't going to fail me as the one in the kitchen had apparently just a few minutes earlier. As I got ready for bed and used the bathroom, I began plotting my trip to Kent. The sheets and blankets on my bed felt soft and inviting as I slipped into their welcoming embrace; soon warming around me and offering further comfort and assurance to my tired and addled brain. Sitting up, I pulled the blankets to my chest and placed the pillows behind me against the headboard in an effort to support my neck and back as I spread out my notebook and paperwork in front of me. As I sat there pouring over my notes, I felt my eyes becoming heavy, urging me towards the sleep my mind and body craved. Putting down my pen I leaned back against the pillow, allowing my eyes to close momentarily. "Just a couple of minutes and I'll be ready to go again."

As I lay there, my mind drifting between the events of the day and the detail of our family tree, I became aware of a bell ringing; it was a church bell and one I'd heard before. I felt a bright glare against my eyelids and opened them expecting to see my bedroom light but caught my breath as I found myself staring up at the sun. I struggled to my feet and looked around me; I was in a field. Looking to my left I saw sheaths of corn stretching out before me, blowing to and fro on a gentle breeze; the only thing interrupting this golden vista was a large oak tree standing proud about a hundred yards away. I turned my head to the right and saw a river trailing slowly away from me into the distance; the running water offering up a pleasant gurgling sound as it rippled over some stones lying on the bank nearby. As I stood there watching the river sparkle against the sun and make its way across the field, I heard the bell toll out again. I turned and looked to the far side of the bank opposite and there it was, the church. I recognised it immediately along with the surrounding countryside from a previous dream I'd experienced in the early days of my first deciding to research our family history. But if I was dreaming then why did the sun feel so warm against my skin, why was I able to reach out and take hold of the ears of corn growing in the field around me and, more especially, why could I hear the church bell ringing so clearly in my head; unless perhaps it was my alarm clock informing me that I'd already slept the night away and it was time to get up? Shaking my head in an attempt to clear these pictures from my mind and transport myself back to the safe environs of my bedroom I sensed the cornfield begin to spin around me and the sky darken. I felt myself falling backwards and reached out to grab at the swirling stalks of corn in an effort to steady myself. As my head hit the ground and I drifted towards unconsciousness, I became aware of that now familiar voice calling out to me once more; "Help me Charles." Everything went black.

In the darkness I became aware of another bell ringing, this time it *was* my alarm clock. I felt my body jump involuntarily; jolted back into life by the loud clanging noise. Opening my eyes, I looked around and breathed a sigh of relief at finding myself back in the familiar surroundings of my bedroom. My body shuddered as I felt a chill run through me. I looked down to see I was still sitting up in bed as before but with the blankets now having moved away from my torso, leaving my upper body naked and exposed. Although it was summer there was still an early morning chill in the air and, presuming I had lain in this position for much of the night, I wasn't surprised to be feeling a little cold.

Dragging myself out of bed I washed and dressed quickly, my mind still struggling to gain any sense or meaning as to the detail and significance of my apparent dream. It had been a dream that, in part at least, I'd experienced before and yet was still no nearer understanding. It was also a dream that, for the first time, was unsettling me at a far deeper level than simply disturbing my sleep.

Chapter Thirteen

The next couple of weeks flew by as I made the final preparations for my trip to Kent. It was the summer break now and it felt good to be away from uni and all the additional pressures that were associated with my being there. Life in Leicester was great but the continual commute between uni and home, along with keeping both my parents and tutors apprised of all the work I was doing, certainly as far as Mum's family tree was concerned, was beginning to take its toll. I was ready for some down time in more ways than one even if my trip to Sowfield had been arranged, in part, to further my efforts at discovering more about our dear departed ancestor. That said I was also looking forward to enjoying the local countryside along with the pleasures of a pint or two of the local brew. Simon had offered to come with me and, initially, I'd considered this to be a good idea, what with us being best friends and enjoying each other's company so much, but on reflection decided what I really needed was some me time and so declined his offer. I had spent the past few months answering seemingly endless questions from Mum and Dad about my work and, when I wasn't at home with them, I'd been researching various family history sites and census results in preparation for my exams and further discussions with my tutors at uni. And so, apart from taking up Dad's offer of finance towards my trip and accommodation, I decided I would be answerable to nobody but myself over the next few days. I couldn't remember the last occasion I'd been entirely on my own without recourse to anyone else. This, coupled with the fact I'd never been to Kent before, confirmed it would be the perfect opportunity for a little one to one time with only myself for company.

Of course, I wouldn't feel truly independent until I was physically on board the train and, as expected, Mum wasn't going to let me go that easily, insisting, as she did, on coming to the station with Dad to see me off.

"Are you sure you've got everything?"

I smiled at Dad and shook my head. "Yes Mum I've got everything. How do you think I manage at uni? You don't check on me every time I go there, do you?"

"That's because I look through your case before you leave just to make sure you've packed…"

I stepped back in disbelief. "Mum, you don't?"

She'd clearly betrayed her own secret. "Well, I'm a Mum remember, and Mums care about their children; we like to look after them."

"But I'm not a child anymore and I can look after myself; *do* look after myself, and pretty well I thought; or did until now."

"I know and I'm not saying you don't, it's just that…"

Dad held up his hands, partially in protest but also in an act of personal submission. "Don't look to me for help, Charlie, she's just the same when I go away, rummaging through my case or bag to make sure I've packed enough socks, hankies and the like."

Glancing at my watch, I jumped in before Mum could respond. "Look the train will be off in a minute so can you leave your domestic until I'm gone." I opened the carriage door and, swinging my backpack over my shoulder, lifted my case onto the train. "I'll let you know when I get there."

Mum thrust her hand into the shopping bag she was holding. "Here, I packed a few sandwiches and treats for you." She smiled. "And you can't say I don't do that for you when you go off to Leicester because I do, and very grateful for them you are as well I seem to recall."

"Thanks Mum." I leant forward taking the package in one hand and squeezing her arm with the other. "Love you."

She put her arms around me and gave me a hug. "Love you to Charlie, never forget that." Moving back slightly she took my face in her hands. "Sorry if I fuss too much, it's only because I care."

I smiled and gave her a kiss on the cheek. "I know."

Dad, knowing that Mum never did like goodbyes, stepped forward. "Come on you, the lad's only going away for a few days, he'll be back before you know it; certainly sooner than if he was off to university." He winked at me and tugged at Mum's arm. "Remember, sometimes he's away for a whole two or three weeks before he returns to your nest Mother hen."

She smiled and stepped back. "I know, but it doesn't stop me missing him." Turning to Dad, she grinned. "You on the other hand can go off for as long as you like. I'll even pack your case for you."

Dad threw his arm playfully around her shoulder and pulled her back from the train. "No chance of me coming with you, is there, Son?"

I looked back over my shoulder as I boarded the train and laughed. "No chance, you married her, so you have to live with her."

I watched as Dad drew Mum into him and kissed her lightly on the forehead. "You're right; she's not that bad I suppose."

The guard shouted to stand clear as the last few doors banged shut. A sense of excitement ran through me as I put my head out of the window to wave goodbye. This was it; I was on my way to make new discoveries about my family, perhaps even about myself. The train lurched forward.

"Bye, Mum, bye Dad." I put my fingers to my ear mimicking a phone conversation. "I'll call you later."

I watched for a moment as they waved. "Bye Charlie, have fun."

I waved back before closing the window and moving along the carriage to find myself a seat. The train wasn't busy so I placed my case by my feet and put the backpack on the seat next to me. Sitting down I looked out of the window to see the last sign on the platform disappear from view as we cleared the station.

"Free at last," I thought, smiling to myself. Of course, I'd left home a hundred times before on my way to uni, but this felt different, more like the first day I'd travelled there, with that same sense of anticipation and of the unknown about it. I knew where I was going and why of course, but as to what I would discover when I got there that, as it had been on my very first journey to Leicester, was an entirely different thing. This was to be a new adventure and one I was really looking forward to. It felt as though I was about to discover the missing piece of a jigsaw, and once in place our family picture would be complete, at least as far back as 1846.

I sat back and looked out of the window again, the English countryside flashing past me as the train gathered speed; the hypnotic rhythm of its wheels taking hold as they rattled along the tracks echoing their repeated verse, *You're going to Kent, You're going to Kent.*

I smiled recalling how many times in the past, as a child, I'd made up similar rhymes with Mum and Dad as we travelled by train to the coast for our summer holidays. With this recurring mantra playing in my head I felt my eyes becoming heavier as the sun beat through the carriage window creating the perfect conditions for me to drift off to sleep. Once more my mind hovered somewhere between real life and events imagined. Suddenly I felt my chest tighten as a sensation of dread and foreboding overtook me. I opened my eyes and, looking down, saw that my hands had blood on them. As I recoiled in shock, I noticed a man dressed in black lying on the floor of the carriage in front of me bleeding badly from a head wound. Was it his blood on my hands? I reached out towards him as he turned his head, straining to look up at me. I couldn't see his face clearly with blood running freely across his forehead and down his cheek, and the outline of my own body casting a shadow across his. He struggled to move his arm as he attempted to reach out and take my outstretched hand. "Help me Charles." I gasped and drew back my hand, a feeling of panic and fear sweeping through me as his words registered in my subconscious. I knew this voice; I had heard its mournful cry many times before but never like this, never so visually or dramatically. I felt my head swim and my vision blur as I attempted to get to my feet in an effort to escape the horrific scene before me. As I struggled for breath and to get away, I became aware of another voice calling out to me.

"Tickets please."

My head jolted back as I looked up, the sunlight blinding me momentarily and causing me to blink as it shone in my eyes through the carriage window. I attempted to speak but my mouth, like my brain, was befuddled and I could do no more than splutter a few incomprehensible words to the man standing in front of me. It was the train guard. "Sorry, I was, I mean I…"

He smiled reassuringly. "I'm sorry to wake you, sir. I did pass by a few minutes ago and saw you were asleep and thought I'd leave you as long as possible but, as we're getting near to London now, I won't have another chance to check your ticket." He reached out his hand. "So, if I could see it please?"

I smiled and rummaged around in my pocket, thankfully finding the aforementioned ticket. Handing it over I ruffled my hair in attempt to stir my head back to life. "Wow, are we nearly there already? I must have really gone over." I smiled again as he handed me back my duly punched ticket.

"No problem sir." He nodded towards the window. "About another fifteen minutes I should think." He smiled as he turned to leave. "Just these last couple of carriages to do and then I'll be getting a bit of a rest myself, I hope. I'm on earlies this week." He tapped the face of his watch. "Started at six so I'm feeling it a bit an' all now." He smiled again and touched the peak of his cap. "Enjoy the rest of your journey."

Nodding my appreciation of his good wishes, I pushed the ticket back into my pocket. "Thanks." I watched as he walked down the carriage, my mind still adjusting to its rude awakening. As I turned away and looked out of the window, my thoughts returned to my dream. "At least it had been a dream," I reasoned, recalling this wasn't the first time I'd experienced these sleep induced imaginings. "I'll be glad once I discover the truth as to what really happened to dear old George, at least then I shouldn't be bothered by any more of these flights of fancy and awful nightmares." I smiled. "Must have been tired though, having slept for most of the journey." I gave a cursory look at my watch. "Just enough time to eat Mum's sarnies."

I spent the next few minutes gratefully munching my way through the, by now, warm peanut butter and jam sandwiches Mum had packed along with a large slice of fruit cake. "Glad she knew I was only joking about her fussing over me," I mused. "She makes the best fruit cake ever." I reached into my backpack and pulled out the plastic bottle of water I'd brought with me and took a large swig to wash down the last of my cake. As I folded the paper bag which had contained my sandwiches and returned the half empty bottle to my shoulder bag, the train's tanoy system crackled into life.

"This service will be arriving at London Paddington in five minutes. Please make sure you take all your luggage and belongings with you when you depart the train. On behalf of British Rail, we would like to thank you for travelling with us this morning and wish you a pleasant onward journey. Five minutes to London Paddington, thank you."

I looked out of the window again and noticed how the lush green of the English countryside had been replaced by the more austere brick work of the rows of houses that sat alongside the track. The closer we got to Paddington the grimier and grubbier some of the houses looked, although I put much of this down to the fact that the earlier sunshine which had warmed the carriage for so much of my journey had now disappeared and been replaced by heavy grey cloud that was threatening to give way to rain at any moment.

"Great, a downpour, just what I need. I should have listened to Mum when she said not to pack my jacket at the bottom of the case." I looked up ruefully at the ever-darkening sky. "Too late now, I'll just have to get wet."

As the train trundled to a halt so, as if prearranged, the heavens opened and I, along with my fellow passengers, made a dash for cover. Most of them had the advantage of only travelling to London for the day on business or pleasure and therefore, unlike me, didn't have the extra burden of a heavy suitcase to drag along the platform, all of which meant I was one of the last to reach the exit gate where an officious looking British Rail employee demanded to see my ticket. At least this part of the station was under cover and so the few minutes I spent retrieving my ticket and showing it to him was less uncomfortable than it might have been had I still been in Peterborough where parts of the platform remained open to the elements. I also took advantage of the opportunity to check with my, slightly less than accommodating, rail assistant as to which platform I required for my onward journey to Sowfield. Perhaps it was my bedraggled look and obvious discomfiture at having to lug a slightly sodden suitcase behind me along with my, equally damp, backpack that brought about a brief moment of caring and understanding in his demeanour towards me. Looking at his watch and then glancing towards the station's large clock to check his timing he nodded towards, first, my case and then into the distance.

"If that's not too heavy and you're up for a bit of a dash across the station, Son, there's a train for Sowfield leaving on Platform six in four minutes, but you'll need to be quick."

I grabbed my case and began the allotted dash to platform six, glancing over my shoulder briefly as I did so to offer heartfelt gratitude for his assistance. "Cheers, thanks a lot."

Thankfully, I'd kept my ticket in my hand and was able to wave it at the collector as I reached the gate. The gods were clearly in my favour as he beckoned me through.

"Another thirty seconds and you'd have missed it mate," he said, nodding towards the train which was straining at the starting blocks ready to leave. "Go on, jump on the back and make your way through to a seat once it's moving." I'd only just slammed the carriage door behind me as a whistle blew and the guard on the platform raised his flag, the train lurching forward in instant response to his instruction. I fell backwards dropping my case to the floor and hitting my head on the carriage wall, but at least I was on board and out of the rain which was now lashing against the outside of the train as we cleared the station. I made my way along the first carriage which appeared to be full of ladies who'd, seemingly, been on an early morning shopping trip to London accompanied, as they were, by a variety of bags set against their legs and seats, all bulging with their purchases and leaving no room for the casual traveller, such as myself. As I passed by each occupant gave me a less than welcoming stare clearly designed to let me know the opportunity of sitting next to a wet and dishevelled young student was one they were happy to forgo, especially if it meant being parted from their precious shopping bags, even by a few inches.

I continued to make my way through the train and, after passing a number of other wet and disgruntled passengers, was pleased to see a notice indicating the buffet car was situated only one carriage further along. Had I found a seat in shoppers paradise earlier I might not have noticed this and therefore missed out on the chance of a cup of tea which, following my recent exertions, I determined to be a well-deserved treat, and one I would take full advantage of once I'd found a place to park both myself and my bags.

A few minutes later, I was safely ensconced in the quiet of an almost empty carriage, having found a seat and treated myself to a piping hot cup of tea along with a large Danish pastry. The pastry was a bonus, and whilst it may not have been up to the standard of Mum's fruit cake it still came in a pretty good second.

As I worked my way through the delicious gooey indulgence, washing down each mouthful with a swig of tea, I glanced out of the window again. Looking up I noticed the rain beginning to move away and the sun force its way through ever widening cracks in the rapidly dispersing cloud. I smiled and settled back in my seat to enjoy the remains of my tea and pastry. Sitting there watching the sun take centre stage in the sky once more my thoughts wandered back to our family tree and all I'd learned about Mum's forebears during the past few weeks. They were stories from our history I now felt comfortable and familiar with but whose final chapter still alluded me. I felt excited at the prospect of what I hoped to discover during the next few days. As I sat there allowing my mind to drift and focus on the positive, thoughts of the earlier soaking I'd received and detail of my equally uncomfortable dream began to fade.

Chapter Fourteen

"Sowfield, this is Sowfield." The words reverberated in my head as I came to, roused once more from my slumbers, having dozed on and off for the last twenty minutes of the journey. The train jolted to a halt, throwing me forward in my seat, as I rubbed the sleep from my eyes.

I threw my backpack over my shoulder and, lifting my case from the train, stepped onto the platform. Not knowing what to expect I was still surprised at how rural the station and its surroundings appeared to be. I felt as if I'd travelled back in time to the late 1950s or early '60s as I gazed around the sleepy looking station with its tired and somewhat dilapidated wooden ticket office situated at one end of the platform. There was a large unkempt Buddleia bush growing from the side of a hedgerow adjoining the platform that forced me nearer to the edge than I would have liked as I made my way towards a slightly dishevelled looking ticket collector waiting patiently by the side of his faded wooden office. Glancing behind me I realised I was the only passenger who had departed the train.

Arriving at the end of the platform I placed my suitcase on the ground and reached into my jacket pocket for my now crumpled ticket.

"Nice afternoon Sir." I looked up to be greeted by the portly rail official who, raising his gaze above the half-moon glasses perched on the end of his nose, smiled warmly at me. I returned his greeting and nodded, musing to myself how well his appearance suited this particular outpost of the rail system. His British Rail cap sat slightly to one side of his head as if placed there as a last thought on hearing the train arrive and suddenly remembering it was his responsibility to be there to greet it. His jacket was partly unbuttoned, and his tie looked as though it had been knotted previously and then simply pulled over his head rather than tied evenly around his neck, with one side of his shirt collar forced under the tie rather than tucked beneath it as would traditionally be the case.

I pulled the ticket from my pocket and handed it to him. "Yes, it is a nice afternoon, certainly now the sun's out. There was a bit of a downpour in London earlier," I replied, pulling my jacket forward to show the odd damp patch still apparent on the shoulders and sleeve from their earlier soaking.

He laughed. "It does that in London."

I wasn't sure how to respond, wondering if he was suggesting that it never rained in Sowfield or that he simply wasn't a fan of London.

"I'm from Peterborough, we get our fair share of rain there as well," I countered, feeling duty bound to say something but realising in the same instant how irrelevant my comment was.

"I saw you struggling past the Buddleia," he continued. "I've been telling them up the line for weeks it needs cutting back but they haven't done anything about it; bugger it is."

I looked behind me at the clearly untidy and unloved bush. "I didn't really notice it." Now I was lying as well as talking rubbish.

"This is one of the stations they don't know what to do with." He nodded in the general direction of the empty platform and then back to me. "Too quiet they say, not enough passengers to keep it going. You're the first today, apart from the early commuters that is. They'll be back later, but apart from the two of them…" his voice trailing away as he shrugged his shoulders and looked down at my ticket.

"So they don't know what to do with it then," I asked, feeling obliged to show an interest?

Looking up he pursed his lips and nodded. "Yeah, always been a quiet station, well, as long as I've been here and that's thirty years." He smiled. "Retiring in another couple, so they can do what they like with it then."

"What about the commuters?"

"The top bods say that Ashford is close enough for them to get to. If they go down that route, I reckon they could well close us down." He laughed. "And you know what her ladyship Thatcher's like, I reckon she'll privatise the whole lot soon, she's already sold off Sealink and the British Transport Hotels, so it's odds on she'll go after us next." He nodded towards the station sign secured to the lamp post above his office. "Won't be any need for little stations like Sowfield then."

Although I'd never been to Sowfield before I suddenly felt empathy towards it, along with its troubled representative.

"Doesn't seem very fair?"

He smiled again. "Life isn't always fair though is it? Still like I say, a couple of years and they can do what they like." He pointed to my case. "You here for a holiday then?"

"No, well, maybe a bit of one." I smiled, wondering why we were actually bothering to have this conversation. I decided as I was likely to be the only visitor to arrive in Sowfield today, and maybe for some time, the prospect of talking with anybody from the outside world was, for my inquisitor, an opportunity not to be missed. "I'm a student researching my family tree, and I've come down to Kent to find out some more about one of my ancestors."

"Local then, were they?"

"It seems so, or at least *he* was, a vicar. Mind it was a long time ago, back in the 1800s."

"Vicar eh." I watched as he rubbed the side of his head, further dislodging his cap as he did so. "That'll be St Mark's then I should reckon, that's the oldest church round here."

I suddenly became excited by his response. "That's right, do you know it?"

He pointed towards a hill situated beyond a field on the opposite side of the platform. "Just near that hill it is, 'bout a mile, you can't miss it." He looked down at my case again. "Where are you staying?"

I shook my head and smiled. "Not sure. Actually, I don't know; maybe a local B and B or a small hotel if there's one nearby?" I looked at him again, hopefully. "I don't suppose you could recommend anywhere?"

He paused, stroking the stubble on his chin and chewing his lip as he considered my request. Clearly enjoying this fleeting moment of perceived esteem in my eyes he nodded thoughtfully. "Well now, let me think." Then, as if in response to a sudden flash of inspiration he took his hand from his face and pointed once more to the field and hill beyond. "I reckon Linda's your best bet."

I stood for a moment waiting for him to continue before breaking the silence. "And she is?"

He shook his head in self admonishment. "Sorry, of course I was forgetting you're not from round here are you?" I smiled again and nodded, questioning whether I had actually done the right thing in asking him and wondering if I might be better excusing myself and seeking advice elsewhere.

"Linda has a smallholding on the other side of the field, just a spit from St Mark's it is, suit you down to the ground I reckon." He lifted his gaze, peering over his glasses again, and smiling at me. "If she's got a spare room you won't do any better than her for a bed, especially being so close to the church an' all."

I decided to give him another chance. "Sounds great, does she do breakfast as well?"

"Does she." He puffed out his cheeks. "It's having the small holding see; she's got chickens and the like, so there's always plenty of fresh eggs."

"And she's happy for people to stay?"

"Well, only on recommendation. She doesn't do it full time, just if someone needs a bed now and then and there's no room at The Blacksmith's Arms. That's the pub in the village; it's on the same road as Linda's. In fact, if you get as far as that you'll have passed her place. It's okay though, small for a pub mind and a bit more expensive than Linda and all." He smiled at me knowingly. "Student you said wasn't it? I reckon you'll be looking for the best deal then, unless you're from one of those rich families where money's no object?"

I nodded, returning his smile. "The best deal sounds fine to me. Should I ring first to see if she can put me up?"

Attempting to add further credence to his assumed authority, at least in my eyes, of being the local fount of all knowledge he stood to attention and, pulling back his shoulders, looked straight at me. "You stay here and I'll give her a quick call for you."

"That's very kind, are you sure, I don't mind…?"

He raised his hand to silence me. "Don't you worry yourself lad, be my pleasure. Like I said, she only takes folk on recommendation so probably best I be the one to call."

I watched as he disappeared into the ticket office only to reappear moments later. "What's your name, son, so's I can let her know who it is that'll be calling?"

"Charles Benton…Charlie Benton." I smiled. "Everyone calls me Charlie."

He nodded and walked back into the office.

"Sounds like you might have fallen on your feet here, Charlie my lad," I thought as I waited patiently for my rail transport saviour to bring me the news I was hoping for.

A few minutes later he emerged again minus his cap, thus revealing a head of thinning grey hair and a large bald spot in the centre.

"All sorted." He smiled; an obvious look of pride spread across his face at having accomplished his task. "You're in luck lad; Linda says she can put you up and that you're just to mention my name when you arrive. Her place is called Meadowfield Farm, although like I say it's more of a smallholding really. The meadow itself stretches behind her place and up towards the hill, but you'll see the sign alright on the gate outside."

"Sounds great, thanks."

His voice suddenly took on a more serious tone. "Linda's a lovely lady, lost her husband to cancer a while back so she's on her own now if you get my drift?"

I shook my head. "I'm not sure I do, although I'm sorry to hear about her husband of course."

"What I'm saying is that folks round here look out for each other, what with it being a small community, and Linda's an important part of it. She takes people in to help with her bills and the like when she's a bit short, so she's not looking to be messed about or taken advantage of." He looked directly at me. "Do you get me now?"

I nodded my understanding of the point he was making, and of the high regard Linda was obviously held in locally. "Of course; I promise she won't get any trouble from me. Like I say, I just want somewhere to get my head down and maybe the odd meal now and then, if that sounds alright? Apart from that she won't even know I'm there." I thought for a moment sensing the need to reassure him further. "I can leave my mum and dad's address if you like so you can check what I'm saying is true?"

He looked me up and down for a moment chewing his lip once more. "No, you're alright, I believe you, just be aware that's all."

"I will, and thanks again." I looked towards the hill. "About a mile you say? I reckon I can walk that alright from here." I looked up at the afternoon sun beating down as it dried the last of any dampness from my clothes. "The walk'll probably do me good after all the sitting down I've done over the past few hours."

"I should think so too, a young lad like you. I'd have run there when I was your age." He looked at my case and backpack and laughed. "Well, maybe not run exactly, at least not with that lot."

Picking up the case and walking towards the exit gate next to his office I glanced at the steep pathway winding its way up by the side of the station. I puffed out my cheeks in anticipation of the trek facing me and turned to ask one final question.

"Does she have a last name?"

"Who?"

"Linda? It seems a bit rude just to use her first name when we've never actually met."

"Oh didn't I mention it; it's Wells, Linda Wells." He tapped the side of his nose. "Just remember what I said though right? She's a good 'un is Linda, and folks round here wouldn't take kindly to seeing her messed about."

"As I said she won't get any trouble from me, I promise."

"Good lad." He pointed up the slope. "You just turn right at the top and keep walking. There's a couple of turnings left and right along the way, but you just stick to the main road and you'll be at Linda's in no time."

I looked towards the hill in the distance and raised my left arm to shift my backpack to a more comfortable position. "Thanks again."

Offering him my hand I smiled. "I'll see you on my way back in a few days' time if all goes to plan."

"Take care of yourself lad, and I hope you find whatever it is you're looking for."

Nodding my appreciation of his good wishes I turned to face the slope stretching out before me. "I hope this is the only climb I have today," I thought, making my way up the steep incline towards the main road; my case and backpack suddenly feeling a lot heavier than they had previously on level ground.

As I reached the top of the path and turned right, I put the case down and shook my hand in an attempt to encourage the feeling back into it having been trapped under the case's narrow handle and causing some of my fingers to go numb in the process. Standing upright to stretch my back I stared ahead of me. "Flippin' heck, main road did he say?" I was looking at little more than a lane with a thick high hedge running on either side as far as the eye could see. I took off my backpack and jacket remembering, as I did so, the bottle of water I'd brought with me from home and that was still half full. Gulping down a great mouthful of the now warm liquid I poured a little of what was left onto my hands to splash on my face and neck. I shook my head allowing the drops of water that were running down my cheeks to spray into the air around me. "That's better." Lifting up my backpack and placing it over my shoulder again, I tucked my jacket through one of the arm supports and picked up my case ready to begin the mile-long trek towards my promised bed for the night. Although I felt hot and sweaty under the weight of my luggage, I was also enthused by all that had happened over the past half an hour or so. I'd arrived safely at Sowfield without too much hassle, apart from the drenching I'd received earlier in London. Additionally, I now had the promise of clean and inexpensive accommodation for the next few days and, even better; it was apparently only a stone's throw from St Mark's itself. I grinned as a trickle of perspiration ran down the side of my face. "Result all round Charlie boy, the gods are smiling on you again." I looked up at the sun and laughed. "In more ways than one."

It took me just under half an hour to reach my, now very welcome, destination. I had, as forewarned, met with the option of a few alternative diversions along the way but had, also as instructed, ignored them in favour of staying on the, so called, main road to Meadowfield Farm. At last, there it was in front of me. It was the sort of scene one expects to find on the front of a box of chocolates or jigsaw puzzle; a picturesque, thatched cottage with caramel-coloured roses growing along the outside wall and around the front door. The small leaded windows were contained within white freshly painted wooden frames set against the thick stone walling of the building itself. There was a large tabby cat lazing peacefully in the sun outside the front door which half-heartedly raised its head in curious response to the creaking of the wooden gate as I lifted the latch to enter. Closing the gate behind me I watched as the cat turned away again, stretching itself briefly before returning to its slumbers. I glanced a little further down the road, noticing a church steeple peeping from behind a row of equally attractive cottages. A tremor of anticipation ran through me. "That must be St Mark's."

As a backdrop to this idyllic scene was the hill I'd kept at the centre of my focus as I made my way along the road from the station. Now, less than a few hundred yards away I was able to appreciate up close the blaze of summer colour it provided with daisies, buttercups, and wildflowers swaying lazily in the breeze against a backdrop of lush green grass growing up and over the hill itself as far as the eye could see. I stood for a moment taking in the simple beauty of this breath-taking vista before me. At the base of the hill was the meadow that had been described to me. In it were a few cattle grazing contentedly, oblivious to my presence. "Mum would love this," I mused, wishing I'd brought a camera with me so I could take a picture to show her when I got home. Thinking about this, I realised my greater folly in not actually having brought a camera with me anyway. "Idiot, how much simpler would it have been to take some photos of the church and its records to refer to when you get back rather than having to write everything down or subject it to memory?"

As I walked down the path towards the cottage, still berating myself for this lack of foresight, the door opened and a slim attractive woman stepped out to greet me. She had lightly greying hair tied up in a bun and was wearing a full-length, cream-coloured pinafore with frills around the edge that covered her dress. From what I could see the dress itself appeared to be a mixture of colour but predominantly blue, although I couldn't tell exactly with it being hidden beneath her apron. She had a welcoming smile and appeared younger than her hairstyle and colouring suggested. I liked her immediately, and even more so when she spoke.

"Charles Benton?"

I returned her smile. "Yes, although everyone calls me Charlie."

"Well, I'll do the same then Charlie, if that's alright with you? I don't know if Harry told you, but my husband's name was Charlie?" She laughed. "Well, actually it was Charles the same as yours, but everyone called him Charlie as well. He always said Charles sounded a bit pompous, but of course if you…"

I shook my head. "No, Charlie's fine, honestly. And I agree, I always think Charles makes me sound a bit posh, like Prince Charles, and I'm not, a prince or posh, if that makes sense?" I laughed. "The only time I get called Charles is either by my tutors or if I'm in trouble with Mum and Dad."

We smiled at each other again as if bonding in some deeper way even though, at this stage, we had done no more than exchange a few words of polite greeting. I was the first to break the silence.

"I was sorry to hear about your husband."

Placing her lips together she put her head to one side. "Harry told you then? He's a good man, likes to protect me from awkward conversations, but it's been a few years now so I…"

She paused. I could tell from her expression the loss of her husband may have taken place some time ago but that the pain was, for her, as real today as it had been at the time.

"Even so, I was still sorry to hear about it."

"Thank you, Charlie, that's kind." She paused, wiping her hands down the front of her apron. "Harry says you're after a bed for a night or two is that right; something about you being a student?"

I took it from her continued references to Harry she meant the ticket collector at the station. "Yes, he… Harry, suggested you might be able to put me up?"

"Happy to do so, it'll be nice to have a bit of company. Do you know how long you'll be here exactly?"

"Just a few days, I think. I'm doing some research for a project I'm working on as part of my degree course."

She smiled. "Sounds exciting, although I can't imagine what there is worth researching here in sleepy old Sowfield?"

"Actually, it is exciting, well, at least I think it is, or will be if what I'm looking for turns out to be true."

As we stood chatting to each other the cat stretched out its legs again and, yawning, rose to its feet and sauntered into the house.

Linda smiled as it disappeared from view. "Looks like Rover's had enough of the sun."

"Rover?"

"I know, who calls a cat Rover?" She turned and nodded towards the open door. "It was my husband's idea." She shook her head and grinned as if recalling the event. "Pretty much as soon as we got him Charlie suggested Rover because he would disappear for days on end and then just as suddenly reappear on the doorstep as if nothing had happened meowing and looking for food. The first couple of times it happened we thought he'd had an accident or been run over but, after a while, we just got used to his coming and going, his *roving* around." She turned slightly, a look of melancholy on her face. "He's much more stay at home these days since Charlie died. It's as if he feels he needs to be here with me, looking out for me, if that makes sense?"

I smiled. "They say animals have a sixth sense so maybe…" I shrugged my shoulders as if to demonstrate my understanding of the point she was making, but also recognising I wasn't really sure of what I was alluding to. There was a brief, slightly embarrassed, silence between us.

Linda, realising this particular topic of conversation had reached its natural conclusion, patted her apron and looked down at my case.

"I'm sorry, Charlie, you must be exhausted after walking all that way in this hot sun with that heavy case and shoulder bag, what sort of host am I?" She beckoned me forward. "Come on in and let me get you a cold drink. I bet you could do with a sit down as well couldn't you?"

I nodded my agreement. "That would be nice yes, thank you."

I followed her into the house which struck me as dark and a little chilly after the warmth and brightness of the summer sunshine outside. The small windows let in defined shafts of light that outlined certain objects or areas of each room, similar to those you might expect from a spotlight, with particles of house dust drifting slowly through them. The hallway was narrow with the lounge door open on one side, revealing a small but welcoming space that had an old green settee set in the centre of the room partly covered by a deep red throw. To one side of the sofa was a large brown leather armchair with a matching footstool set in front of it. The flooring, as with the rest of the downstairs, was made up of large grey flag stones with the occasional rug placed randomly across them. These were of differing sizes and colours, with most looking a little threadbare but equally at home in their surroundings. On the other side of the hallway was a small room containing a dark wooden dining table with four chairs set around it. These were each covered with boxes of various sizes. Linda pointed them out as we passed by. "I've been having a bit of a clear out recently, Charlie's stuff in the main." She stopped and turned to look at me. "I hadn't felt able to do it before."

Before I could speak and offer any words understanding or condolence she turned and walked along the hallway again. "Still not sure what I'm going to do with it all, but it's a start."

The stairs were situated on the right at the end of the hallway. They wound their way up in a spiral effect denying me any direct view of the landing or floor above. Again, a single shaft of light from an upstairs window shone down the staircase, defining its corkscrew appearance. The stairs themselves were of bare dark stained wood at the sides, covered centrally with a heavily patterned carpet. Again, this had seen better days with obvious signs of wear throughout its red and green paisley pattern.

Although on first sight Meadowfield may have presented itself, at least from the inside, as a home in need of some general redecoration and repair, it also had a hospitable feel about it, along with a welcoming, almost tangible, sense of amiability. As we entered the kitchen, which was situated on the left of the hallway directly opposite the stairs, the perception of conviviality and warmth I was experiencing towards the cottage was heightened still further. This room was larger than the two we had passed in the hallway but also played host to another heavily patterned rug which, along with its frayed off-white tassels at either end, covered much of the grey stone flooring. There was a large wooden table in the centre of the room with six matching chairs set around it. Each chair had a small, patterned cushion positioned on it for added comfort against the hard-wooden base. I noticed Rover had found one of the cushioned seats to his liking and was curled up in a ball on it, purring contentedly and happily ignoring our presence. There was a large Aga cooker on the back wall just to the left of the door as we entered the room. Opposite was a substantial white Belfast sink set into a solid wood surround. It had a sloping wooden drainer running along the working surface which contained an assortment of plates and dishes. Above the sink was a large single pane window overlooking a small back garden with the meadow, farmland, and hill stretching into the distance beyond. There were old fashioned painted wooden cupboards on two of the walls and a stable style back door at the far end of the room on the left; the top half of which was open offering a view of a well cultivated vegetable patch and a small array of outbuildings.

"What a lovely room."

Linda nodded in appreciation at my comment. "Thank you, I like it as well. Charlie and I used to spend a lot of time in here plotting, planning and the like, especially in the winter when we would stoke up the Aga and get it going full blast, it was really cosy then." She smiled and pointed towards Rover who was still sleeping peacefully on his chair. "And, if it was very cold outside, we would spend the whole evening in here, along with his lordship of course."

I nodded towards the window above the sink. "Is that new, it looks bigger than the other windows?"

"Yes, well, not new exactly, it's been there a few years. It's the one concession we made to modern life when we moved here, having that window put in. It was so dark before, a bit like the rest of the house, especially on a cloudy day. You've probably noticed that already from the hallway? Anyway, because we liked being in here so much and because it overlooks the hill and most of our land, we decided to have some of the wall knocked out and put in a bigger window so we could enjoy the view. I'm so pleased we did; I really like it." She paused for a moment looking out of the window and taking in the landscape. Still a little unsure of myself in her company and not knowing how best to respond I gave a little cough to break the silence.

"I think it's lovely, very…"

She turned and smiled, recognising my slight discomfiture. "Sorry Charlie, I was in a bit of a daydream there." Rubbing her hands together she wiped them down the front of her apron. "Now, come on, let me show you to your room, then I'll make us both a drink and we can talk about how long you might want to stay, and you can tell me all about this research you're planning to do." Smiling warmly, she added. "Mind, as I said before, I can't for the life of me imagine what it is you want to research here, nothing ever happens in Sowfield." Before I had a chance to answer she moved past me and back into the hallway.

"Pass me your shoulder bag and I'll take you up." She looked down at my case and laughed. "I'll let you carry that one. I've been having a bit of a tidy up in the garden and my back is telling me I've done enough heavy lifting for one day."

I moved to put the backpack over my shoulder. "It's fine Mrs Wells I can manage both, really."

"No, I'll be fine as well; I just don't fancy lifting a big case that's all." She smiled again and began her ascent of the stairs. "And it's Linda."

"Sorry?"

"Linda, that's my name. I never did like being called Mrs Wells even when Charlie was around, except if we went to some function or other and that didn't happen very often." She paused, turning to look down at me. "Of course, a small part of me will always be Mrs Wells, Charlie's wife, or widow now of course, but the rest of me is quite happy simply to be known as plain old Linda. So yes, if it's alright with you, I'd rather you called me Linda just like everybody else does."

Smiling up at her, I noticed the light from the landing window shining down against the back of her head, glinting through the strands of her hair, and presenting a halo like effect around her face.

"An angel in every sense of the word," I mused. "And certainly an answer to prayer for this tired journeyman in providing somewhere to stay while I was in Sowfield."

As we reached the top of the stairs, she paused for a moment. The same slightly threadbare carpet stretched out in front of us to the end wall where the window that was throwing its welcome light along the landing and down the stairs, was situated. There were two doors on the left of us and another two opposite on the right. "This is the bathroom," she said, opening the first door on the left to reveal a surprisingly good-sized room containing a bath, sink, and an old-fashioned toilet with a wooden seat. Above it was a white painted cistern and metal link chain hanging down from its side to flush the loo. The floor was covered with pale pink patterned lino along with a darker pink candlewick style matt positioned by the side of the bath and matching pedestal mat set around the base of the toilet. A toilet roll holder was connected to the wall on one side and a towel rail on the other with a bright green hand towel hanging over it. There was a small white shelf above the sink which held a variety of sprays, hairbrushes, and pots of differing potions and creams, all clearly designed for use by a lady, and which reminded me of Mum's toiletries that filled a similar space in our own bathroom at home.

She looked at the shelf and smiled. "Living on my own I only have myself to think about these days, hence all the female clutter. Charlie always moaned there was never any room for his shaving gear and so on. I used to tell him to put up another shelf or better still a cupboard but he never got around to it, and once he became ill, well…" She turned to face me. "I'll move some of it into my bedroom to make a bit of room for you."

I shook my head. "No really, I'm just grateful for a bed. I can live out of my suitcase for a few days no problem."

"Well, we can talk about that later." She moved to close the bathroom door. "If you're desperate or the bathroom is occupied there's an outside loo next to the back door as well. It's got my boots and a few gardening bits in it, but it works, and if nature calls…needs must and all that." She laughed. "It's come to my rescue on more than one occasion when I've been outside working and not wanted to walk muddy boots through the house."

I smiled. "Thanks, I'll remember that."

Moving forward she opened the next door along the landing. "This is my room."

I glanced inside; the walls were painted white but looked tired as though they hadn't been decorated in a while. In the middle of the floor I could see a double bed with a patterned multicoloured bedspread on it. There was a dressing table set against one wall which had a fixed three-piece mirror attached to it. The surface of the unit was also covered with various jars and bottles. I noticed both the frame of the bed and the dressing table were made from the same matching coloured wood, as was the double wardrobe which stood against the back wall. Again, the bare wooden floorboards had been stained and covered, in the main, by a large plain rust coloured rug. The room appeared cheerless, almost sad, and I felt a wave of sympathy for my host run through me as I remembered how light and colourful my own parents' bedroom was, and of the shared laughter that emanated from it at times.

She closed the door and grinned. "Apologies for the mess."

I smiled back at her. "You should see my room. Mum says it couldn't be untidier if I let a bomb go off in it."

We laughed, enjoying the shared release of any nerves or of feeling the need to impress each other that may have been evident earlier.

"Thank you, Charlie."

"What for?"

"For making me laugh. I haven't done that in a while." She took a sharp intake of breath.

"Sorry, I didn't mean that to sound like I'm sad or feeling sorry for myself all the time, it's just…" her voice faded.

"It's fine really." We smiled at each other again, both unsure of what to say next but jointly aware of the others understanding. After a few moments Linda broke the silence.

"And this is your room over here." I followed her across the landing as she opened the door to the room directly opposite her own. The walls were cream in colour with a single bed set against the wall facing the door. The bed itself had a solid wooden headboard and was covered in a plain light blue bedspread. A faded picture of a country scene, not dissimilar to the one outside the cottage, hung on the wall above the bed. There was a chair positioned against the wall behind the door along with a single wooden wardrobe standing next to it. On the other side of the doorway was a small chest of drawers. I was thankful to see a sink set against the rear wall beside the bed with a hand towel hanging from a rail next to it. A small window was situated above the sink that overlooked the meadow and hill beyond. At least I would be able to wash and clean my teeth without having to worry about being too long in the bathroom, and of course I would have a glorious view to enjoy at the same time. There was a much smaller rug, than in the other rooms, placed in front of the bed for which I was grateful, along with the comfort it would afford my feet when getting up in the morning, as opposed to setting them directly onto the bare wooden flooring.

I placed my case on the floor and looked out of the window. "What a lovely view,"

"Yes, it is isn't it? Even on a dull day it still offers the best outlook, that's why I've made it the guest room." She smiled. "Might as well provide my visitors with good value for their money, not that I have that many."

I felt a sudden pang of guilt. "Of course, money, I'm so sorry. How much should I be paying you? It quite slipped my mind."

"Oh we can talk about that later, downstairs." She took a step back towards the door. "I'll leave you to unpack while I go and put the kettle on, or would you prefer a cold drink?"

"A cold drink would be great, if that's okay, some water or squash whichever's easier?"

Turning to leave, she grinned. "Of course, I should have thought, you must be hot and tired after that walk from the station? Take your time though Charlie, no rush; I'll see you downstairs when you're ready."

"Thanks Mrs…" I caught myself. "I mean Linda."

I watched as she closed the door and turned to unpack my case. As I sorted through my clothes, placing my pants, socks, and handkerchiefs in the small chest of drawers I considered again how fortunate I'd been in striking up a conversation with Harry the ticket collector, and in having him recommend Meadowfield Farm as somewhere to stay. There didn't appear to be any formal B&B's locally and certainly no sign of a hotel, although the Blacksmiths Arms might, as Harry had intimated, also have been able to provide me with a bed for the night. Even so, I was sure the welcome I'd have received there wouldn't have been anywhere near as warm and genuine as the one extended to me by Linda. I also took comfort in the fact she was clearly pleased to have some company herself.

I finished unpacking and placed my shoulder bag and case next to the wardrobe. Turning on the cold water tap on the sink I splashed a little on my face to freshen up. I lifted my head and, drying my face, glanced briefly out of the window at the meadow and hill beyond. The late afternoon sun had begun to sink a little lower in the sky and was casting an early shadow across the meadow as it moved slowly and inexorably behind the hill. A sense of contentment and wellbeing ran through me as I stood watching the light start to fade and evening approach. This had been a good day and, for all the earlier hustle and bustle in dodging the rain and rushing to change trains in London, had ended well. I smiled inwardly to myself and glanced around the small but comfortable room once more before making my ways downstairs. As I did so I ran my hand against the thick stone walling, speculating how many others must have done the same thing over the years as they made their way up and down the stairs in this delightful old farmhouse. Entering the kitchen, I noticed Linda was busying herself in laying the table for our meal. "There you are." She pointed to a glass on the table. "You're drinks ready. Orange juice okay?"

"Great, thanks." I picked up the glass and quickly downed its contents.

"Gosh you were thirsty, would you like some more?"

"No, thank you, that's fine, but you're right I was thirsty. Sorry if I appeared rude by guzzling it like that." I laughed. "Mum would have probably told me off if I'd have done that at home."

"Well, I won't tell her if you don't." She smiled. "I'm just starting to think about tea. Is there anything special you'd like? I bet you haven't eaten much today with all that travelling?"

"Whatever you're having will be fine with me, please don't go to any trouble. You didn't even know I was coming until a couple of hours ago so…"

She waved away my protestations and continued to organise the table for our meal. "Nonsense, it's nice to have you here. I prepared a stew earlier for myself and made enough for tomorrow as well so that's all sorted then. And it's no hardship to pop another couple of potatoes in the pot." She looked up at me. "I'm presuming you're happy to eat stew. I know a lot of you young people these days are becoming vegetarians. There's a young girl nearby who stopped eating meat a year or so back after that Band Aid concert. I wasn't sure what she meant when she told me? I thought Band Aid was some sort of plaster until she explained it. I'm afraid I don't keep up much with modern fashions or pop music and the like."

I laughed. "Thanks, stew sounds great. I don't think I'd survive long at home if I went veggie, my dad likes his meat too much and so does Mum, although I am eating more fish these days."

"Well, I can get some fish in if you'd prefer that for another evening?"

I shook my head. "Like I said, please don't go to any trouble, whatever you serve up will be fine." I laughed again. "Mum says I'm like a human dustbin when I'm at home, I eat pretty much everything she puts in front of me." Pausing, I looked directly at her. "Seriously, I'm just grateful to you for letting me stay, so please don't put yourself out on my behalf. I'm happy just to fit in with you and eat whatever I'm given."

Smiling, Linda motioned to a chair beside the Aga. "Well, if you're sure, but really it's no trouble. Now you sit there and have a rest, you must be tired after that walk from the station. Dinner will be ready in about an hour."

I nodded towards the sink as I moved to sit down. "I always do the washing up when I'm at home, so I hope you'll let me do the same here?"

Throwing her head back, she laughed. "I should think not. A paying guest washing up, that doesn't sound right at all."

"Please, I'd be happy to." I eased myself onto the kitchen chair and felt the heat from the Aga warm against my leg. "I actually enjoy washing up, honest. If Mum was here, she'd tell you the same thing. And anyway, paying guest or not this is still your home and I'd like to do my bit, if you'll let me?"

Moving towards me she nodded approvingly. "Alright if you insist, but we'll do it together."

"Great." I shifted slightly in my chair. "Talking of Mum, could I use your phone to ring home? I said I'd call and let her know I'd arrived safely and where I was staying just in case of…well, you know what Mums are like?"

She smiled, but I sensed it was polite rather than heart felt.

"Of course, the phone is in the hall on the small table behind the front door, help yourself."

I stood up and moved towards the door. "Thanks, I won't be long."

The number didn't ring for more than a minute before Mum answered. I imagined her sat by the phone waiting for my call, worrying because she hadn't heard from me earlier. It was good to hear her voice, and I spent the next few minutes telling her about my journey and of my good fortune in talking with Harry and of being guided towards Meadowfield; also, in how welcoming Linda had been.

"Your dad'll be pleased to hear that Charlie, I'll let him know all about what you've said when he gets in." She paused. I knew what was coming next. "Now, I'm only going to say this once but, remember to be polite and help out where you can; she's a lady on her own and doesn't need you being untidy or leaving everything lying around in a mess like you do at home, alright?"

I took the phone from my ear and, staring at it, shook my head. "Mum, how do you think I get on at uni? I've lived away from home for the past couple of years now remember."

"My point exactly. And if your room there is still in the same state it was that time your dad and I came to visit you then, well…all I'm saying Charlie Benton is that Mrs Wells doesn't need you treating her home the same way as you do ours, or leaving her bedroom in the same mess you do at university."

"Thanks, Mum, love you too."

"Now don't act all hurt, Charlie, you know what I'm saying."

I laughed. "I do; and I've already offered to wash up the tea things."

"Good."

"I'll call again in a couple of days to let you know how I'm getting on, okay?"

"Thanks, Son, you know your dad and I will be thinking about you. I hope everything goes well, and we look forward to hearing all about your adventure when you get home. Take care and thank Mrs Wells from me for looking after you so well."

"I will, Mum, bye."

"Goodbye, Son…love you."

I heard the line go dead and smiled to myself. I'd recognised from the slight break in her voice that she'd started to become emotional. Mum was always the same when saying goodbye to me or anybody for that matter. It was as if she was saying goodbye forever. That said, it was also one of the things that endeared her to Dad and me. The fact she cared so much about others may well, on occasion, have appeared overly sentimental but it also demonstrated the genuine concern she held for those she loved. I put the phone down and walked back to the kitchen where Linda was leaning over the sink peeling potatoes.

"I've decided to make mash," she said, holding up a freshly peeled potato. "Did you get through alright? I thought I could hear you talking, although I wasn't listening of course."

I smiled. "Don't worry about it, no secrets there. Yeah, I spoke to Mum, she was fine. She wanted me to say thank you for taking me in." I laughed. "She told me to mind my manners and to keep my room tidy, so let me know if I'm failing to keep the house rules or she'll be down here apologising to you personally and reprimanding me at the same time."

Placing the potato on the draining board Linda turned to face me. "She'll get no complaints from me I'm sure Charlie."

I laughed. "Thanks. Can I do anything to help?"

"I don't think so, everything's pretty much under control. You just sit down again and relax."

"Actually, if it's alright with you I thought I'd wander down to St Mark's to have a look round before I go there tomorrow. I presume it's open to the public during the week?"

"St Mark's?"

"Yes, the church. I saw the steeple over the other houses as I arrived."

She grinned. "I know where St Mark's is Charlie, I'm just interested to know why you want to go there, is it to do with this university work of yours?"

206

I suddenly realised we had spoken about pretty much everything else except the actual reason I'd come to Sowfield.

"I'm sorry, I should have said. Yes, it's to do with my studies. I'm researching Mum's family tree as part of my degree course in Genealogy and Family History."

Linda wiped her hands and sat down, gesticulating for me to do the same.

"Family tree, how interesting. Does your family come from Kent then?"

I moved to sit opposite her, laughing as I did so. "Well, not exactly, not unless you miss out a few generations, a hundred and forty odd years' worth to be exact."

She shook her head and looked at me quizzically. "I don't understand?"

I smiled apologetically. "I'm sorry that wasn't fair, let me explain. In dealing with the part of my course work that looks at family history I decided to base it on my own family or, to be exact, Mum's side of the family. I've already done quite a lot of research and discovered that most of them, certainly for the best part of the first hundred years or so, were from the Midlands. That said, we actually live in Peterborough, but that's another story altogether."

Linda looked even more confused.

"Sorry, I'm not doing very well here am I, let me start again." Taking a breath, I paused to gather my thoughts. "Okay, as part of my degree course at Leicester University I'm researching Mum's family tree. I've already discovered the history of most of her family line dating back to the late 1800s but, when I delved a little further back, I found that her great-great-grandfather was from Kent."

Linda leant forward, her body language and expression demonstrating a genuine interest in what I was saying. "What, from here in Sowfield you mean?"

"Well, in a way yes, he was the vicar here."

"At St Mark's?"

"Yes." I decided not to talk about his having supposedly been murdered there, at least not for now, and certainly not until I'd had the opportunity of gaining a bit more evidence from the church records themselves. That's assuming such records actually do exist and, if so, would then, provide the necessary evidence to confirm the story one way or the other.

"So that's why I've come here, to try and find as much evidence and information about him as I can. I'm just hoping they keep the details of past clergy and so on at the church."

Linda folded her hands together on the table and smiled. "How exciting for you, and for us in the village as well, that's if he was the vicar here of course. I do hope so Charlie, for your sake at least." She smiled again. "It's a long way to come if not. Still, maybe I can help point you in the right direction. Well, not me personally but perhaps towards someone who can, or at least should be able to, Joyce. She goes into the church every morning to check everything's okay. She also looks after the admin side of things for the vicar when he's not around."

"Joyce?"

"Sorry yes, she's the church secretary." She laughed. "And the church cleaner, along with undertaking pretty much every other job that requires doing at St Mark's. The church only gets a small congregation these days you see, what with less than a hundred people living in the village now, and barely a third of those attend services, certainly on any sort of a regular basis anyway. Roger, he's the vicar, has three other churches locally that he's responsible for and so only takes a service at St Mark's every third week or so. It's a pity in a way as it used to be really busy. It was a vibrant part of the community in its day with lots going on. But I suppose like everywhere else these days the traditional church service is becoming a thing of the past, what with all the modern church buildings coming along and pop bands performing in them instead of the good old-fashioned organ being played. We still have an organ at St Mark's but even that isn't used every week. Joyce's husband Fred plays it when he can but he's no spring chicken anymore and he's not been well of late either. I should think the services would pretty much grind to a halt altogether if it wasn't for the two of them supporting Roger and keeping everything going."

"Obviously they're locals then, Joyce and Fred I mean?"

Linda laughed. "You could say that. They've lived here for as long as anyone can remember. Their cottage is just a couple of doors along from the church itself."

"Do you go, to St Mark's I mean?"

Linda looked down at the floor as if considering her reply. "Not anymore."

I sensed I'd touched a nerve, although was unaware of exactly what I'd said to cause her obvious discomfiture. "I'm sorry I didn't mean to –"

She interrupted, lifting her head and looking towards me. "It's fine, you weren't to know, it's just…well, I haven't really been since Charlie died, haven't felt able to."

I immediately felt embarrassed at having upset her. "I'm so sorry. Look, it's none of my business; really, you don't need to tell me anymore, I shouldn't have said anything."

There was a momentary silence as we both struggled to move forward in our conversation. Eventually Linda took another deep breath and spoke in a soft and considered tone.

"The other room upstairs, the one I didn't show you was our son's." I could see she was struggling.

"Really, like I said, you don't need to tell me any of this."

She forced a smile. "No, I want to; it's been a while now and sometimes it helps to talk about it." Taking a handkerchief from her apron pocket she blew her nose. "Living on my own I tend to bury my head in the sand at times in an effort to forget what happened, so reminding myself occasionally does me good, brings me back to reality."

I felt awkward, but equally that I should provide the listening ear she was obviously seeking.

"David, that's our son, died only a few months after he was born. A cot death we were told, unexplained with no one to blame, just one of those things the doctors said but, as his parents, we struggled to accept that…I still do I think." She paused, putting her hand to her head as if collating her thoughts. "We put him down after his bath and kissed him goodnight." A gentle smile spread across her face as she embraced the memory. "He snuggled down under his blanket as always and then…when I went to check on him a couple of hours later, he was dead."

"I'm sorry."

Smiling at me she continued. "It's not your fault Charlie, just the same as it wasn't ours but, I've never felt that entirely to be true, at least not for my part anyway. I think as a Mum you always feel you could…should, have done more."

She paused, leaning across to stroke Rover who was still fast asleep on the chair next to hers. He jumped a little at her initial touch before settling once more into a contented slumber, purring at the same time as if to demonstrate his approval of her attention.

"We buried David at St Mark's. Charlie and I used to go there every day after that for a long time, changing the flowers on his grave and talking to him, telling him how much we missed him, that sort of thing. After the first year though it became harder to go, at least it did for me. I just felt the baby we'd both known

209

and loved wasn't there anymore and that simply visiting a piece of ground no longer offered the same degree of comfort it had in the days when we first lost him. To me it felt as though we were going out of habit. And, although his body may have been there David wasn't, if that makes sense? He was still alive in us of course, in our hearts and thoughts, but the little boy we'd known and loved was gone." She looked at me, tears filling her eyes. "That might sound mawkish but I didn't want to think of him like that, dead and decomposing in the earth. I wanted to remember him as he had been, even for those precious few months we had with him, a lively little boy with a beautiful smile. I couldn't do that when I stood by his graveside, and so I stopped going. Charlie went for a while longer but eventually we began to have arguments about it and so he stopped going as well, mainly for me bless him, but I think he was also beginning to struggle with demons of his own."

I no longer felt awkward that I may have embarrassed her but more a genuine sense of sadness for her loss, and for the burden of guilt she was clearly still carrying on so many levels.

"Look, it's nothing to do with me but I don't think you should beat yourself up about it so badly. Like you said, it wasn't a result of anything you did or didn't do yourselves. Tragically cot deaths do happen; my parents have a friend who lost a baby under similar circumstances, although I would never compare their grief to your own."

I wanted to reach out and take her hand but recognised that wouldn't be appropriate. She smiled again, acknowledging my sorry attempt to comfort her.

"Thank you, Charlie."

"Presumably you and your husband found a way forward eventually, a way to continue with your lives?"

She stared into the distance for a moment, deciding whether to draw this particular line of conversation to a close or to explain herself further; she chose the latter.

"We tried for another baby but without success, and so eventually found our solace in making this place, Meadowfield, the main focus of our attention." She looked around the room.

"You've probably noticed much of the décor is rather tired and ready for updating?"

I didn't want to embarrass her further but recognised the truth in what she was saying. "I think it all looks lovely, really homely."

She laughed. "Thank you, Charlie, that's very tactful, but I can see as well as you can that a fresh lick of paint wouldn't go amiss, and I don't just mean in here; the whole house could do with redecorating." She paused again. "My Charlie did make a start a few years back, but then he became ill and things like new wallpaper and freshly painted woodwork became less important. He had an early diagnosis of cancer, but we thought the doctors had got on top of it and, what with the various drugs he was taking appearing to work, were hopeful he would make a full recovery but…it wasn't to be. Eventually the cancer came back with a vengeance and he died within a few months of its return." She nodded towards the kitchen door. "When he became really sick, we moved him into David's room and made up a single bed for him in there, partly so I could get some sleep but also for him as he struggled to get comfortable. He also found it difficult to cope with the various drugs he was taking and the effects they were having on him. They often made him feel sick, and he felt guilty in my having to care for him all the time." Looking directly at me tears filled her eyes once more. "As if I would have done anything else? But he could see I was getting tired as well, although I tried my best to hide it from him. Eventually we did have a nurse come and stay over for the last few nights of his life while I tried to get some rest. It was nice of them, but I never really managed to sleep; how could I, knowing Charlie was dying in the room next to me. The only thing it did allow me was the space to cry and shout silently at God for allowing this horrible disease to attack my man and take his life in such a terrible way."

I wanted to interrupt and put an end to her obvious distress but recognised she had begun a story that she needed to complete, no matter how uncomfortable it might be for me to be party to.

"After he died, I had Charlie buried in the same plot as David. I wanted them to be together again, to look after each other." I watched as a tear ran down her cheek. "I went there a few times after that but quickly felt the same way about Charlie being there as I did about David. I didn't want to think of the two of them lying cold in the ground but rather I wanted to remember them as I'd known them in life, smiling and happy, and so I stopped going altogether." She looked at me. "I haven't been there since." Taking a breath, she exhaled slowly, the effects of having recounted such a difficult story etched clearly in her expression.

"I'm sorry." I recognised I'd repeated myself but was struggling to find any real alternative expression of condolence, especially for someone I'd met only a few hours before and whose life story was unfolding before me at a pace I was finding difficult to absorb or respond to in an appropriate way. I also understood now why she'd struggled to react positively towards my earlier remark about her knowing what it was like to be a mother.

"To be honest Charlie I was never much one for going to church anyway, and now knowing the two loves of my life are lying cold in its cemetery I find even less reason to go there. I prefer to remember them here at the farm where they lived and were loved." She smiled. "And so, in a rather long-winded answer to your question no, I don't go to St Mark's, but I'm sure if you want to know anything about it or its connection with your family then Joyce will be only too happy to tell you. She gets there around half nine, same as she has for the past four hundred years since the church first opened." Laughing, she added. "Well, to those of us living here in the village it seems as if she's been there all that time anyway?"

Rising from her chair and flattening down her apron with the palms of her hands she smiled contritely at me. "Sorry Charlie, I don't know where all that came from. I apologise for loading my tale of woe on you like that, please forgive me?" She moved back to the draining board and picked up the potato she'd been peeling again. "Now, tell me more about what it is you're hoping to discover here in Sowfield while I get on with cooking this dinner?"

"Perhaps we could talk about that later over tea if that's alright? I really would like to have a quick walk around the village and have a look at St Mark's if you don't mind, even if it's only from the outside for now. I just want to get a feel for the place. It might help as well when we talk later, if that makes sense?"

She laughed again. "Not really, but of course, off you go. And take your time; I can always put this on hold."

I stood up and smiled, relieved to see her spirits had lifted again. "No, that's fine, I won't be long." I glanced out of the kitchen window. "Anyway, another half an hour or so and the sun will be fully behind the hill. I know it won't be dark exactly, but I'd rather begin my search properly tomorrow in the morning light; a fresh start and all that."

"I'll see you soon then." I watched as she placed the freshly peeled potatoes in the saucepan on the cooker. I felt my tummy gurgle. I was ready for something to eat and a good meaty stew sounded the perfect recipe to end the day.

"Thanks Linda, see you later." I moved towards the hallway.

"Here you can go out this way," she countered, pointing to the stable door. "Just lift the latch when you come back, I'll leave it unlocked." She glanced down at Rover who was beginning to stir. "Looks like his lordship's nearly ready for his tea as well; we'll see you when you get back."

Chapter Fifteen

Closing the kitchen door behind me I paused to look up at the hill, noticing the sun beginning its final decent behind it and casting a lengthening shadow across the meadow below. I breathed in deeply, sucking the warm evening air into my lungs as I made my way around the side of the cottage to the front path. As I did so I became aware, once again, of the heady scent from the rambling rose growing around the front door and facia of the building, exhibiting its beauty and fragrance to all who passed by. Closing the garden gate, I turned left and made my way past a row of traditional stone cottages on both sides of the road, each with their own well-tended garden and neatly cut lawn. As I continued down the road, I noticed one or two more recently built houses tucked in alongside the cottages and thought how out of place they looked. "That's progress for you," I mused as made my way slowly towards the church. Behind the houses on my left stood the hill which dominated the horizon for as far as the eye could see apart from the large open meadow spread like a lush green carpet in front of it but that now, in the early fading light, was taking on a darker hue. Although the hill appeared to occupy so much of the surrounding area it did so, not in a threatening way but more, as if it were reaching out to protect the village, watching over it and providing a safe haven for all who lived within its compass. I turned my head both left and right as I walked along the high street glancing, occasionally, into some of the cottage windows, their frames providing little more access to the slowly receding daylight than had been available through those of Meadowfield Cottage. Some of the occupants had turned on their house lights already, furnishing the rooms with a warm and welcoming glow against the onset of dusk and affording me a glimpse of the life lived within. About halfway along the street stood a larger building with a broad frontage and small leaded windows supported in freshly painted black wooden frames. I looked up and saw a sign hanging in front of me, *The Blacksmiths Arms*. This was the pub I'd heard about that might, potentially, have provided me with accommodation had things not worked out with Linda. Stepping forward I looked through one of the windows and noticed a small bar at the back of the room set with a variety of optics behind it. There was a young lady stood behind the bar who was serving a pint of beer to a man sat on a tall wooden stool. He looked like a farm worker of sorts, wearing a jacket made from harsh sack like material and with trousers that were tied around his ankles exposing a pair of heavy-duty boots on his feet. I stepped back and, looking up at the building itself again, made a mental note to ask Linda about its origins as it had more the appearance of a small barn rather than that of a conventional public house. As I continued my way along the narrow street, I noticed the church spire stretching high above the roof tops, up into the evening sky. It held my gaze until, as I turned the corner at the end of the road, I was faced by St Mark's itself. I thought, on first inspection, what a large imposing building it appeared to be and momentarily questioned why a church of this size would have been erected to serve such a small parish and, presumably, its correspondingly small congregation. I then remembered my earlier research which had shown St Mark's initially being built to serve a wider region and community than just Sowfield and its immediate populace. As I moved nearer, I noticed a couple of small cottages standing almost within the grounds of the church itself and reasoned these to be the ones Linda had spoken of where Joyce, the church's secretary, lived. I glanced towards the first cottage as I passed by and immediately became aware of a set of eyes watching me. I turned and smiled at the woman peering at me from her front room window. "That'll be her," I thought and waved in her direction. Clearly undecided as to whether acknowledge my greeting or pretend she hadn't seen me she chose the latter and, retreating from the window, disappeared from view. "See you tomorrow Joyce," I mouthed as I continued towards St Mark's and the large wooden gate standing in front of it. The frame of the gate was attached to a tall wooden post on either side. These in turn were connected to a low brick wall that ran for a few yards in either direction before appearing to meld into a raised grassy knoll that surrounded the church's border as far as the eye could see. Beyond the gate was a pathway leading to the church's main entrance. To the right of the pathway was a low grassed area containing a few gravestones and a well-established oak tree. Set at the base of the tree, beneath its spreading branches, was a modern looking wooden bench. On the left of the path was a more established graveyard set with numerous headstones and memorials to the deceased. This filled an area stretching behind the church and into the distance beyond. As I reached out to open the gate my head began to swim and the ground beneath my feet appeared to move, spinning out of control, coming up to meet me. Falling backwards I threw out a hand to take hold of the gate and steady myself. I stood for a moment, gripping tightly onto the gate post and, breathing in deeply, sought to regain my composure, waiting for the giddiness to pass. As I did so a voice called out to me. My body shuddered; it was the same voice that had visited me on so many other occasions and which, no matter how hard I tried to ignore, was becoming all too familiar to me.

"Help me Charles."

Attempting to rid myself of the words echoing in my subconscious I shook my head and moved away, closing the gate firmly behind me and stepping back into the road. What was happening to me? Was I simply tired after the day's exertions or was I going mad? I paused, continuing to suck the evening air deep into my lungs as I contemplated all that had happened since leaving home earlier that morning. It had certainly been a long day and, whilst I might hold some serious misgivings about what had just happened, the one thing that wasn't in question was that I was indeed both tired and hungry. "Things will look different in the morning," I mused, forcing a smile in an attempt to reassure myself as to the logic of this assertion. Then, having decided my investigations were now complete for the day I turned and made my way back to the safety of Meadowfield Cottage and Linda's stew. Whatever else might be troubling me I was definitely looking forward to a hearty meal as it had been some hours since I had eaten properly? Perhaps this had been the source of my momentary light headedness and associated disorientation? I concluded that whatever the cause, filling my stomach, for now at least, was priority enough.

As I opened the door and entered the kitchen I was immediately comforted by its inviting welcome, along with the enticing aroma of the hot meal being prepared. Although it was summer, with the sun fading a little quicker now, there was still a hint of freshness in the evening air and so it was good to feel the warmth afforded me by the Aga and general ambience of the cottage itself.

Linda had changed and was now wearing a colourful dress that better presented her trim figure which had previously been concealed beneath her working clothes and apron.

"How did you get on?"

Not wanting to revisit my earlier experience at the church gate I smiled and nodded positively. "Great, I think. It seems like a really quaint village; lots of nice cottages and well-tended gardens, although I saw one or two new houses as well."

Linda smiled. "You can't halt progress; at least that's what the Council said when a few of us protested about those particular houses being built. A developer bought that bit of land off Ted Jones. He's a local farmer, or at least he was until he sold up and moved to Sevenoaks to be nearer his daughter. Those two houses you saw are the first of four that are going to be built there. The foundations for the other two are down as well now, so they should be finished by the end of the year; that's what we've been told anyway."

"I suppose that's not too bad considering some of the new housing estates you see around these days?"

"Depends on how you view the changing world I suppose Charlie, and whether you like living in Sowfield as it is, which most of us do I hasten to add."

Realising there were factors here to be considered that I clearly had no understanding of I decided to move the conversation on. I glanced at the table, noticing it was laid out ready for our meal. "Is there anything I can do?"

"No, you're fine thanks, I think I've got it all covered." She smiled. "It's just nice to have someone else in the house to be honest; it gets a bit lonely at times with only Rover for company."

We both looked across to the cat who was now stretched out in prime position on a rug in front of the Aga.

I laughed. "He doesn't seem to be much of a conversationalist either; I think he's been asleep most of the time since I arrived here."

"He won't be happy in a moment when I shift him out of the way. Honestly, the times I've nearly tripped over him with a hot pan in my hands while I'm cooking or serving a meal." She smiled down at the clearly contented and slumbering ball of fur. "Mind, I wouldn't be without him." Looking towards me again she laughed. "Apart from when he brings his little gifts in for me of course that is."

"Little gifts?"

"It's farmland mostly round here Charlie, so there's lots of different places like barns, sheds, and so on for birds, mice, and various other assorted wildlife to make their homes." She nodded towards Rover. "He often brings in some sorry looking furry or feathered creature for me and drops it at my feet as some sort of trophy offering. Sadly, they're quite often still alive, which means I have to put them out of their misery, much to the consternation of Rover here who feels they should be left for him to torment until they either give up the ghost and die out of sheer terror, or because he decides it might be a better idea to eat them."

I felt myself shudder. "Sounds lovely."

"That's nature for you." She laughed again and threw a glance towards the Aga. "Thankfully, the meat in our stew arrived in the more traditional way. We have a great local butcher, Roy, who's been serving the village for years. I keep a few sheep here at Meadowfield, along with a goat or two, mainly to keep the grass down, but once a year I let one of the sheep go to Roy. He kills it for me and joints it up and we do some sort of barter deal instead of me paying him any money." She smiled. "Life's simpler here in the country Charlie, or at least it's meant to be."

I felt a growing sense of warmth towards Linda; she was clearly a lady who had experienced some major challenges in her life but, for all her struggles, had made a go of things and I admired her for that.

I looked on as she moved towards the Aga, reaching out her foot gently towards the cat. "Come on Rover time for you to move." He opened his eyes and looked up as if to say, "How dare you, I was in the middle of a dream." Linda shook her head and nudged him a little harder. "I mean it Rover, move!" The cat, clearly miffed, got to its feet and walked towards the back door. "Let him out will you Charlie? He'll go off and sulk for a while now, or worse bring back one of his half-eaten trophies later for us to admire. I'm never quite sure whether they're meant to be a peace offering or simply designed to get his own back and annoy me?"

I duly opened the door and watched as Rover trotted out without so much as a purr or meow by way of thank you.

"Thanks." Nodding towards hall door she continued. "You go and wash your hands, and this will be on the table by the time you get back."

Making my way up the stairs I reflected, once more, on how fortunate I'd been in chatting with Harry earlier and in him pointing me in Linda's direction.

"A good meal and a proper bed to boot, you've really fallen on your feet here Charlie boy," I mooted to myself as I reached for the light switch in the bathroom. The light flashed on and off momentarily, both surprising me and causing me to blink. As it did so the white painted wall in front of me appeared to melt away becoming more stone like in appearance. I flicked the switch again, this time the light stayed on, illuminating the bathroom once more as it had appeared originally. I shook my head, dismissing the brief vision as a trick of the light, not wanting to accept it as anything else and certainly not as another of my escalating illusory imaginings. As I washed my hands my thoughts turned to Mum once more. It was good to have spoken to her and assured her all was well. I knew she worried about me when I was away so being able to tell her I was safe, well fed, and had a proper bed to sleep in would not only comfort her but also guarantee some peace and quiet for Dad as well.

Making my way down the stairs I felt a fresh wave of excitement run through me. Tomorrow I would be visiting St Mark's and, hopefully, learning more about what had actually happened to my great-great-great-grandfather.

Entering the kitchen, I was greeted by the sight of a large dinner plate groaning with food sitting on the table, the size of which would have fed a small army let alone one young student from Peterborough.

"Gosh that's a plateful," I exclaimed, immediately regretting my outburst, fearing it might be taken the wrong way.

Linda looked embarrassed. "I'm sorry if I've given you too much; just leave what you can't eat. Charlie always liked a big meal in the evening, said he was ready for it after a hard day's work, so I just assumed with the long day you've had and all that travelling you'd be…" She smiled apologetically as her voice trailed away, leaving me feeling even more uncomfortable about my comment and lack of consideration for her feelings when making it.

"No, it's fine really, I am hungry." I laughed and tried to make light of my earlier remark. "I often say the same to Mum when she serves up a big meal, but somehow I always manage to clear my plate, as I'm sure I will do tonight; it looks delicious." Patting my stomach, I pulled out a chair from under the table. "Mum says I'm a growing lad and need feeding up. I think she assumes I don't eat at uni and spend all my money on beer instead of buying the odd meal along the way as well."

Linda laughed. "And do you? Spend your money on beer instead of food?"

I raised my eyebrows and grinned. "Probably more than I should."

"Then think of this meal as my joining forces with your mum and doing my bit to feed her growing lad."

I was pleased we'd been able to deal with my unwarranted outburst in such a friendly way and felt more relaxed as I sat down to face my mountainous plate of food.

"Would you like a drink? I think I've got some wine somewhere?"

"Not for me thanks. I'd love a glass of water though if that's okay. Shall I get it?"

"No it's alright, you stay where you are." I watched as she filled two glasses, placing one in front of me and the other by her plate on the opposite side of the table. "I think I'll join you."

Reaching forward Linda indicated the condiments. "Salt, pepper?"

"Just a bit of salt thanks," I said shaking a little on my food. "Is your bathroom light playing up? It flickered a bit when I turned it on just now."

She shook her head. "No, I don't think so; I put a new bulb in just the other day."

"It'll be me I expect, probably just didn't flick the switch properly."

The next few minutes were spent contentedly doing battle with our meals.

Pausing to take a drink, I was the first to break the silence. "This is delicious, thank you."

"You're welcome. So what else caught your attention in the village?"

I thought for a moment. "I was struck by how large the church was. It seemed bigger than I'd imagined, although I know from my research that when it was built originally it was intended to serve a wider community than just Sowfield."

Linda swallowed her mouthful of food before resting her knife and fork on the side of her plate. "You're not the first visitor to think that Charlie, but, as you say, when it was built St Mark's served a much bigger area than just the village, most of it farming, and dating back to the 13th century and beyond. Ashford is only a few miles down the road and used to play host to regular market days held in the High Street." She laughed. "Not these days of course. I'd like to see them try what with all the traffic coming and going around the town, and with all the shoppers there. But, in those early days farmers and those with smallholdings used to go to Ashford regularly for the market trade and, with Sowfield being nearby, it was decided it would be the perfect location to build a church big enough to serve all those who lived in the area and worked on the land, including those who didn't have regular access to Ashford itself. There's also St Mary's in Kennington. A lot of people living in Ashford in those days would have gone there as well. That was built long before St Mark's though; it dates back to something like the 10th century. Then there's Christ Church but that was built later, around the mid-1800s. And of course, over the years with roads improving and the introduction of motorised transport, cars, buses and the like people were able to travel much further afield, certainly to those other churches if they wanted, all of which means poor old St Mark's has been left with a lot of history but not many visitors. I'm not sure exactly how many they get for a Sunday service these days but, as I said before, I doubt it's more than thirty, and that'll be on a good day, say for Easter or Harvest Festival. Christmas still sees a few more turn up of course. But then again, a lot of people go to church at Christmas don't they, for the nativity and the carols and so on? Charlie and I used to enjoy the Christmas service as well but…" She fell silent momentarily, her expression becoming more sombre. "But not anymore. In fact, I'm not sure I've been inside the church or attended a service there since Charlie died. Like I said earlier, I don't think of him and David as being physically there anymore." She turned her head and glanced around the room. "If they're anywhere they're here with me at Meadowfield, and in here." Tapping her chest, she forced a smile. "Sorry Charlie, I'm not sure where that came from, but we're not the best of friends St Mark's and I, or maybe I should say God and me. After all that's happened, I'm not sure he's all he's cracked up to be."

Unsure how best to respond I just nodded and returned her smile. "You seem to know quite a bit about it though, St Mark's that is; its history and so on?"

"That was Charlie, he knew all about the churches round here, he was a bell ringer, had been for years even before we got married, and not just at St Mark's but all over. He used to go on trips to other parts of Kent with his bell ringing friends, even further sometimes." She laughed. "I used to tease him about it." She paused again taking a long drink from her glass as she embraced the memory. "He loved bell ringing; it was the one thing, apart from working on our land that he truly cared about." She smiled again. "Along with David and me of course."

Taking a break from my food I leant back in my chair. "Never fancied it yourself then, bell ringing I mean?"

"No, it wasn't for me; I didn't share his passion for it, or the church. He had a strong faith my Charlie although he never shouted about it. But I always struggled to find room for God, especially after David died. Charlie said he didn't understand it either but had to believe God had a plan for each of us. He said there would be something we would learn from losing David, something that would make us stronger as a couple. He liked to think David was with God now and said we could take comfort in that." She took a deep breath, tears forming in her eyes. "That was one of the few occasions we disagreed. I said I knew we all had to die at some point but taking our baby at just a few weeks old and ripping apart our hopes for his young life well, I just couldn't see what comfort there was to be had in that..." Her voice trailed away as she reached for her handkerchief.

I allowed her a moment before speaking. "I'm sorry I didn't mean to upset you."

She wiped her face with her hand.

"You didn't upset me Charlie; it's just that sometimes..." She smiled. "It's just that sometimes it comes back and bites me and I struggle a bit, but it's nothing to do with you, really." Sitting upright in her chair she placed her hands on the table in front of her. "So anyway, in answer to your question, no, I've never really been a church goer, Sunday's or any other day of the week come to that, but Charlie enjoyed it, at least his bell ringing, so I just let him get on with it. And as I said before, apart from placing fresh flowers on their graves from time to time I've never really found any reason to go back there, nor wanted to."

I shifted in my seat slightly, loading another helping of carrot onto my fork as I did so. "But you used to go, even if it was just for the Christmas service and the like?"

"Yes, and to watch Charlie ring the bells occasionally." She paused and took another drink. "And to bury them of course."

I didn't want to appear insensitive but was still keen to learn more about St Mark's itself.

"Do you remember much about the church itself, about the inside; what it looks like and so on?"

"Not really, except that it had a lot of old wooden pews in it. When I first went to support Charlie and his bell ringing, we just went in through the main door and then walked through the church to the bell tower. After he'd finished, we came out the back way, out of the belfry entrance. As for the other times I went there, I remember there was a nativity scene around the altar at Christmas, but that had been erected especially for the service." She smiled. "There were lots of children there as well, dressed up as Mary and Joseph and shepherds and so on." Her smile faded. "But as far as going there for the funerals is concerned, well to be honest, I was too upset to notice anything, certainly anything that has stayed with me anyway." She paused, looking at me apologetically. "Sorry, not much help, am I?"

Swallowing a mouthful of mashed potato, I shook my head. "No that's fine, I'll find out for myself when I go there tomorrow."

222

Linda waved her fork in my direction.

"So come on then, tell me more about this family tree of yours and what it's got to do with St Mark's? A former vicar was a distant relation of your mum's wasn't it you said?"

I wiped my mouth and pushed my plate to one side, having demolished at least three quarters of the mountain of food Linda had placed in front of me. "I'm sorry but I can't eat anymore. It was delicious really, but I'm full up."

She smiled at me cautiously, a slight look of hesitancy on her face. "Not too full for a bit of apple pie, I hope? I haven't made it especially though, so don't worry if not. It's the remains of one I started last night but there's still plenty left for us both to have a piece, and I can soon knock up a bit of custard?"

I could feel my bloated stomach urging reason but my head argued otherwise; apple pie was a particular favourite of mine and far too good an offer to refuse. "Just a small bit though, I really have eaten well, thank you."

Linda grinned at me. "You're just like my Charlie when it comes to puddings; maybe all men are the same? You say you're full up but the minute a jam roly poly or apple pie appears you manage to find just enough room to accommodate it."

"Maybe all women are the same as well," I countered. "Mum says the same thing to Dad and me when I'm at home and she serves up one of *her* apple pies."

She laughed again and nodded towards the table. "Tell you what, let's get rid of this lot and give our tummy's a bit of a rest while we talk before we start again, okay?"

"Sounds good to me."

I helped clear the table, placing the plates and cutlery on the draining board ready for washing while Linda prepared the apple pie and custard.

"I passed the Blacksmiths Arms when I was out earlier. I thought it looked more like a bar built in a small barn than a proper pub though. It didn't look very big?"

Linda walked towards the Aga, a saucepan of milk in her hand. "Is real custard alright, I prefer it to the tinned stuff some people have these days, never quite tastes the same to me?"

I nodded my accord. "Couldn't agree more, and the thicker the better if that's okay?" I suddenly remembered I was a guest. "Sorry I didn't mean to –"

Linda interrupted. "No apology necessary, I'm with you on that one. If it doesn't stick to your ribs it isn't real custard that's what I say."

We laughed together as the milk began to warm on the stove.

"The Blacksmiths Arms," she mused, "now that's a story in itself. As I said before, back in the early days Sowfield was a good meeting place for travellers, farmers and the like when they were on their way to Ashford or somewhere further afield in the county, maybe even up country. And, you've got to remember, those were the days of the horse and cart, there were no buses or cars back then, which meant pretty much every village of any size needed its own blacksmith and Sowfield was no different. By all accounts it was very popular with the locals and with the passing trade. It did a lot of business. But as time went on so the demand for horses to be shod and cartwheels to be fixed fell away, so the old blacksmith's forge and home were knocked into one and converted into a pub bearing its name. If you go in there before you leave, you'll see one of the original anvil's still on its stone plinth next to the bar. Some of the locals apparently spit on their hands and slap the anvil on their way out; it's supposed to bring good luck, or so I'm told, although I've never done it myself, so I don't know if it works or not."

I watched as she mixed the custard and milk together in the saucepan creating a thick creamy yellow glue-like substance. "That looks fantastic, just how I like it."

Lifting the pan from the heat whilst still stirring the contents Linda moved towards the table. "And me. Bring the bowls will you Charlie?"

I picked up the two bowls of apple pie from the work service and placed them on the table, attempting to give myself the smaller portion but failing miserably as both were brimming with the delicious looking sweet. I watched as Linda encouraged the thick yellow substance out of the saucepan and onto the pie, covering it entirely.

"There you go, get that lot down you."

I sat staring at the contents of my bowl wondering how I was going to manage to eat it all but determined to give it my best shot; apple pie and custard presented as invitingly as this doesn't come along every day.

Linda took a mouthful of custard and winced. "Oh, that's hot. Better give it a minute Charlie, you don't want to burn your mouth."

I pushed my bowl to one side, relieved to gain another few minutes grace before assaulting my digestive system once more. Leaning back in my chair I smiled inwardly as I stretched my legs out under the table. I hadn't felt this relaxed for some while and, although determined to make the most of my time in Sowfield, I allowed myself to embrace the moment. It hadn't been the best start to a day, with all the rushing to and fro at the various rail stations but as I sat in the warm and welcoming surroundings of Linda's kitchen a deep sense of calm and peace swept over me. I took a deep breath, exhaling slowly and deliberately, allowing the pressure and stress of all the work I'd undertaken in recent months to escape me. Looking towards my generous host I smiled.

"This is great, Linda, I mean really great. You've taken me in and fed me and, well… I just feel really relaxed, so thank you." I laughed. "And thanks again from Mum. Like I said she's really pleased that I've found somewhere safe to stay that isn't a pub, although I can't think why? And, somewhere that is serving delicious homemade food as well, it doesn't come much better than that." I laughed again and waved my hand across the table, gesticulating towards the bowls of apple pie and custard that lay before us. "She'll be thrilled when I tell her about this lot, no alcohol *and* proper food; she'll probably write to thank you personally I should think when I get home."

Linda nodded, acknowledging my compliment. "Thank you, Charlie, but, as I said earlier, this has done me good as well. I think you arrived at just the right time for both of us, you needed somewhere to stay and I needed something, someone, else to focus my attention on apart from just myself and Rover." She smiled wistfully. "It gets lonely here sometimes if I'm honest, and living with only your memories for company is not always a healthy thing to do. I need to remember there's a lot more going on in the world than just my concerns here at Meadowfield, and you've helped me to do that, so thank you as well".

I forced my spoon into the skin now forming on my custard and watched as it broke, allowing the thick creamy mixture below to flow through. My mouth salivated as I placed a spoon laden with apple pie and custard into it. "Mmm, this is delicious."

Clearly touched by my compliment Linda smiled appreciatively as she lifted her own spoon to her mouth. "You're welcome; I'm pleased you're enjoying it."

We sat in silence again for the next few minutes savouring our dessert, the only sounds being heard were those of our spoons clinking as they made contact with their respective bowls. Eventually we both sat back, patting our stomachs.

"I think I've overdone it a bit as well Charlie. I apologise again if I gave you too much?"

I smiled and licked the last of the custard from my spoon. "You did, but I'm certainly not complaining. I do insist you let me wash up though, guest or not."

"Alright but not just yet, let's allow this lot to settle first, then you can wash, and I'll make us both a cup of tea, how does that sound?"

"Perfect, but before we do anything else you must tell me how much I owe you for letting me stay?"

She puffed out her cheeks. "How long will you be here do you think?"

"I'm not sure, possibly two or three days if that's alright? It depends on what I find out at St Mark's tomorrow, and whatever else I might discover while I'm here."

She looked at me and smiled, placing her hands on top of the table again.

"I'll work out the money side of things later if that's okay, and I promise to be fair. As I said earlier you've done me a favour by coming here as well, and a favour given deserves a favour in return, or something like that." She waved her hands in the air as if to dismiss this particular line of conversation. "Anyway, enough of all that, what I want to hear about is the reason you're here in sleepy old Sowfield, and about this family tree of yours, and our vicar who's supposedly related to your mum?"

I took a deep breath and leant back in my chair again. "Okay, if you're sure? It's a bit complicated though." I laughed. "Actually, most things about our family are complicated, but that's another story."

Linda smiled politely; clearly unsure as to the inference behind my comment but presuming, quite rightly, it had been intended as a joke. I decided to start again.

"Okay, I think I told you earlier that I'm studying Genealogy and English local history at Leicester University?"

"Genealogy? That's family history isn't it?"

"Sorry yes, family and social history, that sort of thing."

Linda nodded her understanding.

"And so I thought it would be interesting to focus my research on our own family, well Mum's side of it anyway. I've spent the past few months looking back at the different generations through the various family registers, census results and so on."

"And that's what's why you're here in Sowfield, because this relative of your mum's used to live here?"

"Exactly. And the further back I've gone the more I've been able to find out about those I'm related to, where they lived and what they did. Honestly, it's been really fascinating."

I could feel myself becoming more animated as I gabbled on about my research but was also aware I might be going too fast for Linda.

"Sorry if I'm waffling, it's just that once I'm on a roll I don't know when to stop."

She laughed. "It's fine, I can hear how much it all means to you from the excitement in your voice. Now come on, tell me more about what it is you've discovered about life here in Sowfield and our former vicar. When was it exactly?"

I took another deep breath and smiled. "That's the trouble with being passionate about something, you make the mistake of presuming everyone else not only shares your enthusiasm for the subject but also understands what it is you're wittering on about. Anyway, to answer your question, we're going back to the mid-1800s, 1846 to be precise." I glanced across the table at Linda who was nodding attentively. "It all started when Mum told me about a rumour regarding one of her distant relatives, a vicar here at St Mark's, who'd apparently been murdered. By all accounts the story had been handed down through her family for generations but was regarded more as fantasy and hearsay than as having any real credence. Anyway, I thought it was worth following up and decided to trace her family back that far to see if there were any facts or detail behind the story to substantiate it and, if there was, to try and uncover the evidence to prove it one way or the other. My early research did confirm he'd been killed but nothing really about the particular circumstances of his demise. So that's why I decided to come to Sowfield and see what else I could discover about the old boy, and as to whether he really did meet his end at the hand of some would be assassin."

"So you think your mum's relation was the vicar who was killed then?"

"That's right." I felt a tingle of excitement run through me. "It sounds like you've heard that story as well; do you know anything about it?"

Leaning her head to one side she pursed her lips. "Not really no. I mean yes, I've heard about it, but I've no idea as to what's actually meant to have happened. Like I said, I don't go to St Mark's anymore or have much interest in its history, past or present. Charlie did mention it once though I think, saying there was a plaque or something on one of the walls that spoke about a former vicar who'd been killed, but we didn't talk about it at any length." She shrugged her shoulders. "To be honest the tale about the vicar who was supposedly murdered in the village has pretty much descended into folk lore around here. Everyone seems to have their own version of what did or didn't happen, and the more it's been talked about over the years the wider the boundaries of credibility appear to have been drawn, and possibly exaggerated. I've always considered it as being a bit like the story of the Loch Ness Monster, you know, is it true or just a good story? And like I said, for me, I wasn't really bothered one way or the other." She scratched her head and nodded at me. "That said, it'll be worth you seeking out Joyce tomorrow, she's the fount of all knowledge around here, at least as far as St Mark's is concerned anyway. She'll know what's what and whether there's any real truth to the story or not. She can probably show you the plaque Charlie spoke about as well and give you any background on it." Linda looked directly at me and smiled. "Sorry not to be much help, but at least it sounds as though you're in the right place. And, if it does turn out to be true, then I'll certainly be interested to hear more about it from a real live family relation of the man himself." Placing her hands together she raised her shoulders. "Quite exciting as well to think I might have one of his descendants staying in my house. What was his name again?"

"George Anderson." I felt a fresh wave of enthusiasm wash over me and could hardly wait for morning when the next part of my adventure would begin. "I'll certainly seek out Joyce though, thank you for that."

"If she's not in the church for any reason then you've seen the cottage where she lives so just go and knock on her door and say Linda sent you, and that if she doesn't tell you all you need to know then she'll have me to answer to." She tipped her head back and laughed. "I may not attend church regularly but we get on well Joyce and I, always have done, she's good fun. We often tease one another when we meet up, so she'll laugh if you say that to her."

I grinned back across the table. "Thanks, sounds great."

Linda stretched out her arms in front of her and stood up. "I don't know about you but I'm ready for that drink now?" She moved to fill the kettle. "Tea or coffee did we say?"

Getting to my feet I rolled up my sleeves and moved towards the sink. "Tea I think, and my part of the bargain was to wash up if you remember?"

"I do, but you're a paying guest Charlie, you really don't need to."

I laughed. "I will be when you tell me how much I owe you? Until then I'd really like to help. Anyway, I can hear my mum shouting in my ear to do it, she certainly wouldn't let me off so lightly, paying guest or not."

"Well, alright, but remember, I said I'll dry so you must let me do that at least."

We cleared the table and spent the next twenty minutes chatting generally about all manner of things as we washed and dried the dishes.

"So what's Sowfield like, as a place to live in I mean?"

"It's nice enough." Linda paused holding a plate in her hand. "Actually that's not fair, it's great. I've been really fortunate since Charlie died. Everybody's rallied around to help and support me, and not just as Charlie's widow but as a person in my own right." She smiled. "So let me answer that question again. Sowfield is a lovely place to live, very caring and friendly."

I looked on as Linda finished drying the plate, putting it away with the others. "And I like that, belonging, it gives me a feeling of security." She turned and looked at me, a hint of melancholy in her eye. "Don't get me wrong, I'd have Charlie back in a heartbeat, but I know that won't happen and so if I have to be on my own then…well, Sowfield is a pretty good place to be. It is for me anyway." She wiped her hands on the tea towel. "Now then, that's enough about me, let's get that kettle on and you can tell me more about your research and what else it is you hope to find out about us country yokels here in the village."

We sat talking and drinking our tea by the Aga enjoying the warmth it afforded as evening turned to night and the air outside became a little cooler. Our conversation was friendly and relaxed, and at times I felt as if I were at home talking to Mum, with Linda showing similar genuine interest in both my work and my ambitions for the future.

"It sounds like you've pretty much got everything planned out Charlie, and know what you want to do with your life once you've got this degree?"

"Still a way to go yet, best laid plans and all that. But yes, I hope I can make a difference in the world in some way, if that doesn't sound too grand or pompous?"

Linda leant forward. "Nothing wrong with ambition Charlie, especially when it's focused on achieving the greater good. Another drink?"

I looked at my watch. "Wow, is that the time, it's nearly eleven o'clock, we've been talking for ages. No thanks, I'd better get to bed. What time did you say Joyce arrives at the church in the morning, I don't want to miss her?"

"Nine thirty or thereabouts, and she'll be there for a good couple of hours or so I should think. Or, like I say, you can always knock on her door if she's not at the church for any reason."

We both stood. "Thanks Charlie, it's been good to have you here; I've enjoyed chatting with you. I just hope I haven't bored you too much?"

"Not at all, I've had a great time." I patted my stomach. "And a great meal, thanks again for that?"

"What time would you like your breakfast?"

"Oh please don't worry about that, I'll just make myself a cup of coffee and a piece of toast now I know where the bread is, if that's alright?"

"You will not. I'm not having your mother chasing after me because I didn't look after her son properly." She laughed. "Anyway, I'm normally up by six." She nodded towards the back door. "I've got the animals to feed remember, they don't take kindly to being kept waiting for their breakfast, and I doubt you'll be up by then?"

I felt my face flush red with embarrassment. "I can be if you want; I could help with the animals? What time should I set my alarm?"

Throwing back her head she laughed out loud. "You won't need an alarm clock to wake you we have one outside, his name's Oscar."

Linda laughed again, noticing the look of confusion on my face.

"A cockerel Charlie, Oscar's a cockerel, and there's no keeping him quiet after first light. You certainly won't need an alarm clock here I can tell you. Shall we say breakfast for around quarter to eight? That'll give you a chance to wash and dress while I sort the animals out and then we can eat together before you head off to see Joyce."

"Sounds great." I moved to pick up the mugs.

She waved my hands away in protest and nodded in the direction of the back door again. "Leave those I'll do them. Anyway, I've got to check they're all settled down for the night outside." She smiled. "A mixed blessing having a smallholding at times Charlie. Don't get me wrong, I love having the animals around, but they never seem to understand that you might want the occasional early night or perhaps even a lay in on the odd the morning. And there's Rover of course, although he'll probably stay out for the night sulking because I've got company and he's not the centre of my attention. Normally he'd spend the entire evening in here on my lap enjoying the warmth of the Aga or curled up on the sofa while I read a book in the front room."

I smiled apologetically. "I'm sorry if I've upset your routine?"

"You haven't, not at all, Rover just likes me to himself. Like I say he'll probably stay out now to punish me for bringing someone else into the house.

Between you and me I'm not that bothered, except if he stays away for more than a day or two, then he'll bring me one of those half eaten furry or feathered presents we spoke about earlier as some form of apology for having gone off in a huff and sulking. I swear he's got a human brain inside a cat's body at times."

We both laughed again. "Well, if you're sure? And yes, seven forty-five will be great."

"You go on and use the bathroom and I'll be up as soon as I've finished down here. Goodnight."

We smiled, exchanging, I felt, a mutual sense of warmth and bonding between us.

"Goodnight Linda, and thanks again."

As I climbed the stairs, I suddenly felt tired; it had been a busy day and the large meal coupled with the warmth from the Aga had all served to leave me feeling exhausted and ready for a good night's rest. I cleaned my teeth and headed for my room, undressing quickly and climbing into bed. The sheets felt cool against my skin as I lay on my side, bringing my knees up in the foetal position towards my chest in an effort to warm myself. As I lay there thinking about the day and letting the bedding warm around me, I soon found myself drifting towards that semi-conscious state between reality and the world of dreams.

I'm not sure how long I lay there allowing my thoughts to wander in this way before becoming aware of a sudden and pronounced chill in the air. My eyes were closed but I screwed them even tighter, an instinctive fear gripping me as to what I might see if I dared open them. My heart raced and my body sweat as the very air from my lungs appeared to be sucked from me. I gasped for breath, and as I did so my nostrils were filled with a strange, sweet smell. My body trembled fearfully as the perfume like aroma filled my senses causing my head to spin. As I lay there, still too afraid to open my eyes I heard a voice call out to me; it was the same voice I had heard on numerous occasions in recent weeks, its plaintive and mournful cry all too familiar.

"Help me Charles."

Fighting back the desire to respond verbally and in effort to rid myself of both the voice and the sickly-sweet smell hanging thick in the air I buried my head deep beneath the covers. I brought my knees tight up to my chest once more in some form of vain attempt to comfort and protect myself from this would-be tormentor. I'm not sure how long I lay like this, huddled up, too frightened to open my eyes, but eventually the tension in my body began to dissipate, affording me enough courage to raise my head above the covers once more. Having been cocooned under my bed clothes for so long I sucked in a much-needed lungful of air and was surprised to find it both fresh and clean again, no longer filled with the sickly aroma that had, just a few minutes earlier, so disturbed me. The weighty feeling of dread and oppression had also begun to lift and I opened my eyes, albeit slowly, still fearful as to what I might discover. There was no external light reflected in the room and so it was difficult for me to make out any shapes or other discernible features. Being in the countryside there was also no street lighting to speak of and, with no moon present on this particular night either, there was little in the way of illumination coming through the curtains, all of which meant the room itself was left in almost total darkness.

I lay there for some time gathering my thoughts, uncertain as to what had just happened or, indeed, what to make of it. I began to wonder if, perhaps, I had actually drifted off to sleep and that the events of past few minutes had, in fact, been a simple fabrication of my over tired imagination, a bad dream perhaps, brought about as the result of a long and exhausting day, coupled with having eaten too much? I nodded to myself, deciding to accept this scenario, rather than some other, much darker, possibility. Perhaps, with all that had happened during the past twenty-four hours my poor brain had gone into overload and, as a consequence, was now putting me though the agonies of yet another imagined nightmare experience. Yet for all that, I was still concerned about the pace at which these fearsome visitations were increasing, affronting both my psyche and imagination as they grew in frequency and unexplained detail, and, on each occasion, appearing all the more real to me. As the tension in my body eased and my bed became, once more, a haven of drowsy slumber I encouraged kindly sleep to draw me into its restful embrace.

Chapter Sixteen

As predicted by Linda my early morning alarm call was provided by the enthusiastic crowing of Oscar as he called out not only to me but, from the noise he was making, to the rest of the village as well that it was time to wake up and face the day. I rolled over and looked at my watch. It was almost six o'clock and although the sun was already shining through the split between my curtains it still felt an unearthly time to get out of bed. I turned over and pulled the pillow over my head, attempting to drown out Oscar's overtly cheery welcome to the day.

As I lay there dozing in the warmth and security of my bed I mulled over, in my mind, the events from the night before, along with the strange smell I had imagined filling my senses, also the now worryingly familiar cry for help. Whatever they referred to I was none the wiser come the bright light of day than I had been during the hours of darkness. I continued to allow these semi-conscious reflections to drift to and fro in my head until Oscar's call to rise became so dominant it left me with little choice but to obey. Taking a deep breath, I threw back the covers and swung my feet onto the floor. An early start would do me good I decided, along with helping Linda around the farm with a few chores, if required, before heading off to St Mark's and my planned mission for the day.

After washing and dressing I made my way quietly down the stairs just in case Linda was still in bed but as I opened the kitchen door I realised it was I who had been the last to rise. Linda was standing at the sink with her back to me. She was dressed in a short-sleeved jumper and jeans. I also noticed she was wearing a pair of slightly muddied Wellington boots.

"Morning Charlie," she said without turning. "I said you wouldn't need an alarm clock, didn't I?"

"You were right there." I moved towards the Aga which was already aglow and offering its own particular brand of warming welcome to the day. "Is he always as loud, Oscar I mean? Don't the neighbours complain?"

Linda turned to face me and smiled. "Living in Sowfield Charlie means farmyard animals like Oscar and other early morning risers are recognised as part of the attraction in being a country dweller, not the opposite." She laughed. "Or perhaps not, as appears in your case."

"I wasn't complaining, just saying that's all. We don't get many cockerels in Peterborough, or at least not in Gunthorpe."

Linda reached across the draining board and picked up a small basket. "Well, one good thing about having cockerels and chickens is we also have fresh eggs every morning. How would you like yours, fried, scrambled, or poached?"

"Scrambled sounds great, if that's okay?"

"Good choice."

"What about you, what are you having?"

She laughed again. "I've eaten already. I had some toast earlier after I'd fed the animals and got these eggs. It's an early start on a farm Charlie, well, not a farm exactly but it's still an early start when you've got livestock. Like I said before they don't have the same patience as you and me when it comes to feeding time. They soon let you know if you're running late." She broke a couple of eggs into a bowel and began to mix them. "Tea or coffee?"

"Coffee please." I moved towards her. "Here let me do that you've got enough to be getting on with without running after me?"

"It's fine really, but if you insist you can get a plate and a mug out for yourself, that would be a help, thanks."

I moved to the wall cupboard where we had placed the supper things the night before. "Will you have one as well," I asked, holding a mug in each hand?

"Not just now thanks, I've still got a couple of jobs to do." She smiled as she poured the contents of the bowl into a saucepan and moved towards the Aga. "Perhaps later when you get back from talking with Joyce. You can tell me how you got on and I'll be in a better position to sit down with you for an hour. It's always a bit hectic around here first thing in the morning. One or two slices of toast?"

"Two please. I'll put them on while I'm here," I replied, filling the kettle and reaching across for the bread which had already been placed by the toaster.

A few minutes later I was sitting in front of a plate of freshly scrambled eggs on toast and a mug of hot coffee, its inviting aroma matching that of my breakfast. "Thanks Linda this looks great."

She smiled and moved towards the back door. "Always nice to have a happy customer. I'll be in the barn for a while if you need anything, otherwise I'll see you when you get back."

"Are you sure I can't do anything to help before I go?"

"No, you just worry about yourself. I hope everything goes well with Joyce, give her my best."

I waved my fork in the air. "Thanks, will do, see you later."

Smiling again she closed the door behind her. "What a great lady. I wish Mum could meet her, I'm sure they'd get on." I turned back to my plate and laughed. "They both know how to cook a proper breakfast, so that's one thing they've got in common already."

The next twenty minutes were spent finishing my breakfast and clearing the table. As I washed my plate and mug, enjoying the view from the large window over the sink, I thought through the questions I wanted to ask Joyce about George and his time at St Mark's. It felt strange to be so close to discovering the truth about my former ancestor and what had actually happened to him on that fateful day, and yet by the same token still knowing so little about him or of his life here in Sowfield.

As I closed the back door behind me, I looked across to the barn and saw Linda attacking a bale of hay with a pitchfork.

"Do you need any help with that," I called out moving towards her?

She looked up and put her hand through her hair which had fallen across her face. "No, you're alright, but thanks for asking." Raising the pitchfork in the air she waved it at me. "I'll see you later Charlie."

I waved back and made my way to the garden gate, noticing Rover stretched out nearby in the sun. "I see Rover's back."

Linda smiled and raised the pitchfork in the air again, acknowledging my comment. "Like I said he never stays away for long, and thankfully he didn't bring a present back with him this time either."

I laughed, waving in her direction once more. "Bye, see you soon." As I lifted the latch on the gate I bent down and stroked Rover, running my hand gently across his fur. He opened one eye lazily in response to my attention and reached out his paws in front of him, extending his claws briefly before retracting them again and going back to sleep. "It's alright for some," I thought, stepping over him carefully and closing the gate behind me. Pushing my shoulders back and breathing in the fresh morning air I made my way slowly along the road towards St Mark's. Linda had said not to get there before nine thirty but, even having made my bed and washing up the breakfast things to fill some time, it was still barely eight fifty. I paused to look up at the clear blue sky, broken only by the odd white fluffy cloud which, when passing in front of the sun, caused a brief shadow to fall across the ground. The hill behind Meadowfield Cottage and the other houses looked particularly stunning in the morning light, its endless display of wildflowers blowing to and fro amongst the far-reaching field of green. Together they combined, rippling in the breeze, to create a vibrant multicoloured carpet stretching as far as the eye could see.

As I walked alongside the short row of houses towards the church, I looked to the other side of the road and beyond. In the distance I could see a field of corn waving lazily on the wind with a large tree standing to one side that I presumed had provided much needed shelter for cattle, left there to graze, against the hot summer sun in years gone by. I also noticed a river running through the field which glinted brightly against the morning sun, reflecting its rays towards me. "I wonder if that's a tributary of the Great Stour," I pondered, making a mental note to ask Linda when I got back, "or perhaps even a stretch of the river itself." Pausing for a moment, I embraced the panoramic vista stretched out before me. It was both striking and beautiful. It also felt familiar, but how and why I had no idea? I'd certainly never visited Kent before, let alone spent time in Sowfield? I scratched my head, allowing my thoughts to wander as I considered a number of improbable scenarios. Suddenly my mind was jolted back to reality as a car horn beeped behind me. I turned to see an elderly gent leaning out of his car window as he drove slowly towards me. "You're in the middle of the road young man, do you mind moving out the way?"

Looking around, I noticed I was indeed standing in the middle of the road and quickly moved to one side. "I'm very sorry," I gestured apologetically as he drew alongside me. "I'm only visiting and wasn't sure of the area." He looked at me, a scowl of obvious derision on his face.

"That's as maybe, but I'm sure they have roads where you come from, don't they? Perhaps you walk in the middle of those as well?"

I felt my face colour up. Of course, it didn't matter whether I was a visitor or not, he was quite right, roads were not designed for pedestrians to walk in. I waved another feeble attempt at an apology in his direction as he drove past. "Sorry, I won't do it again."

I watched as he reached the end of the road and slowed down. Holding my breath momentarily I prayed he wasn't going to St Mark's as well. I didn't fancy getting into another disagreement with him whilst trying to impress Joyce at the same time. Thankfully, he turned right just past the church and accelerated slowly away. "Thank goodness," I thought as I made my way down the small high street again, this time sticking firmly to the narrow pavement on one side of the road. Although I'd made the same short journey only a few hours earlier, somehow, the bright morning light created a wildly contrasting ambience to the area than that of the evening before. Then, the sun had been setting, causing very different shadows to fall across the buildings than were cast now in the early light of day. I liked Sowfield, it had a welcoming feel to it, or at least what I'd experienced of it so far apart from, that is, my earlier run in with the elderly motorist a few moments before. I looked at my watch, just gone nine fifteen; perhaps Joyce had made an early start and was already at the church? My pace quickened; a fresh zeal to my step as I headed towards my destination.

Pausing briefly outside the gates, I stood and admired the church's structure and historic design, soaking up the atmosphere and trying to imagine what life would have been like a hundred and forty years earlier when George had been the vicar in residence. It was a large imposing looking building, standing tall against the sky, its steeple and bell tower rising well above the roof and adding a sense of grandeur to its already striking presence. The church itself was constructed of stone blocks, granite like in appearance, and clearly built to last well beyond the years it had already survived. I wondered how many births, marriages, and deaths had been recorded there over the years, and especially during George's time at the ecclesiastical helm. I felt a sense of anticipation, coupled with excitement, run through me as I opened the large wooden gate and took my first steps into a world I didn't yet know, but somehow felt connected to. My mind went back to the brief bout of giddiness I'd experienced the evening before when opening the gate and was grateful that, today, in the clear morning light, both my faculties and life in general appeared to be of a sunnier and more settled disposition.

Walking down the path towards the main entrance, I passed through a broad shadow cast by the large oak tree standing proud and erect in the graveyard. Its branches reaching out protectively like green leaf covered fingers stretching across the graves and headstones below them. I pondered how long the tree had been there, presuming it to be some years even before dear old George had been the vicar, considering its height and girth. Pausing again to take in the tree's grandeur I walked across the grass to the wooden bench sited beneath it. It was, as I had suspected previously, a more recent addition to the graveyard with its angular frame and modern contemporary design. There was a small metal plaque attached to the back of the seat that glinted in the sun's rays as they darted intermittently between the tree's leaves and branches, wafting gently to and fro on the warm summer breeze.

In memory of Francis Granville, much loved friend and servant of this Parish. 1892-1978. Now resting with his Lord.

"Eighty-six when he died. George had already been gone forty-six years before he was even born," I said to myself, having worked through the dates in my head. It made me realise how far back I was travelling in an effort to trace this particular member of our family tree. I sat on the bench for a moment, considering how many others had done the same thing over the years when paying their respects to a loved one buried here and reflecting on their life. Maybe Linda had sat here herself crying out to God in frustration at her loss after burying David and Charlie? The seat was perfectly positioned to offer a more extensive view of the river opposite and of the field stretching beyond into the distance. I looked again at the large tree set to one side of the field, reasoning it also to be an oak, similar to the one I was sitting under now; its thick, leaf covered branches reaching out and offering relief to all who sought refuge beneath them. As I sat there, soaking up the atmosphere and delighting in the panoramic view set before me, I was struck, once again, by the sensation of having observed all of this before; but how and when? Then it came back to me. This was the same scene I had witnessed in my dream at home. The only difference being, on that occasion, I'd been positioned on the opposite side of the river, walking through the field and looking across towards the church. A shudder of unease ran through me. I scratched my head in almost disbelief at how clear and similar the topography was, not only in the here and now but also in my memory. Every detail was as I remembered it from that dream apart from the church bell which, for now, remained silent. I stared ahead, lost momentarily, in a haze of bewilderment and confusion. How could all of this appear so familiar when, until a few short months ago, I had never heard of Sowfield, let alone spent any time here? Was I hallucinating again, or was this real? In an effort to rid myself of the growing sense of alarm that was tightening its grip around me, I closed my eyes, breathing in slowly and deliberately. "Come on Charlie boy, there's got to be a reasonable explanation for all of this." I sat listening to the sound of the leaves rustling gently to and fro on the breeze in the branches above me, praying the very real sensation of panic I was experiencing would pass. Suddenly, I was jolted back into the moment by a different and much louder, noise. It was the church bell ringing out from the tower to my left. A shiver of dread ran through me as my worst fears were realised. Now, with the bell tolling out its declaration from above, the detail of my dream was complete.

I stood up and moved slowly towards the church, all earlier feelings of confidence and excitement, as to what I might discover, now replaced by a growing sense of uncertainty and foreboding. Also, Linda hadn't mentioned the bell would be rung this morning but, then again, why should she if it were a regular occurrence? I doubted though it would be Joyce's job or responsibility to ring it, so perhaps there would be someone else there as well. On the positive side, if there was, maybe they would also know something about the history of St Mark's or, even better, George himself. Deciding that any information I could find out, from whatever source, would be useful, I continued towards the large wooden doors that stood at the main entrance to the church itself. The handles were round and made of brass, connected to a heavy latch that clunked open as it turned in my hand. I felt the air cool as I stepped out of the sunshine into what appeared to be some form of vestibule or antechamber set between the outside world and another door a few feet beyond, leading into the main building itself. As I closed the outer door behind me, I noticed two slits in the stone wall on either side, permitting only a small shaft of light to enter this lobby style area. I thought how much better it would have been to have left the main door open and allow the full brightness of day to fill the space. It would also offer a more welcoming feel to the church for other visitors and more regular attendees alike.

Taking hold of a similar, large, rounded handle in the door ahead of me, I turned it slowly and heard the clunk of yet another latch lifting from its rest on the other side. The door creaked as I pushed it open and I instinctively put my finger to my lips as if to silence it. On first sight I concluded Linda had been correct in saying the church had been erected originally for a much larger congregation than could possibly be met by those living exclusively in the village itself, with the interior proving equally as large and capacious as the outside. I stepped over the base of the door frame and onto the stone flooring below, the noise from my shoes echoing around the church as they met with the ground. There were a number of beautiful stained-glass windows set high in the walls around me, each one drawing on the bright morning sun to reflect its part in the bible story through a myriad of colour and corresponding scriptural verse. I looked to my right; there were the two rows of wooden pews Linda had spoken of. Between them lay a walkway made up of large grey flag stones set top to bottom in a diamond effect. There were several padded cushions placed along the base of the pews, each one colourfully decorated with a variety of religious narrative stitched into them ready for the congregation who would use them during Sunday services to kneel and pray on. To my left were more pews and beyond them a particularly long stained-glass window, depicting Christ on the cross. Directly in front of the pews was the main altar. Approximately six foot in length, it had an ornately patterned length of fabric spread across its surface, seemingly, constructed from some sort of gold coloured thread and bearing four short green tassels, one at each corner of the cloth's edging. In the centre stood a gold cross approximately two foot in height. To the left of the altar was a decoratively carved stone font, and to its right a short set of stone steps built out from the wall leading up to the pulpit. This was made of wood and presented an intricate display of carvings set about its frame and surround. I stood for a moment admiring the history of the space around me along with its shape, design, and architecture. There would have been no modern technology to help with its original planning or construction all those years ago, and yet each stone and the manner in which it had been positioned, along with the wooden beams and their intricate carvings, appeared to have been created with an eye for detail that would put many a modern architect's plans and drawings to shame. Looking around me I noticed a small wooden door immediately opposite which I presumed to be a side exit from the church, or perhaps a stairway leading up to the belfry Linda had spoken of? As I stood there, absorbed in reflection and the splendour of my surroundings, I became aware the bells had stopped ringing. The stillness that remained was one that went beyond the simple silencing of the noise and clamour from the outside world. There was a peace about this particular calm that seemed to transcend the sometimes-muted hush of our daily, and traditionally, busy lives; appearing rather to offer a deeper sensation of tranquillity, almost on a spiritual level. A tangible feeling of serenity washed over me, along with a quiet within my heart I hadn't experienced in a long time. I felt entirely relaxed. It was though I'd been brought to Sowfield, and more especially to St Mark's, for a reason, the purpose of which I was yet to discover, but the very fact I had obeyed the call to come was, for now, enough. Little did I know the next few minutes and hours beyond would shatter this ephemeral feeling of wellbeing forever.

I paused to embrace this newfound sense of peace within me, watching as the calming ambience of the sun glinted playfully through the stained-glass windows, throwing alternating shafts of light and shadow across the pews and walls. Suddenly, my carefree thoughts were interrupted by the sound of the small door closing from the opposite side of the church. I looked across to see a short, slightly balding, man wearing a black cassock walking towards the altar. Unsure whether to speak, or what to say if I did, I coughed, the sound echoing around the church walls. The man turned to face me and smiled.

"Good morning. Forgive me, I didn't see you there."

I smiled back and walked towards him. "Sorry, I didn't mean to disturb you. I was just admiring the church and –"

He interrupted me with another broad smile and a wave of his hand. "You didn't disturb me lad, it's nice to see you here. Visitors are every bit as welcome within these walls as are the regular congregation and village community."

We stood, in silence, looking at each other, neither quite sure how to proceed. He was a ruddy looking character, small in stature, but with a ready smile and welcoming manner that immediately warmed me towards him. Although clearly not yet middle aged, his long black cassock, reaching down to the floor and covering his shoes, along with his bushy sideboards, thick dark eyebrows and thinning hair still provided him with the appearance of an older man. I presumed him to be the vicar, noticing the small white clerical tab inserted within the collar of his cassock.

He put out his hand to greet me which I readily accepted and shook firmly.

"I say visitor because I don't believe I have seen you here before. Forgive me though if I am mistaken in that assumption." He nodded, gesticulating towards my sweatshirt and jeans. "Although I think I would remember a young man dressed as you are. This must be a fashion yet to reach us in Sowfield." He laughed. "We are a little behind the times in the village, or at least that is what my dear wife tells me anyway. She loves to read about the busy and colourful existence of those living in London and elsewhere around the country." Looking directly at me he patted the front of his cassock. "I on the other hand am content

241

with a quieter life and more traditional style of dress." He laughed again. "Although Sowfield does offer its own brand of excitement on occasion. That is, if you consider our May fair and autumn harvest supper as reason for high jinx and celebration."

I smiled to myself, looking down at my slightly faded navy sweatshirt, and wondered what he would make of Duran Duran and Boy George if he imagined me to be an eighties style guru?

He shook his head apologetically. "I'm sorry lad, here I am wittering on and I haven't yet asked what it is I can do for you? That is presuming you are not simply seeking sanctuary or, perhaps, a time of quiet personal reflection with God, in which case I will leave you to your thoughts and prayers?"

"No, I'm not here for that, although I do think the church is lovely. I was actually hoping to meet Joyce. Linda Wells told me I might find her here? I'm staying with Mrs Wells for a few days."

He took a step back, a look of confusion descending on his face.

"Joyce? I'm sorry I don't believe I know anyone of that name, unless she is also a newcomer to the village and I haven't yet had the pleasure of meeting her?" He smiled again. "However, I would feel that to be highly unlikely here in Sowfield; news of any recent arrival spreads around the village in no time." Laughing openly, he continued. "There are few secrets kept here, and even less from Seth Thompson, very little evades him."

"Seth Thompson?"

"Our local Blacksmith. Anyone on first arriving in the village tends to find their way to Seth's to get their horse bedded down for the night or, perhaps, shod for the next stage of their journey." He laughed again. "Once he has finished interrogating them, the rest of the village get to know their business in no time. We all love him dearly, but everyone knows if you want to keep a secret don't tell it to Seth or it will be common knowledge faster than it takes to print it in the Kentish Gazette."

It was my turn to feel confused. Perhaps I'd misheard Linda when she'd spoken about Joyce earlier. I tried gain.

"I'm sorry, maybe it's me that's got it wrong, but I'm sure Linda said the lady's name was Joyce. She's the church secretary and warden?"

He smiled at me again. "I am not sure what a church secretary is exactly, and as for a church warden well, I undertake most of the duties required to be fulfilled here at St Mark's. We may have a large building, but we don't have as many visitors as we used to, or might like, not with Ashford growing so quickly and with the new roads and highways being built. People are travelling to other churches in the area to worship these days I'm afraid. There is St Mary's in Kennington for instance. That has become quite popular of late with some of those who used to attend worship here. As I said, it is so much easier to travel there these days and of course the church itself has such a wonderful history, having been established long before St Mark's." He looked around and smiled. "I wouldn't change places though, beautiful and historic though it may be. I love this church and all it means to those who choose to worship here, even if they are fewer in number these days." Dropping his head, he stared down at the floor in silence for a moment. Then, looking up again, he smiled apologetically. "I'm sorry lad I shouldn't have said all of that, I must have sounded ungrateful for God's bounty to us and..." He shook his head. "Anyway, in answer to your question, I'm afraid we don't have anyone by the name of Joyce attending here at St Mark's. Are you sure you have the right church?"

I was beginning to feel even more bemused, not only regarding the detail of the conversation I had had earlier with Linda but now, rather, about my own sanity. What was this well-meaning, yet clearly confused, individual before me talking about? A blacksmith called Seth Thompson. I knew for certain there hadn't been a blacksmith in Sowfield for many years. The Blacksmith's Arms public house stood testimony to that fact little more than a hundred yards down the road. And more over, I was still sure Joyce *was* the lady Linda had spoken about. Yet here I was being told, in no uncertain terms, there was no one by that name employed at the church, nor, it appeared, living anywhere in or around the village. I took a deep breath.

"Look, I'm really sorry if I've got my wires crossed here, perhaps we could start again?"

"Wires crossed? I am not sure I follow you?" I could tell from the expression on his face he was as equally perplexed as I was.

I took a slow deep breath, arranging my thoughts as I did so. "My name is Charles Benton, although everyone calls me Charlie." I realised, even in making this simple statement, I was muddying further the already murky waters between us. "I live in Peterborough and am a student at Leicester University studying Genealogy and English local history; learning about the landscape, family heritage, that sort of thing." I could see he wasn't following my line of conversation at all, let alone understanding any of it, but I decided to keep going all the same. "As part of my course work, I'm researching my Mother's family tree, hence the reason for my coming to Sowfield. Apparently, my mum's great-great-grandfather was the vicar of St Mark's, and so I've come down here to find out more about him."

A growing look of uncertainty and confusion spread across his face as he leant his head to one side and ran a finger around the collar of his cassock.

"I'm not sure I understand very much of what you have just said, if at all any of it but, we are indeed standing in St Mark's Church in Sowfield and so, as far as that part of your story goes, here at least we share some common ground. Do you know the name of the vicar you have come to enquire out about? Perhaps I can help you there. I am quite well versed in the history of the church going back many years." He smiled assuredly. "History has always been a favoured subject of mine."

We may not have been entirely on the same wavelength but at least I was in the right place and, I assumed, if I told him about George, he may just be able to point me in the right direction.

"His name was George Anderson. He was the vicar here until 1846 when he was…"

I stuttered to a halt as my partner in conversation staggered to one side, reaching out a hand to grasp the side of the altar in an attempt to steady himself.

"Are you alright?"

He moved towards an adjacent pew. "I…I think I need to sit down." I took his arm and moved to sit beside him as he eased himself onto the hard-wooden seat. He looked down, his hands coming together as his body slouched forward and shivered involuntarily. Then, without raising his head, he spoke in a gentle but uneasy tone.

"I am George Anderson."

I stared in disbelief at the back of his head. "I'm sorry?"

"*I* am George Anderson; the individual you say you are seeking. I am the vicar here at St Mark's." I watched as he slowly lifted his head and turned to look at me. "I am not sure what it is you want here young man, but if this is another attempt to unnerve me or to steal from our church again then I suggest you –" I interrupted.

"Unnerve you, steal from the church? I'm sorry I don't know what you're talking about, but I can assure you the last thing I want to do is to steal anything from you."

His gaze of doubt and wariness towards me held firm.

"Look, clearly I've said something to unsettle you, upset you even, and…and for that I apologise."

We sat motionless, staring at each other, both hostage to our befuddled thoughts and shared uncertainty of the other, neither knowing how we had arrived at this place and, more pertinently, wondering how to move on without creating further mistrust between us. As we sat there, each committed to his own, ostensibly surreal, version of events I was struck by the sense of having met with him before; more even, that I knew him in some way, but how and where?

Suddenly it hit me and, gasping audibly, I gripped the back of the pew in front of me. I *had* seen him before, his balding head and thick sideburns standing out in my memory. This was the man who, lying on my bedroom floor all those weeks ago, had reached out, seized at my leg, and begged me to help him. But how could that be; that had surely been a dream, a hallucination; this couldn't be real, he couldn't be real?

"You can't be George Anderson," I stuttered. "Look, I don't mean to be rude, but I think one of us is losing the plot here, and whilst I am quite happy to accept it may be me, George Anderson died in 1846 and…"

His demeanour changed becoming curt, even abrupt. "We are in the year 1846, and I assure you young man that I am very much alive." He stood up and looked down at me, his expression now a mixture of assumed authority and palpable scepticism.

"We have endured a few visits from individuals such as yourself in recent weeks, telling untruths about life here at St Mark's, sowing seeds of suspicion and uncertainty about my ministry. I have no doubt, as before, your fabrications are designed to distress me, even persuade me to leave the church, but they will not work; I will not be driven away. I am not sure who is behind these terrible lies but what I do know is that you, and others like you, will not succeed. Nor will you gain possession of any more treasures from this wonderful building. They are held in safe keeping and will stay that way until I am sure these threats towards me, my family, and the security of St Marks are passed. Do I make myself clear?"

I sat looking at him, my mind now beyond all rationale. I felt tears of fear and confusion sting my eyes.

"I really don't know what you're talking about. I've never stolen anything in my life. Well, apart from fifty pence I took from my mum's purse when I was seven to buy some sweets, but I felt so guilty that I gave her the sweets as an apology for what I'd done." I smiled limply at him in the hope of lightening the mood between us, but to no avail. "Look, whoever you are, my name really is Charles Benton and I do live in Peterborough. I'm twenty years old and I've come to Sowfield as part of the research I'm doing into my family's history, and to find out about my great-great-great-grandfather George Anderson." I looked at him again hoping for some sign of a softening in his attitude towards me and acceptance that what I was saying might be true, but none was forthcoming on either front.

"I can prove it to you," I said, reaching into the back pocket of my jeans and taking out the small notebook I'd brought with me to jot down any relevant information I might have gleaned during my visit to the church. I flicked through the first few pages. "Here look." I pointed to my notes. "George Anderson, husband of Elizabeth and father of Thomas Anderson." I looked up at him. "If you really are George then you're thirty-two years old and Elizabeth is twenty-four. The two of you were married in 1844 and you were the vicar of St Mark's here in Sowfield until 1846 when you…" I felt my mouth dry as I considered the impact of what I was to say next.

"When, you were killed by thieves' intent on robbing the church and…" I stopped, realising that far from convincing this gentle man of my true intentions, I was in fact adding credence to his earlier accusation of my being physically involved with the very gang he was alluding to. I looked up expecting another verbal lashing from him in response to what I had just said but, instead, watched as he sat down next to me again, his expression softening noticeably as he did so.

"I still don't know who you are young man, other than you claim your name to be Charles Benton. Nor do I understand how you appear to know so much about Elizabeth and I when, clearly, neither of us has ever met before. However, I am prepared to listen to what it is you have to say; only please do not refer to me as having been killed again as I am clearly alive and in good health sitting here before you, as you can plainly see."

I smiled and shook my head, grateful for the apparent truce between us, although remaining utterly confused as to the conversation and situation I found myself party to. "Thank you, but why are you happy to hear what I have to say now? What's made the difference in how you viewed me from just a few moments ago?"

He raised his hand to his mouth, coughing lightly to clear his throat. "My dear wife has recently given birth to our son; just over three weeks ago to be exact." Pausing to catch his breath, a tear formed in his eye. "I nearly lost her during the birth. There were complications, and it is only through the grace of God and the power of answered prayer that she survived. I confessed to her after the child was born I had thought she might die and, that in allowing such fear to take hold of me, I had failed both her and God. I…"

I watched as, overcome by emotion, he leant forward, a solitary tear falling from his cheek to the stone flooring below. Reaching out instinctively I squeezed his arm to comfort him. My mind was still racing but I couldn't deny my humanity, nor the urge to console him. Recognising my intent, he placed his hand on my own. "Thank you, Charles."

I sat in silence, watching as he took out a grubby piece of cloth from his cassock and wiped his eyes. I waited patiently as he sat, head bowed for a few moments, as if in prayer, until he felt able to speak again.

"Elizabeth assured me that I hadn't failed her or God but had simply shown myself to be human in allowing such doubt to take hold, no matter how brief that moment of weakness. She reminded me God is greater than my doubts, and that He had indeed answered my prayers by allowing both her and our child to live." Moving to sit upright he pushed his shoulders back and, turning to face me, looked directly into my eyes. "And *this* is the reason I am prepared to listen to you Charles." Taking a deep breath, he continued. "Elizabeth and I have, only this morning agreed on a Christian name for our son. Since he was born, we have wrestled between choosing to name him after the great apostle Paul and Jesus' disciple Thomas, eventually deciding on the latter. In part, this was to remind us, whilst doubt and fear are indeed an element of our humanity God is greater than our fears and often-misguided belief that He is unable to achieve all that may appear, to us, as impossible. As you may be aware it was the disciple Thomas who doubted the Lord Jesus had actually risen from the grave following his crucifixion. He said he would not believe until he saw, for himself, the scars on his Saviour's hands and feet made by those cruel nails which had so viciously torn against his flesh." A gentle smile spread across his face. "And, since that time, the world has referred to him as doubting Thomas." He squeezed my arm. "No one could possibly have known of our decision to call our dear son by that name other than God himself, as we have yet to speak of it to anybody but the Father. And so, because of that fact I have to believe therefore you have been sent here for a purpose although, as of yet, I have no idea what that purpose may be? But, in holding onto the belief that God knows better than me, I am prepared to listen to what it is you have to say?"

I took a deep breath. I may have considered myself to be many things but a messenger from God was certainly not one of them.

"Listen, I'm really pleased that your wife and your son survived but as for me being sent on some holy mission…well, I really don't know how to respond to that." I paused trying to frame what I would say next in a way that would neither upset nor offend him, whilst equally recognising I couldn't let this inconceivable line of conversation continue unchallenged.

"I'm really sorry, but I'm finding this whole scenario bizarre to say the least." I pointed to the door. "I walked in here five minutes ago expecting to talk to the church secretary, a lady called Joyce, about a distant relative of mine who used to be the vicar here a hundred and forty years ago as part of the research I've been doing into my family tree and, instead, I run into you. Now, I'm not exactly sure who you are, or what it is you do here at St Mark's, but what I am pretty sure of is that you cannot possibly be my great-great-great-grandfather. I mean think about it…" I shook my head, struggling to verbalise my incredulity further.

He placed his hands together in front of him as if in prayer and looked at me; his face taking on a softer and more considerate expression.

"I am also finding our conversation more than a little strange Charles, but I can assure you I *am* George Anderson, vicar of this church and parish." He parted his hands and reached out towards me.

"I am also not sure what year you think this may be but, once again, I can assure you, we are indeed sitting here together in the year of our Lord 1846."

We sat staring at each other, neither of us doubting the other's sincerity or integrity but, rather, their grip on reality. I knew for myself what I was saying to be true but, within that sense of assured knowledge, a seed of doubt still lingered. I couldn't deny he looked like the man who had appeared in those earlier visitations and dreams I'd experienced over recent weeks and, up to now, had so readily dismissed. Perhaps I was asleep now and this was yet another dream from which I would awaken momentarily, finding myself safe and warm once again beneath the covers of my bed at Meadowfield Cottage. Or perhaps, I was experiencing some form of breakdown brought about through the associated stress of my studies and increasing workload. Whatever else was going on, the one thing I did know for certain was, this could not be 1846 and the man opposite me could not be George Anderson, of that at least I could be sure. I decided to play him at his own game for a while and see what happened. After all, if this were a dream, I would soon wake up and be able to move on.

As I sat there, deciding how best to proceed, he spoke again, breaking the silence between us.

"Why don't you come home with me Charles and meet Elizabeth and Thomas for yourself? We can continue our conversation there over something to eat and drink if you would like? Perhaps some refreshment will help settle your mind a little."

I wasn't sure of his intention in making this offer but recognised immediately that, if I did accept, as soon as we stepped outside the church his story would evaporate into the very thin air on which it was obviously founded.

"Thank you, I would like that."

He rose from his seat and removed a set of keys from the white, rope like, cord tied around his waist. "I will lock the front door before we leave; we can go out through the side entrance next to the belfry. As I said to you earlier Charles, sadly, there are those who wish us ill here at St Mark's, and yet others who would seek to make financial gain by stealing directly from the church itself." He nodded in the direction of the altar. "That cross has stood there for almost two hundred years. It is one of the few treasures not to have been secreted away but left for the enjoyment of the congregation and to the glory of God himself. It was a gift from Sir Edward Barnham who attended the church along with his family in the late 1600s. He owned much of the land in and around Sowfield at the time and provided work for many who lived in the village, as well as those from further afield."

I smiled. "It looks very grand and well suited to its position on the altar. Is it real gold?"

"It is. There are those who say we should sell it and give the money to the poor. But others, and I am one of them, argue that the solace and spiritual comfort it provides to those who worship here is far greater than any monetary value it may have, accepting it to be considerable." He turned to look at me. "And there are others yet again who, as I said, would simply want to steal it and sell it for their own personal gain. At least, in having spoken to you, I am now assured that is not *your* intention as I had earlier feared it might be."

I watched as he moved towards the large wooden doors at the front of the church; the heavy clunk of the key resonating around the building as he turned it in the lock.

"Are you ready?" He motioned towards the side door.

"Yes." I rose from my seat and followed him across the floor. On reaching the side door he opened it and stood back a little. "After you."

As I stepped into the sunshine and stared at the scene before me I felt my heart falter and the breath escape from my lungs. The road that led along the high street from Meadowfield cottage had gone. In its place was a mud track marked with the imprint of horses' hooves and a series of deep thin lines, presumably, made from the wheels of horse drawn carriages, one of which stood by the entrance to a cottage just a few yards from the church. I staggered backwards and reached out my hand, placing it on the wall to stop myself from falling over.

"Are you alright, Charles?"

"Yes, I'm fine," I replied. "The sun caught me unawares and unsteadied me for a moment." This was the first thing I could think of to say as I attempted to conceal the shock and surprise which had gripped me so profoundly when first stepping out from the church. In truth, it had been much more than the simple show of sunlight that had overwhelmed me. I felt my heart race as I concluded this was not a dream but very real.

Could I really be standing in the grounds of St Mark's Church in Sowfield in 1846, a hundred and forty years earlier than I had less than half an hour ago? My mind swam as I tried to make sense of what I was experiencing. A number of the other houses I had seen earlier located along the road were now missing as well; instead, open fields and grassland stood in their place. The majestic hill and meadow behind the church still provided the same glorious backdrop but was now more random in appearance, occasionally wild and overgrown; gone was its earlier softness and uniform rhythm of movement with the grass swaying to and fro against the warm summer breeze. As I looked along the row of cottages that still existed, I noticed the sign advertising the Blacksmith's Arms was also missing from its staging. In its place hung a wooden board detailing the cost of repairs to carriages, the shoeing of horses, and a variety of other services provided by, *Seth Thompson, Blacksmith and Ironmonger for the village of Sowfield.*

Through the fog in my brain I heard a now familiar voice call out to me. "Are you sure you are alright, Charles, you look very white? The colour has quite drained from your face."

I pushed myself away from the wall, shaking my head gently in an effort to clear it from the increasing sense of panic and confusion that was now gripping me; also, in the hope of returning it to the world I knew and which, until a short time ago, I had been a willing and active participant in.

"I…I don't know what to say. None of this was here earlier when I arrived, it was all very different."

I felt an arm move around my waist. "Come along lad let's get you home, you've obviously had a shock of some sort and are not thinking too clearly. I'm sure a warm drink and one of Elizabeth's scones will soon have you feeling better."

We walked along the path to the main entrance of the church and out through the gate onto the rough ground beyond. This in turn led to the mud track, which was now, apparently, the main thoroughfare for all those travelling both in and out of the village. As we walked together, I glanced back at the graveyard. It had also changed in appearance and now contained approximately half the number of headstones than had been there previously. Also, the large oak tree I had admired earlier was now little more than a sapling, its young leaf covered branches reaching out as a child might, stretching out its arms, anticipating the growth of future life to come. As my thoughts tumbled to and fro attempting to make sense of what was happening my companion spoke up again.

"It's not far Charles, this way."

Attempting a smile, I looked across to him, desperately praying this illusion would end and that I might be returned to the reality of the life I had known less than an hour ago. "Thanks; I'm just feeling a bit confused. I'm sure I'll be okay in a minute or two."

"The fresh air should help." Nodding towards me he added, "You've got a bit of colour coming back to your cheeks which is comforting to see."

Not wanting to focus on my increasing confusion any more than necessary I attempted to change the topic of conversation. "Sowfield is lovely." I pointed towards the hill. "You've got some great views."

"Yes, we are lucky to live in such a beautiful setting; I never tire of it, nor do I take it for granted." He smiled broadly. "God has truly blessed Elizabeth and I in allowing us to serve Him in such wonderful surroundings."

We hadn't covered more than a hundred yards when we stopped outside a rough wooden gate leading to a stone cottage that I recognised from my walk the evening before.

"Here we are, Charles." I looked on as he opened the gate and beckoned me in. "This way, lad."

Whilst I was familiar with the house, I didn't recognise it as being the manse. It appeared too small to be the home of the vicar and his family, especially when considering the size of the church and the community it had been built to serve originally. In keeping with the other traditional stone-built cottages dotted around the village it had only small leaded windows set into its walls, along with stained wooden beams stretching across the frontage of the roof and down the sides of the building.

As we walked the few yards to the front door I allowed myself a smile, thinking how much Mum would have liked this miniature cottage garden along with the flowers and vegetables that were growing happily alongside each other.

George took the latch in his hand and, lifting it, pushed open the weathered wooden door as he did so. "Please, come in Charles."

I followed him into a dark lobby area that offered little in the way of light once he'd closed the front door, apart from a single shaft of sunlight escaping through an open door at the other end of the house. I noticed two other doors, one on either side of the hallway as we made our way towards the light. These were both closed and therefore did nothing to alleviate the general gloom of the passageway itself. As we entered the room at the far end of the hall my nostrils were immediately greeted with the welcoming smell of freshly baked bread.

"Ah, it appears you have arrived on a good day Charles, Elizabeth makes particularly good bread. She may even have baked a cake." He looked at me and laughed. "I am a man twice blessed Charles. My stomach is well fed by my loving wife and my soul is equally well nourished by the love and word of God." He nodded as if to confirm his statement. "Yes, I am indeed a man truly blessed."

As he was speaking, I looked around the room and felt another shudder of fearful recognition run through me. I had seen all of this before, or at least the stone flooring and walls. My mind went back to the evening at home in Gunthorpe a few weeks previously when I had gone into the kitchen and the light had failed briefly. In that moment I had seen the very same wall I was now looking at projected before me and, no matter how fleeting that vision may have been, there was no mistaking, in my mind, that I had stood on this very spot at least once before, if not physically then in some other supernatural way. For now, I acknowledged this as being a detail beyond my ability to comprehend. But, even in accepting that, it still felt entirely real to me.

My initial sense of panic as to what had transpired in St Mark's earlier was beginning to dissipate as I too began to feel, like George, that perhaps I *was* here for a reason; but as to what that might actually be, I was still a long way from discovering or understanding. As I stood there trying to make sense of all that had happened in the last hour or so my concentration was broken with the sound of the back door opening. A pretty young woman entered, looking a good few years younger than George. She was dressed in a long black skirt that all but reached the ground with only the toes of her shoes visible beneath it. She also wore a thick cream blouse with a high frilled collar buttoned around her neck which looked rather stiff in appearance. A slightly stained white apron trailed from her waist down towards the hem of her skirt. Her auburn hair, swept into a bun on the top of her head, looked full and thick. Although tidy, there were locks that had come loose and were hanging limply by the side of her face. Noticing her husband was not alone, she put her hand to her head, pushing these strands of hair behind her ears in an effort to tidy her facial appearance. Clearly surprised and more than a little embarrassed to be greeted by the sight of a stranger in her kitchen she turned to George.

"George dear, you didn't say we were to expect company, I would –"

He interrupted her with a loving smile and wave of his hand.

"Elizabeth my dear this is Charles Benton, and no, we weren't expecting him so please don't worry yourself on that count. I found him in the church a short while ago and…well." He turned to me. "I hope it is alright if I say this Charles?" I forced an awkward smile, unsure of what it was he was about to divulge but trusting it not to be derogatory.

"My dear, the poor boy appears a little confused." He smiled at me. "Is that reasonable for me to say?"

We may not have been able to reach agreement on the detail of our stories to date, nor as to the circumstances on which they were founded, but I certainly couldn't disagree with his assumption that I was confused. I nodded meekly in response.

"I invited him home for some refreshment my dear along with, perhaps, one of your delicious scones. I trust that is acceptable to you?" He lifted his head a little. "Although, if I am not mistaken there may be something even more appetising we can provide him with. Is that not one of your wonderful loaves of bread I can smell?"

She laughed, wiping her hands down the front of her apron as she did so.

"You know very well it is, George." She turned to me. "And of course, you are welcome to share whatever we have Charles, freshly baked bread included."

I liked her immediately and, returning her smile, offered my hand. "I'm very pleased to meet you, Mrs Anderson."

She took my hand and shook it; her fingers feeling small and cold in my grip.

"I'm sorry if my hand appears a little cold Charles but I have been hanging out the washing." She laughed. "Whilst the sun may offer its heat to warm our bodies, I am afraid the cold water I have been using to rinse our clothes does not."

I responded without thinking. "It doesn't…feel cold I mean." Of course it did but I didn't want her feeling any more awkward than she probably already was by having an unannounced visitor arrive at her home in the middle of wash day. I knew how Mum would respond to Dad and I if we did the same thing to her without due warning.

Releasing my hand, she stepped back and smiled at me knowingly. "That is kind of you Charles, if not, perhaps, entirely truthful. Anyway, I am very pleased to meet you, even if my husband did not afford me the time to make ample preparation for your visit." She moved to tidy her hair again and smooth the creases in her apron. "He probably forgot to mention me at all I should think. He becomes so obsessed with his –"

George laughed and, waving his hands in mild protest, interrupted again. "That is not fair, Elizabeth. I have been telling Charles all about you and singing your praises, haven't I, Charles?"

Again, I wasn't entirely sure how to respond and so, offering an embarrassed grin, looked down at the floor, shuffling my feet a little uncomfortably as I did so.

Elizabeth sensed my discomfiture. "Don't ask poor Charles to tell untruths on your behalf George, he's a visitor." She smiled at me again. "And a very welcome one as well." Pointing towards a rough wooden chair set beside a small square table in the centre of the room she gestured for me to sit. "Here, Charles, take George's seat, he can sit next to me where I can keep an eye on him." She nodded towards a wooden bench on the opposite side of the table.

I moved to the chair. "Thank you." Not sure what to say next but feeling obliged to engage in conversation with her, I continued. "George tells me you have a new baby?"

"Yes, he's asleep at the moment which is why I have been able to finish the washing and hang it in the garden to dry. No doubt he'll wake soon and cry out for me to feed him again." She looked at her husband and laughed. "He appears, like his father, never to be satisfied when it comes to mealtimes, always wanting a little more."

They exchanged loving glances, sharing the humour of the moment as George moved to the black leaded range and, taking a cloth in his hand, picked up a large kettle from a hook hanging above the stove.

"There is no need to fill the kettle, George, I did it earlier when doing the washing."

"Bless you my dear, but you know I don't like you carrying anything too heavy, and certainly not at present. You are still recovering from childbirth and –"

Elizabeth shook her head and interrupted. "I know what you said George, but I am alright. I had to carry the washing outside and that's certainly heavier than a kettle of water." She glanced towards me, a slight look of embarrassment on her face. "And Charles doesn't want to hear all about our family differences, do you, Charles?"

I laughed. "Don't worry about me; you should hear my mum and dad."

George placed the kettle back on the range. It hissed slightly as a drop of water ran down the spout and met with the hot stove. "You are right as ever my dear, I apologise; also, to you, Charles." He smiled affectionately at Elizabeth. "Do we still have some tea left?"

"A little; certainly enough to share with our guest."

"Excellent. Do you like tea, Charles?"

"Yes, I do, thank you, that would be lovely."

"The two of us travelled to Ashford a while ago for a meeting of the local diocese and, during our time there, treated ourselves to some. We both enjoy it, and as tea is still considered a luxury for many and not always easy to find, certainly here in Sowfield at least, we decided to purchase a small box." He looked at Elizabeth and tilted his head towards me. "The opportunity to share the last of it with you today Charles will prove a blessing for us both, isn't that so Elizabeth?"

"It will indeed." She looked at her husband with obvious affection. "God is truly generous towards us with His bounty Charles. When I think of our brothers and sisters in Ireland starving and with seemingly no end to their misery, my heart aches for them."

George returned her smile and nodded. "I know my dear, this awful potato famine has caused immeasurable horror and pain to so many, but our government is doing all it can to help; although with Sir John Peel resigning as Prime Minister because of the recent Government split over the Corn Laws who knows when or how all of this might end." He turned to me. "We live in turbulent political times Charles, with disagreements amongst our politicians on all sides, as they struggle to agree the best way forward for the Country. We can but continue to pray for all of those affected, and for those in authority, including our monarch, Queen Victoria, to act wisely when addressing the issues before them, together with this terrible food crisis in Ireland."

I dismissed the idea of telling them how the four years of starvation in Ireland they were currently witnessing would irrevocably damage and change the Country's relationship with England, as well as decimating the Irish population at the same time. A million Irish lives would be lost to starvation during the famine, with another two million emigrating to America in the hope of finding food, work, and a better life following the horrific effects of this period in Irish, English relations. It would leave a bitter legacy still felt a hundred and forty years on in 1986 with the ongoing troubles between the two nations.

As I watched the two of them preparing the table and discussing the price and availability of tea locally I smiled to myself, thinking how different their shopping experience would be if they were able to visit our local Tesco in Peterborough. There, they would find shelves full of tea and coffee imported from all over the world and costing next to nothing compared to the prices charged in the mid-1800s where, as Elizabeth had stated, both were regarded as something of an expensive luxury.

George moved away from the range towards the table. "I told Charles we have chosen to name our son Thomas my dear."

I glanced at Elizabeth, her expression changing to one of obvious disappointment.

"Oh, I thought we had agreed to tell Mother and Papa first? After all we only settled on the name ourselves this morning. I did so want them to be the next to know."

George bit his lip and smiled awkwardly. "I know my dear but…" he looked at me. "But, Charles already knew he was to be named Thomas."

A look of confusion descended over Elizabeth's face. "Already knew, but how…?" It was her turn to struggle for words.

"Could I say something," I enquired, feeling the need to explain myself, but also aware I would probably be adding to the growing misunderstanding between the two of them.

George looked at me sensing what I was about to say and fearing his wife's reaction. "I am not sure that is a good idea, Charles, perhaps I should –"

Elizabeth interrupted as she cut a few thick slices of the freshly made bread, placing them on a faded patterned plate. "I think I would like to hear what our guest has to say, if that is alright with you Charles?"

Smiling at me, she leant forward, placing the plate of bread on the table along with a bowl of jam.

I nodded appreciatively. "This looks delicious."

"As I said Charles, God is bountiful in his generosity towards us. We are able to make our own jam from the abundance of fruit that grows in the hedgerows, along with that which is additionally gifted to us by our congregation. I hope you enjoy it."

"Thank you."

"Tell me then," she continued, passing me a knife and plate, "How it is that you say you knew our son's name?" I didn't sense any animosity in her question, more a genuine desire to hear what I had to say. She gestured towards the bread and jam. "Will you give thanks George?"

I looked on as the two of them closed their eyes in prayer. "We thank you Father for this food and for the opportunity to share of your abundant goodness towards us with Charles. Please bless it to our bodies now. Amen."

Although not having any great belief myself I still felt humbled by their obvious faith, and in their desire to share the little they had with me.

Elizabeth smiled at me again. "Please Charles, help yourself." Then, turning away from the table she glanced at George. "And you also my dear; I will make the tea while we listen to what Charles has to say." She touched my sweatshirt lightly as she moved towards the range. "I don't recognise your dress Charles, is this some new style that has yet to reach us in Sowfield?"

George laughed. "I made a similar remark to Charles earlier my dear; you must be losing your eye for the latest fashion."

I looked up and grinned, trusting this would serve as response enough to their remarks about my clothing. In truth, I had no idea what to say by way of an answer without adding even more confusion to an already bewildering scenario. I looked at the freshly baked bread and felt my stomach gurgle. With all that had happened during the morning I was feeling quite hungry and ready for something to eat. I took a thick slice and began to spread a generous helping of jam across it. "Where to begin?" I watched as Elizabeth lifted the kettle from the stove and filled a dark brown porcelain teapot with the boiling liquid; steam rising from it and swirling in the sunlight as the water entered the pot.

"Perhaps at the beginning," she countered, hanging the kettle back on the hook above the range.

I looked across the table at George, a little fearful of his reaction at the prospect my repeating the story I had told him earlier, but also recognising it was the truth; a truth I was also now having difficulty in coming to terms with.

I took a mouthful of bread as I considered the best way to respond. "This is great, thank you; there's nothing like homemade bread. If the smell doesn't get you the taste always will."

"Thank you, Charles." She walked towards the table and placed the teapot on a faded woven mat. "Do you take milk in your tea?"

"Yes please, but no sugar, I only have that in coffee?"

"We don't have coffee I am afraid Charles. As George remarked earlier, many items are still not readily available here in Sowfield and, coffee especially, is considered by many as an expense they can ill afford. Also, we are not very keen on it. I, in particular, find it a little bitter to the taste."

I responded without thinking. "Mum gets ours from the supermarket and…" I stopped, suddenly remembering that neither of them would have any idea of what a supermarket was, let alone as to the variety of goods it might stock and sell.

"Supermarket?"

"Oh nothing, ignore me. Thank you, yes, just some milk please."

I watched as Elizabeth poured the tea, smiling at George as she did so and with him returning her look of affection with a wink of his eye. My mind raced; could I really be sitting in the home of my great-great-great-grandfather? I was struggling to make sense of anything that had happened in the past couple of hours. How could I have left Linda's house after breakfast in 1986 and now be sitting drinking tea with my ancient forebears a hundred and forty years earlier.

What could have happened to create this slip in time? Yet for all I found the whole scenario baffling and nigh on impossible to believe I still had the feeling that I *had* been here before. And whilst there appeared to be no rational explanation for all that had taken place over the past few hours there was still an unsettling familiarity about it. Flashes of recognition about the church, its detail, and surroundings, came readily to mind as I recalled the dreams and visions I'd experienced back home in Gunthorpe, along with the bizarre recollection that I had seen George lying on the floor at the foot of my bed pleading for help. Even here in their kitchen everything appeared to be just as it had been the first time I'd witnessed it during that earlier hallucinatory experience at home. And, although little of anything I had encountered at that time made any sense to me, I still felt relaxed and comfortable in George and Elizabeth's company, as though I belonged here in some way.

My thoughts were jolted back to the moment as Elizabeth placed a cup of tea in front of me. "There you are Charles. Would you like some more bread?"

I looked up and smiled. "No thank you, that was lovely."

Elizabeth sat next to her husband who took her hand and squeezed it. "Thomas has been sleeping for some time my dear, do you think you should check he is alright?"

Laughing, Elizabeth shook her head. "You can if you like George, but I am not keen to disturb him. He didn't sleep well last night and so is probably tired. He will let us know soon enough when he is awake and in need of our attention." She turned to face me. "And we have a guest with us who is about to explain his reason for being in Sowfield. Also, as to how he knows our son's name when we have not, as yet, informed anybody of that detail ourselves." Pausing momentarily, she held my gaze. "At least I hope that is what you are going to tell us Charles?"

I took a drink from my cup. "Well, I'm not sure how to say this…" I looked directly at George. "But, as I told you earlier, I came to Sowfield as part of the research I'm doing for my university degree in Leicester and…"

I could see the confusion in Elizabeth's eyes. "A university degree, I'm not sure I –"

George interrupted. "You might remember me saying earlier my dear that Charles arrived at the church this morning a little confused shall we say, about a number of things, including who I was and as to what year this might be. Unfortunately, at that time I mistook him for a thief. As you know we have had some of the more valuable items removed from the church in recent months and I thought Charles might be one of the robbers come back to steal from us again." He smiled at me. "But clearly he was not."

"I am indeed relieved to hear that." Elizabeth picked up her cup and looked at me quizzically. "My husband says you are confused Charles and yet, even in your confusion, you say you know the name of our son without having met us before?" She took a drink from her cup, her eyes still focused on me. "And you say you are studying at a university in Leicester?" She smiled. "I think perhaps it is I who am confused?"

I finished my tea and took a deep breath knowing the next few minutes would prove difficult for all three of us.

"Before I start, let me assure both of you what I am about to say is true, although I accept much of it may sound fanciful at the very least, if not nigh on impossible to accept as fact."

They smiled at each other with George being the first to speak. "You might be surprised Charles. I have been told many stories in my time here at St Mark's that have erred on the improbable." He nodded at me. "We have a God who deals in the miraculous and answers prayers in ways we cannot always understand or even imagine, so don't underestimate His ability to make clear to Elizabeth and I what it is you are about to share with us."

I puffed out my cheeks. Even if I was to agree with them that God had the ability to speak into their subconscious, I still couldn't accept for one minute that anybody would be able to make sense of what I was about to say, let alone understand it or accept it as reality.

"Okay, here goes." I took another deep breath. "My name is Charles Benton, Charlie to my friends and family; that bit you already know. I am twenty years old and live with my parents, Peter and Irene, in a town called Gunthorpe near Peterborough –"

George interjected. "I have heard of Peterborough, there is a wonderful Cathedral there where…"

Elizabeth tugged at his arm. "George, we must let Charles speak. This is his story and, if we are to fully understand it and help him then we must first hear all of what he has to say."

Nodding his agreement George turned to face me. "I'm sorry Charles, my dear wife is right, please continue. We…I promise not to interrupt again."

"As I was saying, I live in Gunthorpe with my parents, although for much of the time I'm resident in halls at Leicester where I'm studying Genealogy and…" I noticed a look of slight confusion on Elizabeth's face, but sensed her reticence to interrupt my flow again.

"Genealogy is a part of my course, along with English local history. It's all to do with family history, landscape, topography…that's the surveying and charting of certain areas of land and particular localities that sort of thing." Elizabeth smiled and nodded gently as if to intimate she understood, although I wasn't convinced she did, nor that I'd explained myself clearly, but decided to move on anyway in the hope of avoiding any further delays to my story along with any additional potential detours and associated lengthy explanations.

"Part of the course work includes tracing Mum's family tree, that's the history of her ancestry across the years." I stopped for a moment, considering how best to continue. I knew, even if they had been able to understand and follow what I'd said so far, the next piece of my narrative was going to change not only the dynamic of our relationship but, more especially, their perception of me, both as a person and as to my mental wellbeing. I closed my eyes momentarily and took a breath.

"Are you alright, Charles?"

Opening my eyes again I smiled. "Yes, I'm fine, thank you, Elizabeth; just not sure how to continue without making you doubt the validity of my story." I laughed. "Or perhaps even my sanity?"

She looked at me as Mum had done many times in the past when I was struggling to say something or make myself clear. It was a look of maternal affection that exhibited both support and understanding.

"As my husband has stated already, we have both heard many accounts of individual life experiences from our parishioners and, on occasion, the wider community during our time here at St Mark's." She glanced at George, "And, some of those stories have been extremely fanciful in their telling, such has been their narrative and corresponding detail, but we have always sought to see and believe the best in people, as did our Lord Jesus, and so we are happy to hear whatever it is you have to say." She took her husband's hand. "And, when you have finished, we will have a clearer understanding at least of what it is you are struggling with, and as to whether there might be some way in which we can help you." She nodded and smiled reassuringly. "Please, continue with your story."

I felt my heart beat a little faster in my chest as I leant forward, placing my hands on the table. "Okay, the thing is, and I am no clearer as to how any of this has happened than you will be when I've finished but, well...I was born in 1966 and, as I am now twenty that means for me this is 1986." I waited for some verbal reaction or outburst of incredulity, but none was forthcoming. As promised, they remained still, demonstrating no expression other than that of concern for me and genuine interest in what I was saying.

"When I left Linda's house, the lady I've been staying with at Meadowfield cottage, earlier this morning and walked the few hundred yards to St Mark's I was expecting to meet a lady called Joyce who, I was told, is the church warden and secretary." I shook my head slightly, struggling to believe my own account of what had happened let alone attach any sense of reality or credence to it. "But, on entering the church I met George instead. He told me the year was 1846 and that he was the vicar." I looked directly at George. "If that is true then I have, on entering St Mark's, stepped back in time by a hundred and forty years." I noticed a slight change in their expression to one of increasing scepticism. "Look, I'm finding this pretty impossible to believe as well, but I assure you, it *is* true. And the thing is, although I don't know how any of this has happened, I also feel like...like I've been here before. When I first entered the church this morning and saw George, I recognised him, or at least thought I did and that his face was familiar." I paused again, feeling the need to explain my self-further. "I've been researching my mum's family tree for the past few months and during that time I've had a series of strange dreams, hallucinations if you like, both during the night when I've been asleep and, in the daytime as well, if that makes sense? Visitations, illusions, pictures in my mind, call them what you will, but all of them appearing as very real to me, as though I were actually there, living in the moment. I could feel the touch of others, embrace their presence; my senses becoming filled with the aroma and physicality of all around me but, for all of that, I had no understanding of what was happening or why? That is until I walked into St Mark's this morning. As I soon as I saw George, I felt I recognised him from those earlier, almost surreal, encounters. I also recognised areas of the church building as well and..." I looked around me. "And, when I walked into this kitchen a short while ago, I also recognised much of the room itself, the walls, the stove, and the stone flooring." I looked towards my hosts again who, whilst trying to maintain their courteous expression of guarded interest, were clearly struggling to believe what they were hearing.

"I can see from your faces you think I've lost the plot and that all of this sounds ridiculous. And, under normal circumstances I would agree with you but, can I assure you again that what I am saying *is* true, or it is for me anyway. I came to Sowfield because, having studied Mum's family history and corresponding detail of her ancestry as far back as 1846, I discovered her great-great-grandfather was a man called George Anderson who lived here in the village and was the vicar of St Mark's Church. Actually, I did go a little further back in my research just to establish George and Elizabeth's...sorry, your lineage in Mum's family tree."

They glanced at each other, a look of mutual surprise and confusion on their faces. Rather than allow them the opportunity of questioning my statement I decided to continue.

"I discovered that George was born in 1814 to parents Samuel and Martha. Samuel was an agricultural worker, a farm hand, and Martha worked as a seamstress. Elizabeth was born in 1822. Her parents, Henry and Rebecca Moor were landowners with an interest in supporting the church, both locally and in the wider sphere." I looked at them both and smiled. "The two of you got married in 1844 and your son Thomas was born in 1846, the same year that George was..." I paused but knew I had to finish the sentence. "The same year, that George was killed."

I looked at the two of them. There was no clue from either their facial expressions or body language that they were about to react in any discernible way, apart from a slight grimace on Elizabeth's face at the mention of George's supposedly early and gruesome demise. "And that's what brought me to Sowfield, to try and find out exactly what happened." I smiled weakly. "But then I met you and..." Shrugging my shoulders I fell silent.

George squeezed Elizabeth's arm briefly, then letting go placed his hands together flat on the table. "But then you met me and discovered I was alive; so now your story has no ending, or at least not the one you were expecting or, perhaps, hoping for?" I detected a hint of hostility in his voice.

"Absolutely not. I couldn't be more thrilled that you are alive and well, even if it does disprove the story of your untimely death and provide a completely different, but very welcome, ending to my investigations into Mum's family history."

"I hope, for all of our sakes, that is true Charles?" Turning to Elizabeth and squeezing her arm again he continued. "But, even if it is, this whole story about your having arrived from the future is still a tale too far, and one I find impossible to believe; nor does it make any sense?" He sat upright, pushing his chest out as if to demonstrate his taking authority over our conversation. "And, as far as you knowing the dates of our birth and associated detail of our respective families well...those are not a secret; records are now kept of these events, births, marriages, and so on. None of this reveals anything new about Elizabeth and I that could not be found through the most basic of investigations, as you refer to them." I sensed his voice, as well as his manner, stiffening towards me.

"As we have said, Elizabeth and I have been witness to many strange tales and uncomfortable confessions during our time at St Mark's but there has always appeared to be a reason for them, a validity in their being. Consequently, and following much prayer and discussion most of these matters would be resolved, or at least some sense made of them but, as for this story of yours..." He looked at me and shook his head. Elizabeth stroked his arm and smiled at me.

"Of course, we would like to believe you Charles, or at the very least try to understand what it is you are telling us; but simply to say you are from another time and that you have come here to find my husband dead is both unsettling and intimidating to say the least." Turning to George she spoke again, emotion clearly demonstrated in her voice. "Why would you want to see any harm come to this gentle man of God? Even the very thought of it frightens me and challenges my commitment and belief in the Lord's command to love all men and make them welcome in my home." She put her hand to her mouth as a single tear formed in her eye and ran down her cheek. "I think I would like you to leave our house Charles and..." her voice breaking as the tears began to flow more freely.

Clearly struggling to control his own emotions George turned to face me. "There would appear to be no profit gained by your staying any longer in our home Charles." He placed his hand on Elizabeth's arm, stroking it gently as an act of comfort and reassurance. "Unless you can explain yourself fully, and the reasoning behind all you have said so far then I am afraid I must, as Elizabeth has requested, ask you to leave."

I looked at the two of them, both clearly upset and confused by what I'd said, but neither could be feeling any more bewildered than I by the circumstances and events of the past few hours. How could I enlighten them further as to what had happened when I was no nearer to understanding any part of it myself? All I could do was recount the truth as I knew it and hope it might be enough to convince them I bore them no harm or ill will. Also, perhaps, between us, we could find a way to resolve our obvious differences and help facilitate my safe return to Peterborough. I looked down at the table for a moment, gathering my thoughts, before committing myself to one last attempt at an explanation of how I'd arrived in Sowfield and my reasons for being here. Looking up I smiled in the forlorn hope they might listen to what I was about to say with an open mind and accept my intentions towards them as being genuine and honourable.

"I am truly sorry if either of you feel threatened in any way by my being here, that is and never would be my intention." I scratched my head in a vain attempt to bring forth some form of inspirational wording that might help resolve the growing misunderstanding between us; none was forthcoming.

"My name really is Charles Benton and, as I have already explained, I am researching my mum's family tree as part of my studies at Leicester University. This is intended to be a detailed history of her ancestry over the past hundred and forty years, dating back to, this year, 1846." I could see from their expression they remained unconvinced by this latest attempt to placate them. I held up my hands as a gesture of appeal to their better nature.

"Please, let me finish. If at the end you're still uncomfortable with any of the detail of my story, or in my being here, I will, as you suggest, leave, I promise." I noticed a flicker of acquiescence at my proposal in their eyes. They glanced at each other and nodded their accord.

"Very well, Charles, we promise not to interrupt until you have completed your story."

"Thank you." I made another attempt to smile in appreciation of their agreeing to allow me one last chance to make my case. "I will do my best to speak clearly and in a way you'll both be able to understand and, I hope, believe. But, if I'm honest, the truth is, I am every bit as confused by all that has happened since I entered St Mark's earlier this morning as you are." I took a breath, exhaling slowly to afford myself a few more seconds in which to collect my thoughts before venturing to speak again.

"My parents, as I've said already, are Peter and Irene Benton, and it's Mum's side of the family I'm researching. So far, I've discovered her parents were John Pearce, a miner, and Mary her mum. Mary died in 1985 and John in 1940 fighting in the Second World War. He –" George interrupted.

"A world war?" He looked at me, an expression of shock and alarm etched across his face. "There have always been wars and fighting amongst nations, but a *world* war? Surely…"

Elizabeth moved to silence her husband.

"We promised not to speak until Charles has completed his story dear if you remember. Perhaps, when he has finished he might allow us the courtesy of voicing our thoughts and, at the same time, pose any questions or concerns we may have about its detail or authenticity?"

I nodded. "Of course, absolutely."

She smiled politely and took her husband's hand again. I was grateful for her apparent support but also recognised her smile couldn't hide the fact she was still struggling to believe any of what I was saying. Her greater desire clearly remained for me to finish speaking and leave their home, allowing the two of them, along with their simple lives, to return to some form of normality. I decided against trying to explain myself further and to simply continue with what I knew, at least for me, to be the facts.

"My Mum's granddad was William Coulson, and her grandmother was named Anna. William was a miner in Nottingham, the same as her dad John before he joined up and went to war. William died in 1968 when I was two and Anna died a few years before in 1964. Consequently, I never met her, but Mum says she was a lovely lady."

Pausing, I scratched my head again in an attempt to encourage my brain to maintain the detail of what I was saying in the correct order as I was speaking, and without notes. I also recognised all I was saying meant little or nothing to George or Elizabeth, as for them the individuals of whom I was speaking, along with any events pertaining to their lives, had yet to exist. All the same I felt the need to continue, if only to establish the facts once again in my own mind and to add credence to what I was saying.

"William's Dad, that's Mum's great-granddad was…is, your son Thomas. His wife Sarah…"

George was unable to contain himself any longer. "Thomas? You are talking about *our* son, Thomas, the baby who is sleeping just a few yards away in the other room? You are telling us that one day he will be your mother's great grandfather, married to a woman named Sarah, is that what you are saying?"

A strained and emotional silence fell over the room as they looked at one another, each of them fearing what I might say next but equally demanding that

I continue with my story. "Yes…Thomas your son." I looked away to avoid their bemused gaze.

"At fourteen Thomas will begin working on a fruit farm here in Kent. He will continue in that work for the next fifteen years before meeting a girl, a young woman named Sarah who he will marry in 1875. Their daughter Anna, William Coulson's wife to be and your granddaughter will be born in 1878."

Elizabeth cleared her throat and looked directly at me, an expression of frustration and growing scepticism set across her face. "Dare I ask what happens to Thomas and this woman Sarah, or are those particular details not yet established in your mind as part of this improbable tale?"

Feeling both embarrassed and uncomfortable I looked away again. I could readily understand their growing annoyance towards me, also their cynicism as to what they had heard so far; considering it as too farfetched to believe. However, my more immediate concern was fear of their subsequent reaction to what I was about to reveal next.

"Thomas will…" I felt the words stick in my throat and my mouth dry. "Thomas will, be killed in an accident on the farm in 1880 two years after Anna is born and…"

I didn't need to look up to gauge the impact my words had had on the two of them; their audible gasps said it all.

"That is enough Charles, we have heard enough. I am sorry, but I must ask you to leave our home immediately."

I raised my eyes to see Elizabeth weeping openly and George place his arm around her shoulder to comfort her.

"We made you welcome here, gave you food and drink, and in return you repay our hospitality with these spiteful tales of dubious and fantastic proportions, not only asking us to believe them but you add further insult to injury by proclaiming our baby son, once grown, will die in some terrible farming accident. And further, that *I* am already dead when clearly I am not. Sadly perhaps, though it may be for you Charles, what I am, is sitting here both fully alive and utterly reviled by the words and lies you have spoken about us and our son." He fixed his gaze firmly on me; his expression turning from incredulity to one of intimidation and menace. "I am not, by tradition, a man of violence Charles, but your cruel and malicious stories about world wars, death, and alleged murder concerning our family have created within me the very real desire to abandon my sworn pledge to view all men and their transgressions through the forgiving eyes of God and, in so doing, enact upon you some form of physical retribution for so upsetting my dear wife." Glancing towards Elizabeth, now clearly distraught, a deep feeling of guilt and regret swept over me at the obvious pain I had caused the two of them.

"I never meant any of what I've said to upset either of you in any way, I was merely telling –"

George interrupted me again, waving away my protests as he rose from his chair.

"Stop, there is to be no further discussion. You will leave our home immediately; we will not listen to another word. Do I make myself clear?"

I could see from his expression there was no point in continuing to plead my case. I stood up and moved towards the door.

"I am very sorry Mrs Anderson, I truly never meant to cause any upset to you or your family." I looked down at this gentle woman who up until a few moments ago had sought, like her husband, to see only the best in me, but who now wanted nothing more than for me to be as far away from her and her family as possible. George moved to stand in front of Elizabeth as if to protect her from any further potential vindictiveness from me, verbal or otherwise.

"I will show you out Charles." He gestured me towards the door. We walked in silence along the dark hallway. As he opened the front door a baby's cry echoed along the passage. George turned his head towards the sound. "That will be Thomas. We will not be inviting you to meet him." He stood back as I moved beyond the doorway and into the early afternoon sunshine. "Goodbye Charles."

"I'm so…" my final attempt at an apology being cut short as the door closed in my face. I stood for a moment, a feeling of both sorrow and trepidation descending over me. Sorrow that I had upset this affable Christian couple and disturbed their settled lives and, trepidation that, not only did I regret all that had transpired between us but more, with little of what I'd said now making any sense to me either. How could I be standing outside the home of my great-great-great-grandfather a hundred and twenty years before I was born? And if I was, then why hadn't he been the victim of the violent and fatal attack predicted in those nightmare visions I'd experienced at home in Gunthorpe; the same ones set down in the records of our family history?

I walked slowly down the path glancing back only briefly in response to the cry of baby Thomas coming from an upstairs open window at the front of the house. I allowed myself a wry smile. "At least he might grow up to know his father now."

Chapter Seventeen

I walked the short distance back to St Mark's, continuing past the church and along the road towards the fields on my right where I negotiated a wooden bridge set across a narrow part of the river. On reaching the other side I looked up to see the water widen its path and stretch out ahead of me, running the full length of the fields and on into the distance beyond. The next twenty minutes or so was spent making my way along a pathway of trampled grass by the side the cornfield; my thoughts dominated by all that had transpired over the past few hours. Lost in my deliberations and with my head down as I walked, I suddenly became aware of a broad shadow stretching out before me and, looking up, noticed I was standing under the large oak tree I had seen earlier from the church on the other side of the river. I sat down under its wide, inviting branches. It felt good to be out of the heat and direct rays of the sun. Making myself comfortable, I stretched out my arms and yawned. I'd only been sitting there for a few minutes when I felt my eyelids become heavy and close; the warmth of the summer's day overtaking me. My mind relaxed and drifted towards sleep in that ethereal world set between dreaming and wakefulness. I saw Mum and Dad smiling at me. "We love you Charlie, come back to us soon." Even half asleep, I felt a smile form on my face and my hand stretch out towards them. "Love you too; I miss you." Suddenly another voice called out to me; it was all consuming, crashing through the gentle dream like conversation with my parents, shattering my sense of calm. "Help me, Charles."

Although instantly recognising this, now familiar, plea for assistance, on this occasion there appeared to be a genuine sense of desperation about it; one I felt unable to ignore.

"Help me Charles." There it was again; even more frantic this time than it had been a moment before. I opened my eyes, a feeling of panic running through me; such was the tone of fear in this latest cry for help. As I got to my feet a church bell began to ring in the distance. Instinctively I turned my head towards the sound, recognising it to be the same one I'd heard earlier at St Mark's. My mind and body were struck by an overwhelming sense of Déjà vu; I *had* been here before. As the sound of the bell continued to echo in my head, I remembered the vision I'd had a few weeks earlier at home where I'd seen myself walking in this very same field and hearing the same bell ring out. This time, however, there was no natural rhythm to the bell's peal but, rather, it was loud and constant as though it were being rung out to me alone in an unrelenting and desperate cry for my attention. I felt my heart rate quicken and a sensation of dread run through me as I began to retrace my steps along the path back towards the church. Now there was no relaxed pace to my stride but more a desperate race to reach my destination as I ran full pelt towards the frantic sound emitting from the bell tower. As I reached the end of the pathway and approached the wooden bridge to cross the stream the ringing stopped as abruptly as it had begun. I looked around me expecting to see others making their way towards the church in response to the frenzied clanging of bells but there was no one, apart from an old man walking his dog. He appeared completely unmoved by the jarring and desperate call for assistance, almost as if he hadn't heard it.

"You in trouble young 'un," he said, waving his walking stick in my direction. "It be too hot to be running around like that."

"Didn't you hear them, the bells from the church?"

"Bells? Ain't no bells been rung today, least ways not that I've heard." He waved his stick towards me again. "It be all that running in the sun lad, I told you it were too hot for that." He laughed. "I'd be hearing bells ringing in me head as well if I was charging around like that in this weather."

I paused momentarily, partly to catch my breath but also to try and make sense of what the old man had said. How could he not have heard the bells? But equally, if they had been ringing then why wasn't the street full of concerned villagers responding to their desperate tolling?

Was this yet another illusory dream, a figment of my imagination, or was I finally losing my mind and grip on reality altogether. I shook my head. No, I had heard the bells call out to me along with George's panic-stricken cry for help.

I started towards St Mark's again, hastening my step once more and ignoring the old man's advice to move at a slower pace in the hot afternoon sun. On reaching the cemetery I noticed two men hurrying away from the side door of the church, making their way towards the field along with its cover of trees beyond. As they sprinted across the grass, I noticed they were carrying something which appeared to be wrapped in a cloth or blanket. One of the men leapt over the small stone wall separating the churchyard from the field. As he did so the covering fell away slightly revealing a gold coloured object which glinted brightly in the sunshine. It was the cross from the altar; the same one George had suspected I might have come to steal when we first met. I shouted for the men to stop, but this only served to increase their determination to escape as they ran full pelt towards the cover of the trees that stood to one side of the field. I sprinted the last few yards around the side of the building and called out to the men again but to no avail as they disappeared into the woods. Gulping air deep into my lungs I forced open the thick wooden door, my chest heaving as I gasped for breath.

On entering the church my nostrils were greeted with an almost overpowering sickly sweet smell that I recognised immediately as being the same one I'd experienced the night before in my bed at Meadowfield. It was incense. As my eyes adjusted to the light, I heard a muffled cry from behind one of the pews; it was George. He was lying on the stone floor between two rows of seating, the incense burner by his side with smoke rising from it. Still panting from my race to the church I called out to him. "George, what happened, are you alright?"

Moaning and in obvious pain, he struggled to lift his head from the floor. As he did so I noticed a steady flow of blood running down the side of his face. Looking up at me he reached out to grasp my leg, uttering the same words I had heard so many times before in my dreams and subconscious but were now being delivered in person and with desperate intent.

"Help me Charles." My instinct was to turn and run, but I was equally aware that here was a man in trouble and urgent need of medical assistance; I had to help. Still unsure of exactly what to do I took the handkerchief from my pocket and put it to his head in a desperate attempt to stem the flow of blood which was now running more freely from his wound.

I eased him up into a sitting position, placing his back against the side of a pew.

"Are you hurting anywhere else?"

"I think my left arm may be broken," he said, wincing as he attempted to lift it slightly. "They hit out at me with the cross as I tried to stop them and it caught my arm before crashing into my head." He looked at me, blinking as he did so, blood running across his face and into his eyes before dripping down onto the floor. "Thank you for coming back Charles, I'm sorry about –"

I interrupted, sensing his efforts at speech were tiring him, along with the steady flow of blood from the deep wound to the side his head. The pain from his damaged arm, now hanging limply by his side, was also clearly having a debilitating effect on his capacity to communicate in any coherent way.

I got to my feet. "I'll go and get help. Someone to look after you while I go and tell Elizabeth what's happened. Is there a doctor nearby?"

"Yes," he mumbled, struggling to make himself understood as he began to drift in and out of consciousness. "Doctor Mason…Elizabeth will show you were he…"

I was loath to leave him in this state, but knew I had little choice if I wanted to save his life.

Bending down I squeezed his right arm to reassure him. "I'll be back soon." I turned and moved towards the door. "I still don't understand any of this George, but I'm glad I'm here to help."

He winced, the pain from his injuries overtaking him once more as the blood ran down his face gathering momentum and dripping steadily onto the stone flooring creating a pool of crimson red around him.

I ran out of the church, the bright afternoon sun causing me to blink following the dim surroundings of the church sanctuary. As my mind and vision cleared, I stared in utter disbelief at the sight before me. Everything was as it had been earlier that morning after leaving Linda at Meadowfield. There were cars parked in the street once more, the sign for The Blacksmith's Arms was swinging in the breeze; gone was the forge and anvil that had stood there only minutes before. The road running through the village was no longer narrow, potholed, and muddy, but wider and even with white lines painted down the middle. The new build houses and footings had returned, set between the more established cottages and their cheery summer gardens. I was back in 1986!

I stood, rooted to the spot, my body shaking and mind spiralling towards an abyss of total confusion at all that had happened over the past few hours.

Had I really been transported back one hundred and forty years and met up with my great-great-great-grandfather and his family? Was he really lying on the floor in the church just a few yards away from me, bloodied and beaten by thieves? And if he was then this couldn't be 1986, and yet the very real evidence of modern life was displayed all around me. I took a deep breath, shaking my head in an attempt to bring my thoughts into some form of focus and rationale. "Maybe it *had* all been a dream, another visitation of my unconscious mind to some ethereal existence that subsists in parallel time with the real world?" I pondered this theory only for a second, deciding just as quickly that such a premise had the same potential to be true as the possibility of my flying to the moon in the next five minutes.

As I juggled this escalating uncertainty in my mind against the greater concern for my overall sanity, one truth remained; whatever had or hadn't happened since saying goodbye to Linda earlier this morning, the answer lay in the building behind me. I had to go back. I lifted my head and looked towards the sun, attempting to draw fresh energy and impetus from the warmth of its rays. A dark shadow stretched the length of the path towards me as the sun threw its late afternoon light behind the spire of the church. I had seen these same shadows before in my dreams, unnerving finger like silhouettes, reaching out to grasp me. My body flinched as a feeling of trepidation swept over me. I took a deep breath to steel myself for what lay ahead, and as I did so a familiar voice cried out to me again from deep within.

"Help me Charles."

I moved determinedly towards the large wooden doors at the front of the building; these were also cast in shadow now as the sun began to drop a little lower in the sky. The inky black outline of the spire appeared to be pointing directly at me, drawing me towards the church and whatever lay within its walls.

I paused briefly to consider my options. "What if I entered the sanctuary and found myself transported back to 1846 once more; would I be able to return to my own time again as I had apparently done on this occasion? Perhaps I should simply ignore the voice crying out to me and turn away, returning instead to the settled life I knew at university, and at home with my parents in Peterborough? But if I did, then whoever it was pleading with me for help would forever remain a mystery and one that would haunt me for the rest of my days."

I knew I had to go on. Reaching out towards the door I took hold of the brass ring and turned it slowly in my hand. I heard the latch lift and clunk as it had earlier when entering the building for the first time just a few hours before, a memory now that felt like a lifetime ago. I walked through the short vestibule entrance and into the church itself fearing, as I did so, that I would be met by the sight of my bloodied and beaten ancestor still lying on the floor, but it was a very different scene that greeted me.

Although the physical structure of the building hadn't changed there was a sense of newness about the place. It had a modern and updated feel to it. There were freshly cut flowers filling vases positioned at various stations around the walls, along with a series of brightly coloured childlike paintings pinned to a board at one end of the church. Looking to my left I noticed a table containing a variety of Christian booklets and notice sheets promoting the differing services and support groups involved with the life of the church. There was a red carpet running the length of the church between the pews, where previously there had been only the cold stone flooring, the same stone flooring where George had lain bleeding only minutes before?

As I stood scratching my head in disbelief at all that had befallen me, I heard a voice, one that I didn't recognise.

"Good morning, can I help you?"

I turned to be greeted by the sight of a woman approaching me. She was smiling broadly. I estimated her to be in her mid to late fifties, with greying hair cut neatly in a bob around her face. She was wearing a green woollen skirt and brown cardigan which was buttoned halfway revealing a white blouse underneath. As she walked towards me the steps from her heavy brogue shoes echoed throughout the church as they connected with the floor.

I opened my mouth to respond but struggled to find any words. "I…"

She reached out her hand and placed it gently on my arm. "Are you alright?"

"Yes, I'm fine, I think?" I looked around me again still trying to make sense of all that had happened since entering the church for the first time earlier that day. "I'm just not sure I…"

I felt myself being guided towards a pew. "Here, why don't we sit down for a minute, you look like you've had a shock of some sort. Are you sure you're alright?"

I sat quietly for a moment, attempting to clear my head, and deciding how best to respond.

I knew if I recounted all I had experienced over the last few hours she would probably think me as demented as George and Elizabeth must have done during our earlier encounter, if indeed such a meeting had ever actually taken place. My brain was now so addled I wasn't sure anymore what was real and what was not. I decided honesty of a different form was required. I turned my head towards her and smiled.

"I think the church took me by surprise a little, it wasn't what I was expecting."

"Are you a first-time visitor to St Mark's?" She looked around. "It is very beautiful isn't it? It surprises a lot of people when they first come here."

We paused, each taking a moment to survey all that lay around us. Eventually, breaking the silence she offered me her hand.

"My name is Joyce, Joyce Emerson; I'm the church secretary and warden here at St Mark's."

I felt my heart leap in my chest as I took her hand and shook it. "This is her; *this* is Joyce, the woman Linda told me to talk to when I left Meadowfield earlier this morning." I still felt confused but also with a huge sense of relief at being back where the day had begun. I smiled again and gripped her hand a little tighter to make sure she really was here and that I wasn't experiencing yet another delusional fantasy. "My name is Charlie."

"I'm pleased to meet you Charlie." She withdrew her hand and looked at me. "You have a little more colour in your face now, are you feeling better?"

I sat up straight and, stretching my shoulders back, grinned.

"Yes, thank you." I looked around me again. "As I said I was taken aback a little by the appearance of the church, it wasn't what I'd been expecting." That much at least was true.

"What has brought you to St Mark's? Do you have family living in the village?"

"No, I'm not from round here; I'm a student at Leicester University studying family history and genealogy. I'm staying with Linda Wells at Meadowfield Cottage; she recommended I come and speak to you."

"Linda eh. Well, you won't do much better than Meadowfield for accommodation while you're here, that's for sure. She is a special lady is Linda and a dear friend. She's had a difficult time over the past few years and…" Her voice faded. "Well, as I say you won't do any better than Meadowfield for somewhere to stay. You'll certainly be well cared for by Linda."

I knew she was trying to protect Linda by not talking about the loss of her husband and David in case I wasn't aware of what had happened and so, not wanting to add to her embarrassment, I decided to move the conversation on. "Absolutely, she's been great." I grinned. "And she's a brilliant cook as well; I can't remember the last time I ate so well."

"That sounds like Linda alright." We laughed and I felt the potential for any unease between us lift.

"So, is it your studies that have brought you to Sowfield then? Is there something special about the area that interests you?"

"Yes, there is." I looked directly at her and smiled, hoping to encourage her support. "It's a long story but, basically, I've been researching my mum's family tree as part of my degree course and it seems her great-great-grandfather was once the vicar here at St Mark's."

Her expression changed from that of polite inquisitor to one of genuine interest.

"Really, how fascinating. What was his name?"

I took a deep breath knowing the next part of my story wouldn't be so easy to discuss bearing in mind my experiences from earlier in the day.

"George Anderson. His name was George Anderson, and he was the vicar here in around 1846."

Joyce nodded in recognition of the name.

"He was indeed, if that truly is your ancestor." Her expression changed again, this time becoming more solemn. "You are aware of what happened to him I presume?"

I thought I was but, because of all that had transpired earlier, I no longer felt sure of anything to do with my family's ancestry. I decided to err on the side of caution and plead ignorance as to the precise detail of his demise.

"I don't know exactly what happened to him, other than that he was allegedly killed here in the church, is that right?"

She nodded and paused before answering as if to gather her thoughts.

"A pretty gruesome affair by all accounts it was as well. That whole episode was an incredibly sad time for the village. The records we hold demonstrate that George Anderson was a popular member of the Sowfield community, not only in his role as vicar here at St Mark's, but throughout the parish as a whole. He and his wife Elizabeth were great contributors to the life of the area and would often be found helping those in need, whether they were members of the church or not." She paused again, looking down for a moment before returning her gaze to me. "I've learnt quite a bit about him over the years, not only in my role as church warden but on a more personal level as well. His story, tragic though it is, is a fascinating one none the less." She smiled. "He had a real love for the village and its residents. Back then of course it was mainly a farming community with the sale of fruit and vegetables being its major source of income, although there one or two who made their living from more traditional farming pursuits, such as dairy or the breeding and sale of various livestock." She paused and smiled. "George wasn't afraid to muck in at every level either by all accounts, and certainly when it came to supporting his own flock so to speak. There are tales of him stripping to the waist in the summer months along with the rest of the men and helping to harvest the fruit for transporting to other local villages and towns ready to be sold at market. And once the railway came to the area in around 1842 and the main station at Ashford was opened, Sowfield's fruit and veg became in great demand both locally and further afield." She smiled again. "George certainly did his bit on both sides of the pulpit to ensure the farm workers and their families here in the village were fed, both spiritually and physically. Apparently, he would speak up for all of those who worked on the land and wasn't shy of reminding the local landowners of the scriptural premise that demands a labourer is worth their hire, and that they should pay their employees a fair day's wage for their work. By all accounts he became a real champion of the people, although some in higher office were not always so supportive of our radical vicar." She paused again briefly before continuing, her tone a little more sombre.

"George was thought to have had a few enemies amongst the local wealthy elite around the county as well. There were those, shall we say, who didn't like their clearly well-versed vicar siding with the land workers and farm hands, filling their heads with notions of workers' rights and claims to a decent wage for their efforts." She smiled again. "Mind, that's an argument that still runs today of course. Just look at the opposition to Mrs Thatcher and her ideas of what makes up a fairer society for us all in 1986. I'm not sure many of those on the shop floor, skilled or otherwise, would have her name as first on their Christmas card list; certainly not from the mining community anyway."

I returned her smile, appreciative of the fact George had obviously been a man of the people and someone who had stood up so resolutely for the rights of the less fortunate in his community. Mum would be proud to know that, as was I. It was also amusing to hear Joyce drawing the analogy between the manual workers of George's time and the miners of today, another community embracing a direct link to my ancestral heritage, and all good material for our family tree.

"What about the story of him being killed? Can you tell me anything about what actually happened, or how he came to die?"

She moved her head slightly from side to side, pursing her lips as she considered how best to answer.

"I said he wasn't as popular in some circles as he was in others; in fact, there was a suspicion at one time that a certain landowner, who George allegedly upset when defending a worker accused of stealing from his employer, arranged to have George beaten as a warning for him to stay away from matters that didn't concern him. That was never proved though, and in fact was later dismissed following reports the landowner had put up a reward for any information leading to the identity of those responsible for George's death. Of course, he may have done that to allay any suspicion of involvement that might have been directed towards him. But now, all these years on, we'll never know whether that was true or not." She paused again.

"As for how he met his end; records show his arm was broken and that he was bludgeoned about the head quite severely. The attack, as you intimated, took place here in the church, with George sadly bleeding to death."

I felt a shiver run through me as I listened to her description of the very wounds, I had witnessed for myself on George's body just a few feet from where we were now sitting.

Joyce touched my arm. "Are you sure you're alright, you still look a bit unsteady?"

I forced a smile. "No, I'm fine. It's just a bit of a shock hearing what actually happened to him that's all. Please, carry on."

"If you're sure?"

I nodded.

"It seems no one was ever caught or brought to trial for his murder despite that supposed offer of a reward. As for the reason he was so brutally killed well, the story goes that a group of thieves from outside the area had come to the village specifically to steal the church's golden cross." She pointed in the direction of the altar. "It stood there, with the silver salver and chalice on either side for the sacraments. A wealthy landowner and benefactor in the 1600s had it made especially as a gift for St Mark's and the local community. He was a successful farmer and businessman and, as well as supporting the church, he also employed a lot of people who lived in Sowfield and the surrounding villages as well. Everyone knew the cross was worth a lot of money even then and, over the years, some suggested it should be locked away and only brought out for special services on high days and holidays. But there were others who argued it wasn't the sole property of the church, rather it belonged to the people and, as such, they had a right to see it whenever they wanted, especially when they attended services. George was of a similar mind when it was put to him the cross should be locked away because of its increasing value and the growing temptation for someone to steal it. He wouldn't be bowed though, saying it should be seen by everyone as a symbol of the price Jesus paid for us all at Calvary, and that surely *His* sacrifice was of far greater importance and value than that being represented by this man-made artefact, no matter what its material worth. Some accused him of being naïve, but George continued to fight his corner, saying it hadn't been stolen in two hundred years so why should it be taken then?" She sighed. "Sadly though, some items had already been removed from the church, and George's perceived naivety was confirmed soon after as rumours of the cross's value continued to gain momentum until eventually the inevitable happened and it was stolen." Joyce shook her head again. "Its whereabouts remain a mystery to this day, along with the identity of those who took it and killed poor George." Glancing at me she forced a weak smile.

"For me, the saddest part of the story is that his wife Elizabeth eventually moved away to another village near Ashford with their young son Thomas. She tried to carry on here for a while after George was killed but the personal tragedy of losing him, along with the daily reminders of his role in the village and shared sadness amongst the local community, became too much for her and so she left. I'm not sure what happened to her after that, or Thomas, the church records don't make any formal reference to either of them once they moved on, other than in general passing. It was harder to maintain links in those days. There were no phones or computers back then."

Joyce looked directly at me. "Perhaps you have some idea as to what happened to them? I believe you said you were researching your mother's family tree for your studies; it would be interesting to know?"

As I listened to what she was saying, much of it seeming to confirm what I had heard earlier from George and Elizabeth themselves, I felt a fresh wave of uncertainty sweep over me. Should I tell Joyce about my meeting with the two of them, real or imagined and, if I did, what would she say or think of me, other than that I was delusional and required help; a suggestion I was beginning to consider for myself. I decided to speak only about what I'd discovered from my research and leave the events of the past few hours, if indeed they had ever taken place, for another day. I smiled. "I'm not entirely sure what happened to Elizabeth either, except to agree that she moved nearer to Ashford with the intention of beginning a new life for herself and young Thomas. She never married again I do know that. But with Thomas being the next link in the family chain to my mum, so to speak, I did follow his progress. Sadly though, he also met with an untimely and pretty gruesome end similar to that of his father, albeit under very different circumstances."

Joyce put her hand to her lips, her expression returning to one of sadness. "Oh dear, I'm sorry to hear that. What happened?"

"Well, when Thomas was fourteen, he got a job on a fruit farm near to where he and Elizabeth were living. He appears to have been a good worker and did well for himself, being promoted to the role of assistant to the farm manager during his time there. He married a local girl called Sarah in 1875. She worked on the same farm as a fruit picker. Thomas was twenty-nine then and Sarah just twenty-three. They had a baby girl, Anna, three years after they got married in 1878. She was my mum's great grandmother. All appeared to be going well for them until tragedy struck, with Thomas being killed in a farming accident two years after Anna was born. That was in 1880. So Anna never really knew her father."

"That is sad. What happened to Sarah and Anna, do you know?"

"After Thomas died Sarah moved with Anna to live near Nottingham. She had a sister, Ruth, who lived there along with her husband Arthur. I suppose she just wanted to be closer to them as her only remaining family."

Joyce looked a little confused. "Nottingham? That's a long way from Kent; what took her sister there?"

"Arthur was a miner in Nottingham. He'd met Ruth a few years earlier when he'd been holidaying in Kent to get away from the coal dust and the pits. Mind, he could have stayed here and been a miner locally if he'd waited a few more years. Early exploration for coal in Kent began around the same time that Thomas was killed. That said, mining itself didn't formally begin here until around 1896 when another Arthur, Arthur Burr, set up the Kent Coalfields Syndicate."

There was a natural pause in our conversation as Joyce absorbed what I'd said. Eventually she broke the silence.

"It's sad that you've lost family members in such tragic circumstances, but it must be fascinating all the same to find out about their history, and of their link to you and your own family today?"

"Yes, it is. And that's what brought me to Sowfield; to try find out more about dear old George and, hopefully, discover what happened to him?" Again, I felt the desire to speak about the events of earlier in the day but resisted the urge and remained silent.

Joyce stared into the distance for a moment before returning her focus to me and smiling.

"I think I've told you all I can really Charlie, although there is something here in the church I'm sure you would be interested in." She stood up, gesturing to a wall on the far side of the church. "It's over here."

I followed as she led the way, unsure of what it was she was about to reveal but wondering if it might be the plaque Linda had mentioned the night before. My suspicions were quickly realised.

"It's a form of memorial to George that was placed on the wall shortly after he died. It talks of his time at St Mark's and a little of the circumstances of his death; also, the robbers, although it doesn't name them of course. As I said earlier, they were never caught." She stopped and turned to face me. "Did you know about the other man who was thought to be involved?"

My mind raced. "Other man?"

"Yes, his name is mentioned briefly in the church records I believe, although, as with the others, his whereabouts were never discovered. If I remember rightly Elizabeth spoke of a young man visiting them on the day George was killed, declaring him to be some sort of simpleton and…"

I interrupted, hardly able to contain myself. "A young man?"

"Yes, but as I said no trace of him was ever found. It's thought he must have fled the scene after the robbery, as did the others, if indeed there were any others. Some suspected he may have acted alone. And of course, there's Elizabeth's testimony that he'd apparently spent time with the two of them on the day George was killed but, as with all the other theories, there's no physical evidence of that being the case. The only thing we do know for sure is that the cross *was* stolen and that it cost poor George his life."

Reaching the wall, she looked up and pointed to a sandy coloured memorial tablet set out in the style of a scroll of parchment. "There we are. The cost was met by the village as a tribute to George and all he'd done for the parish. As I said earlier, he was much loved and respected here in Sowfield. The whole community mourned his passing." Turning to face me she smiled. "It's funny though how certain areas of the church's history, no matter how important they might have appeared at the time, are now considered as little more than folklore or have even been forgotten altogether in some cases. I suppose that's true for a number of stories and historical events no matter their time or place in history, life moves on and we look less to the past and more to the future." She shook her head briefly. "That said, I do remember when I first started volunteering here at St Mark's I would look at this plaque almost every day, wondering what had actually happened and what sort of person George Anderson had been. But, after a while my interest waned and I began to read it less often, and now, well…to be honest, I can't actually remember the last time I did look at it." She laughed. "Fifty years from now and nobody in the village will talk about me I should think, unless it's to moan."

I smiled. "I'm sure that's not true."

"Thank you for that, Charlie, but I'm not so sure." She nodded towards the far side of the church. "I'll dig out those notes of what Elizabeth is supposed to have said if you like, about that day, and of their visitor; we keep copies here at the church. The originals are stored elsewhere in a safe."

"That would be great, thank you."

Placing her hand gently on my shoulder she smiled. "I'll leave you to read this on your own, what with it being your family and all. I'll be in the office when you're ready." She pointed towards a small door. "Take your time, there's no rush."

Although I was desperate to read what was written on the plaque, I was also mindful of the courtesy I'd been shown. "Thank you, that's very kind." We smiled at each other again and I watched as she moved away, then, taking a deep breath, I turned to look at the tablet.

We, the church members and community of Sowfield do hereby honour the life and memory of George Anderson, husband of Elizabeth Anderson and father of Thomas Anderson, also much loved Vicar of this Parish and of St Mark's Church, who was brutally struck down and killed in this place in the year of our Lord 1846. We pray he will find eternal rest and peace in the arms of the one true God whose name and teachings he sought to proclaim to a sinful world during his time on earth. We pray also for those responsible for the taking of his life, that they might confess their sin and come to know for themselves the love, forgiveness, and eternal life offered to all who truly repent. We ask this in and through the name of our Lord and Saviour Jesus Christ.

I stood for some time reading and rereading the words before me trying to glean some clue as to what had truly happened on that fateful day; a day it appeared I had been a part of and yet knew almost nothing about. Nor did I know what had transpired in those fateful few minutes when George's life had been taken so cruelly from him in that appalling act of mindless violence. I turned and looked at the floor where he had slowly bled to death, but now the colour red that met my gaze was from the length of worn carpet stretching between the pews, and not the crimson stain of blood which had flowed so freely from his head. I closed my eyes and breathed in deeply. Could it be true that I actually *was* the same young man referred to by Elizabeth in the church records? Had George and I really spoken together on the day he'd died some hundred and forty years previously? Or was it all a figment of my confused and increasingly tired mind; a combination of all the research I'd been doing, coupled with too many late nights, illusionary dreams and wild imaginings? And yet, if it were no more than a hallucination or fantasy of nightmare proportions, then why were the circumstances and events of our meeting still so clear in my memory? I wrote down the words on the plaque into my notepad and turned away, making my way across the church to the door Joyce had indicated as leading to her office.

I knocked and was greeted by her cheery reply. "Come on in Charlie."

The room was everything I imagined a church office to be. It had obviously been added to the main building at some point, and although the stone walls had been sympathetically set to give the impression it was part of the original structure it had a modern feel to it that belied this intention, both in style and appearance. There were diary and event planners hanging on the walls along with a print of the face of Jesus that, although tastefully framed, hung at a slight angle, presumably having been knocked by someone as they walked by. A brightly coloured rug was spread across the stone floor with a modern looking desk standing on top of it. This was made from a light-coloured wood and of contemporary design. It was covered with books, bibles, and pens, along with various piles of paperwork including one, assembled neatly, in front of Joyce.

Rising to greet me as I entered the room she smiled broadly. "Ah there you are. How did you get on?"

I wasn't entirely sure how to answer. "Fine, I think. It was interesting to read it and to see how well thought of and respected George obviously was, although it still doesn't really tell me anything about the actual events leading up to his death?" I nodded towards the papers directly in front of her. "How did you get on? It looks as though you found something?"

She sat back in her chair, indicating for me to do the same in the seat opposite her desk.

"Please, sit yourself down. And yes, I have managed to find the copy of what Elizabeth is purported to have said to the church members in the days after George died. We need to remember she was a grieving widow at the time when she gave this testimony and, therefore, would probably have been a little confused as to the actual circumstances surrounding his death. This would have been true for pretty much everyone else in the village as well I would have thought." Smiling, she looked directly at me. "Sadly, there was no Magnum or Dempsey and Makepeace around in those days to investigate George's untimely death. In fact, it was only around twenty years before George died that Robert Peel, the then Home Secretary, introduced his Bobbies on the beat or Peelers as they were jokingly referred to in those early days. Before that there was no formal system for reporting crime, or for having it officially investigated; not outside of the main towns and cities anyway, and certainly not in rural areas or villages like Sowfield. Matters of theft and the like back then were traditionally dealt with by random courts and presided over by the local gentry or landowners. A person's guilt in those days would be decided either by their standing in the community or, in their ability to pay a fine. If you had neither to your credit, as would have been the case for many living in the countryside, the punishment could and often would be quite severe. Even cases as serious as George's murder would have to wait another ten years before being investigated in any depth. I think it was 1857 before the Kent Police force was formally established under the county's first Chief Constable, a certain John Henry Hay Huxton." Joyce leant back in her chair and laughed.

"I only know that because it was the answer to a question we had in a quiz at the Blacksmith's Arms last week. It was about the history of Sowfield and the rest of the county from years gone by." She laughed again. "If I'd have known I was going to need that piece of information so quickly I'd have taken more notice of it at the time."

I didn't want to appear rude or interrupt her flow but was keen to know more of what she'd actually discovered. I pointed towards the pile of papers. "But you think those might answer some of my questions, or at least throw a bit of light on what happened?"

"Not about what actually happened here in St Mark's itself, nobody knows that; but more what Elizabeth remembers as happening in the moments before George left for the church." She lifted one of the pages in her hand. "As I said before, these are only copies of her testimony and would have been written by one of the few people living in the village at that time who were able to read and write. Literacy in the more rural areas of the Country back then was still an issue. And certainly, here in Sowfield it would have probably only been the landowners, or those directly connected with the church, who would have been able to read and write with any recognised authority."

"So, can we actually learn anything about what happened on the day itself, or is it all conjecture?"

"Well, there are certainly no great revelations about the physical circumstances of George's death as I say, but there is something you might find interesting about the stranger I mentioned earlier who supposedly visited them on the day in question. Like everything else I'd pretty much forgotten about him, but I'm sure if there had been a police force around at the time, they would have wanted to question him and ask about his reasons for being in the village."

I moved awkwardly in my chair, fearful as to what Joyce was about to reveal. I was also concerned that the events of the past couple of days might be about to be played out before me once more. And, if so, would finally eliminate the possibility of them being considered merely a series of random fantasies or unexplained imaginings in my head.

Rubbing my hands together nervously I watched as she laid the piece of paper down on the desk in front of her. Smiling, she put on a pair of glasses and pushed them back onto the bridge of her nose.

"I'll just give you the relevant information about the stranger for now, you can look at the rest of the documents later, if you want to?"

I nodded my thanks and waited for her to continue.

"I'll read it as it was written down rather than paraphrasing it, then you can decide for yourself what to make of it."

I watched nervously as she flattened the sheet of paper on her desk.

"George brought the young man into the kitchen and introduced him. He said his name was Charles."

I felt my chest tighten, my hands perspiring as I gripped the arms of my chair.

Joyce coughed slightly to clear her throat and took a drink from the glass of water on her desk.

She looked at me and coughed again. "Sorry."

Attempting to smile, I felt my face stiffen and so nodded in response to her apology, also acting as a sign for her to continue.

"I had been baking bread and invited him to join us for some refreshment. I thought at first he was a polite young man but as he talked, I became more concerned about his mental state and wondered if he might be unwell. He told us he was from the future and that he knew we had named our son Thomas. Initially this made me fearful as George and I had not yet informed anyone of our decision, not even our parents."

Joyce stopped and looked up. "The next bit of what she says is very odd. Indeed, there are separate accounts from certain members of the church fellowship at the time which put into doubt the validity of her story altogether, questioning whether there had ever actually been a visitor to the manse? They felt, perhaps, the overwhelming sense of grief at losing her husband in such horrific circumstances had affected Elizabeth's own mind, along with her ability to think and speak clearly. I can show you those reports as well if you like?"

"Perhaps later," I mumbled, desperate for her to continue with what Elizabeth had said. Especially now it appeared to be at odds with the rest of her account.

"Of course, now, where was I? Oh yes." She took another sip of water and continued.

"Although I was surprised by him saying he knew our son's name I reasoned it to be a coincidence or rather that George had inadvertently mentioned it in passing. I knew how excited he was by our decision to name him Thomas and how difficult he would find it not to say anything to those in the church membership before we had spoken with our families. My fears for the young man's sanity and indeed our own safety were heightened further when he began

speaking of George and Thomas dying. At that point I became quite scared and George told the young man to leave. He showed him to the door and I never saw him again, nor did I want to. George came back into the kitchen and we spoke of what had happened for a short while, agreeing we had done the right thing in asking him to leave. Thomas had woken by this time and I fed him while George cleared the plates from the table. Soon after he left for the church and that is the last time I saw my husband alive."

I sat staring at Joyce, unable to speak, my mind frozen in time as a bead of sweat ran down the inside of my sweatshirt.

"Well, there we are; all very odd don't you think? A strange young man arrives in the village and tells the two of them he is from the future and that George and their son are going to die. I mean obviously he couldn't have been from the future, not unless..." She laughed again. "Not unless he was Doctor Who perhaps?"

I forced a smile, hardly able to take in what she was saying above the clamour of my own befuddled thoughts.

"It's no wonder some considered she may have lost her mind and wasn't thinking clearly when she spoke, what with having only just given birth to young Thomas, and then experiencing the shock and grief of losing her husband in such a terrible way less than a month later." Joyce shook her head and looked at me. "Many of the villagers presumed this young man, Charles, if he really did exist, was probably the same person responsible for stealing the cross. Although, as I say, there were those who considered the whole story about a strange young visitor to be no more than an illusion or nightmare fantasy envisioned in Elizabeth's already tortured mind."

Pursing her lips, she dropped her head to one side. "Other recorded accounts from the day show that by the time George was found he was on the point of death and unable to speak, at least not in any coherent way. Sadly, he died a short while later. All of which means the whole episode remains an unsolved mystery to this day, along with the whereabouts of the cross as well. Although, I'd have thought that would have been melted down fairly quickly and sold on for its value as gold, rather than passed on as an emblem for someone to keep."

I felt her eyes focus on me as I slumped forward in almost total mental exhaustion from all that I'd heard. "Are you alright Charlie, you look like a little pale?"

288

I raised my head, breathing in deeply as I did so. "No, I'm okay, just a bit tired." I nodded towards her desk. "It's been a busy few days, and that was quite a story to take in."

Smiling, she lifted the file from her desk and proffered it towards me. "Did you want to look at the rest of these statements, you're more than welcome to? Although, I'll need to leave you with them if that's alright, as I've got some other jobs to attend to?"

Much as I wanted to read what else had been reported as happening on that fateful day, my greater desire, at this particular moment, was to get away from St Mark's as quickly as possible. I needed to be outside, breathing in the clean country air that lay beyond its walls, also, to regain my senses and equilibrium.

"Thank you, but not just now if you don't mind." I stood up. "As I said, I'm feeling a bit tired, maybe some air might freshen me up a bit. Perhaps I could come back later, or tomorrow, if that's alright?"

Joyce rose and held out her hand. "Of course, you'd be more than welcome. I'd also be interested to hear some more about the research you're doing into your family history, it sounds fascinating." She glanced down. "I do hope this has been of some use to you, even if it hasn't answered all of your questions?"

I took her hand and shook it. "It's been great; you've been really helpful, thank you."

"I'll be here until around four if you do want to come back today. I'm working a bit later than usual if that helps? Lots to catch up on and a christening to organise." She laughed. "I'm wearing more than one of my church hats today that's for sure."

Moving away from the chair I nodded and smiled. "I'll leave you to it then. And thanks again, you've been very kind. I'll maybe see you later."

"I'll look forward to it. It's been nice meeting you Charlie; say hello to Linda for me. Bye for now."

I nodded my goodbyes and turned towards the door. As I walked through the church and across the bright red carpet set between the pews I was gripped once more by the same haunting chill I'd felt earlier when helping George. Ignoring the urge to look down to where I'd left him, both bloodied and battered, I continued towards the main entrance. Exiting the building, I heard the latch drop behind me as I closed the heavy wooden door. Pausing momentarily in the antechamber to regain my composure, I took a deep breath to steady myself before stepping out into the welcoming embrace of the afternoon sun. I felt immediately buoyed by its comforting warmth across my shoulders and back. I stood for a moment with my eyes closed, allowing the fresh, clean air and summer sun to do their healing work on my tired body and mind. Opening my eyes again, I walked slowly towards the memorial bench beneath the oak tree. Although grateful to be outside once more and away from the church, I still felt confused by all that had happened over the past few hours.

"How could I have travelled back in time a hundred and forty years to meet with my great-great-great-grandfather and his family in the very same house that stood just a few yards away from me, but now looked very different with its neatly manicured rose bushes and modern garden?" I sat on the bench and stared ahead, my mind in a complete haze and running wild. Surely, it wasn't possible or logical to truly imagine that just a short while ago I had knelt by George's side in the church behind me as he bled to death. But if that hadn't taken place then how could there be physical written evidence of my alleged visit sitting on Joyce's desk in her office? She had just read it to me unless none of that had actually happened either. My thoughts scrambled again. Would I ever be free from this torment?

Shifting back on the bench I closed my eyes again, allowing my mind to drift as the warm summer breeze rustled gently through the leaves on the wide oak tree behind me. For a moment I was home again in Gunthorpe. I smiled to myself as I welcomed the vision of Mum and Dad talking together in the kitchen, sharing their feelings of excitement with me about the adventure we had chosen to embark on when first deciding to trace Mum's family tree. As I sat there allowing the memory to enfold me as a child might when seeking the security of its mother's embrace my peace was shattered at the calling of my name; it was a voice I recognised immediately and knew all too well, it was George.

"Help me Charles."

I had heard this call for assistance many times before, sometimes more anxious than others, but now there was an urgency to it I had not observed previously; it was the cry of a man, quite literally, fighting for his life.

I turned my head in the direction of the church and listened again, praying the desperate cry for assistance had been imagined but no, there it was again, this time even more agitated and distraught.

"Help me Charles."

As I rose from the bench my legs buckled beneath me, my vision blurring and giving way to a feeling of vertigo and acute nausea. I fell forward, reaching out and grasping frantically at the bench for support, the ground rushing up to meet me as the words, "I'm coming George," formed in my head and everything went black.